SAVAGE FALL

COMPLETE DUET

LANA SKY

KING'S MEN

King's Men

ACKNOWLEDGMENTS

Erica and Mickey, thank you so very much for taking the time to help me perfect this draft. As always, your feedback and expertise have been invaluable. Thanks to Melissa Stevens for such beautiful covers. Thank you, Charity for applying the final touches on this draft, and the many beta readers who provided encouragement along the way.

This story is a dark, twisted romance that contains subject matter that may not be appropriate for some readers including mentions of sexual abuse, child abuse, violence, and mentions of eating disorders.

PROLOGUE

I ONCE LOVED someone as thoroughly as I hated myself, with no distinction between the why and the how. Young hearts are foolish like that, passionate muscles comprehending only obsession.

Mine went deeper than blood, into my soul. I woke up every day knowing I would die for him, and I went to sleep at night lulled by the depth of my adoration. I inhaled devotion and exhaled self-loathing.

Brandt Lloyd was my everything.

And I killed him.

There is no such thing as a school-girl crush. Love that pure stains the soul. It twists you. Changes you.

It defines you.

Until it's gone.

Guilt is a festering cancer I've learned to live with. Its corrosion taints my charming smile and haunts my confident walk. It permeates my beautiful designer clothing.

Guilt is all I have left of him—that and the last words he ever said to me, uttered from across a buzzing courtroom: *"All the king's horses, Snow."*

The meaning escaped everyone else. Papa wrote them off as the ravings of a convicted sex offender. The judge had them struck from the record. His mother merely wept as the bailiff led him away.

But I understood him clearly. Those five little words revealed just how cruel love can be, conveying a promise Brandt Lloyd made to me that day. It haunts me still, an inevitable warning of my ultimate fate.

My betrayal didn't merely cause him untold pain. It sparked his ire—my beautiful boy who swore to be unlike his father.

It heralded his revenge.

He delivered it simply, in the form of a sheet woven into the uppermost bars of his cell two months after his conviction. There was no goodbye. No chance to right my wrong.

Just silence. And my own whispered continuation of his final phrase:

And all the king's men won't put me back together again...

No matter how violent my fall.

ONE

A GOOD ENGAGEMENT party should begin much like an execution, last meal and all. I can hear my "executioner" already, marching toward my room.

"Snowy!" Hunter barges in on cue, snapping me from my thoughts. When he sees that I'm still in my robe, he averts his gaze and mutters a curse—but not before setting a porcelain plate on the edge of my vanity. On it rests a single piece of toast. "Get dressed and then eat something."

"I already am dressed." I shrug the silken dressing gown from my shoulders, revealing the elegant dress I'm wearing underneath. Handcrafted in Italy, it hugs my frame like a glove and costs a pretty penny. A perfect, contrived dress for a contrived occasion.

"And you still aren't ready?" he asks, huffing his annoyance. "For someone about to marry into the *Forbes* World's Billionaires list, you're sure taking your sweet time announcing it. Eat."

I roll my eyes while dragging a brush through my hair. Perfectly conditioned curls refuse to conform to shape. Frowning, I tug harder. More frizz forms, and I can't escape the feeling that even my hair is trying to warn me, throwing a tantrum reminiscent of those terrible days in prep school when hats were my main accessory: *You're doing everything wrong*.

My fingers twitch and the brush lands on my lap, dangling loose strands of bright-red hair. With a sigh, I scrape the curls into the semblance of a coil at the nape of my neck and use an army of bobby pins to secure it instead.

"You look perfect," Hunter deadpans his customary brotherly encouragement. Lest I mistake the words as a compliment, he glances at his watch and then cuts his gaze toward the uneaten slice of bread. "Now, eat. The longer you delay, the more likely it is that some blond bimbo will snatch up Prince Charming, and there go all those investment dollars."

A restless scowl darkens the hue of the blue eyes we share. To enhance his irritation, a lock of blond hair falls from his neat coif, and I squash the urge to smooth it back into place. Like a statue, he is. Harsh. Impenetrable. But, at the end of the day, he's only as strong as his foundation. One wobble and smash.

Any other night, I'd take pride in winding him up; it's the only time I see him act remotely human these days.

"I'll be just a minute," I tell him, ignoring how he's fidgeting in the corner of my room.

His suit stands out in contrast to my navy walls. He's wearing gray: a fitting color to describe my life. Perfectly, wonderfully gray.

After sliding one last pin into place, I finger a loose coil of my hair and let the stubborn twist remain.

"I look perfect," I parrot, observing how my curls contrast with my custom cobalt gown. Their fiery red offsets the amethyst set in Mama's old necklace. I'm a wealth of pretentious colors overall. Red for fury. Blue for power. Purple for prestige.

Hunter claims that I'm in danger of losing my fiancé to some blond bimbo. He's close. At night, I lose Daniel to a lustrous brunette from the south of Spain, Sloane Matías-Sebastián—a woman who just so happens to be my best friend. Though Daniel fucks her for hours in that swanky penthouse of his, I'm the one wearing his ring.

Not because I'm more beautiful—Sloane could wear a paper bag and still outshine me. No, my current status has everything to do with my family name.

"I am Snowy Gale Hollings," I recite to my reflection, watching red lips move over the glossy surface. "That means something."

"Hollings-*Ellingston* if you can hurry up to attend your own damn engagement party," Hunter corrects. He's still scowling down at his watch while flicking invisible lint from his cufflinks.

With our stocks at stake, his nerves are forgivable. He won't lay off me *or* the gin he hoards in his office until the day that coveted ring is on my pretty finger.

Hollings-Ellingston. Now *that* name means something.

"I'm ready," I say, starting to stand.

"Snowy." Hunter clears his throat. "You didn't eat."

Sighing, I snatch up the toast and devour it in three vicious bites. My stomach churns, forced to accept every bit. "Happy now?"

"I'm pleased as fucking punch." Hunter's by my side in an instant, gallantly taking my hand and helping me to my feet. He glances me over and nods almost to himself.

I look decent enough to enter with.

"Now, remember. It's simple." He turns on his heel, all but dragging me to the door. "You smile. You simper. You kiss. Voila. Hollings stocks increase by tenfold tomorrow, and you can stamp the Ellingston name on your stationery kit."

"And the money," I say as dryly as I can. "Don't forget the money."

"Oh, and yes, of course, the money." Hunter beams, oblivious to the candor. We're nearing the stairs now, and he descends the topmost one first before extending an arm to assist me.

I need the help. My dress has a train that snakes behind me, requiring that I use one hand to guide it while balancing off

Hunter with the other. Mama used to say that beauty is all about balance: finding the delicate thread between pretty and pretentious and dancing along it on tiptoe.

Daniel Ellingston is both pretentious and pretty, a winning combination. He's waiting for me at the foot of the grand staircase, a champagne flute in hand. We're so perfect together, he and I. We both lie as easily as most people breathe. We sacrifice comfort for fashion, and we know how to stop a room dead in its tracks with a smile.

Mayfield's best and brightest came out in droves to fawn over our impending union. Society's elites pack the foyer, decked out in the season's latest fashions. They hush as I appear, clutching at their literal and figurative pearls.

At a glance, I only know a handful of them personally.

"Focus," Hunter hisses, tugging at my arm.

Right. I've been staring. My lips contort to display my teeth and project confidence. Then, on my brother's arm, I descend the staircase, tilting my head to display my necklace and the dramatic fall of my dress. Oohs are uttered and aahs exclaimed. Camera lenses flash. One of those snapshots will make the society pages tomorrow.

When I reach the final step, Daniel is there to take my hand. He helps me down to the floor level, and a roar rises from our gathered sycophants.

"You look beautiful," my fiancé tells me before pressing a kiss against my cheek.

I return the chaste gesture with another smile. "So do you."

Sloane certainly thinks so. She's watching from the back, wearing one of those strained expressions only possible when you're dying internally in a public setting. Pearly white teeth and hollow, haunted eyes which perform a slow perusal of Daniel's body. I copy the motion and instantly understand her attraction. His tux is custom made from an Italian designer: a pure black suit with a white silk shirt and a navy tie. Unfortunately, he'd clash with Sloane's ivory, body-hugging dress.

We, however, match. My red hair burns bright against his auburn locks. His navy bolsters my bolder blue. Not to mention, our bank accounts accent each other's perfectly.

As Hunter admitted, I can't forget the money. After all, love is a numbers game—the sum of how much you can stand someone versus being alone. I love Daniel Ellingston. He minimizes my silent hours and fills my time with pretty, simple lies.

He doesn't have a heart to break, and I'm not sure I'll ever find mine to give.

We're a match made in heaven.

We truly are.

* * *

NAUGHTY THOUGHTS RIDE the bubbles of the first glass of champagne I've had in months. My stomach flutters, churning an ominous warning: *Not here, Snowy. Not now.*

Too late. Beautiful. It's that stupid word that triggers the memory: Brandt Lloyd never once told me I was beautiful. Or special. A boy so driven toward morality could never tell a lie.

"You're Snow," he'd reply whenever I fished for a compliment. "You're just Snow."

Messy, chubby, ruddy-faced, acne-prone, dimple-cheeked, awkward, gangly Snow.

And that was enough for him.

Daniel Ellingston goes out of his way to ensure that the whole world knows how beautiful he thinks I am. How special. How clueless. He drapes me in diamonds while sneaking glances at Sloane from across the crowded ballroom of our engagement gala. He tells me all the right things, nuzzled into the nape of my neck. He donates thousands to my favorite charities. Our simplest date consisted of skiing in the Alps. He understands my fear of intimacy and patiently claims we can wait until our wedding night. He's perfect. He's wonderful.

I scream into my pillow every night at the thought of marrying him. Why? He's the best I'll ever have.

The entire world tells me so. Our perfect destiny headlines every tabloid. My brothers have all but staked their livelihoods on it. I've staked my worth on it.

As a Hollings-Ellingston, I'll be a matriarch on par with the Queen of England with none of the societal rules. What else do I have to live for? With no education beyond preparatory school and no career to my name, the title of an investor's wife is the only goal left to check off my ambitions list. It's what my parents groomed me to be: the perfect trophy, fit for a king. Admittedly, the societal norms dictating the lives of Mayfield's upper echelon are far more ruthless than those of a royal court. At least we don't have to curtsy. One must simply learn how to smile as you stab someone in the back.

Much more elegant.

"Snowy?"

I flinch as Daniel's hand settles over my spine, guiding me toward him. My body conforms to the motion and cameras flash on cue. Bingo. There's another front-page photo. I start to drift away, but his palm applies pressure, keeping me by his side.

"Is everything all right?"

"Everything's perfect," I murmur against his lapel. It's the truth. Everything about tonight has been perfect. I've never been happier—my father's definition of "happy," anyway. No scandals to speak of. No bankruptcies set in motion.

Carefully dosed and manageable mirth.

"You seem quiet tonight," Daniel insists.

Odd. We rarely talk in general. I usually sputter off a response to whatever he asks.

Like now. "I'm not sure what you mean."

We both smile as we talk, our eyes fixated on our observant guests more than each other. For appearance's sake, Daniel slides his arm down to my waist, ruffling the silk of my dress.

"You seem distracted." Furrowing his brows, he fingers the loose piece of my hair and tucks it behind my ear. "If you're worried about Ronan, don't be. I have Hunter out looking for him. He's probably neck-deep in a bottle of whiskey, but he wouldn't dare miss tonight."

"Oh, Ronan." I nod, still smiling. Ronan, my other, far less materialistic brother. Hunter has dollar signs in his eyes while, these days, Ronan can barely keep his open or off the casino tables. "He'll be here. Of course."

Daniel frowns. "Should we wait for him to begin the reception of guests?" He nods toward the table of wrapped presents and yet another bottle of champagne waiting to be sabered open. It's a gift from Daniel's grandpapa. A vintage from an obscure year some distant relative participated in during one of the World Wars. The second one, I think.

"No." I fist a handful of my gown and lift it. "We can start now."

Together, we approach the center of the room, where Daniel calls for silence by tapping a salad fork against his champagne flute. The crowd hushes, watching us expectantly, as I face them with my hands folded over my waist, showcasing the coveted ring sparkling on my finger.

"Thank you all for coming," Daniel begins before launching into a speech about how wonderful I am and what an amazing wife I'll make.

A few of our guests absently nod along. Aunt Agatha. Uncle Morris. Even Sloane.

Ten years ago, most of those gathered here barely acknowledged my existence. Before I was perfect, beautiful Snowy—back when I was *just* Snowy. I was an outcast regulated to the outskirts of such balls and parties. Only one person ever stood beside me in the shadows. He held my hand, much like Daniel is now. But he didn't worship me. Honor me. Cherish me.

He knew me. He loved me—just not in the way I wanted. But maybe his love was better in the end. Stronger. What I needed.

For a second—just one—I let myself imagine what it would be like if he were here, in Daniel's place. My dress wouldn't be cobalt, for one. Brandt loved white, and silver, and muted colors. He loved green, like the forests we used to play in and the ivy draping the walls of our favorite hideaway. He wouldn't want a large party to showcase his engagement. I'd have to force him to have one—*it's tradition,* I'd pester. *You must.*

The fantasy unfolds so clearly—minus one detail. Brandt wouldn't be ashamed to put a ring on his "Sloane." He'd never settle for me.

"Darling?" Daniel runs his hand down my side, drawing my attention. "Should we open this one next?"

"Hmm?" I blink. At least four once gloriously wrapped gifts are now on full display, perched on the edge of the table like sacrificial offerings. An engraved cake carver. A vintage bottle of wine. His-and-her wine glasses.

"Here." Daniel passes me a box still wrapped in gold foil. "Open this one, darling."

My mouth aches—a clue that I'm still smiling and have been all along. Like a sleepwalker, I must have gone through the motions. Keeping the grin in place, I peel the paper off, revealing a custom silver frame.

"It's beautiful," I coo, holding it up for everyone to ooh and aah over.

This gift came from the Sebastiáns, I presume given its ornate design. Sloane doesn't seem eager to claim it, however.

She is standing beside a cluster of bleached blondes I vaguely remember from prep school. Daniel must have invited them. A thin blonde with a hooked nose sticks out: Patsy Abernathy. Unease ignites in my skin, licking away at my confident exterior. I haven't seen her in years. In fact, our last meeting had to be around senior year when she insinuated I looked like a pig in my ceremony gown.

Brandt called her shallow once. He hated that I held her and her posse of bimbos in such high esteem. "You don't want to be like them," he always said. "They have nothing to live for but their looks."

Patsy's have held up so far. Her black, form-fitting gown is from the exclusive collection of a Parisian designer. She smiles once she notices me staring and waves as though we're the best of old friends. What difference ten years and thirty pounds lost makes.

"Oh, look at this one, darling." Daniel tilts an open box toward me: another gift from some obscure social climber or relative.

"It's beautiful," I murmur before I even look down. When I do, confusion distorts my rehearsed smile.

Someone sent a book, leather-bound with gold filigree forming the title. I read it twice as my eyes widen; it's a children's book showcasing a single fable.

"Snowy?"

I barely hear Daniel.

Impatient, he curls his fingers beneath my chin, tilting my face toward him. "What's wrong?"

"N-nothing." I stagger away from him, but not without first snatching the book from its nest of tissue paper.

It's heavy, a limited-edition collector's volume. The pages are worn, betraying its prior use. I knew someone who had a book like this. They scribbled in the margins, leaving notes and meaningless phrases. Including one at the very end in sloppy script: *Brandt Lloyd was here.*

"Snowy?"

Footsteps chase me from the ballroom. With my free hand, I claw at the train of my gown and outrun them. This wing of the house is darkened and emptied, and I take the route past Papa's old study and out into the garden.

Warm air replaces the chill of the air-conditioned interior of the manor. Heedless of the uneven stones underfoot, I stagger toward the bubbling fountain in the center of the courtyard and attempt to slow my breathing. Think.

I'm hallucinating. Obviously. That five-second fantasy was a mistake. Brandt's chased me into the real world again. Closing my eyes, I inhale deeply and exhale two words. "He's dead."

My morbid lullaby. My cruel slap of reality. My one anchor in the sea of monotony my life has become.

Brandt Lloyd is dead. My beautiful boy. The only one in the world who could turn a vicious taunt into something magical. Our secret saying.

Slowly, I let my eyes open and focus them on the book cover in my hands.

Humpty Dumpty.

With trembling fingers, I flip through the pages. They're crisp and unmolested, the hallmark of a brand-new copy. At the back, all I find is a gleaming sticker from the manufacturer. No notes. No scribbled greetings. Just painful memories that pinch at my psyche like jagged glass.

"Here," he said, tossing a book onto my lap. "Stop pouting and start learning."

I eyed the book with tears streaming down my cheeks and my hair a frizzy mess around my shoulders. We were in Papa's study. Brandt had entered without permission—like always, he had known where to find me. Once I saw the gilded title, I glared at him. "Nice one. You're mocking me too—"

"Read," he snapped while settling himself behind Papa's desk. Barely seventeen and as lanky as a bullwhip, Brandt resembled a sliver of ivory in my father's hulking leather chair. Somehow, he managed to dominate the space, radiating authority and wisdom. With his long fingers steepled beneath his chin, he fixed me with a stern jab of his brilliant, blue gaze. "Out loud. Go on."

So I did only to wind up exasperated by the end. "So, not only am I fat, but I'm irreparable?" I made it a question because I instinctively knew his aim wasn't to insult.

"All the king's horses and all the king's men couldn't fix Humpty Dumpty," Brandt said, looking down on me from Papa's desk, as shrewd as any businessman I knew. "Only he could do that, someone brave enough to climb on a wall despite the danger."

I swallowed hard and fidgeted in my school uniform, still sniffling and wiping away tears. "What the hell is that supposed to mean?"

He smiled. One of those rare, fleeting expressions only he could give. My breath caught, my heart swelling in my chest.

"It means that you stop fucking pouting and pick yourself up. What is that chant your father always makes you say?"

I rolled my eyes. "My name is Snowy Gale Hollings. That means something. Only," I added haughtily, "all it means is that we're so rich it doesn't matter if I'm fat and ugly. Any day now, he'll give me a voucher for liposuction. The only thing my name means is money."

"No." Brandt stood, unfurling his limbs with enviable grace. No one would ever dare mock him for his appearance. Except, perhaps, to imply he was too beautiful. Too handsome. The dark hair set against his indigo eyes made him far too formidable an opponent. My anger was no match, diffusing from me like smoke. "You're Fiery Princess Snow," he said, eyeing my frizzy wild hair. "That means something. It means that I'll always be there to remind you to pick your ass up the next time some jealous, spoiled bitch calls you Humpty Dumpty."

"Snowy?"

I flinch, suddenly aware of my surroundings. Cold air floods my lungs—not the familiar scent of old books and worn leather permeating Papa's study. My vision blurs, smearing the scenery into a blob of golden tones and dark emerald green. That's right: I'm in the gardens, and someone's approaching from the shadows.

"Snowy, are you all right?"

Like always, Daniel conforms to my side, pressing a chaste kiss on my cheek and wrapping his thick arms around my waist. He's more muscular than Brandt Lloyd could've ever hoped to be. His voice isn't as naturally soothing, however. It takes effort on his part to sound more caring than impatient.

Upon clearing his throat, he tries. "Darling, everyone's waiting. Was it the gift? I will admit it's a rather unusual present—"

"It's nothing." My fingers tighten over the spine of the book. Suddenly, its true intent becomes clear: Someone wanted to remind me of my past. No matter who I may marry or how my appearance may change, I'll always be Humpty Dumpty.

Only one guest would be so bold.

"You go in," I tell Daniel, forcing a smile. "I'll join you in a minute."

"Are you sure?" His thumb traces my cheek, catching me off guard by how tender the gesture feels. Sometimes, he fools even me.

"I'm fine," I reply. Banishing the tears, I swipe my hand across my face and wince. The edge of my ring caught the tender ridge of my forehead, leaving a bitter sting. "I...I just needed some fresh air."

"All right."

He leaves, and I turn to the fountain, running through the pages once again. Humpty Dumpty—my hated nickname. Old Snowy's, anyway. The chubby girl with frizzy, red hair and only one friend in the whole world to cry to. The twist? He merely tolerated her, the daughter of his father's business partner. He just never had the cruelty to send her away.

I swallow hard, fighting the memories back. Then I toss the book into the fountain and watch it float over the rippling surface. Unfortunately for the bitch who sent me this gift, I'm not that little girl anymore.

With my chin held high, I return to the ballroom. Rather than head straight to Daniel's side, I approach the gaggle of women clustered at the back of my family's ballroom. Sloane spots me first, her lips contorting into a faux-friendly smile.

"Snowy," she says, her accent giving my name a musical thrill. "You look beautiful. Is everything all right?"

Ignoring her, I turn my attention to the beautiful blonde standing beside her. "Hello, Patsy," I say.

She blinks beneath the scrutiny and giggles nervously. "You look amazing tonight, Snowy. Congratulations—"

"Was that your gift?"

"Huh?" She cuts her gaze to the table overflowing with presents. A splash of color paints her pale cheeks. "I don't think—"

"You know, I was just reminiscing the other day," I tell her, smiling wide, my tone cordial. "About how much fun we had in school. All those games we used to play. And my old nickname…" I tilt my head thoughtfully and run my thumb along my chin. "What was it?"

Patsy giggles again while glancing nervously at Sloane. But, if she expects a rescue, she's sorely mistaken. The Spanish beauty, and anyone else in the nearest vicinity, is suddenly two steps back from her. Patsy's on an island unto herself.

Once upon a time, I'd have cherished this moment.

Now? I can't stop focusing on her mouth. Rumor had it that Brandt kissed her once, on those thin, pursed lips that spewed such torment against me. Rumor also claimed he rejected her afterward. He could be like that sometimes. Hot and then brutally cold.

A newer memory springs forward, unwarranted.

"Stop it, Snow!" he shouted, shoving me back while wiping at his mouth. The look on his face stole my breath away—I'd never seen him that furious. "Don't you ever do that again."

Blinking, I refocus my attention on Patsy. "My nickname," I repeat when she hasn't replied. "Do you remember what it was?"

Patsy's throat jerks beneath a nervous gulp. "I-I—"

"What a shame that you can't make it to the wedding, Patsy." I frown and shake my head. Then I gather my train in a fist and turn my back to her. "Have a wonderful night."

I cross the room, desperate to ignore the pinch in my chest. Guilt. How long has it been since I felt it—or anything at all? Too damn long. Perhaps I need my medication adjusted again. After all, as Papa repeatedly drilled into my skull: I'm Snowy Fucking Gale Hollings. That means something.

It means I lie all the time.

It means I feel nothing.

It means that money trumps all. Even the life of the boy I loved.

"Darling?" Daniel reaches out the moment I'm close enough, grasping my hand. "Are you all right?" He's still smiling, of course. The expression must hurt—he holds it for so long. Anything to keep up appearances—mustn't let them see any flaws in the façade.

"I'm tired," I tell him before placing a kiss on his cheek. "I think I need to lie down for a moment."

"Now, darling? There's something I thought we could discuss."

Only I can hear the crack in his voice. Displeasure. If I leave now, I'll embarrass him.

If I stay, I'll embarrass him. My chest feels too tight. That damn piece of toast Hunter forced me to eat weighs heavily on my stomach.

He's watching me from across the room, his eyes narrowed in warning. *Play along.* After tonight, with our engagement immortalized in every society page in the country, my marriage to Daniel Wentworth-Ellingston III is all but guaranteed. The influx of new money will help Hunter secure his precious investments, and the house of cards that is the Hollings Estate will remain balanced for a few more generations.

All I have to do is smile.

"I just need to lie down." I escape before Daniel can reply, knowing he can't chase me across the room a second time without losing face. I hear him murmur something charming before he forges onward to open gifts without me.

If only I could have him continue the rest of the engagement in the same way. I'd smile and simper and let him do all the talking.

Left to my own devices, I run. I hide. I let him save face alone.

When I reach the staircase without being attacked by Hunter, I'm reminded once again of how the hierarchy works in this secluded, gilded world.

I'm only worth as much as my ring finger.

I eye the digit in question as I mount the stairs and enter my suite. My steps draw me straight toward the bathroom. *No,* I tell myself, faltering over the threshold of gleaming white tile. The toilet looms in the far corner, watching me. Taunting me.

I should have never eaten that bread.

Hunter always nags me at the worst possible times. To protect his investment, of course. Daniel couldn't know about the damaged goods he would receive until it was too late—though he was fucking Sloane, and she's stuck her finger in her throat more than I ever did.

Did. That's the keyword. I'm healed now. I'm healthy and well-adjusted, no longer that girl driven to extremes in a desperate attempt to feel in control. I am in control. I won't go into the bathroom…

I won't go any closer…

I won't approach the toilet…

I won't lift the lid…

Staring down into the rippling water, I let myself toy with the idea. Just one little purge. I'll feel better. I can't sleep on a full stomach, and I need to be well rested—how else can I put on the best performance? My teeth skewer my bottom lip as my fingers trace the rim of the porcelain seat. Slowly, I lower the lid. Then I turn away and reenter my bedroom.

With one hand, I undo the back of my gown and crawl beneath my duvet, wearing only a bra. Then I reach behind my pillow and find a plastic bottle hidden away beneath the silk. It rattles as I drag it closer and fish two Xanax out. They go down roughly without water. But I'm running out.

With my eyes closed, I inhale deeply and try to forget. Everything. All the old memories and the less vibrant new ones. I sink into the monotony my life has become and let it pull me away.

Deep down I know the truth: without him, I'll always awaken to a nightmare.

TWO

SAVORY SCENTS LURE me from a dreamless sleep. Eggs? And bacon, I think. Along with…

Damn. The hint of cologne betrays that this isn't an ordinary meal, and I groan into my pillow. Barring his daily deliveries of bread slices, Hunter has only brought me breakfast in bed three times in my life. Once on the morning Mama died. The second occurence was the morning after I split my winter formal gown in tenth year and ran sobbing from the ballroom. And, of course, the day of Brandt's trial.

"I'm not hungry," I grumble without lifting my head from my pillow.

Nonetheless, his footsteps persist, creeping over my Persian rug toward my bed. There's a thud, like that of Mama's antique silver tray being set down on my dresser, followed by the hiss of Hunter's heavy sigh.

"Snowy…"

Oh dear. He certainly sounds grumpy. My absence from the party must have caused more of a scene than I'd anticipated. What a scandal.

"I know, I know." I stick one hand out from beneath my duvet and gesture dismissively. "I've brought shame upon the Hollings name. I'll organize a brunch with Daniel to make up for it."

A few simpering looks over tea should cool any remaining embarrassment. Right as rain, we'll send out our glossy, official announcements and plan our four-page spread in the society pages. Publicity is the cure to any relationship strife. At least in my world.

"I'm not talking about the damn gala," Hunter replies.

"Oh?" I stiffen at his tone. "Then what?"

"We… Fuck, I'll just come out and say it: Daniel won't be available for brunch any time soon, Snowy."

"What do you mean?" My mouth wrinkles, and I find myself twisting a wad of sheets around my fingers. Has Sloane's seduction finally won her the coveted prize? "Why?"

"Because he's going to be in prison, most likely. Federally indicted on charges of money laundering and fraud."

I laugh. "Very funny—"

"Would I honestly joke about something like this?"

Alarm draws me from my den of blankets. Hunter rarely sounds like this. Hard. Clipped. So much like our father.

I peel the corner of my duvet back and roll over to face him. He's frowning, and more unease unfurls in my chest. I start to stand, dislodging a small object that rolls to the edge of my bed. Hunter catches it, giving it a shake. The pill bottle.

My shoulders tense with dread. Normally he'd spout off some speech about the perils of overdosing. Today, he tosses me the bottle. "Take two of those and join me in Mama's study," he says gruffly. "I'll get your robe."

* * *

TWENTY MINUTES LATER, I'm seated in the upstairs drawing room while Hunter spreads butter on a piece of toast. He lavishes concentration on the act as if his sole motive for dragging me out of bed was to show off his skills with a butter knife.

Not unload a torrent of information that throws our lives into chaos.

"James only found out last night," he explains, naming one of the men on the Hollings Enterprises board of directors. "The official indictment isn't until Thursday, but apparently, some whistleblower snuck the Feds enough intel to open an investigation that's been ongoing for months. The building's been forfeited, with the newest shareholder already installed. The board called an emergency meeting two nights ago and kept it all a fucking secret."

I swallow hard. He sounds so damn calm. Hunter, with moods so volatile Mama compared him to a thunderstorm, rarely showed this kind of restraint. In fact, I've only seen him like this twice before. Once when Papa cornered him about white residue the maids found on his bathroom sink, and the time a rumor spread that he'd gotten Penelope Granger pregnant.

Burgeoning drug use and scandal seem preferable now. My head spins with everything he told me. I keep replaying the sordid details, pairing them with the gilded elegance of last night.

Did Daniel know then the legal trouble facing him?

Did Hunter?

I ask him.

"Not quite." He continues to swipe the edge of a knife against the toasted slice of bread. Flecks of brown exterior flake off beneath the brutal motion, revealing the softer, white interior. Swipe. Swipe. He wears a hole right through the creamy insides without seeming to realize. "Rumors like that float around all the time in this business. Here. Eat your breakfast."

He shoves the mutilated toast at me. One look at my brother's face and I know better than to refuse. With his more delicate bone structure and blue eyes, Hunter normally is about as different from Papa as someone can be. Well, someone other than Ronan. Though, lately, I see more hints of the old Hollings patriarch peering out from behind his shrewd gaze. It's all in the way he looks at me sometimes. Less like a brother and more like a manager of one of our many properties, seeking out flaws while devising the best ways to hide them.

He's a Hollings, after all.

"Snowy, please eat the damn toast."

I take a bite and woodenly chew while my gaze wanders the room. Of all the places to ruin with his bad news, it had to be this one—the last sacred space in the entire house. Mama used to gather us here to either deliver a lecture or read us stories. Fantasies, usually. The kind involving knights and princesses—Ronan's and my favorites. She would sit in that leather upholstered chair near the window overlooking the garden with her feet propped up on the matching ottoman. Ronan would curl up on the floor while I claimed her lap. Ever the stoic one, Hunter would stand behind her and pretend to be disinterested, but I would always catch him reading over her shoulder.

"Snowy?" He's watching me now, standing near the fireplace. He's holding a book, presumably snatched from the bookshelf, and rifles through the pages without reading them. His fingers shake. The next page he accosts tears. Sighing, he closes the book. Inhales. Then he throws it across the room so violently that it ricochets off the framed portrait of some distant ancestor. "Have you been listening to a fucking word I've said?"

I jump reflexively, but I'm not afraid. "Yes," I reply, surprising myself. I sound so damn casual, as if this is a regular morning occurrence. Though, maybe in our family, such things are. Regular. Like clockwork. Scandal and ruin tick ever closer like a ruthless minute hand. All we ever do is turn back the clock. "I heard you crystal clear: We're ruined."

Scowling, Hunter snatches another book from the bookshelf and noisily flips through the pages as if the text might contain the answers to fixing this mess.

I decide to keep talking, processing the jumble of bombshells he just dropped. "You won't be indicted, thankfully, but Daniel will—and the board is already shaken. They've voted you out with no notice. You knew his 'methods' were questionable, but the returns were too good to resist. So, while you never participated in his dealings yourself, you knowingly allowed him access to much of our stock and assets. When he's convicted—and he will be—we won't be legally vulnerable, but we'll lose everything he had a hand in. The condos in St. Martin. The villas in the Alps. The properties in Frankfurt, Paris, and Milan, and just about everything we own in the States. Have I missed something?"

He remains silent while I take another deliberate bite of toast. My jaw works to chew, and I swallow without tasting a damn thing.

"That, however, isn't the worst of it," I continue. He mumbled this information amid delivering the other blows, but I'm a Hollings. We're trained from birth to decipher truth from lies. "Even if we lost everything, with your connections, we could easily earn it all back. But you sold stock to Daniel before our marriage. To 'sweeten the deal,' I suspect."

After all, his sister wasn't enough to entice such a powerful entrepreneur. Oh, no. Hunter had to play his favorite game; he had to gamble.

"However, without your knowledge, Daniel had the stocks auctioned off in a desperate attempt to buy more time. So, not only are we ruined, but we're destitute."

"Snowy!" He flinches as though I've slapped him. Carefully, he closes the book in his grip and returns it to the shelf. Tension ripples through his shoulders, disrupting the fabric of his tailored gray suit. "What do you want me to say?" he demands.

"Oh, I'm getting to that." I choke my last bit of toast down and fold my hands neatly on my lap. "You wouldn't be telling me all of this if that was where the problem extended. I know all about how this family works."

A web of complex secrets and lies, interwoven with a masochistic need for self-preservation at any cost. Someone bought our accounts, but he, my vindictive older brother, hasn't mentioned who. I hate the knot forming at the base of my throat, blocking the passage of anything solid. Mushed-up bread sits heavily on my tongue. My stomach heaves. Speaking requires twice the usual effort, but I have to say something, if only to accuse him of the worst.

"Tell me that what I'm thinking—what you want me to do —isn't true."

His knuckles whiten as he snatches yet another book from the shelf: a heavy tome on the art of war and subterfuge. It's the resounding theme of every book in this damn room. War. Deceit. Deception. Mama always brought her own, smuggled from where Papa couldn't reach. To her, we were children, but to him?

We were tools.

"Fine," I say, turning my attention to the cooling tray of food. Eggs. Bacon. Another piece of toast. I pile the former ingredients onto the slice using my bare hands. With every messy plop of egg and meat, Hunter stiffens. "So," I begin while arranging my monstrosity on a plate. "Who bought our stocks?"

He doesn't even face me. "I don't know. His name is Blake Lorenz. Apparently, he's some new upstart bastard from Germany. From what I heard, he somehow got the board's unanimous support practically over-fucking-night. God, it's all gone, Snowy. The fucker even bought Bolles."

A shiver runs through me at the mention of Papa's notorious gentlemen's club. Rumors claim that its wealthy members traded more than cigars and gossip there. Most girls had the threat of the boogeyman looming overhead to keep them in line. I had the promise of Bolles and whispered stories of the women traded like cattle inside its walls should I ever consider straying from my parents' wishes.

"Ah…" I stare resolutely at my breakfast creation while running my fingers along the rim of one of Mama's finest, white china plates. I lift it by the painted edge, balancing its weight on my palm. One tilt of my hand sends it on a slow-motion fall to the floor. *Smash!* It's suddenly a million pieces and my brother has the nerve to flinch. "I am not a prostitute!"

"Keep your voice down!" Hunter snaps, but he's even louder than I am. He whirls on me, his fists clenched, his face reddening. "You think I *want* to send my little sister to spy on some opportunistic piece of shit?"

"'Spy?' That's a rich word for it! And why shouldn't I think so?" I demand. "You've done it before. You've *all* done it before. After all, being a Hollings 'means something.' It means whoring yourself out to anyone desperate for a taste of the family name!"

"That is enough!"

I blink. For a split second, Hunter isn't the one glaring at me, puffed up with arrogance and rage. Numb, I slide two fingers down to my wrist, and a hard pinch puts everything into perspective. Papa's still dead; my brother hasn't completed his transformation into him yet.

"All you have to do is ask to see the damn man," he snarls. "As a worried fiancée. Or have you already fucking forgotten about the man you supposedly love?"

"Oh, no you don't. I gave you what you wanted." My vision blurs as my voice cracks on a bleating note. God, not now. I swipe my hand across my cheeks in vain. Warmth coats them a second later. "You said, 'We need investment dollars, Snowy.' So, I gave you Daniel—"

"Yeah, as much good that fucking criminal has done for us, huh?"

"You said we were done with this. You'd never ask me again—"

"I didn't expect the bastard to wind up in a goddamn federal sting, now did I?"

"You know what this feels like!" I can't stop my bottom lip from trembling. *No.* I curl my hands into fists, sinking my nails into the surface of my palms in a bid for control. Hard. Harder. The burning pain isn't enough to combat the ache ripping through my chest. Being used by your brother hurts—go figure. "You *know*—"

"Don't," Hunter warns. "Don't you fucking go there."

I have no choice. "All those times Papa would make you 'golf' with that wealthy French bastard who bankrolled our expansion?"

"Stop it, Snowy." He advances a step, his jaw clenched. He won't hurt me, but I have no qualms about hurting him.

"Or when he had you 'accompany' that rich Swedish bitch with the inheritance he coveted? Remember those 'favors,' huh, Hunter? You hated it!"

"And I did it anyway!" he shouts, my eardrums ringing with the force of it. "Because I give a damn about this fucking family. And I may have had to sit on some pervert's lap and call him 'uncle,' but I never lied. I never got someone *killed* —" He deflates, his face paling, shoulders slumping. "Snowy, I didn't mean it like that. I'm sorry." He starts toward me, but I lurch to my feet.

"Stay the hell away from me."

"Snowy!"

He chases me down the hall to my room, and I barely manage to slam the door before he can push his way in. The second I lock it, the wooden frame rattles, startling me. He must have thrown his weight against it.

"Snowy, open the fucking door!"

I say nothing. Instead, I march to my bed and fish my bottle of Xanax from the sheets. Only two land on my palm when I shake it. I swallow both and head for my bathroom. The woman I find watching me from the mirror's reflection is a stranger. Bloodshot eyes. Bloated, grotesque frame. A Snowy from ten years ago who sold her soul and drove the only boy she ever loved to his death. She's fucking disgusting.

I swipe at her, willing her away. Gradually, she morphs into someone new. Slender. Older. Colder. Someone who would do anything to protect the Hollings name.

Because it fucking *means something.*

Closing my eyes, I inhale raggedly. Then exhale. With my vision still obscured, I run cold water from the faucet and splash some on my face. Then I smooth my hair back into a bun before just letting it fall. The more disheveled I look, the better.

As hopeless as a doomed prince from a morbid little fairy tale, Hunter uses underhanded tricks to get his way. Ronan prefers charm, and Papa employed a mixture of blackmail and intimidation. Meanwhile, my currency was always feeding off the pity of others like a parasite and using it to my advantage.

I leave my cheeks tear-stained and flushed. From my wardrobe, I pick the most modest dress I own in a soft shade of ivory, harkening to my impending marriage. I dress slowly, ruminating over every little detail: a white pair of gloves to convey a delicate nature, a fox fur stole to portray ignorance of my impending poverty. Compiling my ruse is like putting together a costume. I've done this so many times, having performed way too many acts to name. So is the life of a Hollings: a minor role in a never-ending play.

When I finally approach my door, the knocking has ceased. Opening it, I find Hunter sitting on the floor, his back to me. His eyes are as bloodshot as mine are, and his brow furrows as he takes in my appearance while rising to his feet.

"I didn't mean what I said," he starts, placing his hands on my shoulders.

I scan his face, hunting for honesty. There are none of the telltale signs of deception I've been trained to look for. No hints of our father—for now.

"You never said that before," I admit, hesitating over the words. "About me lying."

And he never has. Not even back then when I accused our family friend of the unthinkable.

"And I know you didn't." He runs his fingers through my hair, smoothing my loose curls away from my face. It's something he used to do when we were younger and he took his job as my big brother and protector too seriously. "I'm a fool. I should have never said that—"

"I'm sorry too," I admit. "Though, in a way…doesn't this all feel somewhat like we deserve this? After what Papa did to…"

"No." Guilt flashes through Hunter's gaze before he manages to squash it, as any Hollings would. "Don't go there," he warns, but I can tell from his tone that he's aiming for the gentle route. He strokes my cheek and ruffles my hair again. "The Lloyds were criminals, Snowy."

Criminals. Harrison Lloyd and my father were business partners for years. Until, one day, they weren't. Harrison was accused of fraud, severed from their joint company, and thrown in prison. His son died not long after, though he suffered a much worse fate.

"It feels like karma," I say. My heart churns bitter acknowledgment through my blood. Whatever is happening now, we deserve it.

"Bullshit," Hunter says fiercely. "We aren't like them, and you want to know why? Because we fight for what we deserve. Snowy, I know I promised before, but I can't stand by and watch everything we've built burn to the ground. Ronan won't give a shit. But you and I—" His grip on my shoulders tightens almost to the point of pain, not that he seems to realize. He's staring through me, into the past, reliving all the horrible things he's done in the name of family. "We've always done what must be done. Even if it kills us."

And, now, he wants me to track down a certain German investor and flash a smile or grovel at his feet. Anything to get inside the man's head. He doesn't have to say it.

Our father drilled the blueprint for manipulation into our very souls.

"I don't want to fight anymore," I croak. "And bringing up old wounds won't help us now."

Hunter sighs as I smooth my hand through his neatly coiffed hair and finger his wrinkled lapel. He's right. Ronan lives in bliss while we are forced to dwell in the darkness of our family. Being a Hollings is inescapable for the rest of us.

As Papa repeatedly claimed, it means something.

"You're right," I say thickly as grudging acceptance solidifies in my stomach. "We always do what must be done… So tell me where to go."

HOLLINGS ENTERPRISES LIES in the heart of Mayfield, just a twenty-minute drive from my family's estate.

I gaze up at the towering skyscraper before pulling into the parking garage designated solely for the office's employees. At this time of day, I'm forced into a spot on the very top, and I enter through the main lobby, gazing wide-eyed at the sleek white floors and muted gray walls.

Four paces from the main doors, I'm approached by a security guard who demands to see my ID. As he reads my name, his cheeks redden.

"My apologies, Ms. Hollings."

"Could you tell me where the corporate wing is?" I ask him, shamelessly taking advantage of his guilt.

"Oh." He gives me a curious look. "Top floor, Ms. Hollings. To the left. But it's been busy lately…what with all the reporters." Something in his tone makes me suspect he wants to say more. Persuade me to leave, perhaps?

"Thank you," I say firmly. "And is Mr. Lorenz in?"

The man's stern expression softens, and he shakes his head. "I've been told that he's not taking any visitors, miss."

We'll see about that.

"Thank you." I start forward, weaving through people dressed to the nines in business attire. From the corner of my eye, I catch the guard watching me.

I get the gist of his confusion. My name is on this building, yet I need guidance to find my way around. In fact, I've rarely ventured inside it in ten years. Ironic, considering I cut my teeth on the posh leather furniture in my father's office. His blood, sweat, and tears form the corporation's very foundation, and while the layout may have changed, at its core, it's all the same.

Gray. Sleek. Industrial.

Old memories combine with new fears. When I step into an elevator, I scrutinize the reflection on the mirrored walls. My one talent is on full display: I ooze a pathetic air that just commands pity.

On the top floor, I stop short before the wall of frosted glass separating Hollings's executive suite from the rest of the hall. A brunette secretary watches me from a desk placed near the archway leading to the executive office.

"Can I help you?" she asks, her smile polite but restrained. I don't recognize her as the assistant Hunter sometimes snuck out of his room early in the morning. She must be new.

My brother was right, overnight, this man has seized control of the office with ruthless efficiency.

"Is Mr. Lorenz in?" I ask.

She warily eyes the office door. "He canceled all appointments for today. Can I have your name?"

I shake my head and march past her, ignoring her whispered protests. Blake Lorenz. According to Hunter, I'd find him here. For some reason, I hadn't assumed that his location would be Papa's office. I remember it clearly: a large study with an expansive view of the harbor and plenty of nooks and crannies for a spoiled bookworm to hide in after hours. I think I spent more time here than I did at home once…

I shiver near the door, eyeing the silver bar affixed to the wood surface, now devoid of a nameplate. My trembling fingers curl, but I can't bring myself to knock. Not even as a voice seeps through the door. Deep. Masculine.

"It's too late to have a change of heart now."

He must be on a phone call, because I don't hear anyone answer him. "I suggest you take the plane ticket… What's done is done." The rest of his words are too muffled to make much sense of. I hazard a guess regardless. Could he be calling our investors now, as I dawdle, aiming to liquidate more of my family's shares?

"Mr. Lorenz?" I croak as my knuckles finally connect with the door.

Silence. I strain my ears but pick up nothing. *Wait.* Footsteps approach in rapid-fire succession.

"Who is it?"

I suck in a breath as my spine tenses, my pulse surging. It's surreal to know that only a panel of wood separates me from the man who heralded my family's impending ruin. I wrestle control of my expression. Neutral, vapid smile. I can't scowl or pout. I need to keep up the act. Earn his pity.

I need to win our dignity back.

"It's Snowy Hollings," I say. My voice trembles. Good. I do my best to smooth my dress as I prepare to face my newest mark.

Hunter never gave me an age or even a basic idea of what he might look like, so my brain conjures an image of someone like Daniel. Smug. Arrogant. Perfumed in money and prestige. He'd enjoy a meek tone, I suspect.

"May I have a word?"

Apprehension lances down my spine as a noise cuts the air. Sharp. Clipped. Like teeth clenching, suppressing a harsh sigh. "I said no appointments."

I blow out a breath, confused. Hunter called him "some German bastard," but his accent is distinctly American and his voice dangerously low. Were I poetic like Ronan, I'd compare the raspy baritone to a growl.

"P-please." I force myself to knock again, delicately. "I'm…
I'm begging you."

That usually appeases most men. How they love to lord
their power over those perceived as weak. I eye the
doorknob, waiting for it to turn.

"No," comes the gruff reply. "I'll have security show you
out."

He's not bluffing. Alarmed, I stagger backward, casting a
nervous glance around me. The secretary is staring, her lips
pursed. Near the elevators, the security guard touches his
radio. Thinking fast, I spot a lounge area and perch myself
on a chaise in the farthest corner, hoping to go unnoticed.

Minutes pass without anyone approaching me. For now.

So I watch Blake Lorenz's door like a hawk and do
something no Hollings has ever been forced to do.

I wait.

* * *

OH, Hunter. For the first time, the full weight of our
predicament sinks in and doubt eats through my resolve like
acid. Perhaps it's how my vigil on the couch goes unnoticed
that draws the most unease? A Hollings is never ignored.

Not for a minute.

Especially not for nearly two hours.

The longer I watch the door to my father's old office, the more likely it seems that it will never open. He'll stay locked in there forever out of spite. And, now, for whatever reason, I feel a burning need to see his face—the first man to brush Snowy Hollings aside.

Well, excluding one other. A sudden urge to rummage through my purse sends my hair falling forward to disguise the welling moisture in my eyes. His memory follows me even here: the corporation our fathers built from the ground up.

Until mine stole it.

Hunter may live his life in ignorance, but I refuse to. The morning his old friend found his world torn apart, my father was gloating in the newspapers about his expanded corporate holdings.

The ghost of Harrison Lloyd must be sneering down on our circumstances now, wishing only that my father were still alive to see them.

Enough with the melancholy. I tug at my skirt, bunching the fabric and releasing it as my heels tap out a tune over the floor. It's getting late. The office will close to the public soon. From beyond the windows, I watch the sky gradually darken, which enhances the flashing chaos of traffic lights and neon signs below.

"Mr. Lorenz?"

My head whips around at the secretary's voice, and I notice a man marching past her toward the elevators. My prey, finally out in the open?

Whoever he is, he inclines his head to the secretary but doesn't slow his pace. Apparently, no one is worth his time—and I can see why. He's a monolith of muscle, built like a bulldozer accustomed to barreling through any obstacle. An unsettling sensation turns my stomach into wobbling jelly. Nerves?

He's so much bigger than I expected. Even his suit is too small, and his forearms bulge against the black material. Dark hair clashes with our monochromatic surroundings, and he stands out. An ebony stain over lifeless gray.

"Mr. Lorenz?" Stepping from around her desk, the poor secretary hurries after him. "I have the files you requested…"

There's no time to consider the consequences. I'm on my feet so fast that my hair fans out behind me. In an instant, I'm halfway across the lobby, gaining on the exasperated secretary. She doesn't expect me to snatch the envelope from her shaking hands, and I race after the receding back of Blake Lorenz before she can even call out.

My brain issues a frantic series of commands. *Breathe, Snowy. Shoulders back. Smile wide. No one can resist a Hollings smile.* Even in my Humpty Dumpty days, the expression had some effect.

"Mr. Lorenz?"

He stiffens. Suddenly, I'm in danger of running into him, and I scrape my heels against the tile flooring to find enough traction to stop. Panting, I brush my hand along his forearm to steady myself, wrinkling his tailored suit.

"P-please. I only need a minute of your—"

He turns, and my body severs all connection to my brain. I'm on my knees before I know it, reduced to staring blankly into my past. Thoughts. Fears. Common sense. They all scatter.

I'm dreaming.

I'm dying.

I'm already in hell.

A vengeful ghost looms before me, his blue eyes narrowed over my face. Pinprick pupils take me in with little interest, raking down my heaving chest and swaying frame. Unlike my dream versions of him, he doesn't smile. He merely eyes me with a black eyebrow raised, like I'm something caught scurrying beneath his shoe, not worth the afterthought before he squashes it.

I can't stop myself from breathing his name anyway. "B-Brandt."

It can't be. It isn't.

My brain fights to hammer in the knowledge…

But my body refuses to listen even as I'm struck by subtle differences too glaring to ignore. This man is taller than the lanky Brandt Lloyd. He's older, his dark hair barely tamed by the fingers he rakes through it. A stern jaw anchors stormy features contorted in a perpetual scowl.

"I'm sorry," he says in a guttural tone before splitting into two hulking figures. They eye me coldly, flicking their gazes up and down my body. "Do I know you?"

I can't say anything. All I can do is breathe. And then curl into a ball on the floor as the world starts to spin…

FOUR

"GODDAMN IT, YOU *FAINTED*?" Hunter paces the length of my room with clenched fists and flashing eyes. "And the bastard just left you there?"

His anger holds a whip-like sting, but I'm not stupid enough to assume that it all stems from concern for me. A tiny bit is the result of hurt pride. How dare someone spurn a Hollings?

My only injury is symbolic: a throbbing heart. Such a wounded, frantically beating thing. Shock wars with logic, but both fail to soothe the ache. I know that what I saw wasn't real.

He wasn't real—Brandt, anyway. Blake Lorenz, however, is very much a terrifying reality.

"We're going to sue the hell out of that motherfucker," Hunter swears. "What exactly happened?"

"Nothing," I hear myself rasp in a stranger's voice.

"Nothing?"

It's the truth. I fainted. I woke up in the presence of security, and Blake Lorenz was gone.

"Snowy, say something. What happened?"

"I…"

Hunter grinds his teeth. "Snowy, just spit it out!"

"He looked like Brandt."

"Snowy…" He eyes me blankly, not that I blame him. It sounds so insane when said out loud: The man who bought the keys to the Hollings kingdom overnight looks like the boy from my nightmares, all grown up.

He's taller than I pictured. His blue eyes were colder, darker. The stern mouth, however, dashed all resemblance. No matter how brooding or serious he could be, Brandt's lips always concealed the hint of a smile, just waiting to be teased out by a joke or quip.

Blake Lorenz looked as though he hasn't smiled in years.

"That's impossible." Hunter stands awkwardly, frozen mid-step. His furrowed brow does little to disguise his alarm. I struck a nerve. "Maybe you hit your head harder than you thought?"

He marches to my side and sits beside me. Roughly, his fingers graze my forehead as though searching for a bruise or bump, but the attempts are halfhearted. He's stalling, and I can't understand why.

"I didn't hallucinate," I insist, though I sound more doubtful than he did. My gaze fixates on the far wall as my memory taunts me with images. Blue eyes. Black hair. That beautiful, haunted face. "I saw him."

"You need sleep, Snowy." Hunter withdraws his hand with a sigh and rises to his feet. "Rest the remainder of the day. I'll handle this mess myself. I have an appointment with the lawyers." He heads for my door, puffed up with false confidence. Near the threshold, he looks back, still my Hunter, no hint of Papa in sight—which, ironically, makes this moment all the more painful. Papa was a much better liar. "I'll make this right, Snowy. You don't have to worry."

"I know." I let him go, closing my eyes obediently, as if I could just do as he says. Sleep. Wait.

But, this time, I see Brandt Lloyd behind my eyelids, watching me from across a crowded courtroom. I hear the judge render his verdict. I watch on as my only friend is led away in cuffs.

I see my world crumble—repeatedly.

Before I know it, I'm on my feet, treading the same path Hunter did. This room, with its navy walls and spacious layout, isn't the same one Brandt used to sneak into. My old poems don't cover the walls. Brandt's secrets aren't hidden in the floorboards. No, that room is on the other side of the manor, untouched for ten years. It would be so easy to creep over there now, disturb the tomb-like space. Maybe chasing traces of him could help it sink in.

Brandt Lloyd is dead and gone.

As for Blake Lorenz…

I rack my memory for any hint of that name but come up with nothing. Businessmen have been a staple of my entire life, and I've learned to catalog them as one does a list of poisonous creatures that may lurk in their environment. Lorenz is a name I would remember.

Unless Hunter "didn't think" to mention more than he's let on. I wish I could trust him, but a gnawing sense of dread warns me to find my own answers.

Luckily, he isn't the only Hollings with connections.

The thought repels me, but I have no choice. To buy more time, I change into a pair of jeans and a plain gray sweater before entering Mama's study. The strangest thought comes to me now, of all times: how she hated Brandt. Beautiful and cunning, my mother could charm the venom from a snake. She lavished false affection on everyone—from her husband, to his brooding business partner, to the lowest gardener.

Everyone but Brandt Lloyd.

Her nose would wrinkle in his presence and her eyes would take on a glossy glaze as though he wasn't worth her time. Not that he ever said a disparaging word about her. In a weird way, he seemed to pity her, the belle of every Hollings ball and the star of high society.

"Your mother is lost, Snow," he told me once, almost without meaning to. "Lost people seek out company in strange places. Don't forget that."

I never knew what he meant until now. I'm more than lost. I'm rudderless amid an ocean of turmoil. In the tempest, my mind turns to foolish attempts to save myself. With the phone, I dial a number ingrained into my soul, and I pray that word of my family's ruin hasn't spread yet.

"'Lo?" a gruff voice demands.

My throat goes dry as old memories threaten to descend. After ten years of familiarity with this figure, the sound of his voice alone is enough to make me feel fourteen years old again, listening beyond my father's study as they plotted and schemed, using the lives of others like tokens on a game board.

"Hello?"

"This is Snowy Hollings." My voice shakes. I force a cough to disguise the unease. "I need a favor. I'll pay you handsomely."

More silence. For the first time, I wonder if my game is over before it's even begun. Finally, a sigh comes from the other end. "How handsomely, little Hollings?"

His mocking pet name churns my stomach.

"Name a sum," I croak, "and it's yours. But, first, I need you to find someone for me. A Mr. Blake Lorenz."

"Find? Or *find*," the man wonders, stressing the second iteration of the word.

I shiver at the implied meaning. "I just want information. Who he is. Where he's from. Where I can find him. That's all."

"Fine. Fine." He huffs into the phone. The subtle clinking of glass and muttered conversation give clues as to his surroundings. A bar somewhere? Apparently, he hasn't changed much. Still a lowlife, it seems, lurking on the fringes of society. "When do you want it?"

"Now, preferably." I lick my lips and weigh the pros and cons of upping the ante. Damn it to hell. I'll take the risk. "If you can get me his location within the hour, I'll pay double."

"Done."

I hear another forced exhale. He's smoking, I presume. One of those smelly, old-fashioned cigars, most likely. That scent haunts my nightmares. I remember it tinging the halls at night when Father was up to his worst plans. This man participated in the most heinous. With Brandt on my mind, there's a macabre irony in asking him for any help at all—but I'm desperate.

"Nice doing business with ya, little lady," he drawls, returning my attention to the task at hand. "Reminds me of the good times with your old man."

I hang up, wrenching my fingers from the phone as though burned. Apparently, Hunter isn't the only one in danger of morphing into Papa. Then again, he said as much. Our father made him do terrible things in the name of the family, but he never had him lie. Hunter, for all of his faults, never drove someone to his death. Hunter still has his soul intact.

A blue-eyed boy stole mine, however, and I doubt I'll ever get it back. My only hope is to forget its existence and focus on the here and now. I'm here, in Hollings Manor, the home I've lived in since birth. Now, it's in danger, and I'll be damned if anyone will take it away from me.

Perhaps luck is on our side for once; an hour on the dot, the phone rings. When I answer, I'm given an address before the speaker hangs up, but not without first uttering one last warning.

"Leave the money at the usual place, little Snowy. I'm sure you remember where?"

I swallow hard. I remember, all right: a narrow alley near a bar on the outskirts of the city. "Yes."

Back in my bedroom, I stand before my full-length mirror and pick apart the appearance of the creature watching me from the glass. She's so damn pale. Her eyes are hollow. Her face has lost all color. I don't even recognize her anymore. She's a ghost.

I banish her with a blouse, a skirt, and a diamond necklace. Running a brush through my hair smooths most of my curls. There. I'm myself again, poised and confident. My engagement ring sparkles on my finger, and I stare at it as guilt pangs in my stomach. I haven't even called Daniel. I can't—not yet. I'll do my wifely duty and save us from ruin first.

A sudden realization pinches my heart. Instead of Papa, perhaps I'm following in Mama's footsteps?

Obedient to the end.

The thought haunts me as I slip into the hall and approach the staircase. Hunter must be gone. I don't find him in the foyer or hear him rustling in Mama's study. Still, I enter the back stairway and take the keys to one of the cars rather than call for a driver. Sure enough, I find the garage devoid of Hunter's preferred sports car. Ronan's motorcycle is gone as well—has he even come home yet? I can't recall.

There are more pressing matters now, apart from my wayward brother's downward spiral.

Blake Lorenz.

According to my informant, he's staying at a property just beyond the boundaries of Mayfield. It takes me nearly an hour to find it, nestled among the hills.

A gate bars the entrance, but the wrought iron doors part on cue before I even turn onto the driveway.

The gothic structure beyond them towers nearly four stories, with turrets stabbing at the sky and carefully manicured lawns devoid of any decorative landscaping. There aren't even bushes to add definition to the stark plots of grass, just a stone path stretching toward the massive front door.

I park as close to the house as a can, at the end of a circular driveway. God, it's huge. I'm forced to crane my neck to fully take the structure in. The ornate façade makes it look larger than our expansive Victorian-style dwelling. Utilitarian, almost. There are no lush gardens. No tennis courts or pool. Just trees and silence and this inescapable feeling of someone watching every step I take.

My suspicion is proven correct when I mount the three stone steps leading to the entrance, and the door opens from the inside before I can knock.

"May I help you?"

A man dressed in a black suit bars my entrance. Gray streaks his dark, neatly combed hair, adding a wizened quality to his stern features. From his sharp gaze, I sense he's the type of man who takes his duties as gatekeeper seriously.

I clear my throat, hoping to seem unimposing enough to slip beneath his radar. "Is Mr. Lorenz available?"

"He's out," the man says, angling the door to close it. "If I may have your name, I'll tell him you called."

Behind him, I make out a spacious foyer bathed in shadow. It's nearing sundown, but none of the lamps are lit. Any butler I know would have already had the entrance illuminated by now—unless, of course, the place was kept dark by request. Memory, the pitiful thing it is, gnaws away at my resolve.

I once knew a boy who loved the dark. *It helps me think,* he used to claim. He rarely lit the lamps in his room, even after nightfall.

"Wait!" My hand is sliding between the door before I know it, preventing it from closing fully. The man frowns at the slim digits, but he pauses.

"Please," I croak, fighting to keep the tremor from my voice. "My name is Snowy Hollings. Tell him…"

What? I only have seconds to make my case. Brandt Lloyd was a dreamer. But Blake Lorenz is a businessman. He may claim not to know me—and I'll probably never understand the darkness in his eyes—but I know the business. And I remember my father's old warnings about little girls at the mercy of ruthless men.

Are you this desperate, Snowy? a part of me wonders. Desperate enough to sell your soul?

For the family name? No. But to assuage the fearful pang in my heart?

I'd do anything for closure once and for all.

"Tell Mr. Lorenz that I want to make a deal." I lower my voice deliberately, leaving a suggestive air that has my cheeks flaming.

"Of course, Miss." The butler's stoic expression reveals no hint as to what he's thinking. He merely nods. "I'll relay that information—"

"Let her in, Charles." The newer voice comes from within, mere paces from the door. Deep. Haunting. *His.* If I were keeping a tally, the sound would be the first strike in the "not an apparition" column.

My boy spoke softly, never like this.

"Miss?" Charles stands aside and ushers me in with a wave of his gloved hand.

I step inside a spacious entryway, illuminated by what daylight manages to seep through curtained windows. I can barely see my hand outstretched before me, and deciphering the rest of the interior requires vague guesses and my imagination. Dark. Everything is dark. The walls, the floors, and what little furniture there is. It's all paneled wood, I suspect, containing none of the grandeur of Hollings Manor.

An uncomfortable chill settles over the drab surroundings, thickening the farther inside I follow the stern Charles. Another set of footsteps betrays the brooding figure who allowed me inside, not that Charles appears in a hurry to follow him.

"This way, Miss," he says, his stroll steady.

As my eyes adjust, I'm forced to rely on the sound of his voice more than anything. We turn a corner, entering an even darker part of the house: a small hallway. I nearly sigh with relief when we finally reach a room illuminated enough to see clearly. Then I spot the man seated behind a polished oak desk and regret my newfound clarity.

Here, the heavy curtains have been pulled back from the three windows, revealing an endless expanse of green fields and emerald forests beyond. Waning daylight paints the room's interior in a grayish glow, illuminating the plain leather furniture and wall-to-wall bookshelves lined with heavy tomes.

My fingers twitch before I can help it. It's the kind of study Brandt would have loved. Quiet, secluded, with a breathtaking view to spark his curiosity. His first act would have been to sketch the large willow growing in the center of the field. He would have shaded it carefully in grays and blacks, ensuring he captured every detail.

And in the lighting, his resemblance to the seated stranger is so striking that I almost forget. He really could be my Brandt—bulkier, older, but still him. If only it weren't for his eyes. They're far too cold. Too bold. He strips me of my blouse and slices through my bra and my panties, peering at the bared woman underneath, all without moving a damn muscle.

"Ms. Hollings," he says by way of greeting.

A sharp intake of air is my last-ditch effort to maintain my composure. I don't flinch. I don't even blink. I meet his gaze and try desperately not to react. Shadow drapes him menacingly, exaggerating his height, even while seated. Muscle strains against his too-small suit, ending comparisons to the lanky boy I knew with soft, wavy hair. This man's wild mop of curls can be tamed only by the fingers he rakes through them.

"Mr. Lorenz," I reply when seconds have passed in silence, but my lips fail to form any other words.

I interrupted something. A leather-bound notebook lies open before him, tilted the way someone who is left-handed might. Notes? No…

Confusion flits across my brain before alarm replaces it. My heart thunders, sending blood roaring through my eardrums. Even in the semi-darkness, every line and stroke of an ink pen is startlingly clear: a rough sketch of a lone willow tree.

"Can I help you, Ms. Hollings?" A heavy hand lands over the pages of the notebook, hiding the sketch from view. Deliberately, he closes it and leaves it on the desk. Then he levels that piercing gaze at me, heedless of the paralyzing effect. "You mentioned something about a deal…"

The suggestive tone grates against my remaining shreds of resolve. Everything, from the haunting chill in his gaze to his statuesque expression, reminds me of a bear trap partially concealed in the underbrush. One wrong step and I'll be wounded beyond repair.

"I'd like to know what you would consider a fitting exchange for some of my family's stock," I say, fighting to remember why I sought him out in the first place. Not to recall an old love, but for survival. There's no point in beating around the bush with him. "My brother would be willing to make any trade."

Anger. It flashes across his face so quickly that I almost miss it. His jaw clenches and relaxes, betraying him to be an expert player of verbal poker. Not for the first time, I sense I'm out of my league. Even Ronan, when sober, couldn't compose himself so quickly. But therein lies the real question.

He dislikes my unnamed brother. Why?

"Hunter would be willing to negotiate," I clarify only to flinch. There it is again: a second quick tensing of his jaw, which forces his lips into a thin line.

Hunter has a knack for making enemies, but he also has an uncanny gift of making friends. Mainly because he treats friendship as a business and greases eager palms accordingly.

"I'm not interested in making a deal with your brother," Blake says with implied meaning. "In fact...I'm forced to wonder why you're even here in the first place, and not one of your brothers, attempting to negotiate?"

A damn good question. I turn to the window to disguise my unease. A faint outline of the crescent moon gleams over an ochre sky. The sun is already sinking below the horizon. Soon, it will be nightfall.

And I'm alone with a stranger in his secluded home.

"I-I was worried about my fiancé," I say quickly. "If I can buy back some of our shares, perhaps that could help negate the damage he's caused."

"Do not lie." Amusement tinges his words rather than any harsh accusation. "You're not here for your fiancé."

"Oh?" I look back at him, curious despite myself. The shadows minimize the resemblances to Brandt. Just enough for indignation to drown out any bitter memories. "And what makes you say that?" I ask, jutting my chin into the air.

"I have eyes," he says, shrugging his shoulder. "Otherwise, you wouldn't be hiding your ring."

I swallow hard. He's right. I have my hands folded, with the right cradling the left, shielding my ring from view. Deliberately, I unfurl them, allowing the gaudy diamond to catch the light. It sparkles, a pretty little reminder of all I stand to lose.

Daniel.

Our fortune.

My sanity.

"Maybe I was wrong to come here alone," I admit to him. Whether I intend to or not, my unease is laid bare, clear in every involuntary hitch in my voice.

"You were," he counters, rising to his feet. "I took you for an honest woman over a coy one."

Heat sears through my cheeks. "I thought you didn't know me?"

His tight-lipped expression reveals nothing. "I know of you. And from what I've heard, you don't approach most of your brother's associates to offer *business*, Ms. Hollings."

The thinly veiled insult lands as only the best ones can: leveled at unguarded wounds.

"Oh?" I'm genuinely curious. What rumors has he heard? Terrible ones. I'm assured as much by the way his gaze deliberately flicks up and down my front. *Recent* rumors.

"That you will do anything to protect your family name."

I feel my chest expand before I register holding my breath. Once again, I envision a bear trap, its rusty, gaping maw so close to my tender limbs.

He's testing me. But why?

His gaze is harder to read than ever. So much like Brandt… I never could tell what he was thinking.

But I knew my moral boy better than anyone else. I knew what he expected of me. More importantly, I knew which lines to never cross with him.

His voice chases me from the void. Don't you ever do that again, Snow.

"And what should I offer you, Mr. Lorenz?" I make my voice heavy on purpose. Husky. My fingers drift toward the collar of my blouse, and I watch him with every inch they gain, ignoring my frantically beating heart.

This is wrong. Even Hunter wouldn't have this level of seduction in mind.

But neither does Blake Lorenz. Another twitch of his jaw has my limbs buzzing. With relief? Slowly, he steps from around the desk, his gaze on my trembling fingers. Then he slams his hand down over the polished wood. "Do it."

My heart trips inside my chest. "W-what?"

"Your blouse." He nods curtly to the topmost button. "If you're offering what I think you are, then don't beat around the fucking bush. Undo it."

The bear trap creaks in warning and slams shut. I've stepped on the spring. Whether I move now or later, I'm already caught.

And I suspect with a trembling certainty that he won't let me go.

FIVE

WORDS FIGHT to escape my throat, wasting vital oxygen. "I-I don't—"

"Tsk tsk, Ms. Hollings." He slams his fist against the desk a second time, which makes me jump in place. "Or do you merely dangle your body before men with no intention of offering it completely?" He's angry again. Not indignant, like someone impatient with a cock tease, I suspect, but *offended.*

Like someone who'd expect more from me would be…

My chest aches. It's a foolish thought—I know as much. But hope poisons my perception. Stern features meld and soften. He almost looks like Brandt again—a Brandt who hates what I've become, and God, I'd take his loathing over his absence. The only time my boy ever looked at me in disgust was the one moment I attempted to show him just how much I loved him.

Rasping, my throat works to churn out words. "I…"

"I suppose you do," he says coldly. "Frankly, Ms. Hollings, I don't appreciate having my time wasted." He waves a dismissive hand toward me and nods to the door. "Now, I'll ask you to leave—"

A forced exhale renders him silent, but I'm terrified to know why.

Not that I can avoid the truth for long; like the whore he insinuated I am, I've undone the second button of my blouse. My fingers still cling to it, quivering at the base of my throat and obscuring the same strip of flesh I've exposed.

Daniel has seen me naked. I've allowed him that much.

His heavy-lidded gaze never set my body alight the way one searing glare from Blake Lorenz does. He strips me bare, my outer layer singed to nothing. In his gaze, I don't find the same lustful admiration most men direct toward me. I see hollow irises and pinprick pupils.

I see hate.

"Another," he commands, tightening the screws on this figurative bear trap. "Is this meant to entice me?"

But he's a step closer now, his shoulders hunched, his hands flexing at his sides. In this moment, he can't suppress all emotion. He's furious, a fact that confounds me more than anything. I find myself leaning forward, hunting through his gaze for… I don't even know.

Ten years ago, I bared my soul to a younger man only for him to cringe back in horror. *Stop, Snow!*

I don't know how to respond to silence. My body moves on autopilot, unfastening another button. That muscle in his jaw lurches again, throbbing against his skin.

"Another," he commands.

I stiffen as he grips the armrests of my chair, each knuckle whitening against the dark leather. The kiss of his heat raises goosebumps along my arms, rasping against the silk of my blouse and another exposed strip of flesh.

"Another…"

No. Every fiber of my being warns me not to. I should run. Concede this problem to Hunter like he asked and leave Blake Lorenz to a much more formidable opponent. But my brother isn't the only Hollings to sacrifice: I've traded parts of myself in exchange for favors that make my skin crawl to recollect. I've done despicable, horrible things. None of them have made me feel like this.

Like I'm dangling on a tightrope, one wrong move from plunging to my doom. There's not even a clear, distinguishable reward for my troubles. Just this gnawing suspicion that *something* awaits me at the end of this torturous game—but only if I continue to inch along.

My fingers twitch against the material of my blouse, but a harsher grip keeps them from undoing the next button. Helpless, I look up only to find myself paralyzed by a probing expanse of blue. He studies me. He stuns me, twisting his mouth into a menacing scowl.

"You'd do it, wouldn't you?" His voice is hoarse. With disgust. With...shame? I don't miss how his eyes flicker down to my partially exposed breasts before meeting mine again. "You *would*."

Do what? He doesn't say. Suddenly, he bats my fingers away and a newer force cinches the fourth button of my blouse, tugging on the already taut fabric. I gasp and he waits, still gripping tight. It's like he gives me a second to protest. When I don't, his thumb easily unhooks the next button.

"Look up," he commands before I realize I'm staring at the gaping neckline of silk, watching my skin flush pink against his slightly darker-toned fingers. "Up, Snow." There's a sharp noise, the fingers of his free hand snapping together, demanding my obedience as I flinch.

That name...

"I told you to look up."

When I comply, his eyes are on fire. Flames lick beneath the blue, reminiscent of an inferno viewed through a layer of ice.

My breathing hitches as warning tendrils of heat brush my skin, and cool air tickles the flesh above my navel. Another button easily comes undone.

But stripping me naked out of lust seems to be the furthest thing from Blake Lorenz's mind. Irritation emanates from him, so potent that I can smell it. It's smoke, invisible but no less dangerous. I can't shake the feeling that he's testing me. And I'm failing. Miserably.

Something unreadable pierces his otherwise cold expression: a slight wrinkling of his mouth. A deliberate swallow. Suddenly, he withdraws his hands and nods toward my lower half. "Take it off."

His tone conveys not an ounce of desire. I'm a whore at his command, nothing more. Nothing less.

And I should slap him to hell and back. Scream. Lurch from this chair and storm from this room.

Anything but stare, haunted by fleeting remnants in his features that shouldn't exist. He isn't the ghost of Brandt Lloyd; the man is a demon—a tormented, twisted shell, mocking everything of the boy I knew. Their wry frowns of disgust are similar, but their reactions are night and day. Brandt never suppressed his anger. This man thrives on it.

"Do you want my time or not?" he warns, his eyes narrowing. "Take off the fucking shirt."

I can't move. I can't even breathe. My entire being warns me that I'm delirious. Desperate. Delusional. I see what I want to—no, what I'm terrified to—see. But if my eyes fail me, then my ears must as well.

"Why…why did you call me Snow before?"

His brow furrows. "It's your name."

"No one calls me that."

For the past ten years, I've insisted on being addressed by my full name. I can't bear to have it shortened by anyone—not even my brothers.

"No one calls me Snow—"

"And what should I call you, then, Ms. Hollings?" he questions gruffly. "Or should I say the future Mrs. Ellingston? Why are you here?"

He's turned the tables again. I know what he wants me to say: I'm here to save my family from ruin. Maybe I am—or was.

Tears stab their way out, coating my cheeks in wetness. I feel like I'm in a dream. A nightmare. One of those twisted, seemingly never-ending ones I can't wake up from until I say the magic words. A name.

All the king's men, Snow.

The knot in my throat won't let any words come past it. Just frantic, shallow breaths.

"Say it." He cocks his head, staring down at me from an aristocratic nose. "Say it out loud. Why you're here."

To negotiate.

To beg.

None of those reasons leave my lips. Instead, I obey his earlier request. My fingers skim the edges of my blouse. Quickly, I make work of the last button and then start to slide my arms from the sleeves. The entire time, I watch his face, holding my breath.

Shock makes itself known over his features, despite how he tries to disguise it. His mouth flattens into a hard line. A second later, those blue eyes creep along my bared shoulders, and more tears fall to drench my cheeks.

It's the same way I felt last year when I stumbled across an old box of trinkets I hadn't remembered hiding. Those old smells and memories had struck at full force, all at once.

Now, I remember Brandt the night I told him that Jeremy Caulings II had offered to date me if I sucked his cock under the bleachers. Unbeknownst to Brandt, I'd come close to doing just that. I wasn't proud of myself, but neither did I think I could survive another day of being Humpty Dumpty Snowy, the social pariah. Acceptance was a tempting prize in those days, worthy of even the most demeaning tasks.

Or so I'd told myself. Maybe I even believed it—until I saw Brandt's face the following day when Jeremy approached my locker once he thought no one was looking. With one searching pass of his gaze, Brandt Lloyd had me sussed completely. He told me without words just what he thought: I was better than that. I was too good to debase myself. While he may not date me in exchange, I would never have to debase myself to earn his friendship.

Within the frigid gaze of Blake Lorenz, I see nothing of that reassurance. All I find is dark, stormy blue. And…relief?

"You don't have the balls to go through with it," he mutters.

To himself or to me? I'm not sure. My head is too busy spinning to process anything more than the conflicting sensations assaulting my body. Shame. Guilt. Fear. Pain. Recognition.

Memory is a faulty mirror, showing me hints of the boy I loved one minute and a monster wearing his face the next. It's a resemblance even the cruelest God wouldn't devise. Yet my Brandt could never be so cold.

"Get out," he tells me. "I won't have you waste my time—"

"What do you want?" My words are hoarse and whispered. I'm still holding the edge of one sleeve, exposing my midriff and my lace bra. He does his best to avoid the bared flesh, but his eyes dart down almost too quickly to catch, igniting my nerves with every stolen glance. "Tell me what you want from me." Something dark crosses his features, and I find myself croaking out, "In exchange for our shares."

He laughs, and there's no mistaking it now. His hostility toward me is *personal.* Why? I don't recall the name Lorenz among our family's enemies. But it is a long list, and Hunter's sure to have added to it since Papa died. Maybe he's a scorned investor or a bitter ex-partner?

A part of me doesn't buy it. I'd remember this face.

I can't stop the words from forming in my throat. "D-did you know…" The full question refuses to leave my tongue, and seconds creep by without a response. "Just tell me what you want from me."

He watches me, peeling me apart with those uncaring eyes. It's only when he finally directs a pointed glance at my breasts that I realize what I've said. What I appear to be offering him. Am I? Anticipation consumes my every nerve, making it impossible to rationalize anything else. I need to hear the words come from his mouth. I need to hear him say it.

A proposition my Brandt would never make.

He sighs, drawing himself to his full height, and shakes his head. "You think you're worth so much?"

"Some men would think so," I softly admit.

Our family has other investors, and I know my brother. Hunter probably has them all lined up next if his plans for convincing Lorenz fall through. We'll go over the same song and dance we did this morning, but in the end, I'll cave. I'll offer myself to another banker or tycoon. One of them will say yes…

"I suggest you go see one of them," Blake Lorenz says as if reading my mind. "But first, tell me exactly what you're offering. Say it."

I have no choice. "M-myself."

He flinches. Physically. Before I can even marvel at the reaction, his anger sets in, consuming his features like an inferno. "Say it again."

"I'm offering myself."

His upper lip curls back from his teeth. Finally disgust—but it's nothing like Brandt's would be. Blake Lorenz doesn't believe I'm above debasing myself; he thinks I'm not worth the amount I seek.

I blink and the thread holding me captive snaps. I see the man for who he is: a stranger. Then I look down and register the fact that I'm half-naked before him, claiming that I intend to offer my body in exchange for my family's fortune. Embarrassment washes over me, turning my skin pink. Slowly, I wrench the sleeves of my blouse up and fumble for the buttons.

"I should go—"

"And if I were to change my mind?"

I look up and find him leaning back against his desk, a hand propped under his chin. He observes me the same way I figure another man would a piece of real estate he's considering to buy, tallying up all the flaws and weighing the potential windfall.

"Right here and now. If I were to offer you a single share in exchange?"

"Frankly, Mr. Lorenz—" I look him over and swallow down the knot in my throat. His gaze only conveys malice. "I'd refuse."

"You would?" He watches as I clumsily button my blouse and rise to my feet.

"Yes," I insist over my shoulder. "Goodnight, Mr. Lorenz."

"You called me a name earlier," he says, and I pause near the doorway, rigid and tense. "Why?"

I inhale raggedly, composing what little dignity I have left. "I thought you looked like someone, but I was mistaken." I glance back, meeting his gaze for a split second, before turning away. "You're nothing like him."

Once I'm alone in the hall, I stagger toward the foyer only to find the butler already opening the door to darkness.

"Goodnight, miss," he calls as I race down the steps and into my car.

It takes everything I have in me not to look back.

SIX

THREE DAYS LATER, my world is no less fractured. At least it hasn't completely shattered—until now.

Today is our time of reckoning, and even Hunter is forced to stop resenting me long enough to show solidarity.

"Are you ready?" he asks in the shadow near the door, still visible in the reflection in my mirror. With his chin jutting into the air, he makes a stark contrast to me.

Dressed in white again, I'm the demure bit of light to the imposing darkness cast by his stern suit and his gray tie.

Today, my role is to adorn. Hunter will be the one to respond to the rapid-fire questions and have microphones shoved in his face. He'll be the one to pretend he has all the answers and project an air of confidence to our investors. Like always, he'll have the hardest job of all.

"Where's Ronan?" I ask as I smooth my hair back into a tight coil at the base of my neck. There's no need for diamonds or makeup for this occasion. Within four hours, the Hollingses will be all but destitute, and every vulture within our midst will start tallying up every trinket worth selling. "Hunter?"

I look back and find him scowling out of my window at the gray, rainy morning.

"I don't know," he admits. "But I'm going to fucking find out." Then he storms from my doorway.

I scramble after him, still pinning my hair. "Hunter?"

In the three days since my unfortunate visit to Blake Lorenz, neither my older brother nor I have seen Ronan. Any other time, I'd be alarmed—but Ronan is Ronan. He probably saw the collapse coming a month ago. Rather than do something about it, he did what he does best: drown his sorrows in booze without confiding in his siblings.

But today isn't exactly the best day for him to wind up with Hunter's fist in his mouth.

"Hunter!" I chase him down the hallway and toward one of the back stairs the servants use.

"Where is he?" he growls. Craning my neck, I see one of the maids, Sarah, trapped between him and the wall. "Don't lie. Just tell me where he is!"

Sarah points a trembling finger downstairs, and Hunter takes off again. Damn. I have a sinking suspicion as to Ronan's whereabouts even before Hunter peels down the servants' wing and throws one of the doors open. Sure enough, all six-feet-two-inches of Ronan are lying across a slender brunette.

"Hey!" He yawns and rubs at his eyes before spotting Hunter towering over the foot of the bed. "Wus going on?"

"I'll tell you what's going on." Frowning, Hunter snatches what I assume are Ronan's jeans from the floor and tosses them at him. "We're hours from having our total ruin announced to the public and you've been scurrying around fucking all week."

Ronan chuckles, wrinkling his mouth. He glances at the sleeping girl beside him and shrugs. "We haven't been fucking *all* week. Daisy and I haven't been, anyway—"

"You think this is funny?" Hunter grabs the end of the sheet and wrenches it from the two occupants of the bed, drawing a shriek from the maid, who finally startles awake. "Our entire family is in danger of losing everything and you think this is fucking funny?"

"Right now, I think it's fucking *cold*, Hunt," Ronan says dryly, his legs unabashedly splayed while the woman beside him scrambles to cover her vital areas.

Hunter clenches a fist, and I know how the next scene will play out. Normally, I'd stand aside and let it happen, but now, seeing Ronan like this…

He once was the bravest of us three, the smartest and the most willing to tackle any challenge head-on. *He* should have taken over the business when Papa died—and if he gave a damn, he would know what to do now. All of that changed ten years ago.

And it's my fault.

A sob breaks loose before I can smother it. Tears slide down my cheeks no matter how hard I swipe at them with the back of my hand.

Ronan and Hunter finally turn from each other and notice me, shuddering against the doorway.

Hunter, ever the opportunist, gathers me in his arms first. "Do you have any idea what this has done to her?" he asks, angling himself to glare at Ronan over my shoulder. "Apparently not, considering you still can't drag yourself away from your self-destructive diversion long enough even to give a damn."

"Look, I'm sorry."

I hear a grunt and the thud of footsteps hitting the floor. The next second, a familiar hand is running through my hair and my nostrils flood with Ronan's faded cologne.

"Don't cry, Snowy," he pleads. "Just...just tell me what exactly I should be sorry for."

With a hiss of disgust, Hunter steers me away from him and out into the hall. "Go grab a goddamn newspaper," he snarls at our brother. "Then meet us at the courthouse when you decide whether or not to remain a part of this family."

"The courthouse?"

We leave Ronan there without explanation. Near the back staircase, I glance at Hunter from the corner of my eye. He's frowning, his jaw clenched. Not all of this anger belongs to our brother.

"Think you might have been too harsh?" I ask as I mount the stairs, leaning on him for support. It's been a long time since we've teamed up against Ronan like this—usually, I'm the one at the receiving end of their ire.

Hunter scoffs and gently thumbs my nose. "I'm not the one who hit below the belt," he says, referring to my tears, "but don't wipe them away just yet. We need all the pity we can get."

I flinch at the imagery. But he's right. So I leave the tears drying on my face and allow Hunter to lead me out onto the front stoop. A car is already waiting for us. Beyond the gates of the estate, the acreage of Hollings property stretches on, devoid of a news van or a reporter.

For now. In just a few hours, all of that will change. Our lives will be under a spotlight much harsher than that of grim admiration. We'll be a spectacle, there for the mocking and exploitation.

"Are you ready?" Hunter questions before he descends the topmost step himself, leaving me atop the stoop alone.

I shake my head. "No."

But it's not like I have a choice. Silently, Hunter affirms as much by taking my hand and guiding me down the remaining steps and into the waiting car despite my apprehension.

* * *

STANDING TALL, with his back to the gallery, and wearing a divine gray suit, Daniel Ellingston III pleads guilty to money laundering and fraud—a fact that sends a rumble through the few people gathered to witness and draws a curse from Hunter. He stiffens, his expression tight.

As the judge recites the terms of Daniel's bail, I can't stop myself from asking in a whisper, "What's wrong? Is it Ronan?"

He hasn't shown, as per usual. I'm not surprised. Perhaps Hunter is?

"Nothing," he mutters. "Just… Forget it."

But I know my brother. He's wearing the mask of our father again: that cold, calculating look. The same one Papa was wearing the night he asked me to do the unthinkable.

Suddenly, the courtroom begins to empty, and Daniel is whisked away by his lawyers before I can approach, marshaled toward the horde of cameras outside to give his statement. With fewer people around to overhear, I place my hand on Hunter's shoulder, preventing him from rising.

"Tell me what's wrong."

He grits his teeth. Like a hawk, he watches Daniel's swift exit, and an awful sensation begins to build in the pit of my stomach.

"Tell me, Hunter."

"He pled guilty."

Confusion wrinkles my mouth. "Is…isn't that a good thing?"

Apparently not, judging from Hunter's scowl. "It means the bastard cut a deal." He grabs my wrist and lurches to his feet, all but dragging me from the courtroom after him.

Stunned, I say nothing as we hustle into an elevator and enter the garage of the courthouse, where our driver already has the car within easy access.

Hunter shoves me into the back seat and then climbs in beside me. Once the car starts moving, the reality of his haste sets in. My hair is falling from its neat coil. I'm panting. Sweat beads on Hunter's brow, and he huffs out orders to the driver.

"Take…us…hotel."

A hotel. Not home to Hollings Manor.

"Hunter, what's going on?"

He doesn't even look at me. "Nothing—"

My fist makes little noise as it slams onto the seat beside us, but Hunter flinches nonetheless. "Tell me what's going on!"

But I don't need him to tell me after all. The moment I see the guilt written on his face, it all clicks. The worst possible scenario. Daniel cut a plea deal, meaning he must have implicated someone else. Someone much more enticing than a corporate magnate with a real estate empire at his beck and call.

Someone like a Hollings.

Unease unfurls like a punch in my gut. "You lied to me."

Hunter shakes his head. "Snowy, you don't understand—"

"You were in on it."

No wonder he kept everything a secret until he needed my help to spy on this newfound investor. It wasn't because Daniel was implicated. Hunter was afraid he could no longer trust him.

Because whatever illegal activities Daniel performed, my brother also participated in the scheme.

"And you had the nerve to act like this was all my fault!" I slap him. Hard. The sharp noise echoes throughout the car, but I feel no satisfaction as I pull my hand away. Just a burning, bitter sting. "Our home. Our lives. My relationship. You gambled it all away—"

"It wasn't like that," he insists. "It wasn't supposed to be like this. It was one little investment."

"You've ruined everything!" Those pitiful tears start up again, but not because of my brother.

How disgusting does this make me? I offered myself up to Blake Lorenz on a sick, twisted whim, but now…the bastard would have every indication to believe I meant it. That I needed his pity. His help.

The first man to remind me of Brandt, and I spit on his memory.

"Snowy, what are you doing?"

Hunter paws at the back of my dress, but he can't get enough leverage to prevent me from shouldering the car door open as the driver slows before a speed bump. I brace one foot against the pavement and scramble out, running blindly toward the garage's exit.

"Snowy!"

Footsteps gain on me from behind. I can't outrun him.

But I don't have to.

Another car turns the corner from a different end of the garage. I recognize the sleek sports car, and the moment I wave, the driver slams on the brakes. Panting, I round the car and climb into the passenger's seat just as Hunter comes to a stop paces away. Through the tinted glass, I see him mouth, "Let me explain."

But he had his chance.

"Are you all right?" Daniel Ellingston gives me a wary once-over and smooths his fingers along my messy hair.

I didn't even stop to hear what the terms of his bail were. House arrest? Was his passport taken? Considering he's driving alone, I can't tell, and he doesn't seem willing to tell me. A wary crook of his lips is all I deserve, apparently.

"Snowy," he says throatily, "this…this isn't how I wanted you to—"

"I'm done hearing explanations." Closing my eyes, I lean back against the headrest. "Just take me home."

DANIEL DOESN'T WASTE his breath on explanations. For once, he doesn't ply me with compliments or beautiful, little lies. He lets the silence linger between us, and the hum of his engine reveals more than words ever could.

So much for the powerful union of Hollings-Ellingston. He doesn't even walk me to my door. It's as if guilt and shame keep him rooted in the driver's seat of his shiny sports car, the only object he lusted after more than Sloane.

"I'm sorry, Snowy," I think I hear him whisper, but the squealing of tires drowns him out as I race up the driveway of the manor.

Alone, I enter my house, surprised when no one answers the door for me. The halls sound suspiciously quiet. Perhaps everyone's huddled in the breakroom downstairs, avidly watching the fallout of our ruin play out across the television.

I'm exhausted by it all. The need for sleep draws me upstairs and into my bedroom, where I fall across the mattress wearing only my underwear. It's here that Brandt continues to haunt me, luring me into the past.

"Your mother's lost, Snow," he said while pensively staring out my window.

It was one of those lazy, boring winter days when I'd pestered him into playing board games with me. Our brief sessions never lasted, and we always wound up sprawled in various positions, talking for hours about anything and everything. I had been in the middle of sorting Monopoly money, confused by his sudden seriousness.

"What?"

"Lost people do strange things," he said as a lock of black hair fell across his brooding expression.

I frowned, unable to decide if the assessment was a compliment or an insult. My mother was one of the rare people Brandt never mentioned.

"Is your mom 'lost'?" I snottily countered.

He sighed. "She's blind."

Considering that Roseanna Lloyd was an accomplished pianist who'd played a symphony only the week prior, I doubted he meant in the literal sense.

"Mommy not pay you enough attention?" I snickered.

"She pays me too much attention," he muttered before devolving into a brooding silence.

Poor little rich boy, his mother loved him too much. But the fact just brought up another topic I didn't dare mention. We never spoke of his father.

And I never spoke of mine.

Forrest Hollings demanded silence and obedience over love. He ruled this home with an iron fist, and even now, no one ever enters his study. No one.

I could always hear every footfall echo in that room from here. Every sigh and rustle of papers. Every illicit deal Papa made or enforced under the cover of moonlight.

But the purposeful steps echoing through my pillow now don't sound like him. And Hunter couldn't march so heavily, even if he were stomping…

Alarmed, I climb out of bed and tiptoe to my wardrobe. I grab a robe and tie it around me before creeping into the hallway. Papa's study is right off the main foyer toward the back of the house. This time of night, the hall is empty, the lights dimmed—the perfect environment for old memories to thrive in. Like the ones of a younger, teary-eyed Snowy racing down this corridor after school and sneaking into her father's stuffy, foreboding study—the one place no one would ever think to look.

My favorite hiding place was the small space under the desk by the window. I'd squeeze myself there with a notebook and write down every emotion and childish thought in my head until my ears picked up a familiar sound. Like always, I'd been wrong; one person always knew where to find me.

And it's his ghost I find when I finally round the corner and peek past the open door of the study. Tall, imposing, and engrossed in a book. Brandt Lloyd was never afraid of my father. Apparently, he has no fear of his memory, either. He braces one hand against that infamous desk as though he belongs here, lording over Hollings Estate.

And then he turns to face me and the resemblance fractures.

Alarm, unlike anything I've ever felt before, grips my heart in a vise. "W-what are you doing here?"

Blake Lorenz frowns into the pages of one of my father's books. He closes it slowly, pinning me in place with a single jab of his chilling eyes. "A better question would be: What are *you* doing here?"

I clutch at the edges of my robe as I struggle to convince myself that I'm not hallucinating. A covert pinch on my wrist doesn't snap me awake. "I live here."

"But do you?" He cocks his head and shrugs. His wry scowl almost conveys pity. "Hunter is still keeping secrets, I see."

Still? I'll obsess over the word choice later. I can sense without even running to his upstairs suite that Hunter isn't home. Neither is Ronan. And the servants? I stare down the branch of the hall that leads to the back staircase. Even at this late hour, I've never seen it so dark.

"What do you mean?" I ask him when he remains silent. He lights only one of the many lamps in the room, leaving swaths of shadow that drape the bookshelves. "Why the hell are you in my house?"

"This is my house," he says simply. "Or at least it will be once it's out of escrow."

"Escrow?" My heart sinks to my feet, crushed underfoot as I'm drawn forward a hesitant few steps. He's lying. I tell myself that, even as a part of me admits that his slow appraisal of my father's study is far too smug. "What are you talking about?"

"I'm sure they already handed over the notices," he mutters, frowning. "I guess they didn't bother changing the locks—"

"What are you talking about?" I can't seem to catch enough air. My hand flies out, grasping the door frame for stability. Suddenly dizzy, I cling to it. "Stop talking in riddles and just say it—"

"The house, and everything in it, belongs to me," Mr. Lorenz says coldly. "Everything. Your brother made some foolish gambles. I even own your father's club."

I blink. In this instant, neither of my brothers have ever come close to embodying the spirit of my father like this man. Wrathful. Vengeful. Terrifying.

"You're lying."

He chuckles at my pathetic whisper. "Am I? I suppose we should ask Hunter." He makes a show of glancing around the room. "Though, where is he? The last I heard, friends of ours wanted to ask him some questions—"

"You did this." It's a childish accusation to make. As if one man could be responsible for so much hardship striking all at once. But the look in his eye... It's pure hatred, searing my skin beneath its blistering heat. Flickers of it are visible whenever he speaks of my brothers, but nothing compares to the bright flames in his gaze whenever he looks at me. "Why are you doing this?"

"Enjoy tonight, Ms. Hollings," Blake Lorenz says as he heads for the doorway. "I'll let you have that much." He pushes past me without hesitation, continuing his slow advance toward the foyer.

Pain bubbles up, warring with common sense, as a cry rips from my throat. "Brandt!"

He goes rigid, stopping dead in his tracks. "Don't ever call me by that name," he warns in a tone so chilling that my teeth begin chattering. "I've heard all about what your family did to Brandt Lloyd. What *you* did to him." He looks back over his shoulder. "You killed him."

My knees fail, and I wind up sliding to the floor. Footsteps drift off, and the door opens and closes, but I don't have the strength to stand and see for myself if he's gone.

So I wait, huddled in the hallway, a child once again, waiting for a friend who will never return.

EIGHT

MY FAMILY HOME is in escrow.

My brother is being questioned by the authorities.

My life is in shambles.

And I can't stop smiling.

I wear the expression no matter where I go, clinging to it like a life raft. I wear it during the painful trek up to my bedroom to get dressed and pack clothes before I take one of the cars to the hotel Hunter mentioned. For all I know, the car has been sold as well, but it just makes for yet another location Blake Lorenz can invade in the middle of the night.

I keep smiling when I finally meet Hunter at the hotel and find him half-drowned in a bottle of wine, and my grin remains as he drunkenly tells me everything he failed to mention.

"Sorry, Snowy," he mumbles before taking another sip from his glass. Ronan is a gluttonous drunk, but Hunter is a sloppy one. With his eyes glossy, he resembles Mother more than ever. "I'm stupid. I fucked up. I—"

"You could go to prison," I say.

He flinches and reaches for the wine bottle on the settee beside us. It goes without saying that, by booking this room, my prideful brother is still in denial as to our current circumstances. It's a four-bedroom suite on the topmost floor of the city's most exclusive hotel. Funny, I never stopped to tally up expenses before now, so I don't even know which range to aim at. Thousands? Tens of thousands? Either amount is far beyond our reach.

"I'm sorry," Hunter insists, though he seems more intent on finishing off his bottle than doing anything worthwhile.

"Where is Ronan?"

"Dunno." He lifts his arm in a shrug and winds up collapsing against the back of the settee. "Dumb… bastard…left."

With a sigh, I stand and snatch the wine bottle before he can grab it. "Get some sleep," I tell him, knowing that the request is impossible. My head hurts. The room is spinning, but I do my best to stay upright as I cross into the foyer of the suite and toss the wine in the garbage. Can't fall apart now. Need to focus.

Need to think.

I take up a position on the couch and attempt to do just that. Ronan was the mastermind at plotting—or he used to be. He devised some of the best plans for outwitting Papa's rules or Mama's sensibilities. Once, he was my greatest champion.

And now?

It hurts to think about who he is now, so I move on to a more painful topic. After all, Brandt Lloyd may be dead, but his memory festers on my soul, an agonizing open wound. My craving for misery must know no bounds, because I can't stop myself from replaying the image of Blake Lorenz's face over and over.

I could kick myself for not asking him outright about his past. I could kick myself for visiting him alone in the first place.

Hunter and Ronan, as imperfect as they may be, should take the lead on this matter. After all, their bumbling incompetence got us into this mess in the first place. And I'm…

"Snowy?"

Speak of the devil. I look up and find Hunter stumbling from the bedroom, his cell phone pressed to his ear. One look at his face has my blood running cold. My fingers fly to my chest, anticipating the painful surge of my heart.

"What is it?"

He swallows hard, his Adam's apple bobbing. Bloodshot eyes betray the tears he tried to disguise by swiping them away with his sleeve. I've never seen him like this. Not even when Mama died.

"It's Ronan… There was an accident. His bike."

God, no. I'm on my feet, swaying. The next thing I know, I'm in Hunter's arms and he's whispering words into my hair. Phrases I've never heard him utter.

Prayers.

NINE

RONAN'S MOTORCYCLE is now nothing more than a crumpled heap of metal adorning the evening news. Surprisingly, my brother survived with his body intact, but not his skull. A brutal fracture has caused internal swelling. The only way to slow it was a medically induced coma that reduced him to a living, breathing statue hooked up to tubes and beeping machinery.

"You get some rest," Hunter says five hours into our vigil, only one after Ronan left surgery. "I'll stay with him tonight."

I grit my teeth rather than refuse. Blinking tears back, I run my fingers over Ronan's bandaged hands and finger a lock of his hair. Then I leave Hunter slumped on the chair beside his bed and return to the hotel with renewed determination.

Hunter was right: Everything is going to hell. But we Hollingses are natural-born sinners. We always find a conniving, scheming way to survive.

This fall from grace won't be any different.

Or so I tell myself. In all twenty-four years of my life, I've rarely had to take up the family mantle. Just once before has the fate of everyone rested on my shoulders. The memories flicker behind my eyes, desperate to descend, but I don't let them. I shake my head to banish the past and approach the suitcase of clothing I left by the suite's entrance.

In my haste, I only grabbed a few things. One of them plays into my favor, ironically: a black dress with a plunging neckline, which I don't even remember ripping from its hanger. Maybe some subconscious part of me knows what I need to do before I'm ready to admit it to myself.

I'm still not ready. Gritting my teeth, I enter the bathroom and shower. Then I arrange my damp hair around my shoulders and pull the dress on. Red lipstick would complete the look. Or a piece of jewelry. Something to make my intentions painfully clear.

And what are they, Snowy? A part of me demands.

The sick answer can only be uttered out loud to condensate over the mirror. "I'm selling myself."

Not literally, but I know from experience that there are some assurances even a wink and a smile can garner. Some favors are best left unspoken. Like being seen with a reclusive old baron in exchange for a few "investment" dollars.

I can do this. I've done it before…

But none of those previous moments ever left me feeling like this. Tense. Sick to my stomach. Unable to catch my breath. Perhaps because the stakes have never been higher.

Slowly, my fingers drift to my throat, brushing stray hairs from it. I look at myself as someone like Blake Lorenz might. Like meat. Property. My body doesn't cut a figure in this dress anywhere near like what Sloane's would. My cleavage is all but nonexistent. My face is pretty but nothing exceptional. Up until this moment, the most valuable thing I ever had to offer was my name.

Though there is one other virtue I have left…

Do I have what it takes to put it up for sale?

My heart lurches whenever I try to come up with an answer. So I run instead and head downstairs to the hotel lobby. Armed with only my purse and a pair of heels, I leave in a town car toward one destination, and I nervously wring my fingers until it finally appears on the horizon.

The Bolles Gentlemen's Club was always an enigma to my younger self. It was the mysterious, mystical place where Papa held court over the powerful men of Mayfield. Lives were built and ruined within the four walls composing the brick four-story building. Only the most influential men sought membership here. How has it all fared in my father's absence?

Well, I'm about to find out.

I swallow hard but fail to dislodge the lump in my throat. Elegant settings typically instill confidence in me, but not tonight. My fingers nervously tug at my dress as I struggle to imagine my appearance. Is it too long? Too short? Should I smile? Pout?

Garnering pity is one skill I've always possessed, but lust? Even Daniel chose to slake his with someone else. At the thought of him, my lips contort into a frown and it's suddenly impossible to sit still. Daniel Ellingston, the man I chose to spend my life with, couldn't be bothered to warn me he'd tear it all apart. Am I hurt by the betrayal or more annoyed that I didn't see it coming? I can't tell as anxiety dominates my every nerve.

"Miss?" the driver questions. He's waiting for a cue from me, to ensure that this is where I want to be.

The reputation of this place precedes it. Even this lone driver is aware of what takes place beyond these walls, though I've only heard rumors, most of them from Papa's mouth. "You want to know where dumb girls who soil their families' names end up?" he asked me once. "They end up spreading their legs in the middle of Bolles, desperate for a benefactor."

Tears spring to my eyes. Once again, Papa has an uncanny habit of predicting the worst possible scenario of our misfortune. What would he say were he to see me now? I can picture it clearly. He'd tilt my chin with a nudge from his right hand, grazing my skin with the sharp edge of his signet ring. His cold, gray eyes would stare directly into mine. Then he'd snarl, "Settle only for the highest bid. You're a goddamn Hollings. That means something."

"Miss?" the driver questions again.

Squaring my shoulders, I reach for the door and open it without waiting for the driver's assistance. Two steps carry me over the curb. With my head held high, I march the rest of the way.

Like I'm not dying inside.

Individual pain means nothing in the grand scheme—a lesson all three of us learned at some point. Blood trumps all but one ruling factor.

Money.

I picture a fitting amount as I approach the glass entrance of Bolles, where a man in a black suit stands guard. How much is Snowy Hollings worth, body and soul?

"Madame?" The man pulls one of the doors open and inclines his head inside. He doesn't bother asking for my name. Perhaps he's used to it: a parade of desperate women cycling in and out of these doors.

Where do desperate little girls wind up, Snowy? Spreading their legs inside Bolles.

One step over the threshold of the building and I swear I can sense my father's presence. He dwells within the dark walls of a deserted foyer and the muttered voices drifting beyond a short hallway.

Bolles is different than I pictured: dark, stuffy, and obscured by clouds of cigar smoke. So much for my fantasy of proudly facing a room of lecherous men and picking the least offensive of the lot to save me. Reality is a lot less idealistic.

Instead of a den of shadows, I step into one brimming with heat and sinister overtones that taint the air, richer than any cigar. A chandelier hangs above, illuminating the grand entrance. Up ahead, a swath of light beckons where rich laughter intermingles with muttered chatter.

Somehow, that makes it worse. I'm entering a den of men with no real reason to humor a disgraced Hollings.

I'm entering a world where my name no longer means a damn thing.

I catch sight of myself in a mirror hanging from the wall, which throws my appearance in stark relief. I look so pale against these dark walls. Red rims my swollen eyes—the evidence of too many tears to disguise. No matter. I'll use the pathetic weakness to my advantage.

Turning toward the narrow hallway, I start forward only to feel my heart crawl farther up my throat with every step I take.

When I finally glimpse the club's interior through an arched doorway, the air escapes my lungs and my resolve melts into a puddle at my feet. There's no way in hell I can do this.

Apparently, a woman spreading her legs in Bolles means more than the obvious imagery; it means entering a room where at least fifty of the world's most powerful men sip from crystal glasses while being served liquor by women wearing bits of lace and silk. It means capturing the attention of men who balance a priceless antique ring on one finger and an eager hostess on the other.

It means more than just sex. A woman in Bolles needs to be willing to spread more than just her legs to command attention here.

She needs to spread open her fucking soul.

And you can, a part of me insists. I only need to think of Ronan fighting for his life in a hospital bed or of Hunter drinking himself into oblivion.

My choice becomes clear; there isn't one. I'm a goddamn Hollings.

Blinking pricking heat back, I hone my gaze over any likely suspects. Surprisingly, I don't recognize some of the men. Others…

That's James Marsten in the corner, oil magnate and an old rival of my father's. Would he pay for the privilege to humiliate Forrest Hollings from the grave? If he won't, then the man across from him might. My father negotiated a deal that netted him a huge loss once. My innocence might make a fitting revenge. Or…

I start forward, craning my neck to better survey my options. I barely make it over the threshold before someone grabs my forearm. Hard. A gasp escapes from my throat, but before I can turn to see my assailant, they drag me through an open doorway I didn't notice.

It leads into a small sitting room furnished with black leather armchairs overlooking a lit fireplace. Then I'm let go to stagger to the center of the room, and I whirl around and find a figure chilling enough to stop even my heart in its tracks. Just as quickly, it surges to life again, hammering so fiercely that I can feel my pulse in every fiber of my being.

"You don't belong here," Blake Lorenz tells me, his eyes narrowed.

God, I hate how effortlessly he straddles that painful line between familiar and terrifying. Those eyes belong to me, realer than any memory. But the expression is one from a nightmare. Not even in my wildest terrors could I ever imagine my Brandt so…twisted.

Dressed in a navy suit and a darker tie, the man cuts an imposing figure against paneled wood. My mouth waters and my spine tightens, though I don't know why. Not attraction, I don't think. Maybe it's instinct. I'm in a proverbial den of lions, but this man is something far, far worse.

"What are you doing here?" he demands, feeding me each word slowly, as though he thinks I'm an imbecile.

"Why does it matter?" My voice comes out stronger than I could have expected. My chin juts defiantly in the air while, inside, I flinch at how his jaw clenched in response.

He doesn't enjoy being challenged. Do I have what it takes to keep doing so?

My heart taps out an answer in frantic Morse code: *Hell no.*

"Your family's influence doesn't extend as far as you believe, Snow." A dangerous smirk tilts his mouth. He deliberately clipped my name to unsettle me.

And he has. My fingers tremble. Knitting them into fists is the only way to hide the vulnerability.

"Did you buy the club too?" I wonder only to remember that he did. A sudden realization strikes and I'm compelled to voice it. "First, our business. Then our house. Now, this club… It's almost like you're attempting to emulate someone, Mr. Lorenz."

His head cocks to the side. "Oh? And who would that be?"

Every nerve in my body warns me to tread carefully. No matter what, it's pure insanity to utter one name. "My father, Forrest Hollings."

Blue eyes flash like a whip, and I regret my stupid slip of the tongue.

"Never compare me to him," he commands in a hollow tone.

"Why?" I counter, once again toying with a dangerous possibility. My eyes tell me that this stranger is nothing like the Brandt I knew. But my heart? It's always been a foolish thing. "I don't remember you"—at least not the name Lorenz—"but whatever you have against my family, it almost feels…personal."

A wry smile shapes his mouth, more alarming than his various scowls. "Oh, but this *is* personal. Your family has made more enemies through the years than you can keep track of."

"That's true," I say hoarsely. "But I can't help feeling as though you don't just hate my family."

"Oh?" A black eyebrow cocks into the air. "And who would I hate?"

His cold utterance of my name provides a clue.

"Me." Suddenly breathless, I grapple for air. "It feels as though you hate *me*."

He laughs, but it's quick and fleeting, and it doesn't reach his eyes. They smolder. "That's a very selfish statement to make. After all, one might assume that every one of you Hollings has plenty of sins to atone for."

I can admit as much. Had I only his words to go on, I might believe he feels the same—but he glows vengefully at the mere mention of my family. He ignites when he speaks of me.

"If I did hate you," he adds deceptively softly. "It wouldn't be your family's ruin I was after. Your stocks, your holdings, even your home wouldn't satisfy me."

He pauses expectantly. It's like he wants me to goad him on. To prod. To give him a reason to taunt me further.

I resist for two seconds—but crackling firewood taints the air. Orange flames reflect off his hollow gaze. I can almost see myself in them, slowly burning alive.

"What would you want?" My words rise to a mere whisper.

"I wouldn't be satisfied with your family's ruin." He takes a step forward, catching me off guard. Laughing, he takes another. One of his hands captures the ball of my chin when he's close enough. He roughly tilts my head to the side, surveying me from the newer angle.

I stiffen but allow the contact. A part of me understands the unspoken rules; here, he holds all the cards to both my doom and my salvation.

"If I truly hated you, I'd want you broken," he confesses before letting me go. Narrowed eyes notice how I shudder in the wake of his touch. "I'd want you a shell of who you are. I'd want you quivering in the palm of my hand. I'd want you in pieces. Are you in *pieces*?"

Breathless, I shake my head.

"I can't hear you."

"N-no—"

"There's your answer, then." I can't escape the feeling that he wants to add something else. *For now.* "Now, leave. You don't belong here. Consider your membership revoked—"

"Y-you can't do that!" Indignation taints my voice, giving it a whining tone.

"Can't I?" He levels that dangerous gaze at me again, cutting through any confidence I have left. "Your name doesn't hold power anymore. You'd do best to remember that."

"And you should remember the rules of Bolles," I counter, hating how my voice trembles.

But this is one element where I feel I have the edge. This man may shell out money for the club, but rumors of its ongoings were my bedtime stories, told as a privilege for my brothers to aspire to and an ever-present threat for me to fear.

"Membership is decided by a majority vote," I tell him, parroting my father's old rules. "I have as much of a right as anyone to argue for a place here."

"And what could you want with a membership?" His tone alone should give me pause. It's far too quiet, like the lull before a storm.

Any other day, I'd heed the silent warnings. I'd exercise logic over emotion. But, within seconds, this man already has me questioning everything I've staked my entire being upon. I can't let him go without standing my ground. I can't face myself without doing so.

"I'm going to find someone who can help me save my family's name."

Recognition draws his lips to a harsh line. "You mean to whore yourself."

I wince as if slapped and find myself staring down at the floor rather than facing him directly. Damn him. I should get used to hearing the term, I suppose. Whore.

"You are…"

Does the thought anger him? The grated quality of his voice claims yes. Very much so.

I sense him reach for me, his hand a shadow in the corner of my eye. Inches from my face, he draws back.

"Little Snowy Hollings, ready and willing to suck some rich old bastard's cock rather than join the ranks of us mortals. I never thought I'd see the day."

His crudeness feeds anger I didn't even know I possessed, festering in the pit of my stomach.

"More than that," I spit, lifting my chin. "I would rather spread my legs in the middle of Bolles than watch you tear my family apart."

He holds my gaze for what feels like an eternity, peering deeper than my battered veneer. "Spread your legs," he echoes finally, his face devoid of expression. "How about you spread them for the only man here with any damn power?"

The insult strikes deep. Wrenching from his grasp, I start for the hall. "If you're done mocking me—"

"Do you hear me laughing?" His voice renders me motionless even before his hand returns, latching onto my forearm.

Hope and fear lodge themselves in my throat, forming a repulsive mixture. "What...what do you mean?"

I'm not sure I want to know the answer. Nonetheless, he doesn't hesitate.

"You spread your legs for me."

I blink as the world ruthlessly spins beneath me. *You're insane,* I want to say. My lips part, but nothing comes out. Speechless, I'm wrenched around to face him.

"Name your price," he dares. Fire glimmers behind his eyes again. He's mocking me. Or is he?

My tongue flits along my bottom lip, wetting it. I hallucinate, because I swear he tracks the motion, grinding his teeth.

"My family's shares," I say at last.

He scoffs. "Fuck no. You're not worth that much."

"Then I suppose I'll take my chances with the rest of Bolles."

He still has my arm in his grasp. I tug, but he doesn't let me go. If anything, his fingers tighten their hold.

"And risk another night that poor Ronan's hospital bills go unpaid?"

"How did you—" I bite the question off and choke it down. "His bills, then." Anxiety gnaws away at my skull. The hospital bills alone aren't anywhere near enough. But it's a start. Another day, I can worry about the rest. This would be one less matter pressing down on my shoulders.

Though am I truly considering it?

Blake Lorenz must pick up on my unease. He releases me, swiping at his chin with a thumb. "Do you even understand what you're offering? Or do you think someone will take pity on you and give you the money for free? That's not how the real world works."

He sneers down at me, so convinced that he saw through my master plan. It horrifies me to admit that he has. But I'd rather die than let him know it.

"I'll let my benefactor decide for himself what he wants to do with me," I say, drawing myself to my full height. Even on heels, I barely reach his chin. What I lack in height I hope I make up for in sheer loathing, which I pour into every word I throw at him next. "He can teach me to do whatever the hell he wants."

He raises a black eyebrow, so fucking stoic. "Oh?"

"Yes, because…I'm a virgin." My face heats at his sharp intake of air. "A fact I think someone might find worth far more than a few hospital bills."

And with one reckless act, I just gave away the only valuable card in my hand.

"You're lying." He sounds so sure of that, even as he eyes my body boldly. Just who does he think I am? Though he's already said as much: whore. "And frankly, Ms. Hollings, I'm not interested in—"

"I'm not lying." My fingers drift deliberately down my front, hovering above my navel. "Shall I prove it?"

He visibly stiffens. The line of his jaw, his posture— everything hardens until he's a single solid mass blocking my only exit from this room. Only one aspect of him maintains any motion: his eyes as they chase the path of my fingers before returning to mine.

"Strip."

The room wavers in and out of focus. "W-what—"

"You made the offer," he interjects. "Prove it. Strip."

An impatience crackles from him that wasn't there before, and every instinct I possess converges on a single thought: *Run.*

"I-I don't—"

"Do you want the money or not?"

I jump. He shouted though he doesn't seem to realize.

Gritting his teeth, he nods toward my lower half. "Then take off the fucking dress."

I should refuse. God, I want to. I imagine what it would be like to turn my nose up at him and march from this room. Thrilling. But Ronan would still be on life support. Hunter would drown in his guilt. I'd still be a Hollings with nothing to show for it.

"Don't fucking tease," he snarls.

I've reached for a single strap without realizing it. Blushing beneath his scrutiny, I seize a fistful of the skirt instead. I start to lift it only to catch myself gaping through the open doorway. Anyone who walks past this room can see right inside. Am I brave enough to let that happen?

"No." Blake's closer, blocking my view with his bulk. Flashing eyes hold me captive. "You don't think about them," he warns. "Take off the fucking dress."

I obey, cinching the fabric in both hands and wrenching it over my head. A heartbeat later, I'm standing before him wearing only a lace thong and a pair of heels—I'd forgone wearing a bra from the outset.

Blake Lorenz takes me in with a quick glance, frowning at what he sees. A low sound escapes him. Words? My ears decipher them belatedly.

"There's no way in hell you're a virgin."

What about my body gives him that idea? Looking down, I can't tell. Pale skin greets me beneath unflattering firelight. My hands twitch helplessly at my sides, aching to cover the most vulnerable places. But I can't—and he knows it.

"Move and you won't get a fucking dime." The threat comes as he begins to circle my position while his hands fist the air at his sides.

I keep myself utterly still, facing forward. A piece of my hair is disturbed from behind and I hear him inhale. My mind jumps to the first primal explanation it comes up with. Is he *smelling* me? The curl is released without comment, but his slow patrol continues.

"You mean to tell me that your fiancé never fucked you?"

"We haven't made love," I counter, fighting to keep my chin in the air. "Yet." My voice cracks over the pathetic assurance. As if Daniel will give a damn about me after this.

Even Blake Lorenz has enough tact not to point my folly out. "Why?" he demands, returning to the subject of my alleged virginity. "Don't tell me you were saving yourself for marriage, Little Snow."

"I was." Raw pain bleeds freely into my voice, but there's no hiding it now. I let him taste a hint of the suffering he seems to crave. "I was."

"For him?"

It's a dangerous question. One with no real answer. So I say nothing, but he seems determined to fill in the blank regardless.

He lifts another piece of my hair and fire burns across my scalp—he tugged. "Don't tell me you had someone else in mind?"

Again, his hostility feels out of place. At least in a stranger. My nipples tighten reflexively. Despite the fire, he leaves me feeling cold. Exposed. Vulnerable.

"Does it matter?" I croak.

He lets my hair go and it falls against my lower back. "No." Then he completes his circle, but his expression only alarms me further. Something new alights his gaze, adding definition to his harsh features. "You think you're worth stake in your company, Little Snow?"

I struggle to keep from withdrawing beneath his scrutiny. *I'm a Hollings*, I chant to myself. *A goddamn Hollings.* "I'm sure someone would think so." The boast takes my breath away. Humpty Dumpty's all grown up; she thinks she's worth a fortune.

"Should I let you have the floor?" he wonders, leaning in to hiss each word near my ear. "Auction off the chance for one of those men to rip their way inside you? Mark you?"

I cringe at the imagery. Mother always made love-making sound beautiful. To Father, sex was a transaction. Or a weapon.

"You know where stupid girls go, you little bitch? They spread their legs in Bolles…"

"Look at me." Blue eyes survey me coldly, unamused by my sudden lapse in attention. "Or maybe you want to be bought and sold?"

"Sold," Papa hissed, shoving me against the desk. "I'll teach you what it fucking means to be a Hollings."

My eyes blink rapidly, chasing the memory away. No. I refuse to let the past haunt me here. Instead, I focus on the man before me, and I force myself to nod.

"Yes…"

"Half," he tells me. Confusion descends, but my frown only seems to anger him further. "Half of Hollings shares. But I want more than just your cunt."

My cheeks sear at his word usage—and he knows the effect vulgarity has on me. On him, triumph is a vicious expression of bared teeth and glinting eyes.

There's no more use in pretending to be brave. "What?" I ask in a whisper.

"I own you for an entire year," he proposes, but his frown betrays his confusion. He didn't intend to ask for this. It's a request born of smoldering hate. "All of you. You eat, sleep, and breathe at my beck and call."

"And…" I'm forced to lick my lips again to find enough traction to speak. For all of my effort, I can only string hollow gasps into the semblance of speech. "And you'll give me half of my family's shares?"

It's more than I ever could have hoped for.

"At the end of the year. If you survive that long." He doesn't laugh to taper the threat. It lances between us, stabbing deeper than any form of physical violence.

"You want to hurt me?" Fear has me backing against the fireplace. I trip over the carpet, forced to cling to the mantel for balance.

His expression doesn't waver. There's not even an echo of pity or guilt. "I told you what I wanted from you," he says, nodding toward my chest as though it contains the answer.

He turns on his heel while my brain struggles to piece together what his confession truly means: *If I hated you…*

I'd want you in pieces.

Near the threshold, he tosses back, "I don't want a fucking martyr. Innocence doesn't suit you. Come to me only if you're willing to earn your goddamn keep—but you don't tell your brothers or your accountants. You tell no one. You have a day to decide."

He returns to the heart of the club, leaving me there, nearly naked and trembling.

His hate clings to me.

My doom.

My salvation.

TEN

I WISH I were selfish enough—no, foolish enough—to play the victim. That would make this so much easier. I wouldn't have to taste the bitter sting of my desperation. I wouldn't crave my destruction.

Papa trained his missionaries well. We've all sold our souls to protect his name. Is either sacrifice worth it? No answer comes to me in the snatches of fitful sleep I find on a recliner in Ronan's hospital room. He doesn't stir the entire time I'm there. Despite the tubes snaking from his body, he's never resembled Mama more…

I fight to forget the comparison and return to the hotel alone. After dressing in a pair of jeans and a sweater, I claim a secluded booth in a nearby café and savor my freedom by watching the day unfold around me. Life is such a different game outside of the upper echelons of Mayfield. Here, a smile isn't a carefully honed weapon. Tokens of love or friendship are exchanged freely, and young women meet their lovers without any visible hints that one has bought and paid for the other.

Do I fear what awaits me should I take Blake Lorenz up on his offer? Five cups of coffee fail to give me the courage necessary to settle upon an answer.

In the end, it's not like my feelings matter. I'm a Hollings. That fucking name trumps all.

But I refuse to let my brothers die for it.

As the sun sets, I finally leave the café and return to Hunter's suite. I find him passed out on one of the loungers in the main room, clutching what looks like legal papers to his chest. Unsurprisingly, the scent of wine hangs over him like a cloud. My heart heavy, I press a kiss to his cheek rather than wake him.

Maybe one day I'll make him atone for his role in our downfall. Then again, maybe this is merely sweet revenge; after all, I'm the one who ruined our lives first.

With that thought in my head, I shower and dress in a new gown, one of the Parisian creations meant to be worn at the rehearsal dinner for my wedding, of all things. Why I packed it, I'll never know. It hangs loosely on me. Barely a week of destitution and my body is already starting to show it.

At least the hanging neckline reveals plenty of cleavage. Thin breasts rise from a visible rib cage. How appealing. Once dressed, I turn away from the mirror and leave a note for Hunter, explaining that I'll be gone for a few days and not to worry.

Then I begin my descent to the lobby via the stairs, extending every second as though they're truly my last. My lungs flood with the fresh air once I make it outside, and I consider taking Hunter's car, the only vehicle yet to be repossessed, but wind up taking a cab instead.

I track my journey through the back seat window, riveted by the rolling hills and fields I've viewed a thousand times, but never like this. I'm no longer a fairy tale princess but a captive pauper. Hollings blood forms my chains, and my jailer is an evocative shadow of my past with motives yet to be revealed.

When Hollings Manor finally appears on the horizon, I barely recognize it. Draped in darkness, a few days' absence have stripped it bare of twenty-four years' worth of memories.

And Blake Lorenz taints every stone. I feel his presence during the solitary walk up the front path, the one lined with the flowerbeds Mama meticulously oversaw the planting of. I sense him lurking within the hallowed walls, though he isn't the figure who opens the door for me. Unsurprisingly, he's made short work of assuming control of the estate. Charles greets me as formally as though he's controlled this entrance for years.

"He's in the study," he says after ushering me inside.

This time, he doesn't lead the way there. I'm forced to travel down that hallway alone. The lamps flicker at their dimmest setting, and I find only one lit in Papa's study.

Or what used to be Papa's study.

All but two of the bookshelves have been removed, allowing more natural light inside. The desk has been moved closer to the window, angled for its seated occupant to best observe the view.

Which puts his back to me. From my position, I can't make out what he's working on. Documents? He shuffles them noisily before casting me a cold appraisal over his shoulder.

"What the fuck are you wearing?"

It's wrong, but for a split second, my mind goes to Daniel. All of those fawning looks and searching glances. Never once did he…scowl.

"Change," Blake growls, returning to his paperwork. Hunched shoulders close him off further from me—and, by extension, this very room. "There's clothing in your room upstairs."

Clothing? The prospect of an outfit chosen by him is too terrifying to question out loud. Numb with apprehension, I return to the foyer and mount the ornate staircase, feeling like a stranger.

For the first time, I see the house as I figure a newcomer might. So big. So empty. There are no family photographs hanging on the walls or personal baubles strewn about. Our name was our identity, but the irony is that Blake Lorenz didn't have to remove much to strip our presence from the walls. Some of the paintings are missing. The lights in the upstairs hall were left dim. And my room…

It's been desecrated. Gray walls have replaced my beloved navy. Utilitarian white sheets cover my bed instead of my dark silken ones. My wardrobe is gone. In its place stands a metal rack upon which only a few items hang. Thin, terrifying things.

The loss of my personal touches lands with unexpected damage. I wince, blinking rapidly against a sudden burn. Slowly, I suck in gulps of air and creep closer to observe the newer clothing.

I finger a white bit of lace material at random. The sewn-in tag proclaims it's in my size, but when I strip my black dress and pull it on over my head, I must hold my breath to yank the hem over my waist. It clings to me, nearly see-through. The bubbles in a bathtub are more conservative.

"I told you to change, not linger."

I turn and find Blake glowering in the doorway.

He narrows his gaze at my appearance, seemingly unimpressed. "You call this a body worth a fortune?"

My cheeks sting as though they've been slapped. His doubt now is a far cry from the man who gaped at me last night.

"What do you mean?" Self-conscious pain creeps into my voice. I can't stop my hands from smoothing over my waist, noting the uncomfortably tight fit.

"Daniel Ellingston has low standards, apparently. Take it off."

I swallow hard, grasping at the taut fabric. "W-what?"

"Take the fucking dress off," he commands in a tone far softer than his words allude to. It's dangerous. "Now, before you fucking tear it."

Woodenly, I strip the slip. I have it halfway over my head when an ominous rip comes from the seams.

"Jesus Christ, take it off!"

I shimmy out of it fully and leave the ruined garment slung over the side of my bed. "I'm sorry."

He says nothing.

"I-I… It must be a different size."

Again nothing.

I gather up the nerve to look at him directly. Eyes like fire rake freely over my hip and up to my exposed breasts. My first instinct is to shield myself with my hands, but he shakes his head almost imperceptibly. Like he doesn't even realize he's done it.

His throat contorts around a hard swallow. "It's the correct damn size," he says as his stare claims mine. "But *you* aren't."

"W-what?"

He shrugs, turning his attention to my room. "Until you can wear the clothing I provide, you wear nothing."

God, despite everything, a laugh trickles out of me, high-pitched and breathless. "You're not serious."

"I'm not?" He faces me again, but this time, his eyes never leave my face. With barely disguised disgust, his upper lip curls back from his teeth. "Oh, I fucking am. Allow me to let you in on a little secret…" He even leans in close, basting my cheek with his breath. "Unlike the rest of the goddamn world, I'm not enamored with Snowy Hollings. In fact, you're not the first person on this side of the country I want to fuck. You're not even the second or the third. I don't give a fuck what other men may have tolerated when it comes to your appearance"—he gives a pointed glance to the body in question—"but make no mistake. Do you want your shares? You earn them. I won't tailor my tastes for anyone. If you stay, you must meet them. Understood?"

"If I stay?"

He shrugs. "I'm not desperate enough to force you. Hell, your virginity isn't worth a goddamn penny to me, though if you stay, you keep it intact unless *I* decide to rectify it. The moment you find you can't adhere to my expectations, you leave."

And any promise of money is withdrawn. He doesn't say as much, but it's all in the unspoken rules of the game. Money is the prize and my body is the game board—only he controls every piece in play.

"Ruin another dress and you'll know the consequences." He snatches up the damaged dress. Another tear comes from the fabric as he cinches it tight, his knuckles whitening. "I'll give you a week to fit into the clothes."

With that, he leaves, slamming the door behind him. But he can't be serious.

He can't be…

A glance around the room reveals no other clothing. All of my fancy dresses and designer ensembles. Did he burn them? The prospect of such a malicious act blows my mind.

Numb, I sink onto my bed, drawing the edges of my sheets around my naked frame. I don't cry, refusing to allow a single tear to fall. I remember instead. What it's like to sacrifice everything for the sake of Hollings blood.

This isn't the worst thing I've ever done. Not even close.

ELEVEN

I DON'T SLEEP. Despite how heavy my eyelids have become, I can't get comfortable in this strange open cell where I once spent ten years of my life. My brain refuses to accept what my body is forced to realize: my home, my world, all of it is gone overnight.

Blake Lorenz holds the keys to this new reality.

And he wants to make sure I know it. His scent lingers in the air, heavy and fragrant. Stifling and potent. I find myself inhaling deeply, trying to decipher every nuance.

God, he's harsh even in incorporeal form. My nostrils itch with the burning sting of his presence. There's none of the softness I seek. Nothing like…

Stop. I clamp down on the thought before it can unfurl. There's no point in dreaming. My only goal from now on is surviving. Though, funnily enough, I didn't stop to consider just how I'd do so. Blake Lorenz demanded an entire year, and I sold my soul without stopping to consider the logistics.

Dread grips my heart even as a tired laugh trickles from my lips and onto the sheets. I didn't even ask him just what he'd expect from me. Sex? Last night, I would have suspected as much, but now? I run a trembling hand down my front, pinching flesh over my stomach. There's enough to form a cushion between my fingertips…

Years ago I'd do the same thing to measure how much bigger I was than the other girls. A giant, ungainly Humpty Dumpty. Memory plays a dangerous game. Brandt was the one who caught me first, exposing my dirty secret. I still remember how he looked, observing me hunched over a toilet with a magazine clutch in my fist.

There was no judgment in his gaze—that was the worst part. He just shook his head, his voice breaking like I'd never heard. "Snow, you're perfect already. You're perfect…"

A cold sensation washes over me, and I lurch upright while pinching myself on the wrist. *Stop.* God, I haven't thought like this in so long. Not since…well, ten years ago.

I scramble from the bed, surprised to find a faint streak of pink stretching across the sky beyond my windows. I use the illumination as a guide to return to that rack of clothing. I select a different dress and attempt to slip it on. Way too tight. I don't even dare risk pulling the fabric over my hips for fear of tearing it. Another dress fits no better.

Size two. Size three. Four.

Shit. My heart pounds as I enter my bathroom, wary of what I'll find in the mirror. Still the same Snowy, it seems. Thin. The lines of my rib cage press insistently against my skin. Perhaps that's where the newfound gain comes from? My heart aches, swollen a million times its normal size. If I were a decent woman, the discomfort would be out of concern for my brothers.

I turn away from my reflection in disgust. Nervous energy drives me into the hallway. One step beyond my room and I remember my current state of dress as cool air assaults my skin. I glance back at my bed and consider grabbing the sheets.

Until you can wear the clothing I provide, you wear nothing.

Grinding my teeth together, I forsake any covering as I creep through a seemingly deserted wing and down the servant's staircase. Even the back halls are deserted. Did he fire everyone? Guilt racks my spine. Some of our staff had worked with my family for years—yet another casualty to our downfall. In a year, would they be willing to return? I make a promise to myself here and now to ensure they do. Everything will be just as it was. Everything…

Except for this house. Within a day, Blake Lorenz has altered it irreparably. My father's study is a far cry from my old refuge. I linger in the doorway, unsure if it's even the same room. But yes, it's the final door in this section of the house, right off the main entrance.

Papa's presence has haunted this room for so long, but overnight, he's vanished. I can't tell if that's a good or bad thing. Honestly, the shiver racking my spine feels the same. But it's not Papa I picture as I creep toward my old hiding place—the mahogany desk—and run my fingers along its surface.

Despite the cold, I leave streaks of sweat over the wood. My fingers shake. Clenching them by my sides, I turn to the bookshelves. Oddly enough, Blake Lorenz seemed to have left the chilling selection intact. Books on war and revenge.

But years ago, I snuck a sliver of peace into this refuge. After all this time, I'm not sure if the book is still even there, hidden beneath the desk, tucked in the tiny gap left by the drawer. But there it is. I slowly pull it out and curl up on the floor of the cramped space. It's hard to read in the shadow, so I rely mainly on memory, but my mind soon drifts to the person who gave me this gift.

It was a joke, I think. A mocking play on his nickname: Princess Snow. A book of fairy tales spanning numerous continents and ages. I settle on one without thought and wind up running my fingers over an in-depth illustration of a round egg-like figure perched on a stone wall. Humpty Dumpty.

I think I read that excerpt at least ten times before I finally notice the footsteps approaching the room. Charles? Or another servant?

No. Those slow, heavy steps trigger the eerie sensation of falling in my stomach. Only one man affects me this way.

"I know you're in here," he says from the doorway, but I can't shake the feeling that he's speaking more to himself than to me. Animosity wafts on the air, clashing with the memory playing in my very soul.

I've found you, Snow. I know you're in here...

"Get out."

I unfurl my limbs and crawl from beneath the desk. He's wearing black: a plain shirt unbuttoned to reveal a sliver of muscled flesh underneath. His feet are bare, his hair tousled. Going off his frown, I suspect he forgot his own declaration? His eyes narrow as I stand, dropping the book.

My hands fly to my breasts, but not quickly enough. He eyes me shamelessly, from my exposed nipples downward. With every inch traveled, black pupils dilate in that terrible way mothers warn their daughters about in hushed tones.

"I'm leaving." I grab the book and circle the desk only to falter when he doesn't move from the doorway.

He jerks his chin instead, down to the object clenched in my fist. Something flits across his face too quickly to name. Recognition? I hold my breath as he scans the cover.

"Leave it."

My fingers tighten over the leather spine. So many memories have already been forfeited. Can I bare to give up this one as well? A lump forms in my throat.

"It's just a children's book," I say. "It's not—"

"I said leave it."

I lower the book to the desk's surface, but I can't take my eyes off it. My feet refuse to move, rooted to the Persian carpet.

"Someone gave it to me." Why I tell him as much, I don't know. Brandt Lloyd was a presence I thought I had exorcized from my life a long time ago. Lately, it feels like his memory is stronger than ever, thanks in no small part to the man tormenting me while wearing his face. "Please—"

"Enough."

I jump as he advances on me. Alarm jolts through my skin when snatches the book from my reach. He opens it at random and rips a page right from the middle. Another. Then another. As I watch, he crumbles them one by one and tosses them to the floor at my feet. When he turns to another page, my heart lurches to my throat and I can't silence a cry.

"W-wait!"

"What?" He scowls down at the page, devoid of recognition. Though, if I'm not mistaken, the line of his jaw tightens further.

"Not that one," I say. I'm begging.

He captures the title page between his thumb and his forefinger. Then he releases it and shoves the book against my chest. "Get out."

I race for the door.

"Wait."

Clutching the book to my chest, I linger on the threshold.

"Come here."

I turn to face him, biting a refusal back. Already, he's seated behind the desk. In the dim light of dawn, he almost resembles Papa, scowling in disapproval of my mere presence.

"Sit."

When I approach one of the leather chairs positioned near the door, he shakes his head.

"No. There."

The desk itself? When I reach it, he says nothing. Instead, he turns his attention to one of the drawers and fishes a stack of paperwork from within. Slowly, I turn and brace one hand against the wood. A sharp intake of air cuts the silence, but I'm too breathless to make the sound.

I look back and find blue eyes watching me, centered over my lower back. Self-consciousness washes over me, and my toes twitch toward the floor. "I can go—"

"Sit." His tone leaves no room for argument, clipped and cold.

I lower myself without facing him, forced to rely on my hearing to guess his motives. He's breathing harshly but still shuffling his papers. Every now and again, I hear the scratch like that of a pen over parchment.

"Read," he tells me after what feels like an eternity.

My book? I warily eye the pages, annoyed beyond reason when tears blur my vision. He can ask me to strip and I do it without hesitation, but this? This book contains a soul, one too sacred to desecrate. So I attempt to flip to another story.

"Don't," he snaps before I can completely turn the page. "Read it out loud."

I fight to swallow down the lump in my throat. "H-Humpty Dumpty sat on a wall—"

"Louder." For a world-renowned businessman, he doesn't seem eager to question why a grown woman is clinging to a children's book. There's nothing in his tone I can interpret. No inflection. No hint of emotion. He might as well be talking to the wall about the weather. A wall he despises. "Keep reading."

So I do, straining my voice to carry. Miracle of miracles, the tears welling in my eyes never fall. They merely obscure the pages until memory is all I rely on. "And all the king's horses and all the king's men failed to put him back together again."

My voice rasps as my words echo back to me. It's been so long since I've read this book. So long since I've smelled the scents locked within the pages. I swear I can feel him. Hear him promising to be by my side always. Where kings and men failed, Brandt Lloyd never would.

"Get out. And leave the book."

This time, I don't question. I let the book fall from my lap and escape the room before he can call me back. Seconds later, I'm locked in my room, crouched on the bathroom floor, sobs ripping from my chest. Then the tears finally fall, like hundreds of tiny daggers. All of them carry the weight of ten years. God, even reading a simple story to a stranger feels like having salt ground into my open wounds.

My fingers register the loss of the book, uncomfortably clenching together. I sink them into my hair to distract myself from the resounding ache, braiding it into a long plait that falls between my shoulder blades.

The lack of clothing feels even more apparent here, with the cold tile biting through my thin panties. They're delicate lace, not practical in the slightest. The woman who picked them out did so with panty lines in mind. She wasn't a heartbeat from poverty, forced to cater to the whims of a psychopath.

A psychopath who has yet to tell me what he wants from our arrangement.

The thought of not knowing stings worse than any crude remark or jab about my weight. I'm not his type, but in what context? His type of woman in general? Or perhaps sexually?

But therein lies the rub. He seemed more willing to fuck me in Bolles than in his private home. Though, admittedly, not in the slow, lazy way Daniel and Sloane did the one time I caught them in bed. They were so engrossed in each other that they didn't even notice me spying from the doorway before I crept out of his house. Daniel savored Sloane the way I used to enjoy the melted, runny bits of chocolate I'd smothered in my pocket during class. It wasn't perfect, but in a pinch, after a grueling math session, nothing in the world could compare.

Blake looks at me like a starving man who loathes chocolate, forced to decide between starvation or sustenance. His mind chooses to die, but his body overrules him. Those eyes betray him.

I'd prefer Daniel, who would make love to me like a connoisseur devouring the finest box of chocolates. Sure, he'd always have another treat in mind, but for the moment, I'd make do.

Men like Blake Lorenz never settle for a piece of what they crave.

I can still feel his fingers roughly dragging over my skin. Each one left imprints seared into the muscle underneath. He's too cruel for possession. No. I feel marked instead— like a condemned building, forced to remain a hollow shell of myself until a wrecking ball finally puts me out of my misery.

A task Mr. Lorenz seems willing to avoid for now.

I can hear him down in Papa's study. Rustling. Shuffling. Writing. One of those many documents might hold the key to proving that my family's circumstances were manufactured. A confession, maybe? One can only hope— literally. It's all I can do but pray for a miracle. Exhaustion and shame form a powerful elixir. The longer I sit, curled and scheming, the more tempting one of my insane plans seem. Break into the office and find what I can. Evidence. Anything.

Turn the tables on Blake Lorenz.

But even thinking of him is a dangerous game.

Someone's approaching my door as if conjured by the allure of his name bouncing around my skull. He doesn't knock or even open my door right away. I can sense him there, hovering in shadow, breathing in my scent. Hating every drop.

"Unlock the door."

Shit. I lurch to my feet and twist the doorknob myself. He shoves the door open the rest of the way, and I barely manage to duck out of its path.

The man who ruined my entire world stands in the center of my altered room, frowning at the decor. My sheets are mussed, a crumpled bit of lace still on my floor. Heat prickles my cheeks as his attention lingers over every mess.

"You are not a kept woman, Ms. Hollings," he tells me. Hate undercuts every word, and suddenly, my room is stifling. "You are not a guest. You are in my employ, and I expect you to earn every dime."

Earn? My stomach churns at his ominous use of the word. "H-how?"

He meets my gaze with an unnaturally blank expression. "To start with, where the hell is my breakfast?"

"B-breakfast?"

"You have one hour." He storms into the hall before I can question.

Does he mean for me to cook? Dazed, I find myself chasing him, rounding the hallway just as he descends the first few steps of the grand staircase.

"Coffee, black," he snaps. "Toast with butter. Eggs over easy. Don't burn a fucking drop. Understood?"

He continues down the steps without waiting for confirmation, his shoulders so rigid that I could carve pieces of him off and chisel a new man from his solid frame. One who wouldn't hesitate to return my family's fortune if I asked.

There's an art to seducing men. Sloane could—and has—used her body to enact almost anything that she wants from the opposite sex. With my family name, I had success with as little as a smile. But Sloane's body couldn't overcome greed, and without my money, I have nothing—as best evidenced by Blake Lorenz's indifference.

Still, some women have worked with far less. If being a Hollings means something, as Papa insisted, then that should translate, money or no.

"An hour, Snow." The warning comes from below. I startle to awareness and catch sight of him near the base of the steps. Watching me. "An hour."

The moment his presence finally fades, I start down the steps and begin a dizzying trek to the kitchen. He must have fired Alice, the old cook who had served the Hollings table since before I was born. I find the kitchen empty and so cold that my teeth chatter. Here, I have no clue where to begin.

Coffee? As far as I know, it magically appeared in my mug every morning. In fact, the only Hollings with any semblance of knowledge around a kitchen is probably Hunter. It's not like I can ask him now, even if he's sober.

Biting my lower lip, I survey the kitchen and rely on logical guesses. Forty minutes later, I have brownish coffee-flavored water cooling in a mug, a plate full of flakey, blackened bits that were once eggs, and toast burned on one side but nearly untouched on the other. Red with shame, I gather the meager offerings onto a tray I found in a cupboard and approach the study.

I find him hunched over the desk, his back to me. A stack of papers once again serves as his main focus. He pours over one while beckoning me closer. Silently, I place the tray down beside him. He gives it a curious glance and shrugs.

Apparently, I'm dismissed.

Alone, I return to my room and watch the world beyond my window. Rain streaks across my view of the gardens, neglected after just a few days without treatment. For a man who purchased a multimillion-dollar property, Blake Lorenz appears to have little interest in running it. Does his hatred toward my family extend to the very property itself?

I can't imagine that kind of malice. Then again, I can't imagine a man as unreadable as Blake Lorenz. Money. Sex. Power. Which one drives him? All three?

A woman like Sloane might know how to exploit at least one of those desires to her own ends. But me? I've never had to work for anything in my life. I either had it handed to me or, as with any Hollings, I simply took it.

Inhaling deeply, I turn to the rack of clothing again. One of the garments is a dress that fits if I keep it rolled up at my waist. Wearing it, I'm able to face myself in the mirror and devise a plan.

A year is too damn long. Someway, somehow, I need to ensure that Blake Lorenz gives me my money sooner.

Eyeing myself warily, I smooth my hand along the lacy material. It's only as my finger catches the light that I realize I'm still wearing Daniel's ring. Some fiancée I turned out to be. I sold myself to another man without even stopping to consider just what that would mean. For Daniel. For myself. So much for being a Hollings-Ellingston.

I turn away from my reflection, fighting a lump forming in my throat. Nervous energy has me pacing my room in circles. It's approaching noon of my first day of self-imposed servitude, yet I still have no clue as to my duties. He had me cook. Does he intend to make me his maid?

I'm more terrified by the prospect than I care to admit. Servants are invisible, relegated to dark corners and hidden spaces.

He can ignore a servant.

Though he seems determined to do as much regardless. For hours, I hear him at work in Papa's study. Shuffling documents and scribbling in pen. I'm hypnotized by the various sounds, lulled into a daze.

Until the sound stops and my nostrils flare with a newer sensation.

"I told you not to wear a damn thing until you can fit into the clothing."

I lurch upright. I was lying on my bed. Did I drift off? My eyes sting to bolster that suspicion, though the reaction could have something to do with the figure watching me from my doorway. Darkness paints him in liberal doses of obscurity. God, he could be Brandt. He could be the devil.

But he's neither. Just a means to an end—it's how my father taught me to see anyone who isn't a Hollings. As an obstacle to either conquer or step over. I size him up in a single glance and make my decision.

I'll conquer him no matter what it takes.

"I'm sorry." I let my hands drift to my throat, fingering the neckline of the garment. After shifting into a sitting stance, I ease it over my head. I should be the one in charge of the act, but his scrutiny washes over me like lava, burning. Searing.

"Come here."

Slowly, I haul myself to my feet and approach him. When I'm mere inches away, his hand lands over my shoulder, grinding his presence into the muscle and bone beneath.

"You don't disobey me. Do you understand?"

I nod, unsettled by the grating tone. No man has ever spoken to me like this. Frankly. Honestly. With curt words conveying a warning he doesn't bother to disguise beneath frilly language or charm.

"The moment you piss me off, I'll have you on the street. Do you understand me?" The hand on my shoulder creeps to a position behind my throat, guiding the direction of my gaze. I'm forced to meet his directly: fathomless pools of indigo and hatred. "Say it."

"I-I understand."

"And you understand the only reason why I would even consider giving you a single dime?"

Do I? I find myself nodding all the same. "Yes."

"Say it."

"I…"

He laughs. "Because you are a mere commodity of the Hollings brand, bought and sold like a piece of trash, and I've always been a completionist."

THE TRUE DEPTH of the insult doesn't sink in until nearly a minute later. When he's already turned his back on me and sauntered down the hall.

Trash.

Hollings.

Like I'm a toy he bought on a whim.

"No." I voice the refusal to a blank wall, aware that he's listening. His heavy steps trail off nearby. "N-no, I'm not."

I follow him, expecting to find him sneering, ready to deliver a cruel retort. Not scowling with impatience.

"Is that so?"

"I could go to someone else." It's an option that sounds more appealing by the minute. I could return to Bolles and find someone else. But there's one small matter only Blake Lorenz can offer.

"Do it," he says through gritted teeth. His eyes flash almost with glee. "I'll have your home burned to the ground before you can even spread your legs."

I wince at the imagery. "It's just a house."

"Wrong." He advances on me but pauses when he's close enough to touch—not that he does. "You're a Hollings. You know what that means."

I'm not sure I do anymore. Nothing but dread and harsh memories taint the walls of the house, nullifying the good. Mama's study. That space under Papa's desk. My old room —those are the only parts of Hollings Manor worth saving. Could I bear to watch them burn?

I don't need to hear Blake's callous scoff to know the answer.

"You'd fuck a stranger to save this place," he tells me, his voice ringing with confidence.

I would. I will.

"Houses can be rebuilt," I croak, though I'm not sure if I'm trying to convince him or myself. "I don't need you."

"Oh really?" A shadow distorts his hard features, darkening the hue of his irises. "Then get the fuck out. Leave."

I aim my trembling limbs toward the stairs, intending to do just that. It doesn't matter that I don't have clothing, or a car, or a house to run to. As he crudely put it, I'm a Hollings. I'll find a way. I must find a way...

"And what a shame when Ronan gets taken off life support. Or when Hunter is led away in cuffs."

"What?" I come to a dead stop at the base of the steps, panting with the effort it takes to breathe. "You wouldn't."

"Try me. I own everything in your fucking life, Snow. I can smash it all to pieces, but I'll let you oversee when and how. So leave. Just know that the moment you step foot out of that door, I'll fucking set your entire world on fire."

"Why are you doing this?" I can't even shout. Or scream. I just whisper, horrified by the figure watching me from the top of the stairs. His face is so beautiful that it hurts, and I now understand the true meaning of hell. It's not fire and brimstone. It's *pain* draped in Armani and perfumed with hate.

It's Blake Lorenz manipulating me like a puppet.

It's this cold, deep pinch in my gut that warns me there can only be *one* reason why, no matter how insane it sounds inside my head.

"Only one person in the world could hate me so much…"

"Oh?" He shrugs again. "And who would that be, Snow? Fucking say his name."

But I can't. "One person you could only dream of becoming."

He laughs at that. Throws his head back and chuckles deeply. "And why would this so-called 'dreamlike' man hate you?"

"Because…" I nervously lick my lips. In the space of a second, his expression changes. His eyes flash and his upper lip curls back from his teeth, baring them in a snarl. "Because I told the entire world what everyone always thought he was."

"And what was that?" Danger laces his tone, warning me to stop.

But I can't. "I told the world he was a monster."

He blinks, his face blank, almost canvas-like, before rage paints it in strokes of red. "And he showed the world that you're nothing more than an ugly, selfish, disgusting little bitch."

Stung, I turn for the front door and cross the foyer in seconds. With trembling hands, I paw the door open and brace my bare toes over the stoop, assaulted by the frigid chill.

"Run, Snow," he calls from behind me. "Go! Fucking run."

And cause your family's ruin, his cruel tone implies.

My body twitches forward, but at the last second, I turn before I can step fully over the threshold and run headlong deeper into the house instead.

I pick a direction at random, aware only of the fact that someone is fast on my heels. Their steps are heavier than mine. Steadier than mine. When I trip over a doorway and flail for balance, they're already entering the room in my wake.

"Get away from me!"

I'm in Papa's study, of all places. The desk is the only structure capable of being placed between us. So I lunge for it, but he reaches it at the same time. The drawers are on his end and he wrenches one open and rummages inside it while my heart plays a sickening melody. When he withdraws a pair of silver scissors, my pulse stutters to a violent stop.

"Come here." He parts the blades with menacing slowness.

"No." I stagger back out of his reach, but my shoulders strike the firm ledge of a bookcase, trapping me between him and the door. There's no escape.

But he doesn't want to corner me. He wants to desolate me. Cold, blue eyes convey my utter destruction as he braces his weight against the desk on the flat of his hand. "I said come here."

My gaze fixates on the scissors he's holding. The twin blades gleam, dangerously sharp. No one's threatened me like this before. Correction: No one's done so this openly.

"You have five seconds," he warns.

"Are…are you going to hurt me?"

He stiffens, his jaw snapping shut. "Come here."

He won't hurt me physically anyway. It's a suspicion I can't explain, and I don't care to examine it in full.

"Three seconds."

Woodenly, I force my legs to move, bringing myself as close to the desk as I dare. When I'm within his reach, he grabs my wrist, dragging me around to his side of the desk.

"Get down."

A heavy hand flattens against my lower back, forcing me to lean over the desk, at his mercy. I see the scissors glinting from the corner of my eye, alarmingly close to my ear. The snap of them closing echoes like a gunshot, close to my head but not near any skin. I blink in confusion but then the aftermath flutters against my fingers: long strands of fiery red…

"No!" I try to move only to be pushed down harder.

"Don't fucking move." The scissors open and close again in quick succession and more strands of my hair drift down to coat the desk. Red, vibrant.

"Stop."

He doesn't. Ruthlessly, he shears every bit of hair, grunting with each snap of the blades. More. More. More. Somehow, I don't move a muscle even as tears stream down my face, wetting the wood beneath me.

"I don't want Snowy fucking Hollings," he growls as more locks fall from my shoulders. "If that's all you have to offer, then you might as well leave now. I don't want your goddamn family. Or your money."

Then what does he want? I can't find the breath to ask. With one last violent snap, he slams the scissors onto the desk.

"I want a warm fucking hole who knows who she owes her world to." He growls the words into my ear. "Say it. You need me. Fucking say it."

My body vibrates against the surface of the desk. I'm shaking. Fear and desperation shape my spine, keeping it curved while the remains of my hair coat me, red like ashes. Warmth clings to them still. I can tell from how light my head feels that he cut off inches, leaving me with a length that barely brushes my shoulders. To drill the loss in, he seizes a lock of it, cruelly twisting it between his fingers.

"Say it. Say it or you won't get a fucking dime—"

"I need you."

"That's right." He withdraws with a sigh. "You're damn right you fucking do. Now, clean up this fucking mess."

I hear him leave. Somewhere deeper within the house, a door slams. Silence descends, lasting only a second before my sobs shatter it. They rip from me, wordless and howling.

I don't know how long I lie here, gasping for air. All I'm sure of is darkness and unrelenting cold as I return to my bedroom.

Ice greets me beneath the sheets, a fitting sensation to match the chill encasing my heart. Nothing seems to ease it.

No number of blankets pulled over my frame or any position over the mattress.

For the first time in my life, I wish that Brandt Lloyd really *is* dead and gone, any doppelganger be damned. I pray for as much.

Because the alternative is too terrifying to fathom. Could my beautiful boy have become a monster? My brain shies away from deciding on an answer. Instead, I squeeze my eyes shut, desperate to ignore my shorn hair. Cool air tickles my ears in a way it hasn't in years. My shoulders chafe, assaulted by the sheets.

But the worst discomfort dwells in my head, where Blake Lorenz waits, eager to terrorize me, even in sleep.

THIRTEEN

"GET UP."

The harsh tone jolts me awake. Blake Lorenz is standing in my doorway, radiating a cold, subversive hate. It transcends mere disgust. Maybe this is his way of giving me an answer.

He may not be Brandt Lloyd, but his hate is more than directed at my family. It's me. A fact bolstered by the object he tosses onto my bed before storming out.

I scramble for the item, hunting through twisted sheets. When my hand finally brushes the cool surface, I survey it dejectedly: a small box of hair dye. The woman on the package is a grinning brunette.

And the depth of his newest command slices through me.

He can't be serious. I wait for a harsh order to come from the doorway. Something to cement his malice—but no. He leaves it up to me to interpret his meaning.

And like he told me once before, I could easily walk away. It's not like red hair is what makes me a Hollings—Papa was an icy blond, a trait shared by Ronan and Hunter. Mama was fair-haired as well, but it's not her who I remember running his fingers through his hair as he remarked on the shade. Fiery Princess Snow.

God, I can hear him. You can do anything if you stop letting the world get inside your head.

But I did. I let the world get inside our lives and rip them apart. I let the world destroy him.

Ten years later, I'm finally being punished for it.

My heart aches as I carry the dye into the bathroom. Tears prick my eyes before I even get it open and spread out the materials over the counter. I work quickly, slathering every inch of coppery red in brown dye, though I don't look at myself in the mirror once.

After I shower and rinse, however, there's no escaping my reflection.

Blake Lorenz didn't simply cut my hair. He mutilated the perfect image of Snowy Hollings and left a stranger in her place. Dark hair makes her blue eyes wider, her features painfully young. Jagged bits stick out from a blunt, shoulder-length bob. More tears fall before I can hold them back, but I chase down every one and smear them over the back of my hand.

No. I won't let him see me like this.

I towel off, gritting my teeth against any sobs. Then I remember his rule against clothing and I'm left without a stitch of cotton to hide behind. Just my shorn, tangled hair. Drying it doesn't help any. Neither does brushing it. My curls transform into an unruly heap springing in every which direction, a million different lengths. It's dark. Ugly.

This is how he wants me.

But then why pay for me?

The question haunts me as I pace, circling around my room. Soon, walking turns to jogging. Then running. My lungs burn and my heart pounds as I imagine bits of fat burning away. More. More. More. Sweat drips down my spine, slicking my limbs, and I use my bed as a post to count how many laps I take.

Ten.

Fifty.

A hundred.

Three hundred.

I've lost count by the time I finally see him from the corner of my eye. He's near the doorway, his arms crossed, far enough away that I can't see him unless I turn directly to look.

"Brandt Lloyd," he says coldly.

I flinch and stagger to a stop. The next second, I'm on my knees, hunched over as if the position can protect my heart from any further damage. Pain claws through me regardless.

"You mentioned him," Blake adds as if to drill the fact in: I brought him up first. I asked for it. "Why?"

"You look like him." There's no point in lying now. With my gaze trained on the floor before me, it's easier to admit it out loud. This man looks so much like Brandt.

He scoffs. "As if you even remember him—"

"Of course I do." My head jerks upright. "I never forgot him."

"Oh?" he wonders, his head cocked dangerously to the side. My vision blurs around the edges, but his expression is clearer than ever. He is raw, twisted anger in human form. "Tell me, then. What do you remember, Snow?"

Memories tumble loose from the maze of my thoughts, a million things I spent years tucking away. His laugh. His smile. The twinkle in his eye as he teased me. His scent. His touch. The only time he ever looked at me as anything other than a nuisance.

God, I remember every inch of him.

And it hurts.

"Stop." I turn on my heel, aching to keep moving. Run. When I lurch onto the tip of my toes, he steps forward as if sensing my need to flee, and his nearness alone traps me in place.

"Tell me," he goads in a whisper-soft tone. "Do you remember what a sap he was? How easy for you to manipulate?"

"Stop—"

"Or do you remember the lying?" He took a step closer without my realizing it. Each word strikes my bare shoulder in a burst of searing heat. "Do you remember sitting in the courtroom and looking him in the eye as you told the entire world that he—"

"I didn't lie." The truth spills from my lips, bitter and tainted. I'm not lying. But neither are those three words the whole picture...

"Bullshit." A heavy hand latches onto the back of my skull, wrenching my head around to face him. I blink and his features blur into a mocking blend of light and shadow. "Say it," he demands. "Fucking say it. Tell me he raped you."

On command, my lips part. It's like I'm transported back ten years ago, forced to take the witness stand. I only had to utter three solemn words.

"He raped me."

He shakes his head as a roar rips from his throat. In an instant, the callous businessman melds into a monster, twisted and snarling.

"Say it again," he commands.

I recite my line on cue, sick with self-loathing. "He raped me."

Seconds pass in silence, with only the harsh sound of his breathing to add context to the tension. He's more curious than angry. His gaze hunts my own, scouring over every blink and twitching pupil.

"Fuck you," he says, spitting each word against my skin. "Fuck you, you lying little cunt."

His free hand comes to trace the line of my jaw with surprising tenderness in comparison to the guttural cadence of his voice.

"Tell me how he did it."

My lips spring apart at his command. "With his fingers…"

"Digital penetration" they called it in the court filings, just as invasive as any other sexual abuse. I had the internal bruises to prove it, but my hymen was still intact, a fact made public to the world.

"His fingers?" A dangerous cloud falls over Blake's face, sucking the remaining humanity from his features. He tilts his grip, drawing my face closer to his as he muscles his body against mine.

A sharp breath catches in my throat. He's far too close. Heat radiates off his form, searing my flesh. Naked, I have no protection from his presence. No salvation. With one chilling caress down my cheek, he strips away any semblance of composure I had left. Tears fall, and he laughs at the sight of them.

"Manipulative Little Snow. That won't work on me." His tongue flies out, grazing my jaw, crushing a bead of moisture in its path. He exhales raggedly, savoring the taste as his grip tightens. "I could fuck you here and now and you couldn't cry rape, could you?"

A cold sense of dread unfurls in my belly, sparking a single pathetic thought. He wouldn't.

"Answer me."

"N-no."

"You couldn't." He hisses through his teeth at my answer. "Now tell me why."

Fire crawls through my scalp as his grip tightens further, ripping stray strands from their follicle beds.

"You're hurting me—"

"Answer the fucking question."

Numb with shame, I have no choice. "Because I sold myself to you," I croak.

"Damn right, you did." He lets me go.

Rudderless, I stagger toward my bed, forced to throw a hand out to catch myself against the side of the mattress.

"I tell you to fuck me, you'll fuck me," he says, and I tremble beneath the implied threat. "I tell you to go to Bolles and fuck every bastard there—"

"I'll refuse." How I found the strength to counter him, I'll never know. It could be the glimpse of emotion I catch flitting across his gaze, even now. Something so faint but so undeniable that it challenges his assurances of the opposite.

"Will you now?" he wonders, leaving an awkward silence demanding to be filled.

"Why buy me if you don't want me?"

He throws his head back and laughs, glowering at the ceiling. "Little Snow, always so fucking conceited—"

"Then say it," I whisper. God, I almost sound like I'm begging him to prove me wrong. Deny what I feel in the most primal reaches of my being. "Tell me you don't want me."

His gaze refocuses, honed like a blade plunging deep. "I'd rather fuck Charles than stick my cock in you."

Which isn't an outright denial. In fact... The word usage terrifies me more.

His gaze rakes over me, observing my bare breasts and quivering thighs. Contrary to his insistence, I catch him lingering over the space between my legs as a muscle in his jaw lurches against the taut skin.

"Say it," I request. A part of me won't rest until he does. Perhaps it's vanity? Or sheer desperation. *I don't want you, Snow.*

"I'll take what I'm fucking *owed*, Snow," he tells me, inching a dangerous step forward. "I'll fuck you raw to prove my point if I have to: I own you."

He does. There's no denying it; even if I wanted to be brave, I couldn't. His possession is my only saving grace. But he won't prove it any time soon, I suspect. He'll make me wait. He'll make me suffer.

He'll make me wonder just how he'll break me open.

"Why…why buy me if you don't want me?" I repeat in the pathetic hope of a different answer. Something concrete. Anything but another lie.

"Are you that eager to feel me inside you?"

Alarm crashes down my spine, and instinct drives me away from him. Danger. Mayday. I've gone too far.

He advances steadily, watching with hollow eyes as my calves strike the edge of my bedframe. "Lie down."

Ice solidifies in my throat. I can't breathe. Suffocation begins in excruciating slowness as he waits for me to obey the command.

Because I must. Or run. The latter has never seemed so fucking tempting. I'd race miles to put distance between myself and the man before me.

Anything but stay and wait for him to deliver on the malice promised in his eyes.

"I fucking told you to lie down."

My limbs contort on command. Bending knees lower me onto the mattress as my spine extends, guiding my back toward the rumpled sheets. He's over me in an instant. A harsh shove on my chest pushes me down.

"Spread your legs."

"Not like this." I don't know where the plea comes from—ripped from my soul, it feels like. I know he'll fuck me eventually. I know he'll make it hurt.

But not like this—staring into my eyes, snarling with hate. I can tolerate his violation, but not when he looks like Brandt.

"Is that so?" He sneers, his upper lip pulling back from his teeth, but he withdraws from me, lifting his hand from my chest. "Then how? Tell me, Snow? How do you want to be violated?"

I cringe at the raw hatred in his tone, unable to escape giving him an answer. How? In darkness, with my face pressed against a pillow and my pores forced to absorb his shame. The imagery triggers a memory I don't want to relive. My eyes shut against it. Too late. *Creeping, searching fingers…*

"Look at me."

I snap my eyes open, a slave to his whims. Hovering above me, he's a stranger again. Blake Lorenz, determined to push me over the edge.

"Say it," he hisses through clenched teeth.

"Not like this."

I can't explain the expression transforming his face. Such a creature can't be remotely human. But he is. His humanity is proven in the way his fingers flex at his sides as if grappling with the very air for control. A beast wouldn't fear his nature.

"How, then?" Two harsh syllables betray his crumbling resolve. Against what? I can't tell. I don't want to even decipher the dark motives lurking behind those blue irises. "Say it."

"I don't want you to hurt me."

He laughs, a grim chuckle that invades my pores like poison, burning. Searing. I writhe in silent agony. God, I need to run. Get away. Move.

"And why shouldn't I?" he wonders, creeping closer once again. His hand falls on my thigh, flexing as I flinch.

"B-because you're not Brandt Lloyd." The words take everything I have to choke out, and he jerks back as though slapped.

"And he hurt you, did he?"

Such a quiet, dangerous tone of voice. Every part of me begs me to heed the warning in it. Stop.

But I can't. Words spill over my tongue, impossible to lock away.

"He hurt me," I croak. It's the truth. My boy hurt me worse than anyone ever could. Papa. Blake Lorenz. Hunter or Ronan.

He killed himself and part of me with him. He took his light away, leaving only darkness. I'll never find my way out of this hell, and maybe a part of me blames him for it.

But my words have a different meaning to Blake Lorenz. A broken laugh tears from his throat as he backs away before turning to the door.

"You believe it, don't you?" he mutters, almost to himself. "You think he did it. You think he raped you."

He doesn't finish his statement, but I can fill in the blanks. *You stupid, spoiled, conceited little bitch.* Ten steps carry him to the doorway, where he wavers, his head cocked to deliver one last parting blow.

"You don't have to worry about me coming anywhere near you with my cock," he warns. "I couldn't fuck you even if I wanted to savor the experience of making you bleed. Why?"

He pauses, letting the silence linger and anticipation build until I can almost taste it. Just when the dread reaches unbearable heights, he shoots an unsympathetic glance over his shoulder.

"Because you're disgusting. Every fucking inch of you is repulsive, inside and out. Fuck, even looking at you disgusts me, so forget my previous offer. You have three days to fit into the clothes or your shares are forfeited."

He's gone before the true impact of his words can sink in. Embarrassment comes first, flooding my veins. Hunched over as I am, I can only shield so much of me from view with trembling fingers. I choose my stomach, feeling chunks of fat and flesh.

Humpty Dumpty with no king to save her, just broken pieces.

When I'm sure he's gone, I roll onto my side and stare at the floor, urging myself to run. My legs refuse to obey, and I turn my attention to the yawning bathroom doorway instead. My stomach churns, my eternal enemy. I'm disgusting. I'm repulsive.

I'm a liar.

The latter is the worst attribute of the three. Ten years can shape an ugly duckling into the semblance of a swan, but time can never heal the old wounds she gouged into innocent lives with fumbling intentions. I stare down at the body in question and frown. Then I scream—silently, of course—smothered against my palm.

I'm a Hollings. That means something.

We suffer in silence and take our transgressions to the grave.

Like father like daughter.

THIS TIME OF YEAR, each day feels brief and dark— they're getting shorter, after all. Colder. Warmth comes in the form of blood-red sunsets sprawled over the horizon. But not even a second later, it's gone, smothered beneath the oppressive dark.

Blake Lorenz dwells in my father's study, a midnight creature giving context to the shadows. Their whispers resemble the scratching of an ink pen, chasing me into a fitful sleep.

I emerge from a nightmare, drenched in a cold sweat, gasping on the verge of a scream—but it's a harrowing few seconds before I understand why. Faint moonlight reveals the horror; the monster from my nightmare crept into my room and is hunched near the foot of my bed. Before I can scream, he lunges, pinning me beneath heavy, solid limbs.

If only he smelled like a beast should smell. Not like wind, and rain, and all things clean and distilled. Not like Brandt.

He even feels like Brandt.

His nearness burns like Brandt.

With his mouth inches from my ear, this specter demands one thing. "Fucking tell me why," he growls. "Tell me why you did it, Snow. Just fucking tell me why."

His voice… The way it cracks and splinters. No one could fake that sound. No one.

Heart heavy with dread, I realize I really am in a dream. The truth can be uttered only in my dreams.

"I had to…"

He stiffens, drawing in ragged breaths. "Why?"

"Because…"

Either my imagination picks up where my vision fails or my eyes adjust to the dark. I see him clearly, my beautiful Brandt, all grown up. Ebony hair falls into his eyes, disturbed by raking fingers that tear at it still. I smooth my own along the back of his hand, and a painful lump obstructs my throat. He feels the same.

And if he does hate me, I deserve it.

"Please." Endlessly blue eyes peer into mine, demanding an answer. "Tell me why."

"I…I had to save you."

He cringes at the confession, poised to withdraw—but I can't let him just yet. Not now. My fingers find his shoulders and bite down over tailored cotton. Strange. My Brandt loved tee shirts and dingy, cast-off things fished from secondhand stores. He loved ratty jeans and leather jackets.

But no one else could conform to my body like this, made for comforting when all else seems lost. A part of me aches in recognition. It's been so damn long.

"Stay."

He grunts. Stiffens. Before I can beg again, warm fingers capture my hips. The weight on top of me evens, and a groan trickles into my ear. Too deep—a man's reluctant exhale, not my boy's. Alarm nibbles at the outside of my skull, but I cringe from it, arching into him. Not yet. I can't wake up yet.

"I loved you," I tell him before it's too late. "Everything I did was for you."

"How?" he questions, his teeth gritted.

But therein lies the true price of my soul: I can never tell him.

But maybe I can show him, squeeze him so tight that my knuckles crack, praying I never wake up. I could die like this, holding him so close that it's like he's here. My body clings to him as my eyes strain through shadow, hunting down every little detail.

God, he looks so old. So broken. So hateful.

I blink and he's vanished. But another man has claimed his place.

"Tell me," Blake Lorenz demands in a display of white teeth. "Tell me why you fucking did it. Tell me!"

But I can't.

So he rages. Hard fingers dig into my hips, nails first. My cry scratches at the air, too breathless to be of any substance.

"You love him," he whispers coldly against my cheek. "But he hated you, up until the end. He died hating you."

Heat sears behind my eyes. I squeeze them shut, but he refuses to be ignored. Warmth licks my lips. His thumb. Slowly, he nudges them apart, seeking out my tongue, wanting me to taste…

Blood. Mine. He scratched me that badly, coating his fingertips with coppery red.

"God, you fucking little cunt." Something thickens his voice in addition to the rage. The same instinct spurring his ragged breaths drives his pelvis against mine.

Good, well-bred girls aren't meant to notice such things: straining cocks and barely restrained lust. Blake Lorenz turns it on and off like flipping a switch. One minute, he's cold. The next, he's on fire, crushing me against my bed.

Old fear puts up a futile battle, nowhere near as potent as it should be. He's not Brandt, but my traitorous body doesn't seem to know it. Or maybe my aching limbs just don't care. They feed off the intentions wafting from his skin. A low sound builds in his throat, deepening every time I flinch. Move. Breathe.

"Fuck, you're doing this on purpose." Tortured, broken syllables break from him, one after the other. So hateful. So tormented. "Goddamn it, you smell so good." His nose skims the curve of my throat, inhaling me only to spit me back out. "Fuck, I can't. I won't…"

Too late.

My body registers the slow, deliberate movement before my brain acknowledges what's happening: thick fingers ghosting over my belly, trailing down between my legs. They twitch, my knees fighting to come together, but he's too quick, nudging his own knee between them.

"Open up for me, Snow. I know you feel it too…"

Fear ripples down my spine.

I can't.

Deny him.

Another low groan echoes against the valley between my breasts. Rasping sheets catch at the flesh of my side as he fists one of his hands in them, grappling for stability.

"You're so fucking beautiful," he snarls. "How the fuck can you be beautiful?"

It's magical when he says it. Beautiful, hateful beauty.

"Your breasts," he tells me, crouched like a predator, lathing heat over exposed flesh. "I've dreamt about these fucking breasts. How sick is that?"

I wince as he pinches flesh on my inner thigh, demanding an answer.

A huff of air escapes my lungs. *Yes.* It's goddamn sick. Almost as sick as wondering just how much like Brandt he really is. They smell the same. Feel the same. Taste the same?

A part of me shudders from the thought, but then I doggedly chase it again. God, I still remember. Sweet like the spring rain we played in. Soft, so soft. I could drown in his flavor, though I only got a mere taste.

And he banished me for it.

But Blake Lorenz breathes himself between my parted lips, imbibing me with a teasing glimpse of him. So different. So raw. Masculine, deep, musky man. He's a million things I could never decipher, smoldering on my tongue, demanding I swallow. With Brandt, I needed to savor, but Blake… His essence demands I choke on it, every fucking drop.

"Open your mouth."

He doesn't want to kiss me. I instinctively know his motives as my lips spread, breaths escaping in pitiful bursts. He wants to sample me before he rips me apart.

One stroke of his tongue stops my breath, ripping every ounce of air from my lungs.

"Fuck," he mutters, drawing his tongue along his lips. Anger constricts his pupils into pinpricks.

I taste too sweet.

With renewed interest, he lowers his mouth to mine and every nerve in my body flickers in response. Hot. Suddenly, he pulls away, leaving me burning, his gaze heavy-lidded in disgust.

"Tell me I'm not him."

Not who? Daniel?

No…

My devil wants separation from his angelic counterpart. My lips part to deliver as much, but words won't come. Those eyes. That frowning, wry expression and the subtle tilt of his jaw conveying repressed anger. All of it is so familiar, pieces of a broken puzzle. Deep down, I know they won't fit into the missing spaces left inside my soul. Nothing will ever fit.

"Say it."

Biting my lip doesn't lock the admission inside. "You're not him," I gasp.

He nods, satisfied, and rears back, casting a searching glance along my body as if hunting down every bit of reluctance. "Again. Say his name."

"You're not Brandt Lloyd."

Another nod. "I'm not," he says, boring through me with a vicious stare, making sure I acknowledge it. Accept it. "I'm not him," he repeats as he runs a grasping hand over my stomach. "I'm not him. So I don't…"

Have to love you. Be gentle. Be human. Be soft.

He isn't Brandt Lloyd—he's something far worse.

A cry spills from my lips as he rams his hand between my legs—not quite near my mound, but close. Close enough to awaken old, dirty memories.

"Stupid little bitch. I'll teach you the worth of a Hollings…"

I cringe, avoiding the contact. At the same time…my hip jerks, arching against the tips of his fingers. I hate the reaction roiling through me. Memories try to descend but fade without making their impact, smothered beneath his heat.

"Fucking slut," he murmurs, coaxing his fingers along my inner thigh, ghosting up, up, up. More fingers, brushing, curling. Close. Closer. "Tell me to touch you."

My head twitches side to side. No, no, no.

"Fucking tell me to touch you—"

I have no choice. His gruff, hateful tone is the key, twisting through my jagged soul and forcing me to open up.

"Touch me." My legs drift apart, giving him enough room to occupy. My chest tightens, allowing me to see down to where his wrist disappears between my legs.

His eyes catch me watching, and he doesn't approve, voicing his displeasure in a single grunted word. "Fuck."

He touches me like I'm a broken, dejected thing. He'll never put me back together again—he doesn't want to. I'm damaged goods, but he'll take what's left.

"I could hurt you," he tells me, making it even more confusing that he isn't. Not now. His face portrays his torment as his thumb nudges me farther apart, making me fling my legs aside to let him in. I think he grunts that request so softly that I barely hear it. "Let me in, Snow."

Let me break you open as I promised.

One testing brush along my core and everything tightens. Can't think. Cotton bed sheets chafe my skin, making it even realer that he's crouched on top of me. Watching me. Devouring me in tiny, nibbling glances.

"I…I need to touch you," he bites out as quivering fingers lower and spread. Fire. Ice. My eyelids flutter, chopping his image into distorted pieces. "Fuck, I need to feel you."

He arches forward, his arm flexing between us and the pressure feels unlike anything else. He has me spreading apart around liquid fingers, a gasping little plaything—but it's not how he wants me.

Anger rides his dissatisfied grunt. "How the fuck are you even wet?"

Maybe because my body weeps for him. Against him. Memories swell in my skull, threatening to break loose, but he pushes them back, holding everything at bay but shuddering, shameful, aching sensations. They make me writhe against his hand, my hips jerking greedily. What I want, I don't even know. Perhaps I don't even want it at all. I'll chase it down anyway like a moth to a flame.

He'll let me burn.

"I could fuck you like this," he breathes, rocking his hand with vigor, increasing the pressure.

My eyelids flutter, refusing to close. I need to see him like this, even as tears streak my cheeks. So honest. He's not my Brandt, but someone colder, a stranger who looks at me and groans that I'm beautiful, even as he despises me.

Something breaks from the stroking mass of fingers, pushing more firmly inside. Penetrating.

My head falls back, my mouth opening in shock. "D-don't hurt me."

He chuckles, sounding so tired. A man in a war, fighting a losing battle he can't afford to surrender. My eyes close against him as the invasion tightens, eliciting a deep, searing burn. Then they open again. He's closer, his eyes drinking in every pained reaction I can't hide.

"Yes," he grits out. More tightening. More aching pressure. More primal pain. "Take me even if it hurts. Look at me." He groans when I do, resting his face against mine. "You take me even if it hurts."

But my body has other plans.

Uncomfortable wetness pools where he touches me, easing the burn, making me malleable. Open. Ready. His.

"Jesus Christ, it shouldn't be like this," he laments, rearing back on his knees to gaze down at me in despair.

Pain renders his features more hollow than frozen. He's a skeletal shadow of a man, haunted by the substance glistening on the fingertips he's holding up for inspection. An ebony tongue slides from between his lips, stealing a drop for himself. He licks two fingers. Three at once, hissing as liquid meets his tongue.

"It shouldn't fucking be like this," he mutters dejectedly. "It's like you already fucking know. You know." He lowers himself over me again, placing five wet fingertips against my mouth, forcing me to inhale this animalistic form of myself. "You know who you belong to."

Brandt Lloyd. I want to say it. I need to say it.

But Blake Lorenz has me dangling from a string. With every flick of the sensual line, my spine twitches accordingly. I can fit almost the entire length of his finger now. God, it feels so strange. Like a part of me has been rented out for twenty-four fucking years but only now does the tenant decide to return home.

Lo and behold he hates the building he left behind.

"I'll make you regret," he promises, barely intelligible. "I'll make you wish you could scream. I'll make you pray you could grow to hate this."

What exactly?

Noise first. A low, grating hum: a zipper coming undone. It teases the air, a prelude to this menacing symphony. Fluttering next. Fabric being wrenched up by grasping fists, dragged over a beautifully formed head with a devastating expression. He looks how a murderer does, palming his weapon of choice.

My breath stutters when I spot it nudging apart the fabric of his fly.

I've seen cocks before. I've seen Daniel's, thin and wiry, striving to sink inside Sloane. I've seen larger, jutting menacingly.

But never any like his. Blake Lorenz is a study unto himself. He's large enough to terrify, straining, throbbing flesh rising from a thatch of dark curls. He's beautiful enough to inspire all manner of twisted thoughts. Such as how he'll feel inside me. Soft? Hard?

He strokes his fingers along the swollen head, and his harsh intake of air gives me a clue—he'll feel punishing. Every inch will force its way inside me, and there will be no escape. Gulping for air, I part my lips, my head lolling against the unyielding mattress. Hard fingers sink into my hair, forcing my gaze back to him.

"You shouldn't be wetter, Snow," he tells me, cruelly feeling for himself. Moisture slicks an easy path for his thumb to travel, biting deep. "Fuck, you should be screaming."

But I'm not. Tiny sounds rip from me, too insubstantial to register as anything at all. Maybe broken sobs and shattered promises.

"Were you saving yourself?" he asked me once. But I was. I was.

"Tell me to fuck you."

I shake my head, gritting my teeth, even as he winds down the fabric of his trousers. Bare, hot flesh meets mine, rigid with muscle and coiled sinew. God, he's more motion than man, rippling, tightening, breaking.

"Tell me you want me inside you." It's not a request this time. He drills the command in with a hard nip to my earlobe, drawing a gasp from me. Again. I cry out louder. "Tell me you want this."

But I don't. I don't. I—

He twists his fingers, shoving another in alongside the first. Too much. My spine stiffens, lifting my hips from the bed, driving him in farther. Too far.

"Fuck, tell me to fuck you."

Gritted teeth lock back all sound. I say nothing. Even as he crushes me down, kneeing my legs apart. Even as his hand cups my throat to the point of danger, wrenching my head back so that I have no choice but to stare up at him and watch. Those searching fingers withdraw too quickly, making me wince. Something larger replaces it a heartbeat later, nudging alongside my entrance, demanding to be let it.

"You feel… *Shit.*" His eyes close as his head rears back against his shoulders, baring his throat. Taut flesh reveals every inhale as he groans, grinding his teeth so loudly that the crunch resonates in my bones. "Hell," he rasps after a jarring second of silence. "You feel like fucking hell."

His hips lurch. More pressure, fearfully intense. Can't breathe. Can't think.

My lips fly apart, and terror spills out. "B-Brandt—"

"Not him." Glowering, the monster above me braces one hand beside my head, using it for leverage to drag his length along my folds.

Sickening, searing friction. I see white for a split second, it feels so sharp, this violation. It feels so wrong. So real. So…good.

"I'm not him," he repeats in between guttural groans. "I'm not fucking him."

My heart swells, battered and swollen. The pain makes me reckless. I'll do anything not to feel it.

"Tell me you are." It's a pathetic, dying wish before he rips me open. "Tell me you are and I'll say what you want. I'll do what you want… Just tell me you're—"

The bed lurches with the sudden shift in his weight. Flesh tears. Spreads. Accepts.

"Not. Him." He angles my face toward him, ensuring that I see every inch. Every flawed feature. Every twisted, beautiful pore and snarl. "Not…anymore."

The last part was imagined. I know it. Burning tears erupt anyway, coating my cheeks. My eyes shut against the tide of them, unable to keep a single drop at bay.

He's too deep. Without a damn given for my pain, he claws his way inside me, cramming every bit of himself he can. Deep. Deeper. It's impossible to be filled so much. I'll explode.

But then he moves.

And the world shatters into a million fucking pieces.

Bodies aren't meant to be molded like clay, splayed and kneaded into something new. Fingers tease my flesh in new directions as he forces his way inside me. Heavy hands pin my thighs flat on either side, rendering me immobile as he rocks his weight like a battering ram.

"T-too big," I squeak, squirming against the pressure of his touch. "Too big. Too big!"

He stops moving, his breath scalding my throat. "Do you want me to stop? I will." He groans as if it's the only thing in the world he wants. My rejection. "Say it. I will. Say it…"

My lips part… Nothing comes out.

It's futile. There's no shutting him out. No salvation.

All I can do is move against him, hastening my own destruction. Groaning, he rips me asunder, plundering everything I have. And, shuddering and gasping in the aftermath, I give it to him—every bloodied piece.

"Look." God knows how he's even capable of speech as he wrenches himself from my cleft, drawing a whine from my lips. One of his hands slithers beneath my neck, forcing me to gaze down and watch him. Swollen flesh glistens in the dark. "I own you now," he tells me, gnashing his teeth after every word. "I fucking own you. Say it."

Surrender rides conflicting waves of pleasure and pain. I'm no match. "You own me..."

Hissing, he shoves himself back in, stretching my body around his invasion. It hurts. God, it hurts so, so much. But it's that brutal kind of pain you get from flicking a hangnail or nudging a loose tooth.

Sharp and addicting.

My entire body becomes a wound he gleefully grinds salt into. One thrust. Another. Another.

He brews a storm inside me, too fierce for a weak rib cage and paper flesh to contain. With a cry, something breaks free, spills out.

I'm a puddle of gasoline.

He's a lit match...

Until he wrenches himself free, leaving me on the edge of igniting: tense limbs and rigid muscles.

Through a heavy-lidded gaze, I watch him palm his cock. His fingers grip the shaft, stroking until they find a steady rhythm that has him rocking against a quickly tightening fist. Only when he starts to groan does he finally look down, meeting my gaze. Then it's over. Hot spurts of scalding liquid lash my stomach. My chest heaves as my body registers the substance for what it is: his release.

He stands, shaking some of it from his hands. Then he turns on his heel and leaves, slamming the door behind him.

GOD, I need it to have been a dream. A nightmare. I pray for that reality with every fiber of my soul. But no amount of whispered words ease the wetness between my legs or the throbbing burn inside me.

"I own you now," he told me. "I fucking own you."

His possession is a chain, wrapped around my throat, tugging and pulling at his discretion. No matter how tight it becomes, he'll never cut my air off completely. All the better to watch me struggle not to choke.

I don't know how long I stay in bed before I force myself from twisted sheets and into the shower. Beneath the scalding spray, I scrub between my legs, watching the water run red. The moment I feel some semblance of cleanliness, a knock jars the door.

"Where the hell is my breakfast?" He doesn't shout. He doesn't even sound angry—just resigned: a master rattling off orders to his slave.

"I-I'm coming."

I wait until his steps retreat beyond my bedroom before I climb onto a towel and wipe myself dry. The thought of being naked now has me considering wasting the day, hiding in here for as long as I can. Pale skin reveals too many secrets. Reddened fingerprints on my breasts, handprints on my thighs. Swollen lips, bitten and flushed.

I cringe at who I find looking at me in the mirror. Wild brown hair, haunted blue eyes. The strangest thing of all? Blake Lorenz called her beautiful.

I shiver at the memory as I creep into my bedroom. My eyes go to the rack as my growling stomach takes its cue to grumble at full force. One of them must fit.

Then I see it. Spread across the least rumpled section of my bed is a shift dress like the kind I wore in grade school. In fact…

I tiptoe closer, surprised to find the same worn badge Mama herself sewed onto my sleeve years ago. It still fits, hanging so much looser on my frame than it did back then, a shapeless mass of gray fabric with starched white sleeves and a round collar. It's only once I'm fully dressed that I allow myself to process what this simple gesture means: He doesn't want me naked, either.

My feet, however, are another matter, it seems. I don't find any shoes or even socks to match my outfit, which forces me to tread barefoot down to the kitchen.

I cook the same breakfast I did the other day. This time, I have better luck with brewing actual coffee and creating a mixture of egg and toast a few shades lighter than char black. Like before, I find him in the study, hunched over the desk, papers spread before him.

"Put it there," he commands, gesturing to the corner of the desk.

I obey, setting the tray down after creeping as close to him as I dare. Then I turn on the balls of my feet, intending to scurry out of sight.

"Wait." A thud echoes, the result of a book being slammed down, and he turns, meeting my gaze from over his shoulder. A shiver wracks my spine at what I find. A cold mask has replaced the tension from last night, making him impossible to decipher. "Read," he says before turning to his paperwork again.

Read. It's my book he placed on the desk's farthest edge, its battered cover catching the faint daylight. Too soon. The reminder of Brandt strikes a deep, crushing wound. My eyes blink rapidly as my breathing deepens. Somehow, I regain control.

Ignoring his untouched breakfast, I circle the desk without facing him. I fixate on the beautiful day unfolding beyond one of the windows as I perch myself on the desk's very edge. When the scratching of a pen over paper picks up, I grab the book and deliberately open it to a different page than before: the story of Cinderella.

He says nothing as I read aloud. In this study, the whimsical words of a fairy tale clash with dark paneled walls and Papa's clinical furniture. Cinderella's tale is as out of place here as *War and Peace* being read at one of our flashy Hollings galas. But he listens as my voice breaks, and I stutter words. He's testing me.

Finally, I finish, cradling the book against my lap. I don't dare ask to keep it. Eventually, the shuffling of papers cuts the silence.

"You can leave."

I'm already in the hall when he calls after me.

"Lunch at twelve. Coffee and toast. Bring it to the boathouse."

The boathouse. "Okay," I croak without revealing a hint of the significance that place holds for me. Or maybe I do; it's all in my tone of voice. Hollow.

Alone, I return to my room, my mind spinning. None of his clothing fits, even now. Will he test me later?

Leaving my shift on a hanger, I run and stretch until sweat mists my skin, and in the grueling exertion, I can almost overlook the twinge in my core whenever I bend too quickly.

Until I can't anymore.

Blake Lorenz kept his promise. He broke me open. He got his money's worth.

But will I ever see a dime? One year was his demand, and some deep-seated part of me questions that timeline. A few days have been an ordeal. Now, I understand his phrasing: *if you survive.*

Pacing my room is my only hope of distraction. Beneath my panting breaths, I notice an oddity that takes minutes to register: silence from below. There's no one in Papa's study.

My steps falter as a dangerous plan unfurls in my mind. Do I dare?

Biting my lower lip, I shimmy into my shift without letting myself decide on an answer. Minutes later, I'm inching down the secluded hallway off the foyer, straining my ears for any hint of Blake Lorenz lurking in the shadows.

My nerves lurch at every creak of wood and thud of my footfall, but I reach the study unmolested. Then I linger in the doorway, trying desperately to rationalize the act. Considering that this is my home and my father's study, entering this room can't be considered trespassing. Not even when it reeks of masculine strength and the scent of the forest.

His smell alone acts as an invisible barrier, keeping me out no matter how many steps I attempt to take. The only way to counter him is to hold my breath and scuttle for the desk. My shaking fingers latch onto the topmost drawer and wrench it open. Pages unfold, a neat stack of blank parchment. I try another drawer and find pens organized in neat rows. The remaining one contains the only item of interest: a book, small and leather-bound. But it isn't mine.

A peek beneath the cover reveals that the pages are handwritten. A journal?

Or a ledger.

I tuck the knowledge away inside myself as I replace everything. After returning to my room, I linger until the relentless march of the clock forces me into the kitchen.

Lunch for Blake Lorenz is a drab affair of not-nearly-burnt toast and lukewarm coffee. I arrange the meager offerings on a tray and balance it carefully as I head down the back hallway toward the gardens.

Our estate boasts a waterfront feature Mama always touted: a small, private lake with its own dock and detached boathouse. It lies paces from the main house, nestled amongst a small thicket of trees. The house itself is a one-story brick structure draped in creeping ivy and what Mama called rustic charm. The gentle waters of the lake form a fitting backdrop.

The farther I travel down the stone path, the more my stomach churns. Nostalgia is a bitter pill to swallow in this context. Next to Papa's study, it was my safest hiding place. *Our* hiding place and retreat from the rest of the world.

The Lloyd Estate once claimed the other side of these waters, but I always found the youngest member here, curled up on the windowsill with his nose in a book and a can of soda propped between his legs. Somehow, he could sense me coming a mile away, no matter how engrossed he was or how much I aimed for stealth. He always knew the exact moment to lift his head, meeting my gaze through the windowpanes. A simple shrug would be his greeting, the only invitation I ever needed to join him.

For ten years, that sill has gone unclaimed.

Until now. Déjà vu descends as I spot the figure hunched in Brandt's old place.

The last time I ever saw him here, I was alarmed. A purple bruise covered his right eye, and his lip had been split.

"It's nothing," he insisted when I'd demanded an explanation. But that wasn't the first time I'd found him sporting a bruise of some kind, and he never had to tell me the cause.

That day sticks out now for only one reason. He looked so hopeful then, even bloodied and battered. I worried about his father coming after him, but he shook his head and laughed at my concern.

"Father?" He smiled then, taking my breath away, along with my common sense. "No... That bastard's no father. He's no father."

He seemed so happy despite the morbid statement, and like a fool, I was swept away by the sheer presence of his joy. It was infectious in those days.

His happiness was my poison.

It tempted me to commit a foolish act that ruined everything.

A sudden noise snaps me to the present. I look up and find Blake Lorenz, still hunched before the window. He's consumed by something in his hands, manipulating it as I mount the small, wooden porch. He doesn't look up to see me.

So I'm forced to knock, carefully balancing my tray on one hand. A grunt is his response, resonating through the old wood.

Inside, I find that the main house isn't the only interior he sought to change. My father used this place for storage, keeping old boating equipment and spare toys my brothers and I had outgrown. Empty bookshelves. A pool table. Tons of Hunter's old exercise equipment. Only the latter remains, strewn across an otherwise empty room at random intervals. A few pieces of equipment I don't recognize and must be his own: more dumbbells than Hunter could ever amass during his short stint playing rugby.

Blake Lorenz himself is already hard at work with one of the formidable metal weights, crouched near the window, flexing his forearm back and forth, the heavy weight in hand.

"Put it down," he says, nodding toward a small, wooden table strewn with newspapers and a glistening water bottle.

Instinct tells me to leave the moment I set the tray down as requested. Memory, however, keeps me rooted.

God, this place even smells the same beneath the newer stench of crisp sweat. Like secrets, and spilled soft drinks, and loose bits of popcorn the maids hadn't bothered to clean up. This was one of the few places we could truly be alone. Be ourselves.

It's like being inside a crypt, only the body's missing, desecrated long ago. Just dust and pain remain, cloying in my lungs.

"You can go," Blake says. He never stopped his workout, but he's no less intimidating from this angle than he can seem when towering over me. Yellow sunlight spills over his dark hair, highlighting the ridge of muscle straining against his gray tee shirt and black sweatpants.

"Brandt…"

He stiffens, his knuckles cracking ominously as his grip tightens over the weight.

"Did you know him?"

No response, not that his silence can keep my curiosity at bay. Or my stupidity.

"If you did—did he ever talk about this place?" I add in a rush. Though why? Maybe the masochistic pain mentioning that name out loud brings is what I need to distract from everything else. This tiny room is too damn enclosed, but the manor seems so far away. I close my eyes, and for a split second, I remember the old days. How it felt to be safe, and happy, and…loved?

"No." A callous tone cuts into my fantasy, leaving a bitter sting. "He didn't mention this house. He barely mentioned you. In fact…"

The dumbbell lands with a thud as he stands, rubbing his hands together to brush the sweat off them. Cold blue eyes meet mine without flinching. It's as if last night never happened.

"The only time he ever mentioned you was out of pity, to be honest. The chubby, awkward little liar who ruined his life. Though," he adds, heedless of how I flinched, my eyes welling. His footsteps rattle the old structure to its foundation, jolting me onto the balls of my feet. "There was one thing he did say. That you had a silly, pathetic crush on him. Like a lost, little puppy. You even kissed him once, I think. Hmm? You *threw* yourself at him, a stupid whore, even then."

Hot fingers trace a path down my cheek and pull away wet with tears. He chuckles at the sight and rubs the moisture between his fingers.

"Your emotions sure are fickle, Snow," he murmurs. "Tell me, were you really so fucking wet for my cock, or was it the blood?"

Slapped. That's what it feels like. I stagger back, almost wishing he had struck me. At least I'd have an injury to nurse. But this... Old agony rips me open, yet there's no way to staunch the bleeding.

"S-stop—"

"You want to know what Brandt Lloyd thought of you?" He cups my chin, forcing my face mere inches from his. Hot breath scalds my jaw and creeps between my parted lips.

"You disgusted him. But it wasn't because you were fat, or pathetic—oh no you don't." He tightens his grip when I try to turn away, forcing me to meet his gaze. "He hated you because, underneath the repulsive exterior, you were nothing inside. Just a hollow, little whore."

Tears fall, impossible to hide as he lets me go, but I don't even try to wipe them away. There's no point in hiding the pain.

It's what he craves.

"Shhh," he murmurs, running his fingers along my jaw. His sneer rips any kindness away from the gesture. Instead, an empty gaze swallows me whole, feeding off the shuddering gasps that rip from me. "You think it hurts me to see you like this, Snow? Oh, no." He brings his hand to his mouth, letting his tongue whisk away a glistening tear. At the taste, a grunt rips from his throat. For a split second, his gaze softens and something raw and unreadable peeks beneath the cracks. "You look beautiful only like this. Without that fucking fake bullshit. You can only ever look beautiful like this." He touches me again, clasping my face in both hands to the point of pain. "I'll only ever want you when you're a broken, little shell."

He frowns at the admission, hating it even as he utters it out loud. He'll only want me like this: a shell of the woman claimed by Brandt Lloyd. Glowing with renewed interest, his gaze flicks over me, narrowing at the sight of my shift. He fingers it as if realizing I'm wearing it for the first time, trailing his thumb along the worn collar and brushing the crest of East Mayfield Prep. Then a scowl replaces the hate and my stomach tenses in foreboding.

"Take off the dress," he tells me, hissing the words between us.

My limbs contort woodenly, working to bunch the material at my waist and lift it over my head. The moment I do, he snatches the dress from me and throws it onto the floor.

"Fuck."

The hairs on the back of my neck stand on end at the heat in his tone. It's like gasoline being dripped over an open fire, crackling to life.

His gaze roves me shamelessly before settling between my legs. "I did this," he says, running his hand along my thigh, ignoring how I jump at the coarse contact. Something pink streaks his fingers as he pulls them away. Seeing it, he groans, shuddering with the force of a ragged inhale. "I fucking did this. I own you. Can you feel it?" Bloodied fingers grip my chin, forcing my head back, leaving my gaze in the prime position for him to meet it and pierce through me. "I fucking own you. No one else can take from you what I just did."

A cry catches in my throat. Another hand finds its way between my legs, brushing my sore flesh. Something enters me: his thumb? So big… He splits me open, relishing the way I groan through clenched teeth.

"Fuck, it's like your entire goddamn body knows it," he bites out, sounding pained. His hand thrusts, sliding that penetrating digit deeper. Too deep.

"H-hurts," I hear myself whisper.

Sighing, he brings his face close to mine, resting his cheek against the bridge of my nose with surprising gentleness. He lets the contact linger for a terrifying second, holding my chin captive all the while. As he pulls back, his finger slides again, twisting inside me.

"It should hurt." Harsher thrust. I can't smother a high-pitched whine. Too sharp. "It should fucking *burn*. I split you open." He's breathing raggedly now, dragging me closer so that his knee can occupy the space against my core as his hand withdraws. "I came twice in my fucking fist last night, remembering how you bled all over me..."

My eyes shut against the admission, but nothing can block out the twisted imagery: him hunched over in some shadowed room, pleasuring himself to my pain. Cursing my name, even as his seed floods from him. It's disgusting. It's...

"I loved knowing that I hurt you," he tells me, slicing into my thoughts. "But I'm not the sick one. You are. Why? Because you're already so goddamn wet." He rubs me with his knee, creating dangerous friction. "You're seeping through my fucking pants, and I've barely even touched you."

He must hate that fact, because he shoves me back so suddenly that I stagger into the wall.

"Get on your knees."

I drop down without a second thought, chafing my flesh against old wood as he paces the length of the floor just beyond my reach. Tense, I watch his shadow flicker, his hand ever moving, tearing through his hair. He's contemplating. Talking himself out of something. Or into it. Whatever his final decision, my heart stutters with dread when he finally directs his attention to me again.

"Get up."

I'm halfway upright when his hand falls over my shoulder and shoves me right back down.

"To your knees," he clarifies. "When you pictured selling yourself at Bolles, I'm sure you imagined finding some sappy, rich fuck who'd pet your hair and let you ride his cock. Didn't you?"

He tsks when I don't answer, demanding a response.

Did I? I rack my memories for the truth but come up short. Maybe I never intended to go through with it at all.

"Don't lie." It's like he's in my head, seeing through my denials. "You thought I'd be fucking easy, didn't you?"

He's closer, his feet thudding over the floor. For the first time, I notice he's barefoot. His toes nudge my thigh, making me quake.

"You expected someone to buy you out of pity. Cherish you. Crave you. But do you know what I want?" He sinks to his knees, snatching my chin in the palm of his hand. His bold stare rakes over my innermost thoughts the same way he ruined Brandt's book, like my soul is a jumble of pages beneath his scrutiny, torn at his discretion. Satisfied with the damage, he nods to himself once. "Fuck, I'll have you screaming for me. I'll make you become what I want. I'll change you, and mold you, and wipe away every trace of the fucking Hollings name. I own you."

His nostrils flare, breathing me in. A low sound rumbles from his chest, and he's on his feet again. "Open your mouth."

No. Dread and alarm do a dizzying march down my spine.

It's funny. Daniel praised Sloane's cock-sucking abilities when he thought I couldn't hear. He made it sound like magic, her mouth. He relished every illicit little act.

But Blake Lorenz won't ever call me his champion cocksucker. He simply wants to defile any dignity I have left.

"Oh yes, Snow," he hisses when I hesitate, my teeth clenched. "Open your fucking mouth."

He shoves his pants down to his hips, revealing that he's bare underneath. With his posture tense, he could seem as distant and cold as always. But one part of his anatomy strains toward me, practically pulsating with need.

God, he looks even bigger in the unforgiving daylight. Impossibly huge, with distended veins encircling his length like ineffective chains. Somehow, he fit inside me, stretching me to take him. I don't know how I didn't rip apart at the fucking seams.

"Suck," he snaps, but the monosyllabic command seems to be the only one he's capable of delivering. There's no threat. No detailed description of what he wants. Flashing eyes and a clenched jaw tell me all I need. *Suck.*

I touch him first, hesitantly, treating him like a weapon. Something requiring the utmost care to handle to avoid hurting myself. Hot, silken flesh vibrates against my fingers. One brush and he lurches on the tips of his toes, blowing out a breath. There's a curse in there somewhere, mangled beyond recognizable speech. Suck. Fuck. Suck.

My lips flutter apart and then together again. There's no way he'll fit inside. Not without choking me.

Which is exactly what he wants.

Before I can gather up the nerve to act on my own, his hand fists in my hair, dragging me forward. Up close, his musk floods my nostrils, filling my lungs. Sweat. Heat. A million nuanced, human stenches that should be repulsive. On him, the smell takes on a more insidious purpose, forming a noose that imprints his possession. He owns me—even my body can't deny it, inhaling every ounce of him.

A sharp tug on my hair brings me back to his command. "Open."

Left with no choice, I pry my lips apart as far as I dare, wedging my tongue between them. Should I taste him first? Swallow my pride to make room for his length? I don't get the chance to pick an option.

He lunges forward, shoving the swollen head of his cock against my mouth, forging inside. Reflexively, my tongue attempts to bar his path, swiping the crown, tasting musk.

"Fuck." Corded muscle ripples over his abdomen. The next second, his grip on my hair tightens and my mouth opens wider. Almost too quickly to register, he's sliding inside.

Having him between my legs burned. Having him bat his way toward my throat sears. Bitter shame washes over my skin as he uses me, bucking his hips, groaning with each thrust.

"Shit…"

My hands helplessly twitch against the floor, grappling for leverage. He's going too deep. Too long. I'll suffocate. Can't breathe. Can't breathe! Just as panic sets in, he pulls back, allowing air down my aching throat. I suck it in only to cringe as he adjusts his grip, nudging his length against my bottom lip.

Instinct takes over. My tongue shoots out, cradling him in a way I never thought was possible. Anything to keep him from going so deep. Anything to finish him quicker.

"Shit." He shudders, wrenching on my hair only to tighten in the same breath, locking me in place.

Damn my pride. I close my eyes and lavish attention on every inch of his length. I channel Sloane and the dirty magazines she used to recommend for "tips" after too many cocktails. According to her, men liked desperation. They liked it when you licked like a starving woman offered a Popsicle. Like you'd die without their taste on your tongue.

Like the man in your mouth is the only one in the goddamn universe.

The skill never worked for her, and it doesn't work for me. The more attention I pay to his length, the harder he holds me, until I'm whimpering between eager licks.

"Jesus…fuck…" Thunder. Every word rips from him, bellowed in between groans.

His cock hardens. Twitching. Pulsating.

With only one goal in mind, I find the weeping slit in his crown and tentatively suck.

A monster roars. Suddenly, he shoves me away, but not fast enough. Hot liquid splashes over my cheek, scalding. Marking. Branding. Dazed, I don't even know what the substance is until I see him gripping his cock in a fist. My fingers brush the drying liquid as more spurts lash my chest and the floor.

"Fuck." He staggers back and collapses onto a bench press, his pants still around his knees, his cock deflating. He frowns at the sight of his release glistening on the floor. After a cold glance in my direction, he snaps his fingers. "Clean—no. Lick," he adds before I can even reach for my shift as a makeshift rag. "*Lick*...it up..." His pants echo in the resounding silence, clashing with my own croaking gasps.

Lick.

My tongue shoots along my bottom lip, tasting salt. I cringe at the flavor, expecting bitterness. But, God, it's too rich to decipher in one go. Sloane told me once that cum smelled like bleach and tasted just as appealing.

Blake Lorenz smells like hell in liquid form, taunting me to analyze every drop.

"Lick it up," he commands, quickly regaining control over his voice. Ice resonates in the guttural baritone, daring me to disobey.

Hunched over on my knees, I slowly brace my hands against the floor. Then I find the nearest strip of milky fluid. I can't though. I'm a Hollings, after all. That means something.

But Blake's harsh intake of air reminds me of exactly what it means: We'll do anything for the family name. We'll sell our souls for our company's shares. We'll let a monster violate us, body and soul. We'll lick the evidence off the floor, washing away any trace of his weakness.

I let my eyes close and sink forward, blindly flicking my tongue out. I taste dust at first. Old wood and painful memories. Then...

Salt and musk form a strange mixture over my tongue. I cringe at the taste; it should be disgusting. However, when I swallow the first reluctant drop, my stomach doesn't rebel. Inhaling deeply, I follow the trail of his scent, tasting more. Lick by lick, I wipe him off the floor.

"Jesus Christ." He grates the name into pained, tight syllables. "Don't look so fucking eager." What should sound mocking lands more like a plea.

Don't look so eager. Don't shuffle forward with my ass in the air and my nose scraping the ground. Don't hunt down every trace of him as ordered. Don't swallow him down.

I can hear his breathing, ragged and unsteady as I complete my task. Then my eyes open gradually and I find him still seated on the bench press, watching me through a lidded gaze. In the past few seconds, however, he managed to draw his pants up. Already, a bulge strains against the fabric.

"It will always be like this between us," he says. "You're just a tight, little hole. A receptacle. I don't give a shit whether or not you get off." He frowns as he voices the claim, and something crosses his expression, drawing a gasp from my throat.

On Brandt, I knew that look and what it meant. He wore it whenever he read a complex book or found a puzzle he couldn't solve. Grim determination.

Just as quickly, any semblance of him is gone as Blake lies back against the flat of the bench press, sliding beneath the barbells already in place. I'm not knowledgeable enough of the equipment to guess their size, and from this angle, I can't see any markings. They're huge, however, each one the width of my face.

"Come here."

I unfurl my sore limbs, shuddering as discomfort throbs between my legs. A low, constant burn. If I were alone, I'd run my fingers along the flesh to investigate why. Something must be wrong. With every step, moisture slicks the movement of my thighs.

"Stand there." He nods to the space mere inches from the left circular weight. When I stop before it, he shakes his head. "Closer."

Close enough to practically straddle it…

As if I don't exist, he grips the weight and lifts it, exhaling with the effort, but he doesn't lift it nearly as high as he could. Just enough for the cold metal to graze the space between my legs with every subsequent flex of his arms. Finally, the icy surface brushes my core and I flinch at the invasive touch.

Apparently, this is all I'm good for. Not his fingers or his hands, but a callous act he has no real control over.

My cheeks flame, but I keep my chin in the air, my gaze fixed on the wall across from him. Teeth gritted, I suffer every brief nudge of the weight. He grunts with the effort of maintaining such a shallow range. Soon, the metal starts to sway, brushing harder, jolting me onto the tips of my toes.

I struggle for balance, alarmed when he hisses a harsh breath. Risking my sanity, I glance down and witness him glaring at something below me: the round edge of the barbell, shining with fluid.

"Fuck." He breathes out, and the weight clatters loudly into its frame. His gaze is a physical touch, clawing its way along my innermost parts. "Fuck me, you shouldn't—" He bites off whatever he meant to say. Metal creaks as he adjusts his position and lifts the weights from their cradle again.

This time, the press of metal is slow. Deliberate. Insistent. It grinds into my abused flesh, drawing a gasp from my lips. Again. My teeth chatter, my head rearing back against my shoulders.

"Fuck, that little sound," he snarls in disapproval, and I sink my teeth into my lower lip to smother all trace of noise.

With a rasp of creaking metal, the weight ascends again, slamming into me hard enough to disrupt my balance. I yelp as pain shoots through my abdomen, followed by an echo of fire.

"Grab it," he spits out, still working to lower the weight to his chest and lift it again. "Grab the sides."

I obey without question, wrapping my hands against the bars of metal forming the frame of the equipment. When the weight rises again, he's cruel, lifting it so high that I could sit on it, grinding friction into my folds.

"Fuck."

Metal clangs, so I look down and find him glowering, his jaw clenched so tightly that a muscle in his jaw jumps. His gaze traces me shamelessly, hunting every bead of sweat dripping down my forehead and every trembling bit of muscle. Suddenly, he takes one hand off the barbell and beckons me closer. Using the bench for leverage, I have no choice but to arch toward him, grinding my teeth at the raw heat in his touch.

"Goddamn it." Metal sways and he's on his feet, shoving me against the wall near the bench. "Turn around. Bend over."

The only nearby source of support just so happens to be the windowsill. I grasp it with shaking fingers as a hand on my lower back shoves me down, bending my body at the mercy of the figure closing in on unsteady feet. He bats my legs apart with his foot and slides one leg in the resulting space as grasping fingers find my hips, arching me toward him.

I hunch into myself, sinking my teeth into my wrist as he prods my entrance with something intimidatingly large. One thrust has me spreading painfully open, taking him inch by inch.

Our breaths echo in sporadic tandem, harsh and broken. He fights to shove himself inside, but my body clenches against him, grasping at empty space.

"Shit… It's like you were made for this, Snow," he growls into my ear. "So fucking tight."

Made for this. For him. His palm cups my hip, branding possession into my flesh. He thrusts again, going even deeper than before, ripping me apart.

"Jesus Christ." His teeth nip at my ear as he twitches inside me. My inner muscles spasm at the invasion, clamping down so tight that it's like he's fused to me, dominating every nerve. "Don't," he warns when I smother my whimpers into the palms of my hands. "I want to hear you."

He flexes his hips, sliding out and then ramming back in. Harder. My moan spills from me, too loud to swallow down. Again. Harsh groans echo mine as his hands brace against the windowsill for leverage, crushing his weight against me.

Beyond the window, Hollings Estate spreads out, hues of green and wintery grays. The sight is a mocking reminder of everything the man fucking me represents. Money. Power. Green and ice.

And fire…

It licks at the spaces he has yet to fill, searing, aching. My hips writhe, chasing relief. Fullness. No. Friction. No…

"Goddamn it, if you come…" A growl resonates in my bones as he clasps my hips to lock me in place.

His next thrust jars me forward, forcing my face against the glass. Dust mingles with his flavor on my tongue. Through blurred vision, I make out my reflection. Wide-eyed, hair slicked back, breaths heaving. And the man behind me reveals himself in glimpses and snatches of polished glass.

"B-Brandt—"

"Not him." Twitching fingers encircle my throat in warning. "You say any name"—he bucks his hips to drive in his next command—"it's fucking *mine*. You say my name."

His. My thoughts scatter, and I can't say a damn thing. I can only moan, and shudder, and claw at the peeling paint and unyielding wood.

"That's right," he snarls as my body convulses. "You fucking come for me. Only me."

He drags out every unbearable, grating bit of friction to the point where I lose my voice, forced to croak wordlessly as my vision fades in and out of focus. He doesn't come inside me—I know that much; more hot spurts land against my ass and drip onto the floor. I'm left boneless as he pulls out and lets me collapse to my knees.

"Shit, I should hate fucking you," he admits, his voice hoarse. "Looking at you should make my cock so fucking limp, but it's like…" He groans in exasperation, and I imagine him raking his hands through his hair. "It's like you're in my fucking skin."

He backs away from me, dragging his feet over the floor. I sense him approach the door and then pause near the threshold.

"I want my dinner waiting when I come back," he says between pants, fighting to regain control.

Back from where? I'm not given an answer before he leaves. The door doesn't slam behind him, left to swing on rusty hinges, ushering in the cool afternoon air.

Crouched on my knees, I can't move, even as I hear him march up the trail, toward the main house. His silence is my true punishment. In its wake, there's nothing to disguise my shuddering moans as my body still rides waves of torturous, electric sensations. There's no reprieve from the feeling of his seed drying on my back.

There's no mercy.

SIXTEEN

I'M FREEZING when I finally find the strength to move. Gray overcast light has replaced the hot sun, streaking through the dust floating in the still air. Shivering in my nakedness, I hunt for my shift only to hesitate before putting it on. I'm covered in Blake Lorenz. His essence has dried over my skin, leaving a sticky residue. The thought of soiling my childhood frock is too repulsive to bear. So I clutch the fabric in a fist and cradle it to my chest as I walk the path, wearing nothing but shame.

He's gone. I know it even before I enter the house to endless quiet. Charles isn't lurking in the hall, and shadow makes for tempting cover—too tempting to resist.

I shower first, wasting time by scrubbing myself clean of every drop of sweat and lust. I rub each limb raw until my skin is left pink in the aftermath. That's when I allow myself to pull my dress on and creep back down the stairs, toward Papa's study.

The specter of Blake Lorenz lurks in every flicker of shadow or creak of old wood. This time, I head straight to the desk and open the bottom drawer. The ledger lies untouched, a tempting lure. Could it hold the answer to winning back at least part of my family's fortune? I'm desperate enough to try.

My fingers shake as I clumsily flip the cover open. Subsequent pages reveal little, at least nothing I can make sense of. Just pages of numbers and names that don't register. Accounts?

I tear through the pages with increasing desperation. More numbers. More names. Wait...

I stop on a page, my fingers frozen over the ink. At the top of it is a neat row of more abstract figures and unknown names. I picture the writer settling in this chair, going about his work. Until it happens. His nostrils flare, catching wind of a scent that shouldn't be there. His grip tightens over his pen, leaving a streak of ink across the paper. I imagine him instantly settling on a culprit of the smell. Irritated, he writes their name. Over and over.

Snowy.

Snow.

SNOW.

SNOW. SNOW. SNOW.

I read my name at least a thousand times as dread builds in a pulse at the back of my skull. Some deep impulse urges me to turn the page. I must. I can't. My thumb dances, quivering with indecision. Finally, I turn it and what I find has me jerking back, almost out of the room. My heart pounds, surging blood through my veins. I blink, but the carefully etched words never disappear. They're vibrant as if ground into the page, almost tearing it.

Put it back, Snow.

I snatch the ledger and slam it shut, dropping it into the drawer. It lands with a thud, only something creeps from the edge, dislodged by the fall. Crisp. White. A different piece of paper folded in half. I'm drawn to it without knowing why, risking everything to tug it loose. In the faint light, I can make out a crest printed on the other side of the page. From a bank?

Slowly, I peel it open, and my shaking hands stabilize the document long enough for a quick appraisal. It's an email, but not from an official financial institution, I suspect. In fact, I don't recognize the address.

This is all you need, the sender titled the message. The information added resembles a receipt of some kind, displaying transactions. Three figures are listed one above the other, each a monstrous sum. Beneath them is a single line reading *Hollings account.*

Sweat drips down my back as I fight to remember every figure, down to the last decimal point. Then I tuck the page inside the ledger and run from that room as if the devil himself is on my heels.

Chest heaving, I enter my room and collapse at the edge of the mattress. Could someone from inside the company have sent those numbers to Blake? Daniel? *No.* Even the thought of it is too much to bear. So I ignore the world.

Cold sheets make for a weak refuge. Still, I hide my face in them—a futile attempt to avoid the mess around me. Bloodied sheets. The lingering stench of sweat. Drops of dried fluid scattered across my floor.

He haunts this narrow space as thoroughly as he haunts me. The walls close in, threatening to crush me whole. In the end, I snatch my pillow from the bed and creep down the hall, into Mama's study. To think. To rest my head. To hide.

Her room is the one place it seems Blake Lorenz has yet to desecrate. Her chair is still there in the corner, her books untouched. God, if I close my eyes, it's like she's here, a soothing presence on my damaged psyche. But she's weaker now than she's ever been. Just a faint echo shrouding my battered form as I curl up on her chair and imagine her reading me one of her sprawling tales.

Perhaps one about a princess at the whims of a monster. She'd win in the end, of course. She has to…

* * *

I'M STARTLED into awareness by a feeling I can't name. It crawls beneath my skin, arousing nerves and twisting my stomach. Then I smell him and my gaze swivels to the doorway, where he's bathed in shadow.

"Dinner?" he questions mockingly.

My heart sinks as I scramble upright. Darkness paints the room's interior, leaving the light from the hall as the only source of illumination. The orange glow highlights the dangerous silhouette of the man standing before it. Only the corner of his jaw and one eye are visible, glaring at my prone form.

I must have fallen asleep. The lapse of judgment stings, not easily rectified by jumping to my feet. "I-I'm sorry—"

"Get out."

I stagger past him, retreating to my bedroom. Footsteps echo but don't come near my door. Thank God. Trembling in anticipation, I sit with my back to the door and one ear pressed against the wood. He's in Papa's study, throwing, stomping, storming. Something breaks, shattering like glass.

Did he sense me again, intruding in his chosen refuge?

I wait, my heart hammering in my chest, but he never mounts the stairs. I listen all night for the sound of his approach, long after daylight creeps over the horizon and my room is brought into full focus. Only when sunlight kisses my windowpanes do I finally crawl from my position and rip the sheets from my bed, leaving them piled in the corner. I manage to find the closet containing fresh ones in the servant's wing. It's only as I struggle to fit them over my mattress that I let myself wonder just where he sleeps. Here? In Hunter's old room or maybe Ronan's? Perhaps he's claimed a suite in the guests' wing.

Or maybe he's claimed the old, drafty wing Papa dwelled in until his last breath. Oddly enough, no other room seems fitting.

Vanishing thoughts of Blake Lorenz to the depth of my psyche where they belong, I shower only to redress in the same childhood frock. It's preferable to being naked, and I don't have the heart to test one of my new dresses. Not now.

Remembering my new role to play, I head to the kitchens and start on breakfast. The safest assumption to make is to prepare the same fare I have so far. Coffee. Eggs. Toast.

I've barely taken a loaf from the pantry when its scent hits my nostrils at full force. I can't remember the last time I've eaten. In fact…the only substance to grace my stomach came from Blake Lorenz. Salty, bitter liquid.

Only a chunk of bread shoved almost down my throat can banish the memory. More. More. There's no rhythm to the massive chunks I rip off with my teeth and attempt to swallow. Just desperate hunger. Just weakness. Just a pathetic need to hide from the specter invading my home and my head.

But food can't fill the void. If anything, it grows wider, stretched like my stomach, churning and gurgling in disgust.

"You're only beautiful like this," he told me. "Broken."

Vomit lurches up my throat. I barely make it to the sink before the first heaves come up unassisted. My fingers are needed to chase the rest out, prodding the back of my throat until I'm rewarded with a violent gag and more vomit. I purge myself of every bite, every piece of bread.

But I never once feel clean. Just dirty, filthy Snowy.

And then I hear him breathing heavily in the doorway, watching as I scramble to wipe my mouth with a rag fished from the counter. It's nearly a minute before I gather the nerve to face him.

He eyes my wet mouth and my trembling hands. Then he cuts his gaze to the tray holding his untouched breakfast. "Bring it," he snaps before leading the way into the hall.

I follow on unsteady limbs. Dizziness creeps in as my stomach cramps, annoyed at having been stuffed full and rapidly emptied. The tray acts as an anchor, keeping my body rooted to the floor as my head lolls and thoughts drift. The impenetrable back of Blake Lorenz serves as a moving target upon which to focus my wavering attention, always just beyond my reach.

"Set it down." His voice reaches me like snapping fingers, jolting me from a daze. We're in Papa's study. He's seated while I linger near the doorway. With effort, I lurch forward and place the tray on the edge of the desk. "Sit," he snarls before I can escape.

Heart heavy, I obey and circle the desk to perch myself on the opposite end. His satisfied sigh ruffles loose strands of my hair, making them fan across my cheek.

"Read."

A quiet thump alerts me to the book he places beside me. Blindly, I reach for it, opening to a random page.

Old handwriting catches my attention first as I lower my gaze to the topmost paragraph. Worn ink defaces the margins, notes and messages I'd long thought gone. Blinking doesn't make them disappear as memories itch my vision like sandpaper. This book. This smell.

No one could recreate it.

"Where did you get this?" My voice breaks openly, my pain apparent.

"Did I say you could ask questions?"

I hear a drawer opening and the lazy scratch of a pen over paper next.

"Read."

Streaming tears obscure my vision. My lips part, but nothing comes out. Just a low, plaintive cry I can't contain. It's his. This book is his, all of our memories contained within. My head swivels in Blake's direction. How long has he had it? How long has he run his fingertips over the leather-bound cover, comparing it to mine?

How long has he waited to drop this bombshell?

"I said read."

I can sense his gaze without seeing it. Ice runs down my cheek, imparted by his cruel attention.

"I won't tell you again."

There's no need to guess which story he wants. My fingers woodenly flip to it even as my thoughts drift, carrying me years away from this room and the monster within it.

My voice echoes, sounding ethereal and disembodied. "Humpty Dumpty sat on a wall…"

"You need to stop giving a shit what people think," Brandt told me as he pressed something small and square into my hands. "Read it. All of it, even the ad-libbed parts."

My heart fluttered, confusion washing away any pain I may have felt as I turned to the story in question. My old nickname had the power to cut like a knife—but never with him. His constant support was conveyed simply in a single scribbled line near the story's title: A million men couldn't fix your ass, but I can. I always will.

"Did I say you could stop?"

Blake's voice snaps me back to the present so suddenly that I brace my hand against the desk just to stay upright. Pain rips through my stomach, doubling me over. The book falls from my fingers, landing on the floor, opened to a random page. One containing our banter from ten years ago, mockingly traded back and forth for weeks. Months.

"Pick up the book, Snow."

"I-I can't." The room spins as I slide from the desk and stagger for balance. My hand flies out, knocking books from a nearby shelf in a desperate grapple for leverage.

"Pick up the book, Snow." Footsteps vibrate from the floor, coming from behind me.

"I can't!" It's only a few feet away, repelling me like a physical presence. Brandt Lloyd's ghost dwelling near the desk. *I always will, Snow. I'll always be on your side.*

"Pick up the fucking book."

I blink and a monster appears, wearing Brandt's face.

Narrowed blue eyes meet mine in warning as he braces his hands against the desk. "I won't say it again."

I flicker my gaze to the book's cover, but I'm already scrambling through the doorway. Can't stop. Unsteady feet carry me into the hall, as far from the book as my wavering balance will allow, while tears continue to fall down my cheeks, mingling with broken sobs I can't suppress.

"Get the fuck back here!" He's following me, radiating anger. "Snow!"

I turn, feeling for the wall. Then I run blindly, clinging to anything within reach. A wooden sideboard. A picture frame. The banister. A doorway. Terror keeps me moving, even though it's futile to try. He finds me before I can find a haven to escape to.

His hand latches painfully around my shoulder, yanking me around to face him. We're near the kitchens, in a shadowy space beyond any light source or window.

"You cry for him now," Blake acknowledges, his voice a hiss. "But were you crying then? Huh?" He smooths my hair back and bats most of my tears away. As I blink, his face is brought into focus, a mask of pure hatred. "Do you want to know what they did to him? At that place? How they treated a convicted pervert?"

No! I try to turn my head, but his touch turns brutal, yanking me back to face him.

"They burned him," he says, murmuring each word into my ear. "With cigarettes. The guards used to pass them out just for that, you see. On his back. On his legs. Once—" He leans in closer, and his nails dig in to keep me pinned to the wall. "Once, they tried to show him what rape felt like—"

"Stop it!" I flail, striking his chest. Not one blow draws anything more from him than a chuckle.

"You tied the noose around his neck. You killed him. Say it."

He cups my mouth, forcing my lips apart.

"Say it," he coaxes in a mockingly gentle tone. "'I. Killed. Him.'"

"I killed him…"

Blake frowns as if he hadn't expected the words to come so easily. But how could they not? I've whispered them to myself almost daily. They trickle from my lips a second time just to hammer the point home.

"I killed him."

His grip loosens a fraction and I twist out of his reach. I nearly make it into the kitchens before his voice lashes out behind me, a stinging whip. "Wait."

I have no choice. Even as my heart aches in agony, my soul remembers his promise: my torment for Hollings shares. So I stay here, balanced on the tips of my toes, clutching the wall for support.

"Let's hope you fit into one of those dresses tonight," he remarks coldly. "We're going out."

Out? I cringe at the possibilities. Old Roman leaders used to parade their captives naked in chains. I wouldn't put such an act past him. But the bravery to question him doesn't come by the time I hear him retreat to return to Papa's study.

However, I remain frozen in the hall, half crouched over the floor. Pain and misery form a lump in my throat, impossible to swallow down. Whenever I try, I'm reminded of the earlier episode with the bread.

Let's hope you fit into one of those dresses.

My breaths quicken as I feel my stomach, pinching fat with every inch I travel. My hips. My thighs.

It's like I gained a million pounds overnight.

With renewed determination, I haul myself to my feet and make my way out into the side gardens. Then I run, kicking up fallen leaves with every step I take. My bare feet throb, my chest heaving with effort. I run through the gardens and down to the lake, but in a morbid circle, I return to the same point beneath the shadow of the manor. I'm just another ghost on the Hollings Estate, doomed to forever dwell in every piece of wood and stone.

Just like Mama and Papa.

But they never literally had their sweat and blood drip into the very foundation of the house.

Panting, I finally return to my room, wincing as blisters form over the soles of my feet. Moisture slicks my shift to my skin. God forbid, I've ruined it already. I gingerly take it off, scrutinizing the fabric for flaws before leaving it folded by my bed. Then I shower, running the water as hot as I dare.

He never gave me a time, a fact I refuse to let myself dwell over. What feels like a lifetime ago—though it's only been a few days—preparing for an outing was an ordeal that would take hours. Tonight is no exception.

Or so I tell myself.

He may have cut my hair and taken my clothing, but I'm still Snowy Hollings. My name still means something, though I'm not sure what. I search my hollow reflection and grimace. Poor, pitiful thing. Just a few days after his brutal shearing and my hair looks even worse—jagged and sticking out from all angles. This short, my curls have no definition. No purpose. The only way to salvage an ounce of elegance is to smooth my hair back and secure it with a cream-colored headband fished from a drawer.

Blake Lorenz stripped my room of all clothing, but he left my toiletries untouched. I find enough makeup to dust my sallow cheeks in blush and darken my eyes with eyeliner. Mascara completes the look. For a second, I consider lipstick, but then I remember his last use for my mouth and change my mind. I couldn't bear to waste a single coating of Dior on some part of his anatomy.

Frankly, these four walls, guarded by Blake Lorenz, are starting to take their toll. Days out of society and I barely know what I'll do when I return. Should I smile as Blake suggested? Run and hide?

Sneak away to see Hunter and tell him what I found?

What Blake Lorenz most likely let me find. The suspicion itches away at my skull. The man does nothing without calculation. He left that page for me to discover on purpose. The real question is why.

And I don't want to know. Ignorance is bliss, Mama used to say in response to the gossip swirling around Papa's latest unseemly dealings. But, as she was in so many things, I'm afraid she's wrong.

Pain is bliss—being on the constant verge of tears. At least through my blurred vision, I can't see the hell burning around me.

Or the devil himself.

He comes to my doorway before I'm fully dressed, and I pretend not to notice him there. With shaking hands, I run a brush through my hair again and rearrange my makeup—

anything to avoid looking up. But I'm quickly finding that he can only be ignored for so long. His scent seeps into my lungs, compelling me to seek the source out. Hesitantly, I observe his reflection, which looms behind me, and my heart stops.

Dressed in black, he's befitting of the hellish character I dubbed him as. His hair glistens, slicked back lazily to fully reveal his piercing gaze, which rakes over me from head to toe. He lingers on my slight curves, his mouth a stubborn line—but the corners twitch, betraying his faltering control.

"He loved you, you know."

I tense at the words. Are they a joke? His face reveals nothing, though his gaze seems to focus inward. Within the blink of an eye, he's staring miles beyond me.

"He loved you, even if it wasn't in the way you wanted. He…he thought the world of you." His voice thickens, startling me with its intensity.

My heart throbs in my chest, a guilty, pitiful thing. Suddenly, I'm forced to clutch the counter so hard that my knuckles whiten.

"I'm not perfect." I don't know if I'm talking more to him or to myself. I wasn't worthy of his love. Not then. Not now. "I was never perfect."

"He still trusted you." The weight of his disgust washes over me, apparent in every fiber of his being. His hands shake. If he touched me now, he'd hurt me. I know it. "He believed in you—"

"Then…" My voice cracks on a bleating note. No, a part of me wails. Not now. I've gone so long without dredging up the past or trotting out any pathetic excuses. But the dam of questions breaks. I can't hold them back anymore. "Why didn't he respond to my letters, then?"

I look back, hoping to find the answer written in his harsh features. But I find nothing. Just…confusion? His frown becomes more pronounced, his eyes narrowed to pinpricks.

"What letters?"

I shake my head and turn back to the mirror. "I told him," I hear myself croak, though there's no point in explaining. "I told him everything. I told him—"

"You never sent him any letters." His voice deepens, so assured. So confident.

"I did. I did…"

And Brandt Lloyd didn't believe in me enough to trust that I would never betray him.

"What did they say?"

I look at him sharply. The angry flush I've come to associate with him drains from his cheeks, leaving me breathless. He looks so different stripped of rage. So…human.

"Tell me what they said."

"It doesn't matter. He's gone." My gaze returns to my reflection, tracing the hollow features. I need that lipstick after all, and I clumsily fish it from a drawer and swipe at my lower lip. Light pink only makes me resemble a ghost more.

"Get dressed."

I hear him march into the bedroom, and the door slams a second later. When I gather the nerve to follow in his wake, I find a new dress waiting for me on my bed. It's black, cut scandalously with a plunging V-neckline and two waist-high slits on either side. The tag claims that it's in my size, and I nearly collapse with relief when it fits.

He left shoes for me as well—a pair of my own black heels. Does this mean he's kept my wardrobe somewhere in the house? I don't dare hope. Instead, I enter the hallway and find him waiting for me at the foot of the stairs.

Only now do I let myself wonder where a man like Blake Lorenz would travel with me on his arm. An arm he doesn't look eager to extend. He scowls as I descend the staircase, his gaze flitting over my waist. Is he disappointed that I met his challenge? I expect a frown to prove as much, but he only cocks his head slightly to the side, and I can't shake the feeling that he's intrigued for a reason other than shock.

"He talked about you rarely," he says, and my steps falter.

God, tonight, he seems more willing than usual to use Brandt's name as a knife, cutting deep where he knows it will sting the most. My fingers flutter over my stomach, pinching fat through the satin. Brandt spoke of me rarely, but I can imagine what he might have said. Hell, Blake's already given me a cruel taste.

Fat Snowy.

Ugly Snowy.

Stupid, spoiled, evil Snowy.

"He was always a poetic fucking sap. The way he talked about you, someone might have thought you were an angel."

My breath catches in my throat. I can't move. Having Brandt's memory tossed in my face hurts, but this…

Only a monster would lie so coldly.

"He did," Blake insists as if sensing my doubt. He advances a step, reaching out a hand to finger the skirt of my gown. I shiver at the contact, feeling his heat bite through the satin. "He talked about your eyes, so blue. Your hair. He loved your hair—"

"Please stop."

He doesn't. "Little, lovely Snow." He's closer. His palm captures my chin, tilting my face for his inspection. His eyes smolder as they meet mine, a wealth of disgust. "You were the one damn person in the whole world he thought he could trust. And he died knowing you were a fucking liar, but if he could see you now…" He digs his fingers into the base of my throat, keeping me from turning away. I gasp, but he merely blinks, unconcerned. "He'd probably lose his fucking mind to see you now, still lying."

Our last conversation rings in my ears. The letters?

"I-I didn't lie," I say, forcing the words out as he drags me closer, drawing our faces within mere inches of each other's.

"Oh? Tell me. How did you mail these so-called letters? Did you do it the same night he raped you?"

Heat floods my cheeks. "I gave them to someone I could trust," I admit.

"Who?"

I've never seen him like this. Despite all of his apparent hate toward me, he never looked at me with such raw, burning loathing.

"Who?"

I cry out as his nails scrape the curve of my jaw, drawing blood. "M-my mother!"

Suddenly, he lets me go and I fall back, striking my ass off the middle step.

If anything, he looks more off-balance. His hand grips the banister, his body hunched. For a second, I wonder if he's hurt himself somehow. A heart attack? Then his eyes meet mine and all I find in them is a grim, chilling resignation.

"Elizabeth," he says in a rasping tone. "That bitch."

He pushes away from me and races down the hall like a man possessed. I hear a door open from somewhere deep within the house. The kitchen, maybe? He could have gone into the gardens.

For what?

My mind shies away from guessing the answer. Something is wrong. I sense it in the air—this foreboding pulsation urging me to run. Intending to do just that, I lurch to my feet and stumble down the remainder of the stairs. I come close to the door. So damn close.

Before my fingers can connect with the handle, I turn on my heel and return to my room. My thumb engages the lock. No matter how hard logic wars with my building terror, I can't seem to talk myself out of staying.

That ominous energy in the air drives me to the farthest corner of my room anyway. There, I sink to my knees and wait for the storm that I know is brewing.

What feels like hours later, thunder finally ripples through the silence. No. Footsteps. They resonate through the very floorboards, shaking the foundation of the manor itself. Slow. Deliberate. The closer they come to my door, the faster my breaths trickle into the air until I stop breathing altogether. I wait for the slow knock and his command to open.

Neither comes. Just a few paces from my door, his steps change direction, and I sense him enter a different room. One he has yet to taint.

I'm on my feet without thinking, throwing myself at the door. I manage to get it open and race down the hall, just in time to catch him lingering in the doorway of Mama's study. He's holding something, letting it dangle from one hand. Something long. Wooden, but with a sharp, gleaming, triangular top.

My lungs deflate, and I nearly collapse, but he doesn't seem to notice me—and when he finally raises the ax, I'm not his target.

The blade cuts into the nearest bookshelf with a monstrous sound, sending splinters of wood up in its aftermath. After yanking the blade from the severed shelf, he hefts it against his shoulder and swings it again. Mama's prized landscape painting, hanging above the fireplace, meets its doom next.

Then another bookshelf. The mantel itself. The wall.

I watch in horror as he methodically destroys my mother's sanctuary. It's only when he aims the blade at the floorboards that I realize his intent. He's looking for something.

"What are you doing?"

His eyes cut in my direction, but he doesn't stop his assault. One blow. Another. Again. He rips a hole in the panels beneath the study and peers into the dusty spaces. Frowning, he turns to another bookshelf, the one beside her chair.

"Stop!"

Torn wood tears at the soles of my feet as I lunge, grabbing his arm. Violently, he shrugs me off and continues his assault, striking through books and wood alike. Panting, he comes up empty-handed, glaring at the untouched corners of the room.

Then we both spot the only remaining structure at the same time, and I can't stop myself from racing toward it.

"No! Please!"

His hand slams into my stomach, knocking me to my knees. Wheezing for air, I'm forced to watch helplessly as he raises the ax and brings it down, cleaving the armchair in two. A sound rips from me, melding with the violent tearing of wood and bite of metal.

Then shock renders me silent.

Grunting with the effort, he tosses the ax aside and strolls toward the remains of the chair. With both hands, he rips the seat cushion out, further revealing the small object tucked underneath. A box, I see as he holds it up to the light. It's thin enough to have gone undetected all these years, made of polished wood. Why Mama would hide it here, of all places, I don't know.

But Blake Lorenz seems to have an idea. He inhales raggedly, practically shaking with whatever dark suspicion he has as he rips the lid off and throws it to the floor. He blinks at whatever the box contains before grasping it in a single fist.

My stomach drops as I recognize the stack of at least ten envelopes wrapped together in a strip of ribbon. Letters.

My letters…

He lets them fall, and I lunge for them. I only manage to brush the surface of the topmost envelope before he slams his foot against the floor in warning.

"No." Slowly, he stoops and lifts them off the ground. His fingers hold them so gently that they barely ruffle the fragile surfaces.

Even from here, I can see my handwriting and smell the scent of my old perfume. They're mine, hidden in this room. But why?

Blake laughs, terrifyingly broken. He shakes his head and then crushes the letters to his chest before marching past me, leaving the room in shambles and the ax behind. His voice is a gruff whisper I'm sure I imagine.

"She always hid her fucking letters."

She? My mother? I swallow hard, fighting to make sense of it all. But all I really know is this: Mama never sent my letters all those years ago.

And Brandt never received them.

SEVENTEEN

THIS NIGHTMARE GROWS realer by the day, and I want to wake up. But when my eyes finally open, I am trapped in a ruined world of twisted wood and scattered chunks of an antique chair. Mama's presence is so real that I can see her smuggling my letters into this room and tucking them beneath the chair's cushion. Later that night, she probably brought me into this very room and cradled me on her lap as I cried about the state of my life.

And all along, she knew.

Should I be so surprised? After all, I'm a Hollings. That means something.

I lie.

I cheat.

I steal.

All at Mommy and Daddy's behest.

The longer I stay in the room, the more I feel choked by memories. They wrap themselves around my throat, cinching off my air bit by bit until I have no choice but to scramble to my feet and escape. My first refuge of choice is my bedroom, but I don't know what makes me turn for the stairs instead. The moment my foot hits the floor of the foyer, the hairs on the back of my neck stand on end.

"Snow." His voice comes from down the hall, in the direction of Papa's study.

I find him seated at the desk, but there are no loose pages in sight today. Merely a stack of old, crumpled letters. He lifts one and presents it to me without looking back.

"Read."

My hair lashes the air around me as I shake my head. "N-no." Some things can only be uttered once, either out loud or indirectly. Some truths mean nothing when all is said and buried. Rehashing the past now serves no one. Especially not Brandt. My fingers twitch, aching to reclaim them for myself.

As if sensing the desire, he lowers the letter back to the rest. "I will make you this offer once." His voice inspires goosebumps that rise over my arms. I'm suddenly freezing, and this man—this stranger—seems miles away. "Read the fucking letters. Tell me what they say or—" He breaks off as his hands form fists over the desk. Ropey veins pulse against his skin, broadcasting his racing heartbeat. "Or I'll make you wish you'd gone for the first option."

My throat goes dry at the threat. Forming words at all requires that I lick my lips and inhale deeply. "I can't."

He stands, shoving the chair aside. It flies back and nearly strikes me. I only just manage to lurch out of the way—and right into his path. He grabs my shoulders, shoving me into a bookcase next. The ridge of a shelf bites into my spine, but the discomfort is nothing in the face of his expression. Narrowed eyes stare through me, a haunted, stormy blue.

"You said you told him everything," he says. "You said you had an explanation. So say it. Say it!"

My lips refuse to part, sealed shut. Deep down, I know it's foolish—a childish promise I haven't broken in ten years. I'm a Hollings. My name means something, but what exactly? Mama and Papa are dead, yet their hold on me is a steel chain, tethering me to this goddamn house. Eyes welling with tears, I shake my head. "I-I can't."

"Oh?" He brings his fingers to my cheek, but they shake, grazing my skin. "Then I'll treat you like the lying bitch you are. I'll hurt you, Snow." There's no mocking this time.

I can't escape the feeling that he's warning me more than threatening. Pleading for me to give him a reason not to.

"I-I can't."

His eyes glaze over, his mouth tightening. I almost don't see the slap coming—it happens that fast. The sting burns through my skull, sharp, but nowhere near the strength I know he's capable of. I rub the area with trembling fingers as I watch him, my mouth agape.

"Bend over the table." He claws at his front, tugging at the buttons of his shirt. The first two break off in the assault but he's unconcerned. His arm lashes out next, knocking the letters to the floor. "Now."

Everything slows down to the frantic breaths we trade between us: mine mere gasps, his steady and harsh. There's so much malice contained in that single word: *now*. My gaze flicks to the letters as my fingers ache to grab them. Hide them. Letting a stranger peer over them should be easy, considering everything else.

But Blake Lorenz is a monster. Something in me won't let him have that last, final piece of me. Not if I can help it.

Shuddering with the effort, I manage to wrestle control of my limbs from fear bit by bit. My brain fights to put everything back into perspective. The money. The business shares. The Hollings name.

I told myself once I'd do anything to preserve them, the only things in life that matter. Even as terror gnaws at that resolve, I remember Hunter and Ronan. Is Ronan awake yet? Is Hunter even further within the bottle?

My feet flex against the floor, drawing strength from the polished wood. The first step I take is unsteady, but I don't fall. The next propels me close enough to the desk to cling to the edge of it.

Blake Lorenz wordlessly comes up behind me, casting a shadow that leaves me in semi-darkness. When his hand lands on my lower back, I wait for the violence. Instead, he roughly tugs my elegant gown up. Gradually, my ass is exposed, and I hear him groan, sounding pained. Then his foot forces its way between mine, nudging them farther apart and opening me up to him.

I'll hurt you, Snow.

And he does, but without ever having to touch me. His breath nuzzles my throat as he lowers his face to my shoulder, almost crushing me with his weight.

"I won't say that I wish you took the first option," he growls against my ear, scalding the tender flesh with the heat of his confession. "I need you like this. Hating you…"

Air whistles past me as he draws back. A zipper comes undone, and fabric brushes my exposed back before hitting the floor. His shirt, or so I assume.

"I need you selfish and so fucking stupid." A guttural note edges the words and my heart stutters in anticipation. "I need to fucking despise you."

The desk creaks beneath his weight as he braces a hand against it, inches away from my head. His shadow flickers and then flesh meets the damp space between my legs, biting deep. Splitting. Invading. My scream echoes, but it isn't loud enough to drown him out.

"I need it. It's all I fucking have left." He bucks into me, shoving me almost onto the desk entirely.

His nearness traps me, and I'm forced to accept every burning inch he seeks to bury inside me. Throaty groans betray his satisfaction as his hand fists in my hair, wrenching my head to the side while his lips find mine and devour them, forcing them apart. Like that, he manages to thrust even deeper than before, making me whimper. Muscles spread to conform to his size. The sheer breadth of his invasion leaves me speechless. Senseless.

I can only feel.

"I need to hate you," he says almost reverently against my open mouth. Then he shifts his position, mounting me fully, and begins to move in earnest, slamming my body against the desk with every battering entry. "Fuck, I have to hate you." He pants, biting the words out in between breaths. "Or I'd kill you."

Fear sleepily combats the all-consuming sensation of sex. I blink, grappling against the wood beneath me with trembling fingers.

"I would," he says as I struggle in vain to crawl from beneath him.

With one tug on my hair, he drags me back, using the motion as leverage to sink his cock into me so roughly that my vision goes white and my lips contort in a wordless scream. Everything inside me burns. My toes curl, my lungs gasping for breath.

"I'd have to," he murmurs almost soothingly into my hair as his movements quicken. "You'd...beg...me...to..."

A big hand sweeps along my stomach and eases beneath me. He finds the weeping folds where we're joined and rubs, grinding what feels like a thumb over the sensitive flesh. My spine contracts with every rough pass, like I'm a wind-up toy at his discretion. A plaything.

"Because it's already done. It's already done."

The hand in my hair becomes a vise on my skull, shoving me forward as his thrusts increase. Hard. Harder. It's like his goal is to bore through me, rip me utterly apart. Destroy me for anyone but him.

"You're already mine." He slams into me, his chest folding over my back.

This time, he doesn't bother to anticipate his release. It floods into me, pulse after pulse of burning, unbearable heat. Too much. It seeps through what little space he isn't occupying, dripping down my inner thighs.

I expect him to leave, but he lingers, softening inside me while his fingers continue to twist through my hair.

"Your body foils us both," he whispers. "We both need the pain…but you can't even give me that much."

He pushes back off his hand, and I can hear him unsteadily fishing his clothing from the floor. Dazed, I watch him, my cheek still pressed against the desk.

His bare back is turned to me, rippling with muscle and tension, locked within a shell of paper-thin skin. Damaged skin. Old scars define his hulking shape, adding touches of vulnerability where there should be none. A pang shoots through my belly. Pity?

These injuries aren't the result of an accident: circles of silvery skin indicate deliberate, precise wounds. Burns? If so, ones created by something small. My brain tries to place the weapon as he replaces his shirt. Then I remember.

They burned him, Snow. With cigarettes.

My sharp intake of air draws his attention, but his face doesn't reveal dread or shame. He merely meets my gaze and holds it for what feels like an eternity, chilling me to the bone. An expression falls over his features, one I've come to fear. After adjusting his collar, he snaps his fingers.

"Come here."

Only now do I notice that he hasn't attempted to pull his pants up.

"Now." His voice deepens. It's like he's daring me to run. To give him chase and one more reason to hate me.

Maybe I should. I wrestle with the weight of how easy it would be to give him what he wants. He practically begged me to.

I need to hate you.

Slowly, I unfurl my limbs, wincing as fresh bruises throb over my legs. Much to his apparent annoyance, I cross over to him. His next breath hisses through his teeth as he reaches up to trace tears that I didn't even realize were falling. I shiver as his thumb trails over my bottom lip, nudging my mouth open.

"Clean me off, Snow."

His chilling expression contrasts the unusual softness of his tone. My mind instantly conjures up an image of what he means, and I can't stop my gaze from darting down, finding him partially erect, shining with fluid.

My cheeks flame as a refusal springs to my lips. "I—"

"Yes," he murmurs over me. His hand cups my chin, forcing my gaze up to his. He nods encouragingly, stroking his fingers along my jaw. "Do it."

He wants me to run, I realize with a building sense of helplessness. My stomach tightens as I rock onto the balls of my feet, torn between leaving and staying. Finally, I move, collapsing to my knees.

Almost reflexively, his hand seizes a chunk of my hair, yanking my face up for his scrutiny. I'm stripped bare beneath his attention. Then he draws me closer while fisting his shaft with his free hand.

I fight the instinctive need to close my eyes. I keep them open, watching him observe me, his face that twisted mask of rage I've come to associate with him. My mouth opens and my tongue hesitantly shoots out, tracing the wet crown.

I don't let myself process the taste. I simply obey, using my tongue to whisk liquid away even though it leaves him just as damp as before. My mind shuts down and I move on autopilot without ever stopping to reject the act. His gaze is the only thing to give me context to the moment: eyebrows drawn, mouth curved downward, piercing, empty eyes.

Suddenly, my hair is tugged painfully, which pulls me away.

His breaths thunder from him, his lids lowered. A surprisingly pink tongue flits across his parted lips, tasting my fear on the air. "Open your mouth," he says harshly.

No. Fear crawls through me at the thought of being choked again. My esophagus is still tender from before. Without thinking, I return to his cock, this time licking him faster. Harder.

He grunts in surprise, and I'm sure he yanks chunks of my hair out by the root. Then he stiffens. My hand comes up as if on its own accord, grasping him in a weak fist. Desperate to mimic the tightness of my throat, I squeeze.

"F-fuck." His breathless gasp encourages me to squeeze harder and lavish attention on the places along his shaft that make him grunt. Curse me. Hiss. Spit. "Dammit, stop!"

He shoves me away this time, his hand striking my shoulder. I let myself go limp, watching him grasp his length in both hands. He doesn't stroke, just grips until his knuckles whiten as if he's fighting to stave off any reaction. Then our gazes meet. Collide.

"Fuck!" His head rears back and he spills himself into his palm.

Not by intention.

His anger resonates in my very bones as he steps over me and snatches my dress from the floor and cleans himself off with the satin. Then he tosses the garment aside before snatching up another item. This one, he holds up in the overcast daylight filtering in through the window: one of the letters. His teeth gnash at the air as he grabs the other corner of the envelope, preparing to rip it open. Before he can, he bellows out something unintelligible and throws it so hard that it bounces off a bookshelf.

"Fuck you! Fuck—" He tears at his hair, and his gaze finds mine, narrowed and unsettling. "If you won't read, then you stay in here. You don't fucking move an inch."

He advances toward me, testing the strength of his command. I stay still, lying on the floor. I don't breathe. I don't blink. As requested, I don't move a fucking inch.

Paces away from me, he turns and marches for the door instead. I sense his gaze rake over my prone body one last time. Then he's gone, leaving the door open and exposed to the drafty air chilling the rest of the house. Within days, my warm, familial haven has become an icy crypt, haunted by old memories.

A flash of white catches the corner of my eye: one of the letters strewn beneath the desk. There are ten of them in total. Ten fragile pieces of my soul I'd thought torn away years ago. I'm not ready to reconnect with them now. It feels like ages pass before I gather up the nerve to reach for one and run my fingers over the sloppy handwriting spelling out Brandt's name.

My eyes sear. Blinking worsens the pain, and once again, I find myself weeping, unable to slow the onslaught of misery. The moisture smears the old ink, rendering it illegible. Just a stain of black over faded ivory, much like the way the past stained our perfect Hollings future. Papa always warned me not to dwell and never to regret.

We were Hollings, and that means…

It means…

I grasp through my thoughts for the answer but find nothing tangible. Just pain, and agony, and a growling voice that won't stop echoing inside my skull: *You're only beautiful like this. Broken. Beautiful. Broken.*

You're broken, beautiful Snow.

In my hands, I hold just one tiny sliver of who I used to be. Moving like an old woman, I carefully gather the rest, wiping off dust and grime as best I can with my already filthy fingers.

Papa always kept matches somewhere in his study to light the fireplace when the mood struck him. Usually on the mantel, hidden within the false bottom of a Napoleon statue. It's still there, a tiny figure riding a marble horse. So I crawl toward it and find the book of matches intact, with one remaining.

There's no wood in the fireplace itself. Regardless, I arrange the letters in a neat stack and strike the match.

The topmost one almost doesn't light, stubbornly resisting destruction. When I move the flame directly over Brandt's scrawled name, it finally catches fire.

Layer by layer, my unspoken explanation goes up in flames as I watch on. Burning smoke floods the room, making me cough and my eyes water further. It's the smell that must draw him back. His footsteps rattle the floorboards, rapid in their approach.

"What the hell?"

I turn and find him lunging through the doorway, his chest heaving. When he sees what I've done, he lurches forward and shoves me back. Hissing, he beats the flames with his bare hands before snatching my dress up to vanquish much of the fire. From the smoking wreckage, only one letter survives, and he cradles it against his palm.

"Get the fuck out."

I don't make him tell me twice.

On jellied legs, I return to my room and scrub myself clean. I pull on my shift dress and almost immediately find myself wandering the kitchens, desperate for fresh air. His very presence repels me from the house, banishing me to the gardens—but I don't go far. Enslaved by my promise, I go only as far as the grounds allow me. Walking. Running. Weeping.

My eyelids chafe against sore flesh. I'm exhausted from crying so many tears. They blur my surroundings, reducing the stunning estate to a landscape of smeared gray and emerald green. A cool wind nips at my hair and bared flesh, seeming to shove me along until I reach the wooden path by the boathouse.

He's not here, a fact that gives me enough courage to creep inside and throw myself into maneuvering one of the exercise machines. Without permission. I know I'm not welcome here, but exertion is more welcome than waiting for his next assault.

He wants me beautiful for him. I'll give him exactly what he wants: beautiful, broken, ugly, fractured, selfish Snow.

After attempting to lift weights until my arms burn, I reach for a dumbbell, intending to lessen my load. But when my fingers brush the metal surface, everything blinks in and out of focus. Then I'm falling through the floor, wrapped within a heavy, dizzying cloud. The next thing I know, I'm on my knees, tasting blood.

My stomach churns, an angry, vengeful thing. How long has it been since I've eaten? I can't remember, not that it matters. My body swells around me. I've never felt so ungainly. So clumsy. So stupid.

Stupid.

Stupid!

I'm engorged on Blake Lorenz. He fills me up, more decadent than any cake or sweet. He's poison. I can't keep him out. I can't keep him in. Bile lurches up my throat, impossible to choke down. Desperate, my gaze cuts to the lake shimmering beyond the window, and I tear from the boathouse and stumble toward the dock.

My reflection gazes up at me from the water's surface, so hollow and pale that she glows. Maybe she's not me but a ghostly soul doomed to haunt the Hollings Estate. She watches me sway, looming closer. Farther. Closer.

Alarm runs down my spine before my brain can process it. Panicked, I grasp for the railing, but all I find is air. Then my legs give out, pitching me sideways.

Thwack!

Stars dot my vision, burning bright. I hear a splash. And then silence. Darkness.

And everything fades.

* * *

"NO!"

I flinch at the shout. The way thunder heralds lightning, I know that voice and the danger that tone conveys. Sluggishly, my body reacts to it. My eyelids lift and then lower again, which gives me only a snippet of gray sky and looming trees. It's cold. Wet. My teeth are chattering so hard that I almost can't hear what the bellowing figure says next.

"Don't you fucking dare, Snow," he growls. "Breathe!"

Pressure slams against my chest, knocking me onto my side. Rough earth meets my cheek; I can smell it, grass and dirt. My eyelids flutter faster as my lungs heave, refusing to draw in the air as they should. Each attempt wheezes noisily, gurgling...

"Damn you. *Breathe!*"

Another blow to my chest makes me cough up salty, bitter liquid as my eyes open again. An angel is hovering above me. He's beautiful, his blue eyes wide with fear. For me? Then his upper lip pulls back from his teeth in a vicious snarl and he's suddenly more demonic than heavenly.

"You don't get to do this," he hisses as I'm jostled onto my back so that I'm staring up at the sky. "You don't get to leave me. Not until I let you go. I didn't let you go. I didn't…"

He continues to speak, biting off unintelligible words as my thoughts drift and the world dissipates again.

EIGHTEEN

CLINICAL SMELLS ALERT me to the fact that I'm not in my room. In fact, going off the thinner, warmer air, I don't think I'm even in Hollings Manor. My eyes fight to open, but I wind up getting only blinking snapshots of the room: narrow, quiet, and beige.

A mechanical beeping gives me a vague clue about where I could be. Then I attempt to move and the stiff mattress beneath me confirms it: a hospital room.

Panic flutters through my veins as I struggle to keep my eyes open. Part of the difficulty, I realize, is because the right side of my face is on fire. The constant throbbing triggers tears. Then everything's a blur. My arms and legs feel near impossible to lift. Why am I so goddamn heavy?

"Stop."

I stiffen at the harsh command, but I can't bear to turn my head far enough in the voice's direction to catch sight of the figure standing there.

"Where am I?" I wince. Is that me? My voice has never sounded so high-pitched and reedy.

"They say you fainted," my visitor coldly replies. "Then you hit your head and fell into the lake. It's a miracle you didn't drown."

He sounds so dry. As if my death is a topic no more intriguing than the weather.

Groaning with the effort, I lift my head far enough to see him standing in the corner, despite the pain the movement triggers. His arms are crossed over his chest, his face devoid of emotion.

"My face?" My fingers only twitch at first when I try to lift them. Eventually, I manage to bring one hand to my cheek. Pain flares with the slightest touch, and something's covering my skin, stretching down to my jaw. Gauze?

"A minor laceration," Blake says, but he stares right through me.

Overwhelmed, I let myself fall back against a single pillow. Gradually, more of the room comes into focus: the looming doorway from which I can make out the chaos of the hall. Harsh, artificial light clashes with the natural glow streaming in through my window. Someone pulled my curtains back, revealing a private view we couldn't even secure for Ronan.

My lips part and an inquiry about my brothers springs to my tongue, but I bite it back. Silence builds into a stifling pressure between us—at least on my end. When I risk glancing at him again, he's staring straight ahead, far beyond the confines of this room.

"You died," he says, but his expression doesn't change at all. Almost as if he isn't even aware of the words leaving his mouth. "Your heart stopped beating. I felt it. You died in my arms."

Images fill my skull, lacking context. Cold black. Gray sky. An angel. A devil—watching me suffocate.

Suddenly, he shakes his head and his lips flatten into a firm line. "They suggested you stay overnight," he says, sounding more like the callous man I know. "And that you may have some memory loss."

His silence draws attention to what he isn't saying. He wants me to ask him something, but I don't know what. My thoughts are liquid, too intangible to decipher.

He has no choice but to drip-feed me more subtle hints. "I'll have the remainder of your things forwarded to the location of your choice before the liquidation," he adds, and I frown as my heart picks up speed. Is that hesitation I detect? No. It can't be. Blake Lorenz doesn't hesitate to deliver his cruel bombshells.

And this one is the cruelest.

I don't process it for the longest time, and when I do, it's in snippets. *Things. Liquidation…*

"No…" I shake my head, and the nearby beeping sound must track my heart rate, because it increases, building into a frantic rhythm. "No, no!"

"Yes," he interjects. "Our deal was that you stay with me for the entire year. Even the loss of one night was not in the agreement—"

"You can't do this." My voice still lacks real definition. I lick my lips and attempt to sit upright. "You can't do this—"

"I'm abiding by our agreement," he insists, stepping forward from the shadows.

God, he looks awful. Even the harshest swipe of his fingers can't tame his wild hair. His clothes look damp, and the briny scent of still water wafts from his direction. Because, for whatever reason, he jumped in after me…

That much is clearer now, even though a part of me refuses to believe it: his hands slamming onto my chest, knocking the water from my lungs. My chest heaves at the memories as my rib cage constricts over tissue-paper lungs.

"You can't do this."

"It's already done." He shakes his head, and for the first time, his gaze seems to focus on me directly. He frowns at what he finds. Then he turns to the door, squaring his shoulders.

"Why are you like this?" My voice breaks openly, but I can't even attempt to disguise the pain. I'm sobbing again, gritting my teeth against any sounds that might escape. But a moan does. Then a bleating whimper. I'm so fucking weak that even he flinches at the sound and his footsteps slow. "You knew Brandt…"

It doesn't even hurt to say his name anymore. Maybe now I can finally admit that he's a specter. He's dead and gone, even if the man before me reminds me of him in every inch of his being. My Brandt is gone.

"He wasn't… He was good," I croak.

Blake laughs, but it's a hollow sound that chills me to the bone. "He *was* good," he says softly. "He *did* love you. And he *is* dead. I'll send notice as to where you can collect your things—"

"You promised me."

Again, he pauses near the door, his muscles bulging with suppressed tension. "A promise means nothing in the world of business. You're a fucking Hollings. Don't tell me you don't know that."

"F-fine." I swipe at the blankets, shivering as I'm left exposed in a thin, backless hospital gown.

"What the hell are you doing?" He bares his teeth, his hands flexing at his sides. "Get back into bed."

"I'm upholding my end of the agreement," I state. Which is funny because I can't even support my weight. Whatever happened between fainting and hitting the water sapped my strength. Freeing my legs from the sheets is an ordeal that has me panting and sweat creeping across my brow.

A flicker of motion alerts me to his sudden advance. He grabs my arm, shoving me down so hard that I'm left spinning. "Get back in the fucking bed."

"You can't do this!" Pain unlike anything I've ever felt rips through my chest, outlasting any injury. I see Hollings Manor lost forever and my heart physically fractures inside me. I can feel it beating in a disjointed rhythm. "You can't…"

He heads for the door, and this time, he doesn't look back. "Welcome to the real world," he says. A sigh edges his words. He has the nerve to sound weary, as if he's done me an exhausting favor. "A world where your name doesn't mean shit once it's taken away. Where the ones you love the most can betray you in an instant. Where nobody gives a shit if you howl in pain at the injustice of it all."

He's not speaking about me.

"Think about that the next time you dare to mention Brandt Lloyd's name."

"I loved him." At this point, I'm little more than a broken record, croaking out the same tired line. But the repetition makes it no less true. "Everything I did was to protect him!"

If that assertion bothers him, I can't tell. He leaves, melding into the clinical hallway. But he can't go. Not now.

I kick my legs and strain to bring them over the side of the bed. Somehow, I wind up sitting with my feet braced on the floor. Then I try to stand only to fail. Over and over as time ticks stubbornly on.

"Miss?"

I glance up and find a nurse in the doorway. Her blue scrubs contrast with the white surroundings and highlight the wariness in her gaze. Instantly, I suspect she wasn't here on her own, but sent.

"You should lie back down, honey—"

"I want to sign myself out," I say. "Now."

She frowns but scurries from the doorway. I barely get to relish in my apparent victory when a new figure appears in her place.

"Snowy?"

God, not now.

The man standing in the doorway looks so worn that I barely recognize him. Is it really Hunter? These past few days have aged him well beyond his thirty years. His suit jacket is wrinkled, the white shirt underneath stained with what I hope is coffee.

The smell betrays him: it's wine.

"I'm sorry," he mutters as his bloodshot eyes scan my face and quickly glance away. "I must have the wrong room—"

"Hunter?" I self-consciously touch my face, focusing on the bandage. A minor laceration, Blake said.

"S-Snowy?" Hunter blinks and shakes his head as he comes closer. He snatches my hand up in a grip tight enough to break. "Jesus Christ… What the hell happened?

All I know is I get a fucking call in the middle of the night—"

"My face..." It should be the least of my concern. Still, vanity outlasts everything, even shock. Desperate, I scan the room, but I don't find the hint of a mirror. "I need to see my face."

"That's probably not a good idea. They used those damn old-fashioned stitches." Hunter winces as if he hadn't meant to speak. "Snow..." His fingers cup my chin and gently lift it. They shake. "What the fuck happened? Where have you been? Sh-shit, I should have called the fucking police. A goddamn note. What the hell was I thinking?"

"I'm fine." I shrug him off and struggle to tamp down the panic building in my veins. My breaths are shallow and frantic, impossible to slow. "How is Ronan?"

He glances at the door. "He's fine. Better than expected, in fact. He's been awake for three days. I tried calling you—"

"Miss?" The nurse calls from the hall, holding a stack of paperwork and tugging a portable piece of equipment. "Are you ready?"

I glance from her to Hunter and shake my head. Surprisingly, she seems to take the hint and says nothing. For now.

"I'm starving, Hunt," I blurt, nodding toward my emaciated frame.

Questions he doesn't voice out loud linger in his eyes as his fingers deliberately encircle my wrist, which is something he hasn't done in years. The act was always his tried-and-true test whenever I'd gone too far. He draws away but can't suppress his horrified expression before I catch it.

You're only beautiful like this...

"Snowy?" He strokes my shorn curls. "I'll get you something to eat. Would you like that?"

I nod. "Please. From the cafeteria." I force a nervous laugh. "I can't stand hospital food."

"Yes." He swipes his hand along his pants and then blinks as the realization of our precarious financials dawns on him. Then he shakes his head. "I'll get it. Whatever you want."

I send him off, and the nurse comes forward.

"You have the right to leave," she tells me, as she hooks me up to a blood pressure cuff. "But I'll only recommend it to the doctor if everything is within limits."

I submit to her assessment, warily watching the time tick onward. It's already late in the evening.

I have only until midnight.

NINETEEN

I RACE BAREFOOT UP to the door of Hollings Manor and pound against it with both fists, knowing I'll barely make a sound. Exhaustion rips my nerves to pieces. I'm shaking with the effort it takes to stand. In only a thin hospital gown, my body is helpless against the biting chill. Winter is in the air, and it seems to mock me with its looming arrival: *You failed.*

"Blake!" My rasping shouts battle the wind for supremacy. "Blake!"

The door cracks, opened a fraction from the inside. I nearly collapse against it in relief.

"I'm here," I say in between gasping breaths. "You…can't… turn me away."

"Excuse me?"

I flinch back as if struck. That voice. It's not Blake's cold rasp or Charles's suave tenor. No… The soft tone could only belong to a woman. A young woman, I realize as the light from the foyer ghosts over her delicate features. She's tall and slim, with white-blond hair curling prettily over her shoulders. Her dress is nothing like the wispy garments Blake chose for me, but a modestly cut navy-blue shift. Her green eyes watch me warily, drifting down to my bare toes.

"Blake?" she calls, her voice shaking.

"What is it?"

I stiffen at the gruff baritone before I see him cross the entryway over the woman's shoulder. His hair is lazily slicked back, his shirt unbuttoned to reveal the panes of his chest. On bare feet, he approaches the door, and I barely recognize this relaxed, handsome stranger. Then he spots me, and Blake Lorenz returns with a vengeance. His cold eyes narrow over my trembling frame.

"Masha," he says sharply, causing the woman to flinch. "Wait for me down the hall."

She hesitates, her wide-eyed gaze on my face. "What is—"

"Go," he commands, but the gentle tone differs from the callous way he orders me. He places a hand on Masha's shoulder and steers her in the opposite direction. "I'll be there in a minute."

I watch her scurry away, this beautiful, perfect creature. Not too long ago, I knew how to emulate her. How to charm her. How to intimidate her.

I was her. Innocent and pretty, at a man's beck and call. She even walks the way I used to: slowly and unhurried without a care in the world to delay her steps—or so she lets everyone think.

Blake Lorenz has done his best to destroy me since the day we met, but this… This guts me. I hunch over, clutching at the door for support. I hear him say something. Growl something, but I can't understand what. The world spins for what feels like an eternity as a mocking whisper creeps through my thoughts: *You thought you were the only one?*

"Let go of the fucking door."

I'm clinging to it for dear life, preventing him from slamming it shut. The harder he tries, the tighter my fingers grip the panel of wood. I shouldn't be able to outmatch him, even at my full health.

For some reason, he's not fighting me. "Let go—"

"What are you doing?" My entire body is jostled toward the entryway. Only now do I realize that I'm not on my feet, but being carried in arms like steel over the threshold. Robotically, I peel my fingers back one by one and watch the door rattle against its frame with a bang.

"You stupid little cunt," he snarls into my hair. "I should have you whipped. I should have you…" He trails off, speaking too softly to decipher—because of her. He doesn't want Masha to overhear.

Why that thought resonates so deeply, I can't explain. Maybe it's out of concern. She should know the man she's dealing with.

I don't find her lurking in the room he carries me into—the sitting area just off the main entrance. He switches a lamp on one-handed and then dumps my body onto a leather chaise—but he shoves a pillow beneath my head first. Confusion disrupts the indignation I should feel. That self-righteous need to fight for my property that brought me here. So I meet his gaze as best I can through watery vision, intending to state my case right to his face.

"You…you certainly move fast," I croak without recognizing the sound of my voice.

He raises an eyebrow as his eyes cut to the doorway. If I'm not mistaken, a smile tugs at his mouth before a frown destroys any trace of humanity.

"Is this supposed to impress me, Snow?" He gestures to my body, inadvertently drawing my attention to the fact that the hospital gown is bunched up around my waist, baring everything to him from my thighs down. "I told you: It's over—"

"You claim that Hollingses are liars," I counter, struggling to haul myself into some semblance of a dignified position. I curl my legs beneath me, but I don't feel strong enough to attempt standing. Even I can admit as much. "Maybe we are, but if you renege on our agreement, then you're no better than we are."

He scowls at the accusation.

"You told me that I couldn't miss a single day with you. I'm here."

"That you are." He shifts his position to glower from the nearest window, out at the pitch-dark blackness beyond.

"Though." My tone has him frowning and glancing back, his eyebrows knitted. "I didn't sign up for this."

"To be whored?" he wonders with such callousness that I cringe against the seat cushions. He grins at the show of weakness, but the expression doesn't reach his eyes. It's like he's merely going through the motions.

"To be part of a harem," I counter. The venom lacing my voice is a shock, and not only to me.

"A harem?" he repeats as if tasting the word. He begins to pace with his hands clasped behind his back, oblivious to how his chest remains exposed. I suspect from the way his knuckles stand out in stark contrast to his skin that keeping his hands out of sight is the only way he can stop himself from using them. On me. "Whatever do you mean, Snowy?" He observes me shrewdly. "Did you think that you'd be the only woman I'd fuck?"

My face heats and the rush of blood triggers pain from my injury. I turn away. "Of course not."

Maybe it's the truth. A man who used me for pure entertainment would surely have other women at his beck and call.

"But I didn't sign up for adultery."

"Oh?" Something darkens his gaze, making the hairs on the back of my neck to stand on end.

"I…" Even short, my hair encases me like a veil, giving me enough courage to spit an answer out: "Is she your wife?"

I hear him grunt. Out of shock? When I look up, that unsettling expression has strengthened, rendering his face unreadable. Again, his eyes cut to the doorway and I get the sense that I inferred too much. He doesn't like the conclusion I've drawn about Masha.

But it's obvious he cares for her, even in the way he talks down to me.

"And if she is?"

His nonchalance catches me off guard. Confirmation? Something terrible and sharp twists inside me, and suddenly, all other discomfort is forgotten. I kick my feet out and stand. Too quickly. Only the nearby coffee table can break my fall, and I land hard.

"Jesus Christ."

He grabs me before I can move on my own. Blinking, I find the room spinning once more, morphing into the upstairs hallway and then my shadowed bedroom.

"Stay here," he commands before lowering me onto the mattress.

I'm not sure if my head strikes the pillow by his intention or accident. But he leaves the room before I can decipher any hint of concern.

Alone in the darkness, I wait until I'm sure he's descended the stairs before climbing to my feet. Moving at all is an ordeal I grit my teeth to endure. My head throbs and sweat glosses my limbs as I finally make it into my bathroom, using the wall for support. Here, I switch the light on and prepare to face my expression.

Oh God.

Horror drains what little color remains from my face. That can't be me.

I glance around the room, hunting for another figure nearby who could cast such a ghastly reflection. All I find are shadows and silence. When I hobble to the counter, the person in the mirror does the same, her eyes wide and bloodshot with tears. Her bottom lip trembles, one of the few features I can recognize.

What Blake Lorenz classified as a "minor laceration" requires a bandage taped from my right eye almost to my chin. Spots of blood have seeped through, and I remember something the nurse told me that I shoved to the back of my mind before now: "You'll need to make an appointment to remove the stitches."

My hands shake as I carefully peel the tape back and remove the gauze. Then a gasp of horror escapes me. The area beneath my eye is bruised a violent shade of purple. Through the damage stretches a line sealed with a tiny row of black stitches. Dried and fresh blood cling to the rent skin. Despite everything, a sudden thought makes a bubble of hysterical laughter erupt from my chest. At least Daniel's on his way to prison, because he wouldn't want me now. Not without my money or my pretty face.

I'm still laughing, even as dread claws away every ounce of emotion I have left but shame and dread.

I'm a hollow shell, forced to scuttle back into the shadows of my bedroom.

You're only beautiful like this, Snow. You're only beautiful like this.

"I told you to stay in the fucking bed."

I'm still hovering over the threshold when I spot him standing by my bed, his eyes gleaming through the darkness. I didn't even hear him come in. He approaches me, heedless of how I scramble back, and snatches my arm, dragging me forward before shoving me onto the mattress.

I expect him to leave. I need him to.

Instead, his silhouette stubbornly lingers over the wall, blotting out what little moonlight has managed to seep in through the windows. I hear the rasp of sheets as he draws them back, revealing a sliver for me to slip beneath. Before I can mistake the gesture for one of kindness, he yanks the top sheet from the bed entirely.

"Lie down."

My heart clenches unsteadily in my chest. He couldn't mean to… Not now. I glance at the door, but the question I need to ask won't escape my tongue. My head throbs; my body aches. I couldn't stop him if I tried.

"You're wondering if my *wife* is still here," he deduces, stressing the word.

I grit my teeth, but he chuckles in triumph, sounding more unstable than gleeful.

"Oh, little Snow. I sent her away. If I were to allow her to catch me with a whore, it might as well be one worth divorcing over."

The insult can only sting if I care what he thinks of me. Still, I wince. He chuckles again, or perhaps it's just how he breathes: part growl, part grunt, huffing into the air.

"Don't make the mistake of thinking that I won't fuck you, even like this," he warns, possessively sliding a hand beneath my gown, grazing my thigh. He's warm.

I hiss at the fact, hating the greedy muscles that latch onto his heat. In my absence, the house remained devoid of any warmth.

"You came back to me," he adds as his touch travels higher, swiping aside the hospital-issued garment. He has a clear view of my stomach now. My thighs. Between my legs… "You came back for *this*." He shoves a finger inside me without preamble, and I can't silence my cry.

My back bows, pressing my head against the mattress and triggering a throb in my skull that has me seeing stars. If only the pain were the worst part. Anything but the fire he brings to life with one curling, twisting swipe of that searching digit.

"Because you crave it."

I cringe from the brutal accusation, turning my face toward the sheets. He finds me anyway, sinking his hand into my hair to drag me back to face him. I groan. The world is spinning now, with him at the constant center.

His clenching jaw is my only warning before he mounts the bed, easily batting his way between my closing thighs. With his grip on my hair, he guides where I look—up at him as his free hand shoves between us, flicking my gown out of the way. He settles himself between my splayed legs as if he belongs there, even when I'm dazed and bleeding. Even if I'm half dead. He owns me, and he'll take what he wants.

I shiver as his fingers trace the curve of my rib cage, ghosting up…higher.

"I saw the way you looked at yourself," he admits, his breath nuzzling my breasts as his creeping fingers displace my gown further. "With pity." He laughs as my skin heats with shame.

His hand sweeps over my stomach and hooks beneath my waist, flipping me over. My head lolls at the sudden shift. The doctor warned I could have a concussion and to return immediately if I felt unusual pressure. I'm all pressure, building to a painful, crushing degree. I let my face sink into the sheets, inhaling my scent, alarmed to find it mingled with his.

Already, he's permeated the cotton. "But you don't even know…"

Nails rake down my spine and over the curve of my ass. Right before my thigh, the sharp ridges bite down, drawing a scream I barely manage to smother. Almost as quickly as the assault came, he soothes over the area with his palm. Then he draws it back and smacks the same spot.

"You don't know how fucking beautiful you look like this." He nudges my face toward him and strokes along the line of burning stitches. "It gets me hard just thinking about the things I could do to you," he admits.

With his next pass, he presses against the wound, just enough to make it sting more. "The bruises I could leave over your skin. The ways I could make you scream. Your pain is a drug, Snow." He inhales raggedly, his gaze unfocused. God, that's how he looks now: drugged. "It's fucking hell. And you came back."

I tense in warning, even before his fingers encircle my throat, clenching so tightly that I choke. Then he releases his grip and tugs the rest of the gown away, leaving me bared to him fully.

"You came back knowing that I'd fuck you. That I'd bite you—" His head lowers, teeth bared.

A protest stammers from my lips, but it's too late. He nips the swell of my breast. Laves with his tongue. As air flutters from my lungs, he bites down so hard that my vision goes white for a split second. I can't even form a proper scream— just a gasp. My hand shoves against his shoulder, but he doesn't even budge.

"You knew," he accuses against damp, sore flesh. "And you came back anyway. Say it."

I flinch as he strikes me again. Not to bruise, merely to sting. To feel.

His heavy groan betrays the erection hardening against my lower back. He wasn't lying; hurting me arouses him. My pain gets him off. "Say it—"

"I-I came back."

The obedience doesn't save me from another quick strike to my hip, followed by another chilling stroke of his fingers to seal in the injury. He lingers there, lazily tracing a path to my thigh. I can sense his control fracturing. His hands shake. His breaths quicken, ruffling my hair and drying the sweat slicking my shoulders. Something is holding him back, and my stomach drops at the prospect.

"Tell me what you want from me," he demands.

My answer comes without thinking. "My money. My shares."

My life.

He laughs again as if all of those things are already burned and broken, but there's no real joy in it. Just the hollow echoes of a pain I know I'll never explore in full.

Suddenly, he flips me over again, forcing me to face him. His mouth captures mine before I can even think to resist. He's ruthless, prying my lips apart with his tongue, grunting at my taste. At the same time, I hear his zipper come undone, and he maneuvers me with one hand, positioning my thighs to rest against his hips, with my back arched and my spine curved at his discretion. His teeth capture my bottom lip and bite down hard before he pulls away and slides both hands beneath my hips.

I shiver in anticipation as the swollen head of him seeks my entrance. Flexing his hips, he guides himself into me through force and feel, squeezing past tensing muscle to take me deep on the first thrust.

My head falls back, a moan escaping me, melding with his satisfied groan.

"So fucking tight," he bites out, grinding his fingers into my skin. His next thrust is shallow, almost mockingly so. He's stingy with the grating friction, sending shudders down my spine. "Take it, Snow," he rasps through gritted teeth.

Only now do I register how he watches my hips and the subtle, twitching motions I wasn't even aware of. My body is a traitor, chasing a sensation it shouldn't crave.

"Fuck...*don't*. Don't...stop." He flexes his grip, urging me to him. Slowly. Harder. Faster.

The slap of sweat-soaked flesh makes my cheeks flame. I'd do anything to block it out. My hands scramble at my sides, but one look at him makes me clench the sheets instead.

God, for the first time, it's like he's...open. Endless blue stretches onward, devouring me, inviting me to stare. To gape. What a tormented, hellish creature he is. There's an agony in his gaze he doesn't even try to hide. In fact, he dares me to turn away as he grinds his pelvis into mine, forcing me to take as much of him as I can. My nerves tighten, wanting more than anything to hide from his scrutiny. But I can't. I won't.

He has me drowning all over again, fucking his way into my very soul.

With a curse, he throws his head back, hissing as if furious with his body for daring to climax now. He swivels his hips to stave it off. Too late. He howls as his release floods me, and he slumps with the force of it. I'm pinned beneath him, forced to suffer the full brunt of his weight as his mouth finds the crook of my shoulder. He holds himself inside me, plugging the flow of his seed, making me feel him. Swell with him.

My breaths come in rapid pants, my thoughts scattered. There's none of that terrifying numbing pleasure like before. Just tension. Building…tightening…

"Even now, you still want more…"

I jerk in place as he wrenches himself out of me, gazing down as my thighs draw together. With a harsh shove of his hand, he drags them apart, hunching forward like a predator over prey. There's no warning. No explanation.

He merely lowers his head to the slick gulf between my thighs. I see his mouth open. His tongue protrudes.

Then silence as blood rushes to my ears. Then screaming. Thrashing. Moaning. I'm a puppet on a string, clawing at the shoulders of my master. But he's cruel. He makes me jump and jerk for his pleasure. With stabbing, quick motions of his tongue, he makes me dance like a madwoman over the bed. Then his teeth grind my clit and everything shatters.

The orgasm punches its way out of me without any say. Any reason. I know I'm wetter, releasing a flood of liquid that pools on his tongue. He tells me so, rasping the words in awe, in between desperate laps.

"Soaked…Snow," he accuses before stabbing with his tongue. Then his fingers. Then his cock again until all I can do is lie limp beneath the assault as the wet sounds create a violent soundtrack to every thrust.

Exhausted, he finally collapses beside me, his fingers sinking into my hair like a leash to keep me close.

I don't know if he falls asleep or if I merely lose consciousness. All I'm sure of is darkness and confusion as a shout jars me into awareness.

"Fuck… Get the fuck away from me!"

A hand slams into my side, shoving me from the bed. I land in a heap of twisted limbs, a whine ripped from my lips. I see stars again. Vomit threatens to crawl up my throat, and I clamp a hand over my mouth to force it back down. And the entire time, my assailant rages against me.

"Get the fuck off me! Get off!"

The mattress lurches beneath his weight, and I curl up, a pathetic ball waiting for his next attack. The headboard clamors against the wall as twisted sheets rasp against slick flesh. I suck in a breath and find the strength to finally look up.

Blake is thrashing over the bed, swiping at the air. I flinch as his fist strikes flesh with a thud—but it's not mine. It's *his* stomach. His legs. His side.

He's hurting himself.

"B-Blake..." I drag myself to my knees, clutching the mattress for balance.

He doesn't hear me. His large body dominates my bed, making me question how we've ever shared such a small space. Because we have. For God only knows how long, he was beside me, still inside me.

"Blake."

He grunts, kicking the blankets off, lashing out with clenched fists. "Fuck. Get the fuck away from me!" He swipes through the air and finds his knee, pummeling. Clawing.

Suddenly, I know the source of all those scars.

Alarm makes me reckless. I waver on the edge of the bed, as close to him as I dare. Tentatively, I reach out, ghosting the flat of his back as he twists onto his side. "Blake!"

He continues to writhe, cursing. Groaning. When his head wrenches in my direction again, his eyes open, unseeing, and my breath catches at that endless blue.

"Brandt…"

I say that name without thinking, pressing my palm more firmly against his chest. His heartbeat rails against me, thrumming like mad. He throws off heat, yet he's shivering at the same time, his teeth chattering. That listless look leaves his gaze, and he blinks, focusing on my face.

For some reason, I stay here, a prime target, as every cell in my body urges me to run. There's something about him in this moment that I can't resist. Something about that lost, lonely look, gone in the blink of an eye. I've only ever seen that expression on one other man.

I saw it in a courtroom.

"You had a nightmare," I tell him as his breathing steadies.

He finally seems to realize where he is, and he yanks my sheets off in disgust before lurching from the mattress, naked. He undressed fully without my realizing, and the scars on his back are on full display. Silently, he approaches the doorway, swaying on his feet. Near the threshold, his eyes cut in my direction, hooded and shadowed.

His first impulse seems to be to slam the door. At the last second, he lets it go to swing on the hinges. And I'm left staring after him, confused as to what the hell just happened.

I doubt I'll ever know.

TWENTY

MORNING COMES WITH UNBEARABLE CLARITY. The overcast daylight hides nothing, and neither do my sore, throbbing limbs. I feel everything. I taste everything. I smell everything. Blake Lorenz is a potent mixture of madness that affects all my senses. He's every-fucking-where, and all I can do is suffer him.

I cower in bed until the dreadful moment when I hear him enter Papa's study. There's no steady scratching of a pen to track his actions by. No shuffling documents. Just heavy footsteps treading the same path over and over. I can smell his impatience from here, wafting through the vents. He's waiting for me. But I ignore the instinctive suspicion until the warm sunlight streaming through my window heats my back like a spotlight, demanding I obey my cue.

Surprisingly, when I attempt to move, my body hurts the least. I don't dare assume he went easy on me last night. Perhaps, I'm just adjusting to his brutality. So, while I ache between my legs, it's my soul that throbs the most.

The constant pain resonates through my bones, leaving me hunched over and listless as I climb to my feet and search for clothing. I look everywhere, even under the bed, before I'm forced to admit that the hospital gown is gone. So is my shift dress, though that might have been lost at the hospital. I don't remember him taking either last night, which opens the door to the terrifying possibility that he returned sometime during the night for those very garments. Why?

To leave me helpless, of course, and drive home one point: He still owns me. I came back. I'm at his mercy.

I let myself eye the rack of thin clothing he arranged. Then I stoop for the bedsheet and wrap it around me instead. The small act of rebellion is merely baiting him, but I can't bear the air on my naked skin. Not now. Cotton makes for an effective barrier as I shuffle into the hallway and descend the stairs. Dread weighs my steps down like manacles the farther I wander down that narrow back hallway.

My breath catches the moment I see him hunched over the fireplace with his hands braced on the mantel. He didn't change, wearing the same crumpled clothing he was the night before. His shirt is undone, his belt unhooked over his fly. Dark curls have fallen haphazardly across his face, adding definition to his wintry-white skin.

He has a fire going—a real one this time—with a base of burning logs rather than memories. The orange glow licks at his hollow features, painting shadows in the various crevices.

I stop near the threshold of the study, and he merely glances at me, his gaze cold. Then he returns to staring into some distant place between the mantel and the portrait hanging above it, far beyond where I can follow.

A low sound tears from my throat. No. This isn't how I want him to be—need him to be: cold, vicious, evil Blake lording over my new station in life. He's human like this. He's reachable like this, even if he's mentally miles away.

Minutes tick by and he says nothing to me. Numb and sore, I can't stop myself from approaching the desk, convinced he'll command me to leave at any moment. But he doesn't, and when the prospect of mounting the desk seems impossible in my exhausted state, I settle for leaning against it, watching him.

He's beautiful like this. I cringe from embracing the thought, but there it is, in all its terrible implications. He's beautiful while haunted by something intangible, his muscles drawn tight with tension, his spine curved in rare vulnerability. It's dangerous to associate him with anything close to that word, but looking at him now, I can't find anything else fitting. Terrifying, maybe. He'll always check that box.

If anyone had told me days ago that I'd scrutinize Blake Lorenz for a shred of humanity, I'd tell them to go to hell. In fact, maybe human isn't even the right word. Real. A real man, chased by real shadows in his past, who feels more than hatred toward me.

Just as the thought crosses my mind, he shifts, flexing his hands against the mantel. I wait for a command or a sharp insult. Anything. But he just…sighs. The sound chases the stillness in the air away, and I'm the vulnerable once again, waiting in anticipation of his next move.

I don't know what makes me push my luck. "D-do you want me to read?" My voice is a formless whisper, lacking any eagerness, and when I glance around, I don't find either my book or Brandt's. But something else catches my eye, sticking from the topmost drawer. Thin. White. I grab it without thinking, smoothing my fingers over its wrinkled surface. Ten years of absence and I still remember the turmoil racing through my skin when I first penned these words. It's surprisingly easy to rip it open, ushering the scent of the past into the air.

Blake says nothing to my suggestion, but I find myself following our twisted routine regardless.

"Dear Brandt…" My fingers shake as I unfold the page over my lap. I can't force my voice above a whisper or dispel the tightness in my throat. All I can do is recite the words scrawled over decades-old notebook paper. God, it's the last letter I ever wrote to him, fittingly short. "P-please," I read, tracing the word with the pad of my finger. "Please. Please. Please. Please—"

I jump as he rips the page from my fingers. He scowls at my old handwriting before tossing the letter into the fire, where it's swallowed up and spit out as smoke.

I know the rest of the words by heart anyway. "Please. I love you."

His mouth contorts into a snarl as he draws himself to his full, imposing height. His gaze finds me through a wayward fringe of his hair. Though I expect to find wild anger, he's surprisingly composed.

"You think coddling me awake like some fucking child changes anything?" He sounds genuinely curious, as if he doubted that even I could be so stupid. "Seriously, Snow. Forget the fucking bullshit fairy tales. Life is not a fairy tale—"

"I didn't coddle you awake." How I counter him, I'll never know. Something hardens my spine, rooting me to the spot as he advances and anger peeks through his mask.

"Oh?" He cups my chin with fingers that tremble, conveying a subtle warning: *I'm losing control, Snow. I never fucking had it.*

"Y-yes." Up this close to him, I can't keep the tears from streaming down. It's like he conjures them through his sheer nearness, a creature designed to trigger my torment. "I didn't touch you."

At least not then.

He inhales, his eyes narrowing. Before he can insult me further, I force myself to meet his gaze fully, peering through the darkness.

"I said your name," I tell him hoarsely. "All I did was say your name."

His eyes widen with understanding, and he lets me go as if he'd been burned—only to grab me by the throat before I can deflate in relief.

"Brandt? Oh, Snowy…" He strokes along my windpipe, bathing me in malice. "You don't want me to be him. Why? Let me tell you something about your precious Brandt Lloyd."

I stiffen as he crushes his body to mine, forcing me to bend back over the desk.

"Do you want to know a little secret he never told you? Why he reacted so harshly when you kissed him, even though it was the only fucking thing in the world he craved? The reason why your whore mother hid your letters? How she hid her own letters inside his home? In his parents' room? Under their bed? The bitch got a kick out of flaunting it."

Flaunting what? My mind taunts me with dark suspicions: memories that had no context until now. Wandering the halls during sleepless nights and finding Mama slipping toward the servants' hallway, her blond hair streaming over a gossamer nightgown. The resentful looks she directed toward Brandt. Her anguish when his father was put away. She died not long after he did. From septicemia, they said. But I saw the truth for myself: She wasted away.

She just stopped living.

"Oh, so you *do* know," Blake murmurs, peering into my gaze. He brushes his knuckles over my injured cheek with painful softness. "Her dirty little secret. Did you ever wonder just where, in a family of fucking blonds, you got your hair from?"

A great-aunt, according to Mama. Red hair was a recessive trait in her bloodline. Or so she claimed.

Blake fingers the now muddy-brown curls. "Brandt saw it all. He knew how sick it was for you to pine after him, but he just couldn't put you out of your misery."

My chest heaves in a desperate bid for air. "You're lying."

"You wish I were," he murmurs. "And how sick would it be if I am Brandt Lloyd, hmmm? Think of all the times I fucked you. How much you enjoyed it."

"S-stop!" I squeeze my eyes shut, blocking the sordid memories out. They play regardless. And they play. And play—on an endless loop. "Please stop—"

"Stop?" He draws back. "Yes. Let's stop. This charade. This fucking game. All of it."

He turns to the fireplace, where the remains of my letter are smoldering. He snatches a poker from the mantel and jabs at a log. Wielding the smoking end, he whirls around, pacing the room. Seemingly at random, he fingers the curtains. Then he yanks, sending the green damask crashing to his feet. He stabs the mass with the poker, twisting them both into a makeshift creation. When he lifts it, a single object comes to mind: a torch.

Fear curdles in my stomach. "What are you doing?"

His eyes narrow, pure ice. "What I should have done day fucking one."

"N-no…" Our gazes collide before his attention turns to the fireplace. Terror contorts my limbs, and I lunge for him, clawing at his arms, his hands, anything I can reach. "No!"

He shoves me aside, knocking me against the wall. "Oh yes." With eyes like fire, he turns to the real blaze and bathes the wadded curtain in the heart of the flames. Orange embers dance dangerously in the air wielded by him, a manic magician with my soul at his discretion. He'll make it disappear. Poof, like smoke.

"No!" My scream melds with the burning hiss of paper catching fire as he swipes the lit torch against the nearest bookshelf.

There's no slow spread of flames. It's as if the entire world ignites all at once. Roaring, hungry destruction. Heat slaps my cheeks, building as a newer bit of my family's legacy catches fire and burns.

Before I can swat his hand away, his arm cinches my waist. He drags me from the room like that, kicking and screaming, spreading the fire. Along the walls. The portraits. The scarlet runner over the stairs. He lights it all, laughing as he does so.

Pain and torment rob my brain of everything but the need to wail. Scream. Bite. Kick. Fight. He never lets me go, forcing me to watch.

I'm only vaguely aware that we're in the courtyard now. Cold air tosses my tangled hair, chilling the tears pouring down my face. Eventually, they stop, and my eyes run dry; I'm devoid of anything left to shed.

"Did you think I'd let you keep it?" he wonders mockingly, his voice dripping into my ear. The paving stones of the circular driveway threaten to rob my balance as he yanks me backward, ensuring I watch as orange illuminates the windows of my family home. "Did you really think I'd let this fucking piece of shit remain standing? An eye for an eye, Snow."

It's fitting in a twisted way. My father took his home. He's taken mine.

"I loved you." My voice rings hollow as my legs give way. He's the only thing keeping me upright, and he grunts with the effort, adjusting his grip. The torch still burns, wickedly hot, near my face. I don't flinch from it though. I embrace the prickling sting. "I-I loved…I love…I loved you."

I fall to my knees as Hollings Manor glows brighter. And brighter.

"My father was going to kill you." I heard him hissing his plan to the raspy-voiced man. The same man I enlisted to help me find him. The irony has me laughing. Screaming. "He wanted the company, and you were almost eighteen. He needed you gone."

But Brandt wouldn't be as easy to dispose of as Harrison Lloyd. No, removing the only obstacle in his way required finesse.

"They were going to make it look like an accident. That you got drunk behind the wheel after your father was sentenced. Something violent but swift so there'd be no questions."

I close my eyes to the memories to no avail. Ten years of suppressed pain comes flooding back. All of it. I can't slow the tumult, and my words falter as I struggle to keep up.

"Father...saw me."

Lurking outside his study of all places. My haven. My hell.

"He laughed. Took me into the s-study..."

Can't. I'm shaking my head, fighting against my own conscious. Don't show me. Don't see. Can't go to that dark place.

A hand lands on my shoulder, a silent command. And I break.

"He called me a whore like my mother. He told me he'd treat me like one." Monotone words paint the picture—a stranger's voice, not mine. "He shoved his fingers inside me so hard that I screamed. Threatened to kill me too if I told. I was a Hollings!" I shout it as smoke rises, consuming everything tied to that fucking name. "I was...am a Hollings. If I was going to betray him, then my death might as well mean something."

I still remember the way he looked as he said those words. The way Hunter does in those rare, fleeting moments when his ambition possesses him. The way Blake Lorenz looks now: soulless.

"He wrapped his hands around my throat, b-but…" Something stopped him. He shook his head and let me go, his gaze narrowed as he thought up a different plan. A better one. "I-I thought I was saving you."

I can laugh at it now. How fucking stupid I was. How naïve.

"I thought you'd be safer in prison than dead. My father could have the company, and you would have your life. And…I couldn't say…" My nails scrape the stones, but I find nothing to hold on to. Just more pain. "I wrote to you. God, I wrote to you. If you could use my letters…"

The Brandt I knew would save us both.

"Then you died," I whisper, watching my breath paint the air white. Suddenly, the sky is darker. Hollings Manor is entirely ablaze, roaring its last against an uncaring landscape. "You died, and it killed me. It killed me."

I finally look up and find him staring down at me, his face drawn tight. All of those secrets I'll never decipher remain locked behind a fathomless gaze. I realize now that he never lied to me—at least not about this one fact. He isn't Brandt. He may have been once—but the boy I knew is long since dead.

"I loved you," I tell him. "I loved you so, so much. And you killed me. You're killing me."

He starts forward, and my tired body lurches into action. I'm on my feet, tearing toward the once-envied landscaping now overgrown with weeds. I climb over dried flower beds and cut across the expansive lawn.

He's behind me, panting. Howling. "Snow!"

I run. Trees blur past, growing denser with every step. The sky becomes a maze of crisscrossed vines, and unyielding branches tear at my skin and snatch bits of my hair. I run until I can't stand, and trembling legs deposit me into a heap upon the ground.

But he's gone.

I'm alone.

And, in the silence, I break.

* * *

I MUST HAVE ENTERED some fugue state, because dawn paints the sky when I'm finally found.

"Snowy! Oh, Snowy, thank God."

I'm shaken, jostled from my nest of brambles and twigs. Someone shrouds me in something warm. A jacket? Then I'm lifted into strong, familiar arms. A soft chin nuzzles mine.

"I've got you, Snowy," they mutter. "It's okay."

I stiffen, resisting the firm grip at first. Belatedly, my mind places the familiar tenor and I go limp. "Ro…Ronan?"

I blink to bring his features into focus, doubting myself even as my eyes confirm the impossible. He's really here. Apart from the slight pallor to his skin, he looks just as he always has. Almost. His smile is forced, his gaze pained and a row of bandages crisscrosses his forehead.

Other than that…

He's *here*.

"I've got you," he says, squeezing me tighter, stroking my hair. Tree branches whiz past, faster by the second. "I've got you."

TWENTY-ONE

HUNTER IS PACING my hospital room, clenching his hands into and out of fists. His clothes are still wrinkled, his hair disheveled, but something has changed. In his eyes, maybe. For the first time in so long, they gleam. "I'll kill that son of a bitch," he says. "I'll kill him—"

"Have a seat." Ronan is sitting on the chair beside my bed, his hands folded over his lap. His metamorphosis is more startling than Hunter's, conjuring a cruel cliché.

The blow to the head did him some good. He's the unwavering stone to Hunter's manic, electric energy. In this moment, I realize just how much I missed him. *Needed* him. "We'll discuss legal action later," he says, glancing at me. "For now, we're here for Snowy."

"R-Right." Hunter defers to him and sits at the end of my bed. He absently pats my leg as if ensuring I'm not made of tissue paper. "Snowy…" He swallows hard, but he doesn't get the chance to finish his statement.

"We can survive this," Ronan says bluntly. There's a self-reflection I haven't heard in so long in his tone. My eyes water at the sound. He's my reliable big brother again, even if only for a moment. "We should have never made you feel as though this was your responsibility." He grabs my hand, squeezing it thoroughly. "It never was."

He directs a pointed glance Hunter's way. "*We* will make this right. All you need to do is rest."

Rest. As if it's so simple a task when all we own is a smoldering ruin.

"What about you?" I demand, my voice so faint. I'm too drained to put real energy into it. A part of me is convinced that I'm still living in a nightmare. Any moment, this peace will cease. "Your head—"

"Hurts like hell," Ronan admits, brushing his fingers along the gauze messily wrapped around his forehead. "The doctor thinks I'll be fine after another day or so of observation—"

"As long as he doesn't stage another dramatic escape, that is," Hunter cuts in. "The bastard practically barreled over two nurses and a surgeon on his way out." The pained smile on his lips betrays just how hard he's trying to make a joke. Ultimately, it falls flat. "We heard about the fire on the news and, God…" He stares at his hands, slowly shaking his head. "I've never been so fucking scared in my life, Snowy."

The house. I squeeze my eyes shut against the memory. "What will we do now?"

I don't expect an answer.

Sighing, Hunter concedes to the silence.

Ronan curses. "We're fucking Hollingses," he says defiantly. "That means we always persevere."

I let myself believe him even though my heart aches with the truth: *They* are Hollingses. Dizzy with that knowledge, I close my eyes tighter, sinking into the darkness. But a nightmare waits for me, taking the form of a specter with blue eyes and a haunting gaze.

I own you, he tells me. Did you think I'd really let you go?

<h1 style="text-align:center">TWENTY-TWO</h1>

SOFT FOOTSTEPS DRAW me into awareness. Hunter? Or maybe Ronan, though neither of them usually smell so sweet. Like flowers. My nostrils wrinkle and I open my eyes, prepared to issue a weak attempt at humor.

New cologne?

I blink, registering the glow of blond hair, but the figure is too slim. Too small. Her delicate features catch the sunlight streaming in through my window, which gives her a reflective gleam like that of a porcelain doll.

"Ms. Hollings?" she asks softly. She creeps closer and smooths the skirt of her cream-colored sundress with one hand while brandishing a bouquet of fresh daisies in the other—the source of the smell. "I don't mean to intrude," she adds, revealing the hint of an accent I can't place. "Blake asked me to come."

She places her offering on my bedside table, seemingly oblivious to how I stiffen. My gaze cuts to the doorway, seeking out any trace of his hulking shadow. All I find are clinical white walls.

Still, I'm rendered speechless as Masha casts an appraising glance around my room. Then she reveals another object cradled in her palm.

"He asked me to give you this."

An envelope. Every cell in my body urges me to refuse it—scream, shout, protest somehow before she can place it beside the flowers. My lips flutter apart, but no words come out.

"I'll let you get some rest," Masha says gently with a weak smile that doesn't reach her eyes. The two wide, curious eyes she can't seem to take off my bruised, battered face.

I expect her to walk to the door backward, but she surprises me by turning away. Near the threshold, she pauses, her mouth trembling with a question she can't seem to repress.

"Forgive me, Ms. Hollings, but can I ask you something?"

All I can do is nod. Dread has robbed me of my voice and left me little attention to focus on anything but the envelope.

"How do you know my brother?"

The universe stops spinning in the wake of her words. Brother. Her brother. How do I know her brother?

Brandt Lloyd was an only child. It's why his father resented him so much; his sole heir actually had a soul. What a waste.

"Ms. Hollings?" Poor Masha sounds worried.

But I can't bring myself to answer her. Confusion and terror claw through my chest as I contemplate the impossible. Was he telling me the truth all along?

I'm not him…

My fingers tremble and I remember the envelope within my reach. It tears easily, but inside, I find two pieces of paper. One is painfully familiar: a list of numbers named Hollings account, only this time, my name is at the top of the figures beside the title recipient. Hope forms a painful noose over my throat—but it barely has the chance to grow before I realize that it's unsigned. Unfulfilled. So much money but no way to access it without Blake Lorenz's signature.

The next page doesn't hold the answer. It's a different texture: a photocopy of a small document, so old that it copied barely legible. I have to trace its contents with my gaze for what feels like an eternity before I finally can make sense of it.

A birth certificate.

Brandt Harrison Lloyd was the child's name. Roseanna Lloyd was the mother. But on the line designated for the father…

Instead of Harrison Lloyd, a painfully familiar name fills that space instead. I have to blink twice just to accept the chilling reality.

Blake Alfonse Lorenz.

My first instinct is to deny it. This is yet another twisted trick.

And yet…it makes sense to a part of me buried deep down. In a way, my beautiful boy told me the truth himself. *He's no father*, Brandt murmured once, referring to Harrison. His smile betrayed a joy I hadn't seen in him in so long. *Father? He's no father.*

The truth hits with the crushing weight of the entire world pinning me down: for ten years, I've mourned a boy who, technically, never existed. The heir to the Lloyd fortune was never a Lloyd—and the pitiful Hollings brat who adored him was never really a Hollings.

I don't know how to reconcile these facts. So I don't. All I can do is focus on the cruel olive branch sent my way. Do I dare seek him out to fulfill it?

Or do I burn it?

I stare from the window and let the fiery sunset stretching across the sky give me my answer.

All I can do is endure.

And wait.

Because, as sure as the setting sun, Blake Lorenz isn't finished with me yet.

KING'S HORSES

King's Horses

ACKNOWLEDGMENTS

Erica and Mickey, thank you so very much for taking the time to help me perfect this draft. As always, your feedback and expertise have been invaluable. Thanks to Melissa Stevens for such beautiful covers. Thank you, Charity for applying the final touches on this draft, and the many beta readers who provided encouragement along the way.

This story is a dark, twisted romance that contains subject matter that may not be appropriate for some readers including mentions of sexual abuse, child abuse, violence, and mentions of eating disorders.

PROLOGUE

BLAKE

NUMBERS. That's all these corporate bastards give a damn about. Shares, figures, dividends—goddamn numbers.

How they stack up.

How they fall apart.

Their investments are a house of cards, ripe for one bad shake to send it all crashing down. They make it too easy in the end. Disrupting the entire game with the stroke of a pen is almost child's play.

And with four new companies under my belt this week alone, I've bought the entire goddamn game board.

Even so…

I'm still running out of fucking time.

"Gentlemen." Looking up, I face the four men dispersed around the round table. Some of them scowl while the others sport stoic expressions—for good reason. Unlike them, I'm not clinging to the prestige a few shares can buy me.

The entire company is in the palm of my hand.

And they fucking know it.

"Don't begrudge my shares too much," I say, my mouth quirked, "think of me as merely a new investor, under your wing. After all, I don't intend to impose myself."

Not yet, anyway. When all is said and done, I'll burn this fucking corporation to the ground.

I don't have a choice. Even if *she* gets caught in the middle of the blaze.

Snow. My jaw clenches as the boardroom fades. I can still see her: bloodshot eyes, pale skin. Fiery red hair. Still so beautiful. *Fuck.*

My fingers curl into fists, crushing her memory into the depths of my psyche—where she belongs. But, like always, she claws her way back to the forefront of my thoughts, haunting me. Always.

In retrospect, she was never meant to get caught in the middle. I had it all planned down to the last detail. Takeover the company and then crush it, liquidating its shares—I just didn't expect her to fight me for it.

Though, to be fair I shouldn't have been so fucking surprised. For years, I've heard rumors of the lengths the Hollings have sunk to. 'Favors' the eldest son would grant to someone he wished to manipulate. Hunter would gladly suck cock to climb up the corporate ladder.

But never her. Not Snowy. She was always my naive, selfish, spiteful fool—but never desperate.

Until now.

That frail little creature's all grown up. These days there isn't an ounce of fat on her body but the loss puts her bone structure in sharp contrast. The last time I saw her, she looked more like her mother than ever. Haughty. Spoiled. But even underneath the polish and shine lurks hints of the girl she used to be.

Her hair is just as red.

Her face just as round.

Her lips just as pink.

Snowy Gale Hollings, the girl I once loved more than life itself…

And now, knowing her deception was based on a stupid, childish fantasy?

I shouldn't feel a damn thing.

"Mr. Lorenz?" I grit my teeth and fixate my attention on the man across from me. "Frankly, if you don't mean to impose yourself, then I have to ask. What is the point of this?"

He gestures around him at my impromptu board meeting.

"My plans mirror yours, gentleman," I insist, employing the suave tone that my so-called father did best. Prevent any ounce of emotion from seeping into your voice. Never smile too hard. Blink at random intervals. Harrison Lloyd—the bastard had deception down to an artform.

"It's Blake, is it?" The man directly across from me cocks his head. His hands are braced against the table's polished wood, displaying the gold watch on his wrist and the signet ring on his left hand. He smiles in that way only men like him can. As though everyone with less than a million to his name isn't worth the time on his diamond-studded clock face. "Frankly, I won't question how you happened upon this newest company," he says, staring down his hooked nose. "But now that you have other enterprises under your belt, my associates and I will gladly buy you out of the Hollings shares."

"I think I'll hold onto my seat for now," I reply, matching his smirk—another trick Harrison taught me. Like wild animals, these men communicate in nonverbal cues more than speech. They piss on their holdings and snarl at interlopers, no better than a mangy mutt.

And like any feral beast, they require an alpha's bite to bring them to heel.

"And while my percentage of shares allots me not only a seat at the table, but a right to demand a vote on the chairman, I'll refrain from that choice. For now. Let me cut to the chase. I know you're all aware of the donation I'd like to make in the corporation's name," I say, changing the subject.

"Donation," one of the men retorts. "You mean the very generous *bribe* you've promised to that cuck Antonio Sebastián? I hear he already found another sap to parade around that gala of his. My vote is a no. I say we focus on other matters."

"Oh," I say, nodding. "You mistook me. I'm merely *informing* the board. I'm not asking for permission."

The man sputters, redness blossoming over his hollow cheeks. "Y-You—"

"Enough." One of the men seated beside him scoffs. "Get a hold of yourself, Ramsey," he mutters before turning to me and extending his hand. "Welcome to the board, Blake. I trust you'll fit right in. Only the shrewdest of backstabbing cucks could manage to claim a majority of Hollings shares overnight."

His laugh suggests his words are in jest. But I know that look glinting in his dark eyes. It takes a backstabbing cuck to know a backstabbing cuck.

"I prefer Lorenz," I tell him while shaking his hand. "Blake Lorenz."

"Ah…" His eyes narrow, intensifying their stealthy scrutiny. "You wouldn't happen to be of the Frankfurt Lorenz's?"

"That's the one." I force a cold smile. "My father would be pleased to know that his humble reputation has reached all the way to the States."

"Humble?" The man guffaws so hard he damn near falls off his chair. "Given the way your family has overtaken Europe I'm not surprised Hollings enterprises were your next conquest."

He's equal parts impressed and alarmed. As he should be.

"But there is the question of that messy merger situation back in your country. What's the company again?" He pretends to mull it over, but his eyes are too sharp for true ignorance. "H.E.T.Z Corp? Run by Hanz Zipler, I think? Now *there* is a ruthless son of a bitch. Wasn't he married to your—"

"Are we bringing gossip to the boardroom now?" I ask, raising an eyebrow.

"N-No." The man's cheeks redden, but like a dog with a bone, he digs in. "Though Zipler, he had a big share of your family's company, didn't he? Nearly half."

I flash a smile that makes the bastard gulp. "In my experience, a businessman's fortunes can change at the snap of an even more ruthless man's fingers."

And Zipler's is already between my thumb and fucking forefinger. Case and point: we're at the top of the Hollings building. *My* building. The entire world is exposed below from beyond floor-to-ceiling windows. Everything from the waterlogged harbor to the endless jungle of skyscrapers clawing at the sky. The entire world: that's how people like the Hollings view this lone city. Any other destination is a mere detour, a pretty spot on the map. This place is where their heart lies; the proverbial nest of the snake.

"I thought it was time to try my hand at entering the American markets." I deliberately copy the man's callous tone.

He nods. "I can see that. Jacob Marshall, at your service."

The other men take turns introducing themselves not that I give a damn to remember them all. They sit at this table, in these chairs and dare to look at me like an outsider.

While they dallied in corporate offices, I cut my milk teeth on the walls of this building. Harrison Lloyd may not have been my biological father, but his blood, sweat and tears formed its very foundation. The layout may have changed and the furniture more modern, but at its core this entire fucking complex is the same.

Minus the name: I bet that motherfucker couldn't wait to drop the Lloyd surname from it.

"Blake?"

I flinch at the voice. It's not Emily's, my usual assistant. *Fuck.* Lurching forward, I hone my gaze on the figure at the door and bite down a curse.

Sure enough, Masha has her head stuck through a small crack in the door, her cheeks flushed pink. The other men watch on, barely concealing their amusement and curiosity. I catch one of them eyeing her bare legs and I have to remind myself of one thing: still need his signature. *Can't kill him.*

"What is it?" I demand, fighting to keep my tone level.

She lowers her head contritely, her voice so faint I have to strain to hear her, "I need to speak with you."

"Oh." Any irritation I felt instantly dies. Masha knows better than to interrupt me for anything other than matters concerning two people.

The first has avoided me for two damn months, ignoring every call and letter sent her way.

And the second…

"Well gentlemen," I say, flexing my fingers against the table, hard enough so each knuckle cracks, "I think we should cut this meeting short. I'll be expecting your approval of the donation however."

A second's pause gives any fucker the chance to argue.

No one does.

Standing, I lead the way to the door as they scramble behind me. Masha is the only one who follows me wordlessly into my office across the hall.

"What is it?" I ask, approaching the large oak desk dominating the center of the room.

Facing me, she lowers her gaze, her lips pursed. She's practically swimming in the dress I bought her, wringing her hands nervously over the navy, businesslike frock. With her blond hair scraped into a bun and little makeup, the average onlooker might peg her at sixteen—at the most. Not nearly twenty-one.

Her lips tremble, fighting to coax out words, but she doesn't even have to fucking say it.

"He contacted you again." My hands curl into fists and the closest victim is the wall. *Bang!* My knuckles sear as they meet the polished wood. Once. Twice. Again. Blood streaks my fingers when I finally unclench them. "That son of a bitch—"

"He wants me back," she says, almost in a whisper. Her tormentor needs no introduction. Only one bastard can make her sound this hollow. This empty. "He said… Blake, he'd forgive the debt if I come back."

"That same old lie," I remind her. "And I told you. I would handle it."

"You shouldn't have to!" Her voice is too flat to hold any real emotion so she raises her shaking hands instead. Unsteady, they claw at her neatly arranged hair, ripping strands from the coif. "This isn't your fault."

"Enough!" Irritation makes my tone harsher than I intend. "He was *my* goddamn father too."

The original Blake Lorenz: a man I barely knew, who both saved my life and shackled me to his in the same fell swoop. As a Lorenz, I'm freed from the taint of the Lloyd name.

But my real father had his own demons—a crushing load of silent debt so vast it was basically a death sentence. A burden he gladly shouldered, right to the grave. Anything to save his only daughter.

I could only hope to match his selfless devotion.

But I don't plan on dying anytime soon.

"No," I hiss, meeting Masha's gaze directly. "You're not going back to him. I already have Hollings enterprises and this week alone we've incorporated four smaller corporations."

"But it isn't enough," she says, shrugging her thin shoulders. "Unless you consume every company in the whole city it will never be enough."

"I told you not to worry yourself about that. You leave the business to me." Gritting my teeth, I add, "Want me to make it easier? You don't have a choice—"

"Don't I?" She's jutting her chin into the air, her jaw tight. "You've already lost so much because of me."

"Lost?" I nod to the windows and survey the view, shutting out the grim reality for a thundering heartbeat. The world of the Hollingses lies outstretched before me, kissed by the pinkish glow of mid-morning. "It looks like we've gained to me," I say. "You need a city? I'll buy this one, and then another. However many it fucking takes."

"And what about Snowy Hollings?"

Her name is like a fucking switch. One flick of it and my entire perspective on the world changes. For the worse— power is a simple goal, easily obtained.

But Snow? What I want from her can't be granted via a simple board meeting. Or with money, apparently, considering that in two months she has yet to accept the amount I offered her.

Suddenly drained, I collapse into the leather chair behind my desk. There's a stack of envelopes lying there, along with messy piles of paper.

The irony is a bitter pill to swallow. Once, she claimed to have given me her truth through her letters.

And I can't write a single goddamn one to explain mine. "Don't mention her," I finally muster the energy to reply. "Don't—"

"What happened to her family… It's my fault. You did that because of me—"

"No." I turn to my desk and swipe my hand over the surface, knocking everything on it to the floor. "It was never about you."

Always her. Beautiful, fiery princess Snow. Once, before Masha, I would have given her the world. I promised it to her.

"One day I'm going to live in the heart of Mayfield," she used to boast. "Right in the center! And I'd want a throne, of course. Red, placed perfectly to take in my servants."

"Stop worrying." I banish Snow with a shake of my head and stand. Masha trembles when I cross over to her, wrapping her in my arms. Mouth against her hair, I swear, "I won't ever let him hurt you again. Ever—"

"It would be easier if you sent me back," she insists, her face buried against my chest. "It would."

"But I won't," I say, gripping her tighter. "Don't even think about it."

"Just promise me one thing." Her small hands find mine and pry them from her waist, intertwining our fingers. "Just one thing."

I nod. "Anything."

"Promise me you won't hurt her again. Snowy. Please—"

"I promise." A part of me twinges, knowing deep down that it's a lie.

Snow can run for now. Hide away. Ignore me.

But her company was just the start. Child's play.

She was always the real prize—and some way, some goddamn how I'll make her see reason. I'll get her back, as easily as another fucking business.

Only this time, I won't ever let her go.

ONE

SNOWY

A FLAWLESS VENEER can make anything seem shiny and new again. All it takes is the perfect shade of red lipstick and a smile. But buyer beware: One peek beneath the hood betrays the sad truth.

The poor thing isn't even worth owning for free.

"You look beautiful, Snowy," Ronan insists. He started using this soothing, careful tone after my discharge from the hospital nearly eight weeks ago. "Beautiful. But if you don't want to come, you don't have to."

"I'm fine," I croak, forcing a smile. "Besides, it's just the Sebastiáns' benefit gala. We've gone a million times." Damn. My voice cracks despite my best efforts, and Ronan's grimace conveys what I can't say out loud.

Sure, our family has regularly attended the annual gala—but never once have we arrived penniless and scandalized.

"It's okay if you aren't ready. You don't have to listen to Hunter," he adds partially beneath his breath. "I can handle him."

Oh, Hunter. As he liked to reiterate, we Hollingses have attended the Sebastiáns' annual benefit gala every year since the dawn of time. To avoid doing so now would raise more suspicion than we could weather. After all, paupers must choose their battles wisely.

"It's not just him," I reply softly.

"Forget the rumors," Ronan hisses without looking at me. "The tabloids print whatever crap they can make up to sell papers. But if you insist... I think you look beautiful."

I bite my lip to smother a groan. He means well—I know he does. But the woman in my reflection isn't beautiful by any standards. Her pale skin hides a sickly hue, tainted by secrets she can't reveal. A vicious scar claims the right half of her face, reddened and scabbed, but her eyes draw the most concern: They're empty—despite how wide she makes her smile.

King's men, Snow, a cruel voice reminds me as I rummage through the makeup scattered on my vanity. A dash of pale lipstick doesn't banish dread. *Don't you see? Nothing can put you together again.*

"I'm fine," I insist without taking my eyes from the mirror. *Am I trying to convince Ronan or myself?* "Besides...it's been ages since I've seen Sloane."

"She tried calling you earlier," Ronan remarks, a polite way of phrasing: *she's tried contacting you for weeks.* "If you're not ready to go out, maybe we should—"

"I'm fine," I repeat for the umpteenth time.

"Good. But… Are you sure about *this?*" He fingers the collar of my modest black cocktail dress and my shoulders slump in defeat.

He has a point. The long-sleeve garment resembles something better worn at a funeral. My hair doesn't help matters any, slicked back into a bun as tight as its short length allows. The look is a far cry from the colorful couture creations I'm known for wearing, and the contrast doesn't escape me.

As shallow and stupid as I was just a few months ago, at least I had something then that I lack now. *Hope* sounds far too dramatic a term to describe it. Maybe it's naïveté, I used to be so fucking *naïve.*

Pretty dresses and lovely colors can't disguise the terrible lies drilled into me since birth. Someone clawed them out into the open, and the truth has finally seeped through the cracks.

Two months free from the hospital and I feel no less broken.

Not that I can say any of this to Ronan. Not the truth about my parentage or the real culprit of the man who assaulted me all those years ago. At least when it comes to Hunter, I only need to smile. Like a true Hollings, he'd rather focus his attention on reassembling our broken kingdom than waste time trying to fix me.

"Are you ready?" As if on cue, my other brother sticks his head through my bedroom doorway. He's the ivory contrast to Ronan, wearing a tux in a light shade of gray.

"Yes," I say, contorting my lips to match his grin. "In just a minute."

"Good. You look…nice."

I don't miss the look he and Ronan share before he retreats down the hall, and I watch him go, fingering the hem of my dress. "Maybe I should change?"

Ronan quickly averts his gaze. "You know what, Snowy? How about I get you something to eat before we leave? Give me five minutes." He practically runs off, leaving me trapped before my vanity and alone with the stranger staring back at me.

My brothers aren't the most nurturing of siblings, but *this* hurts the worst of all: the blatant ignoring of the elephant in the room. The way they both look at me as though they're afraid I'll crack at any minute. To prolong the inevitable, they dance on eggshells.

And I'm so tired of the fucking charade.

Then do something about it, a part of me hisses. Frustrated, I push back from my vanity table and turn to the small pile of clothing I left on the bed.

This room is on the top floor of one of Mayfield's premier hotels, decorated to excess. The view beyond my window is enough to command a steep price point—and deep down, I know we can't afford a single night, given our current finances. How Hunter and Ronan managed to avoid having us thrown onto the street, I've yet to discover.

I don't want to.

Maybe the stress of worrying about such matters is why they focus so much of their attention on me? Ronan himself purchased these dresses, paying for them only God knows how. I finger one: a flashy red cocktail dress from my favorite designer's private line. The strip of silk probably cost more than a week in this penthouse suite, and he offered it to me like a paramedic administering a last-ditch dose of adrenaline.

Sighing, I strip my black dress and slip the red one over my head. God, it barely even fits. The neckline gapes over my flat chest and flares out at my waist. Ronan must have gotten a larger size. To drill it in?

Without long sleeves to hide behind, the grotesque creature I've become eyes me warily from the mirror. *He's won, Snow,* she tells me. *Just admit it already.*

And maybe he has.

My hands shake, pawing at the flared skirt as if trying to find my old self lurking in the threads. All I find is loose bits of satin and, as a last resort I fish a pair of socks from a chest of drawers, recalling an old cleavage trick of Sloane's.

Three socks stuffed into each bra cup add some lift to the front of the gown. My hair I leave loose around my shoulders, salvaged by a gold headband. Repeated washes have rinsed out most of the dark-brown dye that had stained it, leaving the once fiery curls a rust-colored hue. A swipe of red lipstick along my mouth makes me look somewhat human again at least.

Maybe I'm not beyond repair just yet…

"Wow!" Ronan exclaims when he returns and finds me adjusting the final touches to my improved ensemble. His mouth cracks into a real smile as he places a plate of crackers on my vanity. "You look amazing, Snowy."

He's still lying. But this time, if I squint, I almost believe him.

"Thank you." I march over to him and take a bite of a cracker without being prompted. Once I've mechanically devoured three more crackers, he extends his arm.

"Shall we?"

Together, we meet Hunter in the foyer, and he does an exaggerated double take of my new appearance.

"Dazzling, Snowy," he says before grabbing my hand to give me a spin. He's a better charmer than Ronan, but his eyes always give him away. It's not my dress he's observing, but my legs, and my arms, and my hips.

Because, without anything to hide behind, there's no escaping the awful truth: I'm a shadow of who I used to be.

Something in my facial expression must change, because suddenly, both brothers stiffen, their smiles even more forced. "You look beautiful," they chirp in unison.

I let them rattle off more hollow compliments and bundle me in my coat before I exit the suite, one man on either arm. Tension taints the air, even if they don't want me to sense it. After two months, there's a reason they're dragging me out tonight, of all nights.

Not even trauma can keep a Hollings from the pursuit of money and power. We're off to see the wizard, with the hopes of making our fortune back—and I'm the last shiny trophy they have left to auction off to the highest bidder.

Considering that my ex-fiancé, Daniel Ellingston, was not only disgraced but fell off the face of the Earth, Snowy Hollings is open to a new master. Let the bids start at zero.

It isn't like they tell me as much, though they don't have to. Ronan keeps stroking my hair while Hunter makes sure to stand by my side, keeping me in plain view, lest we pass a rich, old baron on our way to the car. Who can blame them? I sure can't. We've performed the same song and dance for so long, I don't think they even realize how it makes me feel.

Worthless. Like one remaining sliver of the Hollings Estate yet to be burned to the ground.

"Are you sure about this?" Ronan asks while helping me into the back of a cab. But I'm not the one he's looking at. He and Hunter are communicating nonverbally again, trading loaded glances above my head like I'm not even here. "Maybe it's too soon—"

Hunter and I reply in unison.

"She's fine."

"I'm fine—*seriously*." I disentangle my arms from them both and enter the cab alone.

Something in the atmosphere changes, so potent that I can taste it: nerves. They sizzle from Ronan, obvious in how he keeps tugging at his cufflinks. Hunter fares no better, scowling out the window.

If I smile wider, perhaps he'll stop reaching for my hand every five minutes? I lift my lips at the corners only to feel his palm rasp over mine regardless.

"I can't wait to see Sloane," I say, forcing enthusiasm. "It will be nice to chat with her again. I'm sure she'll have all the usual suspects in attendance."

"Maybe," Ronan mutters, frowning. "But I want you to stay close tonight."

Irritation flares, making me clench my teeth. "Why?"

"No reason," Hunter says smoothly, beating Ronan to the punch. "We both want you to have fun tonight."

"Fun?" Ronan all but growls. Suddenly, he sighs and crosses his arms over his chest. "Damn it. Snowy, there's something you should know—"

"We're here," Hunter interjects while adjusting his tie.

Sure enough, the cab pulls onto the circular driveway of the Sebastiáns' breathtaking Italian-style villa. Towering at four stories and sprawled over countless acres, it's the bohemian counterpart to our family's once-traditional estate.

My throat tightens as I envision Hollings Manor. I haven't seen the property since the fire, but I have no trouble imagining the destruction: heaps of twisted wood and ash. Do I wish it were still standing? Weeks later, I'm unsure of the answer. So much hell lurked within its beautiful walls and gilded fixtures. Maybe it's better off burned to memory.

"Snowy?" Still tugging at the collar of his tux, Hunter exits the car first and holds out his free hand for me. The moment I take it, he clutches my fingers as if I'm a balloon in danger of drifting off. "Are you ready?"

He hauls me forward without waiting for a response. Ronan appears by my side, and between the two of them, I feel like a princess being shepherded to her doom by two executioners. Someone's signed my death warrant, but I won't know who until the very end of this charade.

There's no choice but to keep pretending until then.

Wearing our smiles like masks, we join the press of elegantly dressed guests ascending the curved staircase leading to the mansion's entrance. Up ahead, I can make out Sloane, who's greeting guests while dazzling in black silk. Something that could be regret pinches my rib cage, constricting my heart. I haven't seen her in so long. I'd almost forgotten just how charming she can seem when I don't have a fiancé for her to steal.

Speaking of which, how much of a spectacle do I make without my ring? My eyes trace the crowd with renewed interest only to find curious faces staring back. And no wonder. It strikes me now that this is my first time being seen in public since…

Since before I met Blake Lorenz.

Ronan mentioned the tabloids, but I know he's hidden the most salacious issues from me. Still, I gleaned the gist of them from articles I caught lying in crumpled balls around the suite. Hunter is a criminal. Ronan is a careless drunk, and I got the most dramatic title of all: recluse, suspected of a nervous breakdown over my family's demise.

"Snowy?" Hunter's grip tightens as he lowers his mouth to my ear. "What's wrong?"

"N-nothing," I croak, but I can't stop running my fingers through my hair. Its cropped length offers no protection from prying eyes.

One of the first things Ronan did when I left the hospital was hire a hairdresser to cut it to a proper bob—again, with no explanation of how he managed to pay for it. I don't even have enough curls left to disguise my healing scar.

Humpty Dumpty Snowy's irreparable cracks are visible for all to see.

"Shoulders back," Hunter mutters, and I balk, casting him a wary glance.

Papa used to say that very phrase, though admittedly harsher. "Shoulders back. Chin up. Remember who you are: a goddamn Hollings."

Rather than question his motives, I give Hunter the benefit of the doubt. Following his lead, I lift my chin into the air and hone my focus on the Sebastiáns' ornately carved entryway festooned with creeping vines. It's the only way I can keep moving.

When we finally reach the head of the procession, I hesitate. Inches from Sloane, I'm struck by the depth of my transformation. I used to be like her once. Smiling prettily while kissing wealthy billionaires on their cheeks and showcasing my enticing figure. So intent on her act, she doesn't even notice our approach until Hunter shakes her hand.

"Snowy?" Her brown eyes widen over my frame as her mouth forms a perfectly shaped O.

A heartbeat later, I find myself bombarded.

"Snowy!" Sloane exclaims while burying her face in my shoulder, muffling her musical accent. "I've missed you so much. Come. We have so much to catch up on."

She turns, dragging me toward the expansive foyer. I start to follow, but Ronan's grip on my opposite hand tightens. When I look back, he loosens his hold, but his worn smile only unnerves me further.

"It will be all right," he murmurs. "Just…stay close, okay?"

I nod, but I'm swept away by Sloane before I can question him. She steers me straight toward a gaggle of giggling socialites holding court near the back of her family's ballroom, and my brothers are instantly forgotten.

Unlike my family's stubbornly "old money" taste, the Sebastiáns relish in gaudier décor. Gold walls and white marble floors baste everything in a warm glow. A bit like hell. The moment I catch the first sly glance directed my way, another comparison comes to mind: fresh prey dragged into a lion's den.

Blood is in the air. Sloane does her best to give my hand a reassuring squeeze, but even she can't resist the promise of a spectacle. After my family's downfall and my sudden disappearance, I'm an easy target.

"Snowy!" One of the women we approach wrinkles her nose while casting me an appraising glance.

I recognize her instantly as Patsy Abernathy, my old high school tormentor, still blond and beautiful. Stunning in emerald couture, she poses with her left hand in full view—though it's hard to miss the giant rock sparkling on her finger regardless. The irony of it all almost draws a laugh from me. The last time I saw her, I publicly disinvited her from my wedding.

My, how the tides of fortune have changed.

"How wonderful to see you again," Patsy croons sweetly. She flicks a strand of blond hair from her face, allowing her ring to catch the light. Any more contorting and her poor hand will be one wrong move away from developing a stress fracture. "Such awful news about you and Daniel." She feigns a pout, her eyes gleaming mischievously. "I'm sure you have just the *best* tales to tell about your little getaway. Where did you go?"

The four women positioned around her lean in, watching me avidly to gauge my reaction. Even Sloane.

Dread washes over my skin. I find myself crossing my arms over my chest as if to guard the battered muscle within. *Where did I go?* I went into the Devil's private dwelling, where he crawled inside my head and tore my world to shreds. The worst part?

I allowed him to.

Tears prickle behind my eyes, but it's easier than expected to blink them back. Rage is a welcome antidote to pain. This blond bitch and her hellions have no idea what real agony is. I've crawled out of the flames of hellfire.

A trollop like her won't drag me back down.

My lips contort into an expression I haven't worn in so damn long. The nuances of it greet me like an old friend: a slow, stretching smile and slightly narrowed eyes. I meet Patsy's gaze head on and hold it until she blinks. The moment she does, I clasp her hand in mine.

"Oh, how attention-grabbing!" I exclaim as I brush my gaze over her ring. "A bit like old-fashioned costume jewelry. Not many people are brave enough to pull off that look."

A burst of nervous laughter erupts from the nearest guests. Good. Now to go in for the kill.

Still smiling, I step closer to Patsy and boldly sweep my hand along her shoulder. She shudders, another betrayal of weakness. Three months away from the Mayfield society scene and the tools for navigating it return like instinct. The way most people breathe without thinking, I manipulate. And intimidate. Papa taught me well, after all.

Garnering pity was always my chosen weapon, but not tonight.

"I wouldn't want to bore you about the nitty-gritty details of that mess with Daniel," I say, raising my voice so that it'll travel to every nosy onlooker pretending not to eavesdrop. "As for my family's current predicament, well, I'm so glad you're here. You know better than anyone what it's like to weather a scandal or two." Like one of her father's many public affairs—with women half our age, no less. "But anyway. Let's cut right to the chase."

As Patsy blinks in shock, I move in again, politely nudging her from the center of the conniving little group to claim the spotlight for myself.

"Enough about that," I declare, squaring my shoulders. "Who wants to learn all about my scar?"

TWO

THE LIES WERE ALMOST fun to spin, in retrospect. As far as Sloane and her cohorts are concerned, I spent the past four weeks in Tahiti, where I went scuba diving with a handsome instructor and injured my face learning to cliff dive into the sea. Sure, it's not the most engrossing of tales, but it did the trick.

It'll keep them guessing.

Just like that, Princess Snowy is back on her throne—but the thought doesn't comfort me the way it should. It feels far too easy to smile and schmooze with Mayfield's elite as if nothing ever happened to darken the Hollings's star.

Hell, tonight, I'm even graced with my own eclipse: Sloane's clinging to my side, murmuring all the gossip I missed over the weeks.

"...and then he gave her the money to fix the 'little' problem, of course," she stage-whispers as we pass a politician rumored to be in the midst of a scandal.

Suddenly, she grabs my arm. "Oh, and social climber alert. She's ruthless. Avoid her at all costs."

Her scorn is directed toward a beautiful woman with flowing, black hair, dressed in red. I don't recognize her, and at a glance, dressed in a modest gown, she doesn't trigger any alarm.

"Her name's Riley Haverty. A talk show host who runs some charity," Sloane explains while steering me along. "She's been hounding me for weeks, trying to get an audience with the illustrious Snowy Hollings—"

"A what?" I frown, giving the woman another glance. Caught between two wealthy men, she doesn't notice as Sloane smuggles me past.

"I told her to get in line," the Spanish beauty continues. "Like everyone else. If I have to hear someone ask me about you and Daniel one more damn time. Oh!" She lets me go and wiggles through two elegantly dressed women. "Papa's waving me over," she calls back. "I'll see you in a bit."

I have no choice but to press on without her. One must navigate the social order of Mayfield like a shark in the open sea; you stop swimming and you die.

Upon spotting my brothers on the periphery, I make my way toward them. At least Hunter could easily do all the acting for me; he's been so obsessed with our "reputation" lately. But when I try to meet his gaze, he's too busy chatting up a fellow guest to notice.

Unease spurs me on. Perhaps it's the glittery scenery, but this moment feels like glass. Fragile. It's as if some invisible clock is counting down the seconds until it's shattered. God, I can hear it beneath my heartbeat, steadily ticking away.

Three.

Two.

One.

"Can I have your attention, please?"

I turn, along with the rest of the crowd, to face the raised dais at the back of the ballroom, where Antonio Sebastián is standing before a microphone. His resemblance to Sloane is apparent in his sensual, shameless smile. A wealthy investor, he's a magnate in his own right, with sway almost comparable to what Father once commanded.

But even he can't afford to run such an event alone. The thought only comes to me now: With the Hollings money out of contention, which wealthy family rose to the occasion to claim the mantle of this year's star benefactor?

Given Patsy's gall to confront me, I'd stake my money on the Abernathys.

"I'd like to introduce the man of the hour," Mr. Sebastián begins as if reading my mind. "Without his generous donation, I'm sure the Children's Hospital wouldn't receive nearly the incredible support that we expect to give this quarter." He extends his hand beyond the crowd, toward a lone figure whose entrance must have been perfectly timed to coincide with his introduction. "Please join me in welcoming Mr. Blake Lorenz…"

Icy dread solidifies my limbs, rooting me to the floor. It's as if my entire body conspires to prevent me from turning around.

But it's too late. Driven by an impulse I can't name, our gazes connect, his one of chilling, unending blue.

Standing on the periphery, this mysterious benefactor gleams, a creature formed of shadow, illuminated by a spotlight that settles on him from above. He's dressed in the colors of destruction—a black tux and a blood-red tie—promising more with every step propelling him through a throng of gaping admirers.

Toward me.

I'm already turning on autopilot, pushing my way through anyone unlucky enough to be caught in my path. Shoving. Someone gasps and mutters a curse—I'm making a scene. Embarrassment sears my cheeks, but I can't stop. Not until I'm shrouded in the shadows of the ballroom. Then farther. Farther…

"Stop—"

He grabs my wrist from behind, halting me mid-sprint. Thrown off-balance, I stagger backward into a stone surface. A breathing, stiffening stone surface. We're in a hallway, one that branches toward the front of the house and is devoid of anyone else. When I step forward to escape, my captor grips me tighter.

"Just fucking wait a minute."

His tone sinks into me like a hook, spearing tender flesh. Caught, I'm spun around, forced to meet his gaze. God, it's like looking at a ghost. A demon. I find myself pinching the side of my hip—hard—to reinforce the painful truth.

This man isn't my Brandt. At least not anymore…

"Finally." He hesitates as he flicks his gaze over me, narrowed. "You look…"

I can guess the taunts he doesn't voice. You look broken, Snowy. You look disgusting.

I tug my arm, but his grip tightens.

"Wait."

In the glow of moonlight streaming in through a nearby window, I can only make out the stern line of his jaw, but there's no snarl distorting it. No glare lurks behind his gaze, either. Just shadow.

"We need to talk—"

"Why?" I'm not stupid. Hope is a weak fantasy I easily squash; I may have told him the truth, but in the grand scheme, it means nothing. Ten years of pain have done their damage, and no excuse on my part could ever make up for them. Weeks of reckoning with what happened between us on my own, however, still haven't prepared me for this. Seeing him. Smelling him. Hearing him: gruff but for once devoid of anger. Swallowing hard, I echo my pathetic question. "Why now?"

He flinches. Surprised? As if to compensate for that brief weakness, he steps in closer, towering above me. "You want a reason? How about business? My accountant is still waiting for a call from you."

I cringe, remembering his poisoned olive branch: a sum more than I could ever hope to recover from my family's finances—money we desperately need. And money I've left virtually in limbo, untouched.

"Are you waiting for an invitation?" he questions when I haven't answered. "After all this time, you owe me more than fucking silence, Snow."

Do I? I thought his parting gift in my hospital room was closure enough on his part—a birth certificate, in addition to the account transfer, confirming his identity. Yet the revelation just brought up even more unanswered questions. The foremost being: Why return now?

"What do you want from me?"

He levels his gaze against mine. "All I want is to talk."

"T-talk?" My mouth goes dry with the possibilities. Talk about how he destroyed my family home? My life? My brothers?

Months of silence and it seems fitting that he would choose now, of all times, to make his reappearance. If only to reinforce the truth he drilled into my skull: He'll never let me escape the past.

"I think you've said enough."

"Listen to me," he insists, reaching for my arm again. "Just let me explain. *Please*—"

"Snowy?"

The shout triggers alarm. *Ronan?*

Eyes flashing, Blake hisses, "Fuck, not now. Come with me." His fingers graze my forearm, but I'm already backing out of his reach. I can't let my brother see me like this.

Sensing my chance, I lunge, breaking into a sprint.

"Snow!"

Panting, I run through the dark, and footsteps echo, gaining on my position. Fast. Faster—too quickly to outrun.

"Snowy!"

Ronan. He's the one who grabs my forearm. My brain knows it, but my body reacts impulsively and I jump, wrenching away from him.

"Don't touch me!" I wrap my arms around myself, rubbing his touch away. Overly sensitive skin remembers everything I don't want to—every hateful caress. The cruel words snarled against my spine and whispered into my ear.

You're only beautiful like this, Snow. I'll only want you broken.

"Snowy?"

"I'm fine." My heart slams against my rib cage as fear mingles with guilt. I've never heard Ronan sound so worried. No, so *terrified*.

From behind him, I can see Hunter running, his hair mussed in haste. One look at me and he skids to a stop, his hands held before him.

"It's all right, Snowy," he says in that soothing, calm murmur only he can master. "It's okay. You're safe. We won't let him hurt—"

"I want to leave." God, I barely recognize the high-pitched voice tearing out of me. My hands are shaking. Wringing them together can't disguise the motion though. *I'm* shaking —and this time, I don't flinch when Ronan reaches for me, wrapping me in his arms.

"We are," he says. To Hunter, I hear him mutter, "We should have never brought her here. Fuck him. We'll just call the police the next time he sends another fucking—"

"Enough," Hunter snaps. "Now isn't the time."

I don't even try to follow the argument, as they steer me through the ballroom, past wide-eyed vultures desperate for a glance. He's watching as well—I sense him. Anger and cologne broadcast his location, so fucking close. Behind me? Numb, I can't even find the strength to look. I just eye the floor, clinging to my brothers as they forge a path through the crowd.

When we finally reach the cool night air, I realize I've been holding my breath all along. A bitter chill floods my lungs when I inhale, numbing me to my core.

"It's all right. We're leaving," Ronan insists while shoving me into the first town car that pulls up.

Sandwiched between him and Hunter, I struggle to catch my breath. To catch my senses. The only action my brain seems capable of has nothing to do with logic. Memories seep into the cracks where control has fractured. They taunt me with images, and feelings, and thoughts I've spent two months fighting to smother.

All the king's horses and all the king's men, Snow. No one can put you back together again. You're broken. Beautifully broken.

My brothers try to salvage the damaged pieces. They bundle me in their arms and rush me up to our suite. They ply me with promises of a bubble bath and a warm meal. The moment they leave to let me get undressed, I find myself staggering into the bathroom with the only goal of facing myself in the mirror.

Poor little Snowy Hollings. I was wrong to think wearing a stupid dress and lipstick could hide the damage visible on my skin. Angrily, I swipe the makeup off and sob openly at what I find underneath. A blind person could see it: I'm broken. Hollow. Ugly, selfish little Snow.

I'll always be that little girl who killed the boy she loved.

And he'll always haunt me.

Like a coward, I can't even run. So I cower over the toilet bowl, emptying myself of everything but pain. It's the only way I feel even an ounce of control.

Of something…

"Snowy!"

Oh no. I look up and find Ronan standing in the doorway, and I'd give anything in the world to avoid witnessing the pain lancing across his features.

All I can do is swipe my hand across my mouth, shaking with silent sobs. "I'm sorry," I croak, meaning every damn word. "Ronan, I'm so, so sorry."

THREE

"REMEMBER," the doctor says, standing before me in clinical white. "One session once a week. I look forward to meeting with you, Snowy."

My smile forced, I nod and then turn to the two men behind me. Wearing stoic expressions and gray suits, Ronan and Hunter resemble orderlies more than the disgraced businessmen they are.

"I'll get the car," Hunter explains before exiting the unit alone, leaving Ronan as my sole escort.

"Are you ready?" he asks, eyeing me warily.

I say nothing. Three days of inpatient psychiatric treatment and I'm right as rain. Honestly, I do feel better, even as my brother escorts me from the private, locked unit on the eighteenth floor of the city's most exclusive hospital.

All of those hours spent trapped here made one fact apparent: Blake Lorenz is the least of my problems.

Strange things have a habit of being revealed in family therapy sessions. Like the fact that Ronan and Hunter have been corresponding with a medical team for weeks, even before the night of the Sebastiáns' gala.

"We're worried about you, Snowy," Hunter had the nerve to insist, even while he surreptitiously eyed his cell phone beneath the unit's conference table—watching the stocks, I presume. "Lorenz did something to you," he added, his teeth bared. "If you just tell us what it fucking was, then we can nail the bastard—"

"Your well-being is all that matters," Ronan insisted, cutting him off.

Supposedly, that was their motive for turning their backs on me. Covert photographs of a skeletal stranger fill my medical record, along with secondhand descriptions of my behavior for the past eight weeks. I've lost five pounds, apparently. I've stopped eating. Stopped sleeping. As Ronan relayed to my therapist, he and Hunter were concerned.

Concerned enough to recommend an extended treatment facility outside of Mayfield against my protests. Concerned enough to offer an ultimatum: treatment, either voluntarily or otherwise.

Concerned enough to lie to me all this time.

I can process it all now with an almost detached sense of curiosity. After all, the joke's on me. I thought I'd been doing such a great job of coping. I smiled on cue and danced like a puppet on a string when asked. But the moment I falter on the world's stage? Oh, no. It's time to hide me away.

"Please say something," Ronan urges as he wrestles with a rolling suitcase containing my belongings and attempts to drag it onto the elevator leading to the hospital lobby. The wheels keep getting stuck just beyond the closing doors. Exasperated, he glances up and tries to shove the extended handle of the suitcase down into the body. "Give me a hand?"

I cut my gaze to the gleaming buttons on the elevator's interior, but I can't seem to move. Gradually, the doors meet, blocking off my view of a startled Ronan.

"Snowy!" He lunges a fraction too late.

Ding! The elevator's already descending, and seconds later, I arrive on the first level alone.

A good sister would wait for him to catch up. She certainly wouldn't merge into the stream of visitors with her head lowered to keep from drawing attention. She wouldn't slip down the first hallway she came across with no goal apart from…

What? Running?

Perhaps all I want is some fresh goddamn air. I'm so fucking sick of having my every moment scrutinized and maneuvered like a pawn on a chessboard. I'm so fucking *sick…*

Strangely, the anger I feel isn't even directed at Ronan or Hunter. Every ounce of rage festering inside me has only one target: myself.

"I was angry at the world," a woman says. The veracity of her words makes me freeze, mid-step.

At first glance, I see no one around, and dread gnaws at my nerves. Am I that desperate for validation that I hallucinated it? No. The voice is real, coming from somewhere nearby. A doorway, I realize.

Curious, I find myself drawn closer, peering into what looks like a lecture hall. At a podium stands a beautiful woman with cocoa skin and black hair hanging freely down her back. Dressed in a red pantsuit, she stuns almost as much as her heartfelt words. Her face seems familiar somehow, though I can't place it to a name.

"Do you want to know the worst part?" she asks the attentive crowd seated before her. "Everyone kept tiptoeing around me like I was some fragile porcelain doll. Like I'd cry at the drop of a hat. They thought I was 'depressed' or 'wallowing in despair,' but I wasn't." She shakes her head and hones her blazing, brown eyes on a distant spot, beyond the reach of those around her. "I was angry. And while I may have been raped, that didn't mean I was dead."

Raped. That word triggers alarm that has me scurrying back out into the hall. A bitter ache starts up in my stomach. Guilt? For the first time in so damn long, it feels as though someone is finally voicing what I can't say. How fitting that it only cements reality like a slap in the face: the elephant in the room. Despite how he treated me, Blake Lorenz *didn't* assault me. At least…I don't think I can call it that.

I stayed with him willingly. Even the sex was consensual. *And,* a twisted part of me adds, *you enjoyed it.*

I cringe away from the thought and then find myself leaning against the wall of a deserted hallway, panting. The longer I dawdle, the more elusive my freedom feels. Ronan's probably torn the whole hospital apart by now or called in the SWAT team. I almost feel bad for abandoning him. Almost.

But not too long ago, he abandoned me to be Hunter's babysitter, forced to cater to his fragile ego after our family's company went to ruin. I never consorted with doctors behind his back. I never betrayed him.

"Excuse me?"

Oh no. Soft footsteps approach, and I look up, fully prepared to find a security guard ready to escort me back to my brother. Instead, an amused pair of brown eyes takes me in, gleaming with genuine interest.

"Snowy Hollings," the woman says. "Don't tell me that the one time I stop contacting your family's offices is the one time I'm graced with a meeting?" Her warm laugh dispels any hostility the words may convey.

Regardless, I blink. "Excuse me?"

She's the woman from the podium, I realize. But wait. Even stranger, I think she's the same woman from the gala as well. The ruthless social climber, according to Sloane.

Up close, she radiates a steady confidence even Forrest Hollings would take note of. She tilts her head, eyeing me with a black eyebrow raised. "Or perhaps you were merely minding your own business and the fact you stumbled upon this meeting was entirely coincidence?"

I glance over her shoulder to find that I only managed to take a few steps from the lecture room she spoke in. Soft murmurs allude to the fact that someone else must have taken her place at the podium.

"Look, it doesn't matter. I'm Riley Haverty," she says, extending her hand.

I return the gesture, but she doesn't release my hand.

"I have to say that I've been trying to meet with you for… Well, it doesn't matter now. Can I have just a few minutes of your time?"

Minutes. I cast a wary glance down the hall, but I don't hear the stampede of armed forces on my trail just yet, and it seems Riley Haverty doesn't take no for an answer. Before I can respond, she steers me into the lecture hall, where a petite blonde is speaking to the crowd.

"They told me to just get over it," she says, her voice breaking, "but you can't just 'get over' something that affects you so deeply."

When she finishes, Riley claps the loudest. "I run Haven," she explains to me as the applause dies off. "We focus our outreach on assault victims, male and female, and I have to admit that I have been dying to meet you, Ms. Hollings."

A frown tugs at my mouth. "Why me?"

Riley shoots me a curious glance. "Well, to be frank, you were a witness in one of the most high-profile sexual assault cases in the entire country, accusing not only your longtime friend but the son of your father's business partner. In the years since, you've become a societal icon in your own right. If anyone could serve as a powerful voice to bring attention to Haven and our outreach, it's you."

My stomach sinks and I'm driven a step back. "I don't… I didn't—"

"I'm sorry," Riley says smoothly, her voice soft. "I didn't mean to intrude or bring up uncomfortable emotions. I tend to have what they call 'a blunt approach' in some circles." She laughs. "My only point is that you could be a powerful voice. I'd love for you to lend it to our cause, even for one event. We have a fundraiser at the convention center later this week, and it would be more than beneficial if you came to—"

"Snowy! Thank God."

Oh no. I turn as Ronan appears in the doorway, his hair wild, his eyes glazed with worry.

Heedless of the attention he's drawing, he races toward me and grabs my arm the moment he's close enough. "Don't you ever scare me like that again—"

"I'm sorry," I say over him, forcing a fake smile for Riley's benefit. "I wish I could but...I just... I'm not much of a speaker."

With a polite nod, Riley sidesteps Ronan and starts toward the front of the lecture hall. "I'm sorry to hear that," she says over her shoulder. "But if you change your mind, come to the convention center on Wednesday. I'd love to see you there."

"I—"

"Snowy, let's go." With the efficiency of a correctional officer, Ronan manually steers me to the doorway.

Before crossing the threshold, I wrench my arm from his grasp. People are staring—how shameless. Papa would roll over in his grave. I hope he is.

"I'm not a child," I snap before heading into the hallway alone.

Contrite, Ronan trails behind me, but his concern taints the air. I think I'm more startled by his behavior than angry. I've never seen him like this—not even when my weight reached its most dangerous lows. An irrational sense of dread warns me that something else must be feeding his guilt.

If so, an answer doesn't make itself known during the ride back to the hotel. Once we reach our suite, however, Ronan grabs my shoulder, rooting me to the floor.

"Please, Snowy." His voice rasps, breaking openly. "Please. I know you're angry, and I know you have every right to be," he adds when I try to break away. "You're pissed. Okay. Maybe the treatment center idea was too much. So punish *me*. Go on a wild tour of the strip clubs, or find a cabana boy to scandalize, if you must. Anything but hurt yourself. I can't…I can't take it."

"It's not your fault," I admit. "I just…"

"It's okay."

I'm in his arms before I know it, squeezed to the point of pain—not that he seems liable to let me go, even if I break. For a split second, I'm his sister again and not a fragile piece of porcelain. I'd suffer any bruise to make this moment last.

"We fucked up. I know we did. We should have done more, but it's like you won't even tell us what happened—"

"You don't have to apologize," I admit, hating myself for ever taking my anger out on him in the first place. "I'm sorry. I know I haven't been the easiest to be around lately."

"It's okay." He grips me tighter. "Just give me something to do—anything at all. Please."

Anything? "I want information on the Haven campaign," I blurt out. "And I want to make a sizeable donation in our name. *And*…I want to go to her event this week."

I'm not sure where the sudden change of heart comes from. Guilt? Or newfound shame? Showing my face for a cause bigger than myself is better than skulking around the suite, tormenting my brothers.

"The Haven campaign? *Riley Haverty's* Haven campaign?" Ronan draws back and eyes me, his mouth wrinkled. Rather than give him an answer, I wait until he nods. "Okay. Fine. Whatever you want. But—"

I stiffen in advance of his condition. "What?"

"You meet with your therapist as agreed. Once per week. Deal?"

I nod, my sigh resigned. "Deal."

"Then consider it done."

Just how would he find the money to make such a donation? I try not to care. For the first time in days, I feel some semblance of clarity. Normalcy? Hope?

Maybe Blake Lorenz didn't destroy all of me. Maybe there's some small piece of good left in Snowy Hollings. The least I can do is auction it off for a cause that deserves it.

FOUR

BLAKE

NEARLY A WEEK later and it's still all over the papers. Every tabloid, even the odd mainstream imprint, runs the same grainy photo. Her running, her head downcast, eyes so fucking wide.

Poor, pathetic Hollings girl. That moniker is her identity now, immortalized by the paparazzi in one brutal snapshot —but none of those casual spectators know the real truth behind her tormented expression.

Little Snow was fleeing from me.

She was terrified of *me*.

"Mr. Lorenz?" The intercom on the end of my desk buzzes, distorting the feminine voice coming through it. "You have a call on line one."

I reach out and strike a button on the console so hard the damn thing issues an alarming snap. "Thank you, Emily."

It's about fucking time.

The phone is in my hand before I even register grabbing it, cradling the receiver against my jaw. "Tell me you've done it."

"Damn," a woman replies, her tone crisp. A delicate laugh inserts a false sense of charm that only reinforces the warning I can sense from here. *Watch yourself, Lorenz.* "Perhaps next time answer with a greeting. Something to make me feel less like an awful, preying vulture than I already do—"

"I apologize," I reply smoothly. "Feel free to double my last donation. Satisfied?"

I wait.

She's silent.

"Now…" My fingers curl against the polished wood of the desk as I fish for the right phrasing. There's so many fucking things I need to say. Ask. Demand. In the end, I can only spit out, "is it done?"

"Well, I've met her if that's what you mean," she replies. I hear her inhale dejectedly. She must be alone, wallowing in her guilt.

"I'll triple my donation if you stop beating around the fucking bush." I yank the phone toward me and stand, turning to the view below. The city sleeps, a maze of gray concrete and twisted metal. Somewhere amongst it all, Snow is hiding away. I'll let her—for now, but every mouse has to scurry out into the open sometime. "Did you get her to agree or not?"

"I got her to come if that's what you mean," she finally admits. "And trust that I feel disgusting enough to doubt that even your very generous *bribe* is worth this. Why her? I think the poor girl has been through enough—"

"You don't need to concern yourself with her," I say, forcing more suave politeness into my tone. These days I feel more like Harrison than ever. Always lying, always balanced at the edge of a precipice.

All over a Hollings. The man would have gladly given his soul for Elizabeth, his partner's wife.

But I've already died for Snowy once.

"Just tell me again that spiel you spun before," the woman demands. "I know it's a lie but I'd like to hear it anyway: you won't hurt her."

"I won't," I reply. "Add another zero to my donation if it helps you sleep at night. Just remember our agreement."

I hang up, slamming the receiver against the base. Energy surges through my blood, demanding I pace. Crack my knuckles. Anything but sit and fucking wait.

I've gone from clawing my way to the top, to sitting at the top of the fucking pile, always waiting.

"Mr. Lorenz?" Emily announces through the intercom.

"What?" I snap without thinking, still stuck on Snowy. She doesn't understand now, but I'll make her see. No. More than that… I'll make her come *running* to me.

"You told me to tell you when yesterday's reports came in," Emily says, unperturbed by my tone.

"Right." I boot up the computer on my desk and open the latest email in my inbox. A smug grin is already forming, tugging at the corner of my mouth. Four businesses in two months, not including Holling's INC.

It's a fucking impressive feat.

But not impressive enough. Within seconds of scanning the latest corporate holdings, my smile becomes a frown. "Son of a bitch!"

Where I've taken over four of Mayfield's minor corporations, a foreign investor somehow managed to snag six.

My eyes narrow over the name and I form a fist, slamming it against my knee.

Hanz Zipler.

"Mr. Lorenz?" Emily calls tentatively. "Sorry to intrude, but you have another call. Line 2."

My eyes narrow further as I snatch up the receiver, tearing myself from the reports. "This is Blake," I say gruffly.

"You were supposed to leave her alone." This speaker is a man, his words slurring together. He's drunk, I suspect.

Were I in his place, I would be as well. "All of this… You said you'd leave her alone—"

"And you said you'd stay in fucking Tahiti, or Bali, or wherever the fuck you've run off to," I remind him. "You worry about keeping your head down and scraping together what little pride you have left and leave Snowy Hollings to me."

I hang up and grit my teeth, biting down the rage that feels so fucking constant these days. It sustains me more than blood, it feels like. Hate and anger and everything I've held onto for so damn long.

I could swallow up the entire damn city and it still wouldn't be enough.

I could amass more money than God.

Rule the entire goddamn world.

But claim Snow again? Make her see reason…

Maybe only *that* would ever be enough.

Or fuck, it could just be the beginning of another twisted power play, well beyond my games with Zipler.

We used to play chess, her and I. She relished the complexities of kings and queens, while I enjoyed the classic appeal of it: power and war. Her tactic was to always go after my most powerful pieces, leaving me with only pawns.

And, still, I always won.

Not because I was a better player, she just couldn't stand to ever deliver the finishing blow.

"You show your hand too soon," I used to scold her. "You play softer when you think I'll lose it all. You let your guard down, Snow. When you think I'm on the brink of destruction, you always back down. That only makes it easier to trap you in the end."

If only the world were still as simple as those childish games. The donation to Antonio Sebastián would have made the impact it should have. Snowy would have *willingly* attended the gala and meeting her there would have resulted in a miraculous reunion. Happy fucking ending.

Not this. The look on her face made it clear—I'm still the monster of her story. Now more than ever, I'm determined to do whatever it takes to twist that perception. Turn the tide of the game. Then win.

There is no option other than checkmate.

* * *

SNOWY

THE CONVENTION CENTER is a sprawling complex in the heart of downtown Mayfield, and I spend almost as much time admiring the building as I do trying to talk myself out of entering it. Not because I'm afraid of being seen. I'm not. It's just that the Haven campaign is much more well-known than I would have believed.

Every news organization in the city must be here to cover this event. Cameramen and reporters scour the property, interviewing guests at random.

Damn. I let loose a resigned sigh as I haul myself from a cab. It will be nearly impossible to sneak in unnoticed. Poor Riley. The last thing she needs is a tabloid headline courtesy of Snowy Hollings, the unstable train wreck who made a spectacle of herself at the Sebastiáns' gala.

My brothers couldn't shield me from the rumors for very long. Sloane herself ensured I caught wind of them by forwarding me a text linking an article sensationalizing my sudden departure. *My father threatened to sue,* she'd prefaced the message with. One look at the headline and I sensed the narrative being spun.

DISGRACED HOLLINGS HEIRESS STORMS FROM GALA

God, I barely recognized myself in the grainy photo attached to the headline.

No wonder Hunter looked seconds from tethering me to a leash before I left today. How I'd convinced him to let me go to this event alone, I have no idea. Perhaps the promise of this exact kind of publicity is enough to soothe his nerves —after all, anything to redeem the Hollings name.

Regardless, I soldier onward while clutching my purse to my chest. I'll make this quick—no hysterics, no scandal. Ronan's earned that much of a compromise.

Within minutes, I find Riley Haverty in the largest auditorium, charming a sea of supporters. At a glance, it's apparent that I missed the memo: Everyone seems to be wearing some shade of crimson, and I assume it must be the campaign's signature hue. Suddenly self-conscious, I tug at my sleeves. I dressed conservatively today, wearing just a blouse and a demure skirt.

In contrast, Riley's confidence permeates every minor detail of the décor. Banners promoting sexual-assault awareness hang from the walls, and sneaking insecurity festers the more I inspect my surroundings. Nearly everyone conveys striking confidence.

"Snowy?"

I jump as a warm hand settles over my forearm.

"You made it!"

Dazed, I find myself drawn into a hug by Riley Haverty.

Wearing a blazing shade of crimson, she cuts a commanding figure. "I had a feeling you would. Tada!" She reaches into a leather handbag and withdraws a small square of plastic: a name tag.

I gape, stunned. "I…I can't—"

"And you don't have to," she insists, dragging me forward, deeper into the auditorium.

We draw notice with every step, and I recognize the flash of cameras in our wake. Whether I want it to or not, word of my arrival will spread, and I cringe at how my family's taint might soil such an event.

"I just wanted to present this to you in person. Here—" I reach into my bag for an envelope and press it into her hand. The crumpled thing is damp with my sweat. Ronan came through with his magic donation, though I'm not brave enough to see the amount for myself. "It's nowhere near what you deserve, but—"

"It's more than enough," Riley says warmly. "And you being here is even more appreciated than money."

"Really?"

She winks. "Immensely."

The way she speaks weaves a spell that instantly relieves some of my nerves. Her poise is infectious.

"Stay for a bit," she implores. "Here—" As we approach a table sporting brochures containing information about the Haven campaign, she lifts a stack and hands them to me. "Pass these out. Smile. Trust me—your presence alone goes a million miles."

It's only now that I read the tagline accompanying the branding for this event. **Featuring speakers: Riley Haverty, Chloe Pracile, Amy Harville, and Snowy Hollings.**

I wince. Suddenly, my fingers are shaking too badly to hold anything, and the brochures fall to the floor. "I didn't… I can't speak," I say, stumbling over the words. "I'm sorry if you thought—"

"Oh, damn." Sighing, Riley sinks to her knees and gathers the pamphlets. Then she looks up, biting her lower lip. "I jumped the gun again, didn't I?"

Am I angry? I don't know. My emotions feel too sluggish to reach my brain, as though they're trapped behind something solid. Eventually, I settle on a name for the feeling tearing through my veins. *Guilt.* Out of all of those women, I don't belong here.

"I should go—"

"Please don't." Riley imploringly clasps a hand over her chest. "Please. I… It's just, if you don't mind my pointing it out, you were assaulted by someone close to you," she says, her tone soft. "That's the open secret: Most assaults come from the people we trust the most. Friends. Neighbors. Parents—"

I wince, though Riley doesn't seem to notice.

She clasps one of my hands in both of her own. "I'm sorry if I overstepped. At least listen to a few of our keynotes. I'll apologize for the confusion myself, and I won't drag you on stage without your permission. I promise."

Before I can reply, the lights dim and another woman takes the stage, announcing the start of the event.

"Please," Riley mouths before taking off to the front. "I'll make it up to you."

I waver on the tips of my toes, eyeing the doorway to the auditorium. A part of me wants to leave, remembering Sloane's warning. Or maybe it's just cowardice; here, I'm forced to stand without my mask. I'm just Snowy, a spectator like so many others. Alone, I settle against the back wall and just watch.

The speakers range in ages from barely eighteen to twice as old. Their stories are harrowing, detailing horrific abuse that puts anything I've experienced to shame. As Riley mentioned, there is a disturbing theme: friends, brothers, sisters, fathers, mothers. The worst abuse seems to come from within, and I can't help but picture Papa. I think it's the first time I ever let myself put him in that dangerous context I've avoided for so long: abuser. Denial is a Hollings defining trait, and I've admittedly painted his memory in so many bright shades to make it easier to look back and not…

Scream?

Multiple women verbalize the same conflicting emotions in heartbreaking detail. At the same time, they speak bravely, without flinching from the trauma of their past, and an air of hope settles over the crowd by the time the final speaker delivers her message to thunderous applause. Riley takes the podium next, and as promised, she mentions my family's donation and apologizes profusely for the confusion regarding my speaking.

So I don't know why the hell I step forward, cutting her off midsentence.

"I… Um, it seems she would like to say a word after all," Riley says smoothly while inching back from the podium. "Everyone, please welcome Snowy Hollings."

The applause that follows draws heat to my cheeks. How unwarranted. I'm cheered only because of my name—*that* name. Hollings. A name tied to Forrest and the darkest, most twisted things festering in my soul. How ironic is it that the Hollings name can be coveted by someone fighting a crusade against sexual assault with no clue as to how hypocritical it is that I'm even here?

In a daze, I mount the stage anyway, and I face a crowd of people who should be sniggering. Laughing. Not waiting.

Not listening.

I don't belong here, but no one seems to know it. They sit patiently in the lingering silence as I clear my throat, desperate to find words. In the end, I stop trying, pretending, and acting. I open my mouth and simply speak.

"I don't belong here," I admit before licking my lips to find traction to keep talking. "I'm not…I'm not a victim—"

Applause erupts, and I stiffen, mortified. They misunderstood me, thinking I meant the statement as one of empowerment. If only I were that brave. But I'm not.

"I wish I could say something inspiring or incredible like everyone else," I add weakly. "But I can't. All I can say is… No one wants to label events in their life as t-trauma."

God, I hate that word, but there it is. Traumatic: an event that shatters the world as one knows it. Only now can I finally let myself use it. I inflicted trauma on Brandt Lloyd —and the man I'd grown up believing was my father inflicted similar damage upon me.

Someone in the audience coughs, drawing my attention, and I blink, remembering where I am.

After clearing my throat, I try again. "Why would we? You're a good daughter. Or a good friend. You're doing what you must. If someone hurts you, you deserve it b-because…" I break off, heat searing behind my eyes. God, not now. I blink rapidly, clenching the podium to the point of pain. Before I can run, I spot a familiar face in the crowd. Riley.

"Go on," she mouths, nodding encouragingly. For the first time in so damn long, someone wants me to speak out loud, and I'm finding that I can't resist the temptation, even if it stings.

"If someone hurts you, you think you deserve it. You believe it. Maybe it's true…but… You aren't responsible for someone else's pain. Your feelings matter as well. Your body matters. No one should be allowed to violate it just because they feel they own it."

My teeth clamp together over the last words as I marvel at their ferocity. Who are they directed at? Papa? Myself?

I don't know, and as the crowd responds with applause, I don't have to decipher them.

At least for now.

* * *

THE REST of the event passes in a strange, dazed blur. For most of it, I follow Riley, greeting visitors with my plastic, fake smile. Eventually, she disappears, leaving me alone to my own devices.

And all I can do is stare.

The speakers mingle with the crowd and trade stories with visitors. They offer sympathy and convey emotions in ways even Mayfield's most adept social manipulators never could. They're genuine, and I find myself swept up in the chaos, just as riveted as the average visitor. It isn't until I notice the sky darkening above the glass skylights that I realize just how long I've gone without stressing about Ronan or Hunter's vigilance or fighting my own thoughts.

Haven feels more like a feeling than a name, and I wish I could make it last forever. All too soon, guests begin to trickle one by one from the auditorium until just a handful remain. I find Riley greeting the last few stragglers, but when she sees me, she nearly barrels me over in another hug.

"You are amazing!" she exclaims against my shoulder before pulling away. "You are amazing. Not one, but two donations, both equally generous?"

"Two?" I shake my head, convinced I've misheard her.

"Yes," she insists. "Your associate delivered it by hand not too long ago." Something in my expression must convince her to elaborate. "A man. Tall."

I sigh. Has Hunter gotten in on the action, attempting to buy my trust back as well? Probably. He's certainly charming enough to inspire the flush creeping into Riley's cheeks.

"Dark hair," she adds as a falling sensation washes down my spine, leaving me lightheaded. "Young. Handsome… Snowy?"

"I'm fine," I whisper even as I clutch the edge of a table for balance.

She gently touches my shoulder. "Are you sure?"

No… The word won't leave my tongue, but Riley's already scurrying across the room.

"Let me get you a chair," she calls back.

Movement catches the corner of my eye as a hulking figure steps from the shadows the moment she's gone. Black stubble coats his chin, and bruises beneath his eyes reveal lingering exhaustion. From lack of sleep? Any concern I may feel is all but shattered by the coldness in his gaze.

I've never seen such a hard, frozen shade of blue.

I've never seen someone so furious.

"Don't run."

I'm not sure if I imagined the strained growl. Either way, I'm already racing for the main doors, weaving through the thinning crowd—but I'm not fast enough. Mere paces from freedom, my arm is seized in a grip of iron. One tug has me off-balance. Before I can get my bearings, I'm steered into a narrow room just outside the auditorium.

It's small. Dark. I faintly make out a table and chairs, which reveals it to be a conference room of some kind—an ironic prison for Blake Lorenz to trap me in now.

"Let me go." My breathless whisper lacks any conviction, but he releases me anyway. When my gaze darts to the door handle, however, he places his hand over it, blocking it from view.

"All I'm asking for is five damn minutes."

"For what?"

His eyes narrow into slits. He's wearing a dark suit, which bolsters his true intent: He's not here for an idle chat, but business. "Seriously, Snowy, let's not play this game."

I'm not faking my confusion. "W-what game?"

"I'm sure you know the one," he suggests, raising a black eyebrow. "It seems to always begin with you running from me."

I can't stop smoothing my hands over the front of my blouse, tucking every part of me away from his scrutiny. "Did I…offend you at the Sebastiáns' gala? If so, I'm sorry—"

"The gala?" He laughs coldly, shaking his head. "Don't play coy, Snowy." There's a hard note I can't miss in his voice. Almost a plea. *I'm trying my best. Don't ruin it.*

"Okay, then what do you want?" I demand cautiously. "You could call or send a message. You don't have to ambush me—"

"I don't?" He blinks. "Funny you'd say that, because I've been trying to 'call or send a message' every goddamn day for two months and you've yet to give me a single response."

I shake my head, alarmed by the dark expression crossing his features. "You're lying."

"Am I? It seems your brothers have taken their roles as your gatekeepers much more seriously than you've given them credit for."

"And they shouldn't?" A defensive lump forms at the base of my throat. Ronan and Hunter have been nearly insufferable lately, but it isn't like they don't have a reason to be. "Let's not forget the fact that you had them find me naked, wandering the woods alone after you burned down our house."

"I haven't." He doesn't even wince. It's as if his face is a siphon, designed to filter all emotion. He's so different from the boy he used to be that it blows my mind. Brandt would never be so callous. If anything, he'd sense the tears welling behind my eyes, and he'd already start wiping them away. *King's men, Snow,* he'd murmur to reassure me. *I'll always be there to pick up the pieces.*

"Fine," I say thickly. "Then I don't think we have anything to discuss—"

"Listen to me. I didn't come here to fight with you." The genuine note catches me off guard. "I came here to warn you. Tell your brothers that they accomplish nothing by sending the police to my goddamn office every morning. I'm not the one threatening you, though I think you have a damn good idea who is—"

"Threatening me?"

He scoffs, studying me with a flick of his gaze. "You know damn well what I mean."

"What are you talking about?"

"Damn." A frown distorts his cold expression. For a second, he almost looks human again. Pitying? "They haven't told you…"

I can't keep the exasperation from my tone. "Told me what?"

"You've gone and got a bounty put on your head, Snow," he declares. "A nasty one. What the hell were you thinking, messing with a man like Lyle Harlow?"

Oh God.

The name triggers a dark wealth of memories, both old and new. Lyle Harlow was my father's lackey, known for engaging in criminal enterprises. Though it isn't like I can judge Papa too much, considering that just a few months ago, I consorted with Harlow myself to find the whereabouts of one Blake Lorenz.

"I demand my payment in full, Little Hollings," he warned me then. Only I never sent a dime.

I don't have one to spare.

Suffice it to say that a man who'd murder a teenager isn't above targeting an heiress to avenge a slight. "They haven't told you," Blake accused. Just what do Ronan and Hunter know?

"Did you fucking hear what I said?"

"Y-yes." I turn away from him, crossing my arms to disguise how they're shaking. "But I don't know what you're talking about."

"Bullshit. You went to Harlow. How could you be so fucking stupid—"

"And what if I did?" My vision blurs, and warmth paints my cheeks before I can swipe at the tears with the back of my hand. "Why does it matter to you?"

"Don't."

Alarmed, I look up and find him balanced on the tips of his toes, his entire body tensed like a coil ready to spring. I can almost visualize the ropes of his control snapping, one by one—a twitching finger here, a pulsing vein there.

Pulling his upper lip from his teeth, he growls, "You may not trust me, but at least give me the benefit of the doubt, Snow. Don't you dare treat me like I'm a monster. Not again."

I don't mean to counter him. I don't. But something hot rises in me like bile, impossible to keep back. "You cut my hair. You locked me away. You told me awful, vile things. You destroyed everything I ever cared about. What else does that make you?"

"Fine," he says, his tone dangerously soft. "Then what does that make *you*?"

Any reply I could say dies in my throat. He's right. I helped create the person he's become.

"Maybe I'm even worse," I rasp, regaining my voice. "So blame me. Hate me. Just let me go." I start forward, but he doesn't budge. If anything, he seems to loom above, infinitely taller.

"You need to listen to me. Pay Harlow. You have more than enough money—"

"*Your* money," I reply more harshly than I meant to. The money he made by selling off my family's business shares while making me believe he would let me keep them. Blood money. "I don't want it."

"This isn't the time for fucking pride, Snowy!"

I stiffen as he grips my shoulders and forces me to meet his gaze.

"Do you understand how much danger you're in? Do you know what a man like Harlow would do? He'd make an example of you." His fingers shoot out to graze my cheek, inching toward my healing scar. "He'd hurt you worse than I ever could. Pay him with the goddamn money."

"Let…let me go."

He immediately withdraws his fingers, scowling at the tips —but his opposite hand stays, rooting me to the floor. "You're playing with fire."

He sounds too serious. Too stern. My racing heart wants me to read more into it than I should. There's something ominous in the set of his jaw. It's the same way he looked the day he promised me the Hollings Estate.

"You're lying," I whisper.

"Am I? Or perhaps I'm here to 'abuse' you further? Violate your body? Claim I own it? Admit it: Was all that directed at me?"

My face overheats as I recognize the words of my impromptu speech spit back in my face. When I say nothing, he barks out a callous laugh.

"Of course it was. That was a rousing presentation," he declares, mockingly clapping his hands. "But, even now, you still can't accuse *him* out loud, can you? Say his name, Snow. Admit who really hurt you."

Forrest Hollings. My lips flutter, but words won't come. Ten years of lying and I can't find the voice to speak the truth a second time, even to the one person who deserves it the most.

"I thought so," he hisses. "It's still easier to blame me, isn't it? No matter what righteous reasons you may have had. Fine. I want to hear it from your mouth. So say it. Say I raped you for a second time—"

"Stop."

"It's what you let them think, isn't it?" He cocks his head, his gaze honed with laser focus. "Say it. Use me as your goddamn scapegoat. Tell me I hurt you."

Rape? No. But I can't begin to classify the damage he's done to me in other ways.

"You *did* hurt me." That voice was a stranger's, so weak. So pathetic.

"Did I now, Snow?"

I shiver as his eyes flash a dangerous blue.

"Tell me how."

No. I turn away, but his fingers hook beneath my chin, wrenching my head around to face him.

"Tell me," he commands. "This time, there is no judge. No jury. Tell me how I hurt you. In detail, Snow."

"Stop it—"

"Say it."

"Y-you lied to me," I hear myself croak, sounding miles away. More tears spill down my cheeks without warning, hot and punishing. "You violated me. You made me feel… you made me feel like I was worthless."

"Good." He lets me go, leaving me to stagger for balance. "At least now you know what it fucking feels like. You want to die? Be my guest," he calls on his way to the door. "But if you want to play the role of traumatized victim, try a little harder. Perhaps more tears as you run gasping from the room next time?" He chuckles while rubbing his chin. "Such intrigue swirling around, ever since your little display at the Sebastiáns' gala. Bravo. You certainly had them all fooled. They're whispering about who I am to you. An ex-lover? Blackmailer? High society minds certainly have quite the imagination."

"I didn't even know you'd be there," I admit, my voice thick.

"Ahhh." He rubs his chin, mulling over a different explanation. "Your brothers sure love exploiting your flair for the dramatics. Hunter, I bet."

He laughs again, hollowly. Then he clenches his fist and slams it against the wall between us.

"I publicized that fucking donation," he growls as I jump. "The whole damn world knew I'd be there. Then you show up, after avoiding me for fucking weeks, and you… You act as though *you're* the goddamn one hurting." His voice breaks, betraying something raw and ugly festering underneath. Just as quickly, a cold smile banishes any hint of anger. "Enjoy the drama, Snow," he says while wrenching open the door. "I look forward to hearing all about how I raped you in the tabloids."

He leaves, slamming the door behind him so fiercely that it rattles on the hinges.

All I can do is struggle to remain standing.

FIVE

I SPEND the next three days locked inside my room with only my window to connect me to the outside world.

Surprisingly, my brothers haven't mentioned the treatment facility, and I can't bear to broach the topics Blake brought up. Would Hunter really be so manipulative as to bring me into the man's orbit, knowing I'd crumble?

The answer lurks at the pit of my stomach: He's a Hollings. A part of me doesn't want to go there. Perhaps my brothers are simply worried and the so-called threats against me explain their sudden eagerness to ship me away? I'm not brave enough to ask.

In a bitter compromise, we silently coexist. Mistrust festers, gathering in the air like water swelling behind a fragile dam.

Until it finally breaks.

I wake up smelling the first sign of danger: Ronan's cologne. He enters my room without warning, and when I startle upright, I find him standing by the window, glaring at the streets below.

"Ronan?"

He cuts his gaze in my direction, and I gasp out loud. His eyes glow red—they're so bloodshot.

"What's wrong?" The blood drains from my face. "Is Hunter—"

"Why didn't you say anything, Snowy?" He sounds rough, the way he does when he's been drinking. Or…crying? God, he has been. Drying tears glisten on his skin, and my heart throbs warily. "I would have done something. I…I'd have killed that son of a bitch!"

Oh no. Only a few men could earn this amount of scorn from him. "What are you talking about?"

"This!" He throws something onto my bed that I didn't notice him holding. Flat. Square. A newspaper.

The blazing headline makes me do a double take. Blood rushes from my skull and pools within my overworked heart. I can't breathe. All I can do is read.

CHILLING EXCHANGE REVEALED ON TAPE, screams the headline, followed by snippets of said recording. I see my name. Blake Lorenz's. A list of abstract quotes supposedly from a recording.

"You hurt me."

Numb, I grasp the paper, drawing it closer. Ink smears beneath my sweaty fingerprints the faster I read.

"You violated me… You made me feel like I was worthless."

"Good. At least now you know what it fucking feels like."

Among the sordid snippets, there's no mention of the gala or Lyle Harlow. Just carefully constructed phrases to make it seem like…

To make it seem like Blake Lorenz did more than just torment me.

"Oh…God…" I pinch myself, raking my nails over my skin. But I don't wake up. This is real. Drawing my knees to my chest doesn't contain my throbbing heart. It hammers through my rib cage, leaving me hollow.

"I look forward to reading about how I raped you in the tabloids."

"Are you listening to me?" Ronan is still watching me, his expression agonized. "I knew he hurt you," he says, hissing through clenched teeth. "Somehow, even if you wouldn't admit the details. But never… Why didn't you fucking say something?"

He's joined by Hunter before I can answer. Stern-faced, our older brother flanks the opposite end of my bed.

"The board's put the bastard on suspension," he says, though I'm not sure if he's talking to Ronan or me. "If public opinion trends the way it seems, he'll be gone for sure. He's ruined."

"I don't give a damn about the company!" Turning from Hunter, Ronan lunges for my hand, yanking me upright. "Come on."

I stagger to my feet as he drags me down the hall and throws the door to the suite open. Alarmed, I clutch at the doorway with both hands. "Where are we going?"

"To the hospital," he says, casting me an incredulous look. "Or the police station. Fuck, we have to do something—"

"No!" I wrench out of his grip and pace mindlessly. My fingers tear through my hair as I remember the damage done to it and by whom. He did hurt me, but never in a million years would I do something like this to retaliate.

Never.

"When were you ever alone with the bastard?" Ronan demands. "Is this why… God, we should have never taken you to that fucking event!"

"Ronan, enough." Hunter employs that gentle, stern tone only he can—but there's something off in its cadence. I've never heard this grit in his voice before. This…hate. "Snowy," he says gently, "you will press charges."

"Charges?" Ronan fumes. "I'll kill that son of a bitch—"

"I can't breathe." My fingers clutch at my chest as if physical touch can force air into it. Suddenly, Ronan is by my side, rubbing my shoulders.

"It's okay, Snowy," he croaks. "We'll make this better. I'll fix this."

"We need to put out a statement," Hunter suggests. "Something concise—"

"Please." I pull away from them, heading for my room. "I just...I just need to think."

I might as well have said nothing, because they continue to talk without me. Shout. Argue.

Closing my door only muffles the sounds, not that I can shut out the world so easily. The paper taunts me from my bed. It's as if the honking horns and faint clamor of traffic below carry the vicious rumors directly to my ears.

I look forward to the tabloids, Snow.

Someone must have recorded us. Someone who leaked select phrases to the papers. But why? Dazed and dizzy, I can't come up with a single name. The only thing I'm sure of is guilt. It hammers through my veins in time with my heartbeat. Liar. Liar. Liar.

You've ruined his life twice, Snowy.

Hunter claimed that his spot on the board is already in jeopardy. I should be happy to hear that. Maybe if I were a real Hollings, I would be. Scandal festers like a poison in a city like Mayfield. Losing the company would only be the first cog in the vicious wheel of public contempt. Only God knows what could happen next.

Could he lose his money?

His home?

More?

I'm pacing again, wringing my fingers together, desperate to do something. Eventually, I find myself near my door, feeling along the wood. The shouting sounds fainter now; Ronan and Hunter must be in another room.

Heart pounding, I approach my closet and throw on the first items of clothing I can reach. Jeans. A blouse. Once dressed, I open my door and creep beyond it.

I don't see Ronan or Hunter within view, and I reach the door to the suite without drawing notice. Leaving now is the worst possible thing I could do. I know it, but my body doesn't seem to care. Rebelliously, my fingers clench the handle, turning it before my brain can fully process the consequences. Then I step out into the hall, and the moment I've cleared the threshold, I race into an elevator.

My thoughts are a jumble as I exit the lobby minutes later. Dazed, I find myself flagging down the first taxi I can, but once inside, I'm forced to admit that I don't even know where to go.

Or do I?

Without thinking, I blurt out a single address. Regret sinks in the moment the cab approaches a reclusive manor on the outskirts of Mayfield. Or it once *was* reclusive.

Now, a herd of news vans is swarming outside the gates.

"Holy shit!"

I flinch as the driver voices the concerns I don't dare.

"Are you sure about this, lady?"

Am I? An answer won't leave my throat. In the end, I just nod.

"All right." With a wary glance at me, the driver presses on.

The car barely travels a few feet before unknown faces press against the windows of the taxi. Cameras flash as pounding fists and shouting voices demand answers.

"Do you know Blake Lorenz?"

"I think it's her!"

"Ms. Hollings! Ms. Hollings!"

Thankfully, the wrought-iron gates barring the road part as if on cue, and the driver fearlessly peels through them. Far too soon, the sprawling manor house looms on the horizon. The chaos hasn't reached here, at least. Imposing and dark, the house looks more untouched than it did two months ago.

After paying the fare with what little cash I have on me, I cautiously approach the front door and lift the lion-shaped door knocker. No one responds to the first knock though. Uneasy for reasons I can't explain, I switch to knocking with my fists.

Still no answer.

So I try again, pounding. Banging.

Words meld into my attempts before I can bite them back. "Blake? Blake, please—"

A lock disengages, and the door opens so quickly that my fist meets air. Momentum draws me forward, right into the body of a figure who palms my waist, effortlessly righting my balance.

"I'm surprised you're here."

I look up, inhaling sharply. He's paler than I've seen him yet, outlasting the dark. Mussed hair and reddened eyes betray the depth of his exhaustion. His expression, however, reveals nothing. No anger. No shock, either.

"Come to see for yourself?" He steps back and pauses as if giving me the chance to run.

I should. God knows why I inch forward instead, allowing him to close the door behind me, which drenches us in shadow.

He hasn't lightened his decor any. The house remains dark, but before where his servant, Charles, added at least the illusion of a lived-in dwelling, I now sense only silence. He's alone.

Why that thought makes my heart pound harder? I don't know.

"What are you doing here, Snow?"

"I didn't..." My voice thickens and I swallow hard to strengthen it. "The recordings. I didn't release them. I swear—"

"There's no need to waste your breath," he says.

My heart sinks. This was a mistake. Stung, I start for the door, but his hand brushes my arm, drawing me back.

"Wait. I… I believe you."

"Y-you do?" I blink, unable to recognize the stranger watching me, devoid of hate and rage. God, he looks so damn tired.

Even his lips seem to have barely enough energy to twitch into a frown. "There are other ways you could hurt me, Snow."

How so? By revealing his true identity?

Hooded eyes reveal no answers. Instead, he turns on his heel and wanders deeper into the house. "But maybe now we can talk, at least."

Talk? I follow him despite my better judgment, keeping enough of a distance that he's beyond my reach. I examine him visually instead.

His clothing is wrinkled, a suit that looks more than a day old. His hair has been ruthlessly ravaged by his raking fingers. The disheveled air is such a far cry from the cold, polished man I know him as, and I'm drawn closer by a dangerous step. A single brush of my hand along his forearm reveals crackling tension trapped beneath his skin. I try to pull away, but he turns, grabbing my wrist. One tug lures me closer as his free hand captures my chin, forcing me to meet his gaze. With surprising tenderness, he tilts my face toward his.

"I'm ruined, Snow," he murmurs as if marveling at the term. "I bet you and your brothers are ecstatic. You always did love a bit of poetic irony. I've burned your name to elevate mine, and now look at us both—"

"Don't say that." My heart aches, more so because of cruel memory. *Poetic irony.* It's something Brandt would say. I shake my head to clear it, desperate to stay on topic. "I'm not here to gloat. I just… What can I do?"

Helping him should be the least of my worries. In fact, given everything he's done, I have more than enough reason to hate him. If only my heart knew that too. I look at him and try to only see Blake Lorenz. I *try*.

But his eyes—the brief glimpse of them I catch from behind a wayward lock of his hair—draw a different answer to my lips.

"A press conference," I find myself proposing. "I could say something. Say that my words were misconstrued—"

"No." He shakes his head. "That wouldn't work."

"Then what?" I grit my teeth, desperate to do *something*. Anything.

"There is something…" He turns away as if repulsed by the idea before he's even voiced it. "We'd need to be seen." When I say nothing, his eyes cut to mine, brimming with intensity. "We'd have to convince them that I never hurt you. Or," he adds as if sensing the memories playing on the fringes of my thoughts, "we'd convince them that you've forgiven me."

Forgiven. I stare blankly ahead as my mind spins with the term. After all he's done to me, can I afford such a luxury?

"I'd have to be seen with you," he reiterates. "Could you do it?"

A better question is: Can *he* after all I've done to him? The man who can't seem to look at me without baring his teeth in hatred. Could he set that aside, if only to clear his name?

Lost in thought, I gaze out a nearby window. A drab, gray sky promises a storm. I sense it hovering on the horizon, waiting to break. Every fiber of my being tells me to leave now. Avoid the tempest. Run. But, when I glance over and meet his gaze, something in me shifts. He looks so human in this moment, almost like a stranger. Someone older than Brandt yet softer than Blake. Someone vulnerable.

I nod. "Y-yes. I think I can try."

His jaw tightens, highlighting the gauntness of his features. "Good. I know it won't be easy."

"It won't be," I agree. Swallowing hard, I square my chin. "Which is why I want something in return."

He stiffens. "What?"

"You allow my brothers onto the board when your position is secure." I pause, but he doesn't shout or deny me outright. Odd. Inhaling deeply, I soldier on. "You can hate me all you want, but don't punish them. Please."

"Damn it… I don't hate you." He tears a hand through his hair as if grappling with that admission the same way I am.

My shoulders slump beneath a sudden sense of weightlessness, and I'm forced to cling to the wall for balance.

"Maybe I never did. Maybe…" He sighs, his teeth gritted, and shakes his head. "Doesn't matter. Fine. But, in exchange, I want something from you as well."

"What?" A part of me suspects the answer even before he directs a searching glance in my direction.

"A single night won't be enough. Not to convince everyone. You once promised me an entire year…"

"No." Horror robs my voice of any strength. The protest just resonates as a formless whisper. I cringe beneath the assault of memories: the pain, the humiliation, the shame. The sex. The nights that still leave me jolting awake, gasping at their intensity. I barely lasted a month of our previous arrangement.

"It wouldn't be like before," he says, his tone hard. "I won't… We'd just have to convince them in public. You'd still have your freedom, Snow."

Freedom. My breath catches at how valuable he makes that word sound. As if it's the world's most coveted possession. He's offering it to me willingly. I'd be a fool to turn him down. I sense all of those sentiments in everything he doesn't say.

But then there is the small matter of what he has said. I hate you, Snow. I'll break you, Snow. I own you, Snow. Did you really think I'd let you keep it?

"I want it in writing."

He inhales sharply, betraying his irritation at the ultimatum. So used to holding the cards, he can't stand to let one slip out of play. "I'll write you a check," he says, palming the pocket of his slacks as if he intends to do just that. "How is that for binding?"

"For how much?" I blurt before I can help myself. A heartbeat later, I add, "Nothing you say is binding."

Lightning-fast anger flickers across his face, disappearing almost as quickly. "Well, considering that *you* are the one in control of the situation…"

He waits while I process just what he means.

I can make my own demands.

"I want it in writing," I reiterate. "You guarantee my brothers a spot on the board. And—"

"What else?" he prompts. "Make your demands."

"I want full control over what I wear," I say in a rush. "How I dress. How I act. You demand nothing."

No illicit commands. No demeaning acts. No taunts or vicious games revolving around my weight.

He processes my words coldly, his frown unnerving. "And if I refuse?"

Then so do I. The words spring to the tip of my tongue, but I fail to voice them. On the surface, I could leave him to ruin. But my brothers and I would be no better off. Sure,

Blake could be removed from the board, but there is no guarantee that the remaining members would choose to reinstate a Hollings in his place. I'd still be a pauper with no money to my name, and he'd have no reason to bargain. With one expert twist, he's proven to be a calculating businessman. I have no choice but to play this game at least partially by his rules.

A satisfied gleam settles in his gaze as if he's aware of every thought twisting through my head. "I suggest you meet me halfway," he says. "A better arrangement for both parties."

"And what do you want?" I lick my lips in anticipation of the answer.

"Don't look so worried." It's an admonishment, not a taunt. "I won't have you do anything you don't want to. I simply need…assurance."

"Oh?"

"Of your safety." He's worried. For me? "Do you really think some lax hotel suite can protect you from a man like Lyle Harlow?"

I stiffen at the reference. All this time, I've fought to put my minor indiscretion out of my mind. As long as I didn't think about it, the danger didn't seem to matter. How fucking naïve.

But I won't have Blake Lorenz be the one to remind me of that foolishness.

"Then what do you suggest?" I counter. "That I stay with you?"

What I intend to be a cruel joke lands to a startling silence. Only a second passes before I realize that, yes, that's exactly what he intends. At least he has the decency not to say as much out loud. Instead, he raises an eyebrow and his mouth twitches as if fighting to keep from twisting into a frown.

"Would it really be so unbearable?" he wonders. "You'd be safer with me."

"Safe?" I rasp the word, but even I have enough tact not to mention the obvious.

How safe was I the night he set my home on fire with us inside it? How safe was I every night he tormented me with cruel insinuations or threats of physical violence? How safe am I here, with him now?

I hunt his eyes for an answer but find nothing but shadow. He's more alarming like this than he is raging with fury. At least then I know what to expect.

"The choice is up to you," he says on the cusp of a sigh. He even has the nerve to shrug—but I know him, this strange, vengeful creature he's become.

My heart lurches at the thought of just what he could have in store. There are so many corridors here for him to chase me around. So many rooms to hunt me in. So many chances to finish what he started.

"We wouldn't stay here." He scowls at the hallway's enclosed interior. "I own a penthouse downtown. It's centrally located. You can continue your affairs from there."

My affairs? I suspect he's referring to Haven. Good. I force myself to add, "I'd also like you to make a regular donation—"

"Done," he says, cutting me off. "But I want you to suggest to Riley Haverty that I become a primary benefactor."

I choke on any smugness I may have felt for leveraging Haven against him. "W-why?"

He shrugs again, turning to stare out the window. "You're not the only one with crusades. Riley Haverty is a shrewd businesswoman, but she's very wary of her contacts—for good reason."

"And, now, given the current news cycle, she wouldn't consult with you in a million years," I surmise.

"Something like that."

"Fine." It feels so strange to speak in such businesslike terms. I never was a part of the corporate world like my brothers. I never wanted to be. How ironic that I've been forced overnight to learn the ways of the boardroom, but they're applied in secret with a man who makes me tremble. I'd laugh if the prospect weren't so utterly pathetic. "So, what now?"

"Now..."

I stiffen as his footsteps grace the wood in tandem, drifting in my direction. Warmth alludes to the hand he brushes against my shoulder. Gently, as if he's aware I'll cringe from his reach. A part of me doesn't mean to. But my reactions to him are based on pure instinct. Muscle memory. I cringe. I shiver. I endure.

Surprisingly, he lets me scuttle away to a distant end of the hall. After a heartbeat of silence, he advances just a single step—to reinforce his presence, I suspect. He may pretend that I hold the cards, but there's no illusion here; he still runs the game.

"Now, we make our first move," he says, suddenly switching to a tone that reminds me of Papa. Calculating. "The world will be watching, demanding answers. I say we circumvent them. We take our 'relationship' public for a quiet night on the town, as if the rumors mean nothing."

I frown at the imagery. Only he would propose such a thing —someone with a wealth of confidence who has never been the butt of a cruel joke. Though maybe he has. I keep forgetting the truth behind his current persona. The differences between him and the boy he used to be are so vast that it's easy to forget they were the same person once. My beautiful Brandt Lloyd whose world I plunged into hell.

"Okay," I say thickly. "Just how do we do that?" I look over my shoulder and find him staring pensively into the air, stroking his chin with the pad of his thumb.

"I have an idea in mind. Leave the arrangements to me."

"I thought *we*"—I stress the word—"were in this together."

"We are." He sounds surprised by my doubt. "But just... just let me take the lead just this once. I promise to consult you from then on."

I find myself gritting my teeth, anxious at the thought. In the end, I don't have much of a choice. "What am I supposed to do?"

He smiles, but there's no joy in it. His eyes remain distant, focused on something far beyond me. "In the meantime, you play the part," he says. "It's best if you get dressed here, however, given the current circumstances."

A part of me agrees, unwilling to cross the horde of paparazzi alone. "But," I start, "I don't have any clothing here."

Somehow, I know even before I see the slight tilt of his chin that he's one step ahead, like always.

"I have a few things that may be in your size," he says softly. "They're upstairs. First door on the left."

Things of his sister's? Another woman's? I don't have the nerve to ask. Instead, I jump at the chance to escape him, even if it's just by a few yards.

The upper level of his home is no less intimidating than the entrance. Shadows drape the winding hallway, and most of the doors are closed, including the one he directed me to. I open it warily as my stomach knots at the thought of what may lurk behind it.

Once I finally peer inside the room, a gasp escapes my throat. Someone unloaded racks and racks of designer clothing into what must have been a guest room.

All are mine. The shoes stacked neatly on the floor are mine. In fact, the longer I stare, the more I recognize every item from my old room at Hollings Manor.

My dressers.

My vanity.

My old mirror.

So this is where he kept them.

I don't know if I'd prefer he'd thrown it all away. This wardrobe belongs to a stranger, one who prioritized beauty over compassion or common sense. She lived her life looking only to sparkle, heedless of the damage she left in her wake.

I don't know who I've become in the few short months since having this persona stripped away.

Drawing in a ragged breath, I step into the guest room and close the door. After a moment's pause, I lock it. Then I wander from each rack of clothing, surveying my options. So many things to choose from, yet none of them catch my eye. In the end, I select a modest navy ensemble with a high neckline and long sleeves. I suspect, even before I strip my outfit and pull it on, that it isn't what Blake Lorenz had in mind when he ordered me to play my role.

He wanted Snowy Hollings, the charming socialite. But it's getting harder and harder to be her.

Sure enough, when I finally creep from the room and approach the staircase, I find him watching me from the bottom step. His expression reveals nothing. Neither do his eyes as they perform a slow perusal of the body-hugging yet simple dress. Finally, he nods as if to convey: *As you wish.*

"I made us a reservation," he says.

Only now do I realize that he's changed as well, into a simple black suit with a crimson tie. We don't match in the slightest, a fact that lingers at the back of my mind. He's dressed to kill, while I'm…

I'm dressed like prey who's already been savaged.

"Wait." I turn on my heel, leaving him in the foyer.

Upon returning to the blue room, I head straight to a rack I initially overlooked. Hanging near the very back is a gown I once purchased with one sole purpose in mind: capture my ex-fiancé, Daniel Ellingston. We needed the money, and like the perfect tool, Hunter put me to the task. I did my duty well enough that within one meeting I'd already secured a date and a slew of roses hand-delivered to my home the following day. Now, it's merely a befitting piece of armor to wear into this new war. Blake Lorenz doesn't own me—not anymore.

This time, I dress slowly, ensuring that every curve is accented perfectly by silk and lace. I find an adjacent bathroom and arrange my hair around my shoulders. Left with no makeup, I pinch color into my cheeks and bite my lips until they redden. With one last glance at myself, I return to the front of the house.

Observing the man watching my descent, I know I've done my duty well. He clutches the banister so tightly that his knuckles whiten. *Damn.* I'm not sure if he truly grates the word between his teeth or if I imagine it. Either way, his blue-eyed gaze hunts me with every inch of space I cover between us. When I finally reach his side, I shiver before he even attempts to bring his hand against my lower back.

"Not here," I croak, loathing the fear I can't contain. Not here, alone, where his nearness grates on what little composure I have left.

Without a word, he approaches the front door and opens it, revealing a car already idling in the driveway. A single nod ushers me after him and into our first battle.

I CAN TASTE the tension on my tongue as the car starts down the driveway, approaching the reporters gathered at the front gate. Once more, eager faces press against the windows, fighting for a glimpse beyond the tinted glass.

"You get used to being a public spectacle," Blake explains, eyeing my trembling hands. "Show them fear and they become relentless."

A hard swallow contorts my throat. "I remember."

Admittedly, my father's legal team kept the worst of the reporters at bay back then, but the boy I accused of the unthinkable wasn't so lucky. No wonder he seems so unaffected by the chaos around him now.

"We'll have dinner," he says as if sensing the direction my thoughts have taken. Obsessive control is perhaps the one trait of Brandt's he still possesses, only magnified times a million. I sense the chains of his plan wrapping around me, tethering me to an unknown outcome. "Then I'll have your things brought to the penthouse."

I don't miss how he avoids the defining nature of said penthouse: *his* penthouse.

"That's not necessary." A night tops. That's how much I'll give him. A night spent awake, hoping my brothers don't beat their way inside with their bare fists—or with the aid of a SWAT team. Speaking of Ronan and Hunter... "My brothers want your blood, you do realize." And for a good reason. "How am I supposed to convince them that we are not only reconciled, but cordial? They think—"

"Leave it to me," he says. I'm alarmed by just how confident he sounds, though at a glance, his expression reveals nothing. "And I will go ahead with having your things moved. Unless you've decided to purchase new clothing."

"Shopping hasn't been my focus as of late," I admit. "And I wouldn't want to impose—"

"Don't fight me on this." There's no anger in his tone, a fact that only unnerves me. He sounds so damn serious. As if, somewhere beneath that frosty exterior, he may give a damn about me.

Or maybe it's his image. If I get murdered by Lyle Harlow, he'll be the one suspicion falls upon first.

"You really think I should stay with you?" I find myself asking.

A harsh exhale escapes his clenched teeth. I look over and find his hands tightening into fists only to suddenly unfurl and settle over his lap.

"I'll let you decide that for yourself after tonight."

The offer feels less like a show of faith and more like an ominous dare. Still, I say nothing during the rest of the trek into the heart of Mayfield.

By "handle things," it quickly becomes apparent that Blake meant "ensure that the world knows exactly where to find us."

Our destination is visible from blocks away due to the paparazzi stationed at the building's entrance. I vaguely recognize the restaurant as one of the most premier establishments in town. Blake Lorenz must still carry enough sway, even while disgraced, to command a table here. Especially now.

"This shouldn't take long," Blake assures me as the driver cuts through the calamity to bring us as close to the restaurant's entrance as possible.

How he knows as much, I don't dare ask. Instead, I fidget, tugging at my gown, suddenly aware of its low neckline. What an affront to anyone who'd dare pity me as a victim I make: stepping out with my supposed abuser, wearing the dress of a foolish socialite as if oblivious to scandal. Perhaps that's why Blake seems so satisfied by the costume change.

As the driver parks and circles around to his end, he reaches for me, but I flinch out of his range.

"I'm fine."

His low sigh cuts the air, resonating restraint. "Appearances, Snow," he says simply.

Left with no choice, I force my hand against his, and he grips it tight. Then, together, we exit the car to a myriad of shouted questions and statements.

"Ms. Hollings! Is it true that you…"

"Is it true that he…"

"Mr. Lorenz, are you a predator?"

To his credit, the man weathers it all with barely a frown to show for it, but he tightens his grip, ruthlessly steering me forward as strangers crowd in.

"No one will harm you," he swears.

Almost as if on cue, imposing men in suits swarm from nowhere to flank us on four sides, keeping the crowd at bay. He wasn't lying about being prepared.

I can't escape the suspicion that he's planned everything, down to ensuring that a restaurant employee would usher us inside while firmly keeping all others out.

"Reservation only," he mutters.

Together, we enter a partially deserted dining room filled with just a few couples who barely look up from their elegant meals. Odd. Even the poshest of socialites I know can't resist the obvious allure of a scandal. Unless, of course, they weren't socialites at all.

Confused, I glance at Blake from the corner of my eye as he leads me to a table in the room's very center. Draped in an ivory tablecloth, it serves as the perfect stage for a couple's intimate dinner.

"Why do I get the feeling that nothing in this room is authentic?" I ask in a fitting stage-whisper.

He shrugs before gesturing to the waiter approaching us with a bottle of wine. "That's because it isn't. The other diners are actors and the waiter is in my employ."

"Are you serious?"

He raises an eyebrow, but I can't tell if he's amused or joking. "Have a seat."

Resigned, I claim the chair he's pulled out for me and watch him circle the table. Seated, he towers over the elegant table setting—a baron lording over this room and all inside it.

"I thought we were supposed to be convincing?"

A slight quirk tilts his lips. Just as quickly, he's blank again, eyeing me as the waiter fills two crystal glasses with wine. "That will come later. Trust me."

I swallow hard. "Fine. And in the meantime?"

He nods to our empty place settings. "Try to relax."

It's like he's in my head, sensing the nerves I can't suppress.

I cast a wary glance around the room, taking in its muted but chic color scheme of black and silver. Last I heard, most had to wait on the guest list for months to earn a table here.

Barely a few months in Mayfield and Blake Lorenz has already scored the chef's table.

"You came back." I clear my throat, unsure of how else to phrase it. Came back. As if he ever had a choice in leaving. "How… Your sentence. They told me that you…"

He reaches across the table for the wrapped silverware in front of me and effortlessly unfurls the white napkin from the utensils. Without prompting, he sets my fork and knife on either side of my plate. Then he flicks the napkin into the air but stops short of placing it on my lap for me. Instead, he sets it aside and withdraws to his end of the table.

"It's complicated," he says carefully. I don't miss how he reaches up to adjust his tie, a rare display of unease. "I'd rather not discuss it here."

"Oh." Am I disappointed? Or was I so foolish to suspect he might feel obligated to tell me something about his past? A gap of ten years separates who we are now from the children we used to be. I'd give anything for at least a glimpse at what the darkness in his gaze shrouds—if only to know how to better protect myself against it. "How can you even sit there?" I wonder, a blunter way of phrasing: *I thought you hated me. Despised me, even.*

His mouth twists into a wry frown. "I'll let you know the answer when I figure it out myself."

Fair enough. At least it's not a lie: *I forgive you.* "So…" I clear my throat, hunting for a change in conversation. "You have a sister?"

His fleeting frown warns me of yet another topic determined to be off-limits. "I've had them cook your favorites," he says rather than mention Masha.

I turn and find a waiter carrying two meals on a tray. The first is a modest steak adorned with grilled vegetables. On the other is a small pile of pasta primavera paired with a toasted piece of French bread. A small slice of strawberry shortcake accompanies it.

"You remembered," I say thickly. "Thank you. But I'm not hungry."

Something unreadable darkens his expression. When I don't touch my food, he doesn't reach for his, either. We're at an impasse, watching each other from above steaming plates.

"You're afraid to eat in front of me," he says suddenly.

My cheeks flush, and I shake my head. It's like I still hear him hissing into my ear: *He hated you, not because you were disgusting.*

"For what it's worth…I apologize now for—"

"We can discuss it later," I blurt. Only belatedly do I realize that I've just thrown his own words right back in his face.

His eyebrows rise slightly as a low chuckle rumbles from his chest. "Little Snow, always so manipulative." Suddenly, he pushes back from the table and begins to unfurl his silverware. "Ask me what you wish as you enjoy your meal. Our 'dinner' won't seem convincing if you don't eat."

Ah. I don't dare question the tit for tat. My stomach churns at the thought of eating now, of all times. But I'll do anything for answers. Slowly, I break off a piece of bread and bring it to my lips. "Blake Lorenz," I say before taking a bite. After swallowing, I add, "Who was he?"

"My real father," he says. His fingers manipulate his bundle of silverware. Within seconds, he has the utensils free and the napkin folded neatly on his lap. "He was a prominent businessman in Germany. My mother must have had the affair before she married Harrison Lloyd. After my conviction, she contacted him. He used his influence to have 'Blake Lorenz' enrolled in the facility as my cellmate. Not long after, 'Brandt Lloyd' committed suicide and Blake was released on a technicality. His only stipulation was that I leave my life in America behind."

"So you moved to Germany." It's not hard to picture him then, maneuvering the foreign landscape. He was always adept at mastering most social situations.

"I kept abreast of what happened in Mayfield," he says. "I knew when my mother died, and Harrison Lloyd. And Elizabeth..."

My mother. A woman I'm starting to realize he knew better than I ever did. "Why didn't you ever tell me about her?"

He cuts his gaze down to my plate. Reluctantly, I scrape a bit of noodle onto my fork and take a bite.

"Would you have believed me?" he counters as I swallow. "I hated Harrison Lloyd. Your world *revolved* around Forrest

Hollings."

And, in a way, it still does. Papa rules our entire lives from the grave, dictating our one worth—as a Hollings always. I wonder now for the first time if he ever suspected the truth. Perhaps knowing I wasn't his child made it easier for him to hurt me…

"Snow?"

"Hmm?" I blink back tears, looking up. He's watching me, and I'm not brave enough to wonder for how long. "My mother. You always knew about her affair?" I ask while stabbing at another piece of food.

"For years," he admits. "And I didn't tell you about her for obvious reasons."

If my life revolved around Forrest, then it was balanced upon Elizabeth. Thinking of her in anything less than a flattering light stings. All of those memories feel tainted by the awful truth. She lied to me. Even worse, through me; she ruined Brandt irreparably.

"I would have never given her my letters," I admit around a lump in my throat. "If I had known, I would have—"

"I know." He grabs his knife and carves a slice from his steak. It's rare inside, leaving a pinkish smear of fluid across the plate. "It won't be easy, but… I'm trying to put that in the past."

But can we? I can't stop my fingers from tracing the right side of my face, the scar still healing there. His eyes catch the motion, and the knife rattles to the table. Suddenly, his hand cups mine.

"I never wanted to hurt you."

The depth of the admission unnerves me, almost as much as my reaction to it does. I stop breathing. Thinking. His heat is a trigger to a million sensations, each one more destructive than the last.

"Yes, you did," I find myself replying. Very slowly, I pull away from his touch, guarding my wound with the flat of my palm.

A sharp noise cuts the air like that of teeth clicking together. Then his throat contracts around a hard swallow. "I did," he says.

And we ignore our plates in unison.

Sweat drips down my back, seeping into the priceless gown. Thinking we could normally coexist in any capacity was a mistake. Too many secrets taint the air. Too many old emotions burn when disturbed. My eyes sting, but blinking hastens the tears forming. Far too quickly, they seep from their hiding places and slide down my cheeks.

"Shit, *enough*." Before I can react, he's closer, swiping at my tears, frowning as he does so. "So much for forgiveness, huh?" he murmurs, scowling at his glistening fingers.

I can't find the words to argue, and he says nothing else. Neither does he remove his hand, and I don't have the strength to pull away. In his eyes, I see a vortex of emotions impossible to decipher. A part of me wants to try anyway, anything to understand him. Guilt? Remnants of anger? Pain?

Sighing, he tilts my chin against his thumb, observing me from the newer angle. "I'll admit it now," he says, his voice a rasp. "I didn't seek you out before solely to warn you about Harlow. There's something else. I want something from you."

My stomach falls. Smashes into pieces on the floor. I inhale raggedly, wary of what he could say. A real apology? Something far more sinister?

Indigo irises search mine as his lips finally part. "I want us to start over, Snow—"

Breaking glass and a monstrous thud add an eerily beautiful melody to his plea. Suddenly, he draws back, rising to his feet—just in time for a bulky blur to ram into him, knocking him off-balance. I blink in shock as the "blur" rapidly takes on more human characteristics: blond hair, blazing blue eyes, flying fists, striking any part of Blake they can reach.

Oh, God.

"Ronan!" I shout, but he doesn't seem to hear me.

He keeps fighting, pummeling Blake, who does his best to block every blow. Growling, Ronan catches him in the mouth with his knuckles. Blood flies, splattering the fronts of expensive suits.

"Ronan, stop!" I stagger to my feet and paw at his shoulder. Grunting, he shrugs me off. Another of his blows lands with a thud, this time in Blake's stomach. "Stop!"

Maybe it's my scream that does it, but Ronan suddenly stumbles back. At the same time, he grabs my arm, wrenching me around to face him. "What in the hell are you doing here with *him*?"

I'm struck dumb as my brother glares from me to Blake.

"I see you near her again, I'll fucking kill you—"

"Stop it!" I manage to break his grip, and I scramble out of his reach before he can grab me again. "Ronan, calm down."

I barely recognize him. Blood speckles his chin, but it's not his. No, the only bleeding figure is the one currently watching the exchange while swiping at his mouth with the back of his hand. His bottom lip is split, and redness around his left eye tells me it won't stay any color but purple for much longer.

"Get over here, Snowy," my brother demands.

My chest constricts around fragile lungs, which makes it impossible to suck in air. I only have enough breath to croak, "Ronan, it isn't what it looks like. What the papers printed were lies. He never hurt me—"

"Snowy." He's begging, something I rarely see him do—and never like this. Veins bulge against the skin of his neck as his hands clench into fists. His gaze cuts to Blake again, and I scramble to put myself between them.

"I promise I'll explain!" I say, placing my hand on Ronan's chest. "Just trust me. Please. Trust me."

"Then come home." He reaches for me, but I once again evade his reach.

Why? I don't know. If there was ever a reason to ignore Blake's proposal, it's this: I can't bear to see Ronan so furious.

"I will," I tell him, my voice breaking. "But just give me time to explain. I promise I will."

"We need to go."

I stiffen. Blake doesn't even have to speak in my ear for his voice to resonate through me, invading every nerve. From the corner of my eye, I see him paces back, still swiping at his bleeding mouth. The reminder is clear: I have a bargain to uphold.

"Like hell!" Ronan bares his teeth and postures as if preparing to lunge. "You aren't taking her anywhere, you sick piece of shit—"

"*Snow.*"

"W-wait." I glance at my brother, willing him to listen to me. "I'll be okay. I promise." Turning from Ronan, I extend my hand to the man behind me. "Let's go."

He's by my side in an instant. Before I realize it, we're hurrying from the restaurant doors, with Ronan close behind. When I hear him shout, I look back and find that

Blake's bodyguards have appeared from nowhere to keep him at bay.

"He'll be fine," Blake murmurs into my ear. Without giving me the time to protest, he ushers me into the back seat of the car and the driver takes off.

Neon streetlights cast the back seat in a reddish glow. Only as my vision blurs do I finally register the moisture slicking my cheeks.

"Do it now," I say, my voice breaking. "Uphold your end of the bargain and put them back on the board. Do it now!"

He already has a cell phone against his ear. After a few minutes of murmured conversation, he hangs up and tosses the phone onto the seat between us. "It's done."

My shoulders slump. A sliver of power perhaps wouldn't be enough to console any other brother, but I know mine. Intrigue alone will buy me more time to explain. What, exactly? I'm not sure.

Perhaps how I lost my senses enough to trust Blake Lorenz for a second time.

"Where are we going?" I ask, not recognizing this part of town where skyscrapers tower above.

He casts me a glance that could be described as equal parts amused and irritated. "Home," he says. "My penthouse. I took the liberty of having your things delivered."

Despite my having explicitly told him not to. For now, I don't challenge him. Instead, I try to decipher every twist and turn and remember every street name, just in case I have to make my way back to the hotel on foot. Normally, I'd laugh at such a dramatic thought. However, going off the blood still dripping from the mouth of the man beside me, I think the theatrics are warranted.

"You're hurt."

He frowns and brings a hand to his bottom lip. The fingers come away red, glistening in the glow of a passing streetlamp.

"Oh God, here." I run a hand down the side of my gown but find nothing useful.

Motion catches the corner of my eye, and I find him fishing a handkerchief from his pocket. He holds it awkwardly between his chin and his chest as if unsure whether to clean himself or…

"Let me." I snatch the cloth and shift closer, pressing it against the worst of the bleeding.

He flinches, his eyes tracking every movement of my fingers.

"You'll have a scar," I tell him, impressed by the veracity of the wound. Ronan has a vengeful streak, but I've never seen him attack someone before. Not even the bullies who taunted me all those years ago. No, that honor always went to another boy who once punched a bully who'd lifted my skirt in grade school to see how fat I was underneath.

Something in my face must change, because my fingers are gently batted away.

"I've got it," Blake says, adjusting the cloth to staunch even more of the bleeding. Protocol would dictate that I apologize to him on Ronan's behalf.

But I don't.

In silence, we endure the rest of the ride until the car enters a secluded parking garage and comes to a stop near an elevator.

"The suite has a private entrance," Blake explains as he exits the car, this time without reaching for my hand.

I follow him warily, tense for reasons I can't explain. It's quiet here, which is an eerie contrast to the chaos of his home in the hills and the restaurant. He must keep this residence unlisted, a prospect that unnerves me more than it should. Just how many secrets is he hiding?

Speaking of which.

"Is Masha here?" I wonder, feigning innocence. "I'd hate to intrude."

Blake enters the elevator, leaving me to follow. "No," he says without looking back. "I have her staying someplace far beyond the city."

Fair enough. I picture what little I can remember of the blond waif who claimed to be his sister. She's beautiful, that much I'm sure of. And she's young.

"You're doubting if I've told you the whole truth."

I jump and look up. His narrowed gaze meets mine unflinchingly.

"She is my sister," he reiterates without voicing my suspicion out loud. "My half-sister, but my sister nonetheless."

"How old is she?" I ask, watching him strike the button for the top floor.

"She…" He hesitates as the elevator car lurches beneath us. I'm seconds from admitting defeat when he sighs. "She's twenty."

"Oh." I swallow hard. So she *is* young. "And she grew up in Germany?"

"Exclusively," he says, eyeing the doors, his jaw rigid. "I met her there when she was still a child. Twelve, I think."

Which makes for a two-year gap between his supposed death as Brandt Lloyd and his rebirth as Blake Lorenz. In the end, I decide against commenting on that point. Instead, I tilt my chin, observing him as closely as I dare.

He's different when he speaks of Masha versus anyone else, even me. There's a softness about him. A wariness, as if he isn't sure just what his face might reveal.

"Speaking of Masha…" He surges forward, leaving me to catch up. "She helped me design this place. I hope you don't mind the décor."

We follow a short hallway that leads directly into a spacious foyer.

And my mouth drops open.

Once upon a time, I used to babble to Brandt Lloyd about my hopes and dreams. I told him that I aspired to be an astronaut; in space, no one would give a damn about my weight. I told him about my dream home: a high-rise overlooking the heart of the city. *Like a castle for a princess*, I used to quip. One decorated in shades of emerald and gold, our favorite colors. But not gaudily, of course. Natural. Like a snapshot of a forest taken the split second before winter sets in. When everything is that silvery hue of stillness, and the air smells so clean that you can taste it. When greens never look greener, and the earth still holds that summery warmth.

"Masha" must have been there to overhear all of those silly daydreams, because the interior of this room feels ripped right from my fantasies. Gray marble floors add contrast to earth-colored walls. Black accents and silver fixtures cast a warm yet chilling atmosphere that demands any occupant to curl up with a book in one of the welcoming nooks. So many books line the shelves along a wall that opens onto a sitting room with floor-to-ceiling windows.

It's breathtaking. Literally. My hand flutters to my chest as if aiming to force air into it.

"I… It's beautiful." I don't mean to sound so damn awestruck. Neither can I stop myself from approaching the view and bracing my hands against the glass.

Something nearby catches my attention: a red leather chair angled toward the incredible swath of the city laid bare. Ice runs through my veins, displacing some of the wonder. "I'd want a throne, of course," I boasted once. "Red, placed perfectly to take in my servants…"

"I had a feeling you'd enjoy this." Blake seems unaware of my sudden realization as he comes to stand by my side. A rare smile shapes his mouth, visible in his reflection off the glass. Smug. "It's yours."

A watery laugh trickles from my throat. "Thank you, but I can't afford it."

"I'm serious." A sudden shift in his stance draws my attention a second time. He's standing rigidly, surveying the world glittering down below. "If you need a reason to trust me, then here: It's yours."

"Stop it!" I push back from the window and turn on my heel. The unfamiliar layout looms before me—so much for the hysterics. If I were to make a dramatic exit, I wouldn't even know which way to go. With my shoulders back and my breaths ragged, I settle on the next best thing and march toward the mouth of the foyer. "You don't have to ply me with expensive gifts or favors." Then a cruel thought strikes me, drawing a gasp from my lips. "I'm not the same selfish little girl I was—"

"And I don't want to hate that girl anymore." He seizes my arm from behind, yanking me against a body made of steel.

"D-don't!" Agony strikes a wounding blow on my heart. "Stop… Stop mocking me—"

"I'm *not*." His arm cinches my waist before I can run—and something keeps me from resisting. Perhaps it's how he sounds? Ragged breaths rake the air near my ear, betraying fracturing control I doubt he ever had a full grasp on. "I hurt you. I know I did," he rasps. "And I… We'll do this your way. Retribution. An eye for an eye. Tell me what you want from me. I'll give it to you. Anything—"

"All I want is the truth!" I sag against him as my voice echoes in the cavernous space, high-pitched and thready.

Rather than laughing, he nods, sliding his nose against the groove in my neck. "And you'll have it," he promises. "You will. I swear it. But I need something from you, Snow." He sounds like a drowning man begging for a lifeline. Rope. A bullet to the brain. Anything to ease his misery. Slowly, he loosens his grip on my waist but doesn't draw back. "I need five fucking minutes. That's all. Show me what I've lost. What I need to earn back."

His heated tone sends blood rushing to my cheeks. "You think… You really think you can ask me for sex—"

"Of course not." He scoffs, offended by the idea. "But I need… Show me what I've lost."

What he's lost? I pull away from him and find myself backing toward the window. Cool glass braces my spine, drawing my attention to just how thin this dress is. How fragile. Even so, it's thicker than my skin when it comes to him.

He wants to know what he's lost?

The moment I reach for a strap, he sucks in a breath. My thoughts run together, jumbled and incoherent. Lowering part of my dress is a foolish, stupid act. But it's all I have. The words won't come. Just tears. Just this pain contorting my features in ways I can't control. Slowly, I loosen the second strap and let the gown slide down my arms. I'm thin enough now that it falls without resistance and pools at my feet.

He told me once that he'd only want me while broken. While ugly. *His.* Apparently, he never lied in that respect. His jaw goes slack around a guttural groan, and he eyes me openly without shame, raking his gaze over my heaving chest and my trembling limbs.

I start to cover myself only to freeze when he shakes his head. Bitten-out words reverberate like thunder.

"You're so fucking beautiful…"

My cheeks heat at the raw tone. If only beauty weren't pain when it came to him. It's wrong, but I do it: I compare them. Brandt cherished and coddled sweet, lovely, beautiful things. Blake crushes them—something he seems inclined to do to me. I don't miss how his fingers twitch at his sides before he wrestles them against his hips.

"I won't touch you," he warns before surging forward, swallowing the distance between us.

My breath stills in my chest as I watch him advance, quivering on my heels. His eyes meet mine, the pupils dilated, while his body cages me against the glass. With our chests separated by just a fragile inch of space, he inhales me, bracing one hand against the glass near my head.

"Show me what I've damaged, Snow," he begs, his voice hollow. "Show me. I swear I won't touch you. I know I've hurt you. Tormented you…" Warm breath tickles my cheek, sending a ripple through my entire body, down to my toes. "Torment me."

My eyes shut, blocking his expression out as tension floods the air, soaking into every pore. Torment him? He desolated me. Not because of what he's said, or done, or inflicted. But because…

I'm weak.

I can't stop aching for what I'll never have, and I tell myself the brutal truth over and over. I'll never hear his voice reach that familiar, warm cadence. I'll never hear his laugh again, not like it was: soft and freeing. I'll never taste that innocent, sweet flavor that used to linger on his skin. I'll never taste Brandt Lloyd again. I'll never hear him groan…

Like the sound rumbling near my ear now. He'd sound softer, Brandt—never so hard. So empty. So hungry. Brandt Lloyd never lusted after me. He'd never watch me slide my fingers beneath the waistband of my panties just to test his response—explosive. Curses meet their doom, ground between clenched teeth.

I've never touched myself in front of anyone, not even him. Sweat slicks my skin, making it easier to follow the invisible trail down my stomach, toward the cleft between my legs. My cheeks catch fire at a sudden thought. How pathetic. This is as close as I'll ever get to my beautiful boy: a twisted reflection of who he used to be breathing his taint into my skin.

"Fuck," he rasps. "You're killing me."

Good. Some sick, vengeful part of me latches onto the genuine pain in his voice. I rock my hips against my fingers, biting my lip at the feeling. Hot. Wet. Then I stiffen in shock and draw my fingers away, the cold air licking at the moisture, raising goosebumps.

"Fuck." Something slams against the glass, rattling it, but he doesn't touch me. He keeps his promise, and I fight to uphold mine.

Torment him.

After what he's done to me, I want to take him up on his whispered exaggeration: I want to kill him. But I'm not sure how. Only that he groans again as I peel my panties down my legs. He's even closer now. His ragged breaths form a disjointed melody, counting the seconds down. With my bare ass against the window, I arch my hips, ensuring he can see every inch of the heated flesh. Torment him? With that goal in mind, I lazily flick my fingers along the heavy folds, relishing in the sensation he's denied himself. A low moan rips from my chest before I can swallow it down. My eyelids flutter, but I refuse to let them open. Not yet.

I rub, cupping myself against my palm, hating the fire that flares in response. God, his attention feels like groping, greedy fingers spreading me open for his pleasure. All I can do is retaliate, grinding my touch wherever I feel his gaze travel. Lower. Lower. Deeper…

"J-Jesus Christ." He barely sounds human—some growling creature salivating over a bone he can't have.

My body is a dirty traitor, however. It resists the finger I try to ease inside, clamping down, craving something larger. More forceful. Destructive.

"You're…killing…me…Snow." He sounds like he means it, which makes my heart despair. He sounds like he's enjoying every vicious bit of torture.

I bite my lip and forcefully ram the tip of my thumb inside. My gasp is swallowed by his growl. Vibrations ripple through the glass, but he never touches me. Not even when I give in to his plea. I rub. Twist. Curl. Fuck myself on the ridge of my own fingers. I let him watch. I let him moan, smothering the sound against what I assume is his palm.

Eventually, my body can't take any more. Fire ignites along my spine, forcing it to curl. Rudderless, I writhe against the glass. My knees buckle. Thoughts dissipate. When I regain my senses, I'm on my knees, shaking as footsteps resonate through the floor. Gasping, I look up and find him swaying on his feet, crossing the foyer.

"Get some rest," he croaks to me. "Your room is the first on the right, at the top of the stairs. I'll sleep in the study tonight."

A study that I assume is on the first floor, which gives me some ounce of distance from him. Alone, I haul myself to my feet and redress. Then I ascend the winding staircase, clinging to the banister for support. The top-level sports another breathtaking view of the cityscape, and leather chaises are positioned for viewing at the end of a wide hallway lined with several closed doors. I approach the one he directed me to and then grasp the handle.

I doubt Masha had a hand in designing *this* room, considering that its blue walls resemble the exact color scheme of my old room in Hollings Manor. The oak furniture is similar, and the door to the walk-in closet is open far enough to reveal my clothing hanging neatly on its racks.

I'm too overwhelmed to examine his motives for this gesture. Another taunt? I just close my eyes while locking the door behind me. Then I sink to the floor, my back pressed against the wall. I don't strip my gown or my heels. I don't seek out a comfortable position.

I test him, listening to his footsteps seep through the floor. And a strange thought sinks into my belly and won't leave: He picked this room for a reason, the one positioned directly above what I assume is his study. He knew I'd hear him through the walls. I could track his movements.

At the same time…

Even while alone, I'll never be able to ignore his presence.

SEVEN

BLAKE

I SPENT ten years pushing her away. Every thought. Every memory. I never looked at a picture of her. I never read an article.

For so damn long, I dwelled on the image of that silly little girl who threw my love away, and I purged that specter of everything that made her human.

Her smell.

Her touch.

The thought of her just triggered rage. Hatred. And I relished it.

She was the reason I fought so fucking hard to the top. The reason for every bastard crushed in my wake. My father's legacy was a fitting excuse, but it was her—loathing every inch of Snowy Hollings made each victory ten times sweeter.

One day, I'd swallow her entire world fucking whole.

But now…

The faintest hint of rose-scented perfume colors the air, even in here. My nostrils flare, hunting every last trace of the shit and I feel my brow furrow at the cloying aroma. It's her mother's smell. The old Snowy hated the scent of artificial flowers—she preferred to smell them fresh, drenched beneath a spring storm, or stolen from her family's gardens.

The Snowy Hollings I knew, was a writer, not a socialite. A girl who preferred to spill her emotions in poetry and stories scribbled in the margins of her father's books.

She was silly and so fucking trusting.

She was so damn *forgiving*.

I could ignore her on a bad day. Forget to walk her home. Casually insult her by accident with my careless fucking mouth.

She never once held any transgression against me.

To be fair, I always knew the right words to say, or gestures to make. I always knew *her*…

My pocket jolts, snapping me from my memory. Someone's calling and my jaw clenches. Only a handful of people in the entire fucking world would be so bold to disturb me this time of night.

One glance at the ID and I'm on my feet, my heart pounding so hard I can feel my pulse in every goddamn fingertip. "What is it?" I demand, answering.

The voice on the other end comes in snippets. "You promised. You promised me," a woman insists, sounding faint.

"Fuck." Panic rouses my pulse into a frantic, pounding rhythm. "Masha? Where are you?"

"You promised..." She must be outside. Rushing traffic snarls at her words, obscuring most of them. "Everything... my fault—"

"Where are you?" I lurch toward the door, fighting to keep my voice steady. "Tell me!"

"...never let me go," she insists, her voice broken by static. "I'm so sorry, Blake. He'll never...me go."

* * *

SNOWY

SHOUTING jars me awake and I scramble to my feet, struggling to get my bearings. Faint gray light adds little definition to my surroundings. For one cruel, sickening moment, I almost forget. I'm in Hollings Manor again, waking up late. My first instinct is to scramble into my bathroom to wash my face, but the moment I cross the threshold, reality returns. This layout is twice the size of my old bathroom, with a sunken tub and gold fixtures. In fact, every detail of this room seems designed to add a charm reminiscent of a deranged princess in a dark fairytale.

Shivering, I splash water on my face and rub my color back into my cheeks. I finger my hair and consider taking a risk by washing up even with Blake still so close.

I hear him pacing down below. Marching. Shouting?

Alarm draws me to the bedroom door. With my ear pressed against it, I can't make out what he's saying. Just the tone of how he's saying it: growled, frantic words bellowed in quick succession. He's arguing with someone. Then a terrible vision pops into my head: either Ronan or Hunter storming in, ready for a second round of what happened in the restaurant.

I'm already in the hallway before I can weigh the benefits of staying in hiding. In the pale light of dawn, I easily find my way to the staircase and into the foyer. There, I find him pacing just beyond the hall, a cell phone pressed to his ear, and his usually stoic expression radiating fury.

"What do you mean she's gone? Find her!" he snarls before rattling off a phrase that I don't think is English. "Did he call, that son of a bitch? No…the manor? What the hell was she doing out there? No, it doesn't matter. Don't let her out of your sight." A heartbeat later, the phone is flung from his grip and smashes against the wall inches from my head.

"Shit…" He deflates as if noticing me for the first time. A trembling hand does its best to rake a mess of black curls from his forehead only to make him look more disheveled. "I didn't see you. I-I have to go." He storms across the foyer to snatch a coat from a hook near the entrance. After shrugging it on, he cocks his head in my direction without turning around. "I'll be back later. Have your run of the place. Your breakfast is in the dining room."

Then he's gone, slamming the door in his wake.

It's like the very walls exhale the moment he's gone, and the beauty lurking in the muted color scheme makes itself known without the threat of him here to consume my attention. God, it's so beautiful. So dangerous. He turned my nostalgia into a weapon.

Or a cage.

Alone, I watch the world rouse from a sleepy trickle of traffic into a full-blown torrent of people and machines surging toward various goals. It's a view of the world I never got from my window at Hollings Manor. Though I always dreamt of moving to the heart of the city like the stereotypical socialite.

In the end, I never left home. I had to be smoked from the ruins of it, thrown into this louder, gaudier setting. Ironically, I can't even take the reins of my newly upended life. People are watching. Waiting. Once again, I'm at the mercy of the men in my life to make all the bad things disappear.

The catch is that they rarely do. If anything, my problems only seem to multiply.

Left with no other options, I retreat to the navy bedroom and shower in an effort to take my mind off the darker thoughts. I dress in an old cream blouse and a cobalt skirt. I brush my hair and find a case of makeup with blush to dust on my cheeks. Then I scowl at the person I find watching me from the mirror's reflection, and I dare her to do something.

Blake claimed that this was a partnership, not a captive situation. It's time for him to prove it.

With renewed determination, I return to the lower level and hunt the various rooms for one in particular. It doesn't take me long to find it: a study tucked near the back of the suite. Here, he kept the decoration minimal. There's just a desk and a chair flanked by bookshelves filled to the brim with leather tomes. The view, however, is second only to the one in the living room. The waterfront gleams in the glow of early dawn, and hints of sunlight ripple over the water. Rolling hills in the distance create a humanizing backdrop as both a warning and a comfort: Mayfield isn't the end-all-be-all. There is a whole world waiting beyond its boundaries.

I don't know how long I let myself stare before the sound of a door opening and closing snaps me into awareness. I turn just in time to catch a figure stepping over the threshold. He pauses, his gaze flitting in my direction as if he hadn't expected to find me here.

He looks even worse than he did before he left. Exhaustion weighs his features down despite the wary frown his mouth contorts into. "You don't have to go hunting for answers this time, Snow," he says, sounding hoarse, as though he had worn out his throat from shouting. "Let's attempt honesty, for once. Whatever you need, you can ask for it."

"I wasn't snooping," I truthfully admit, running my hands over my skirt. Still, I can't resist testing his claim. *Whatever I need.* While I look at him, only one burning request comes to mind. His eyes are bloodshot, and he doesn't seem to realize how tightly he's clutching the doorknob. Not out of anger, but for balance—he's that damn exhausted. "Where were you?"

He flinches. *Damn.* I can almost hear the thought cross his mind. He didn't stop to consider I'd ask about him.

"I'm glad you're awake," he says, approaching the desk. "There's one matter of business we can get out of the way now. Your terms, in writing, as requested." He opens a drawer and withdraws a folder that he places in front of me.

A quick glance reveals everything we discussed laid out in legal terms. Considering the events of last night, he must have had this drafted by a legal team and delivered all on short notice. The man works fast.

"We can sign to make it legally binding. Or base it on my word. The choice is yours."

I eye that beautiful mouth, which is still sporting a bruise left by Ronan's fist. He doesn't even seem to notice the pain or the nice black eye shaping up on the left side of his face. Settling on an option takes mere seconds.

"Give me a pen."

Without a word, he fishes one from his desk and hands it to me. I sign my name on the last page of the documents, and he does the same. Begrudgingly, it seems. Something he said once sticks out to me now. "Honor means nothing to a Hollings."

Even now, he still doubts me.

"I'll have a copy made for you," he assures me before returning the documents to his desk. "And now... I would like you to uphold your other end of our bargain."

"Oh?" I cock my head, wary of the answer.

"Lyle Harlow." He withdraws a cell phone from his pocket and offers it to me. "Call him. Tell him you'll square the debt, no matter the amount. I'll take care of it."

And, later, exact vengeance for every penny? I don't dare question him out loud, but his eyes narrow as if aware of my suspicions.

"You gave me your word," he reminds me. "You put it in writing—"

"I'll do it." I force myself to take the phone, but I can't bring it to my ear just yet.

Blake sighs. "If you want me to, I'll—"

"No." I shake my head. "It's just... I'd like to be alone."

He frowns. I can tell from how the corner of his mouth twitches that he wants nothing more than to refuse. But something in my expression must change his mind, because he turns to the door instead.

"You have five minutes."

I waste the first one trying desperately to catch my breath. Lyle Harlow isn't just a monster looming over my present, but a very real one from my past. Seeking him out before was one thing, but now? Dread forms a pitiful lump in my throat, impossible to swallow down. Not that I have a choice.

Four minutes.

My fingers shake as I punch in the number I know by heart. Surprisingly, the call is answered on the first ring.

"Who is this?" a gruff voice demands.

"I have your money," I croak without giving my name.

A gruff bit of laughter is his response. "Little Snowy Hollings," the man murmurs, lingering over my name. "Most people who don't pay end up having nasty accidents."

God, he sounds too calm. Too…smug.

"Well, I have your money now," I tell him through gritted teeth.

"And you're too late. Someone's already bought your contract, little Hollings."

The world crashes to a halt. My stomach turns, fighting with my heart for supremacy. "W-what?"

"Don't sound so disappointed," Harlow croons sweetly. "We'll be seeing each other soon, Little Hollings. I'll make it worth your while."

He hangs up, and I drop the phone, paralyzed as it slides beneath the desk.

"Snowy?" A fist rattles the door. "What's wrong?"

"N-nothing." I sink to my knees and all but throw myself under the desk, hunting for his phone. I hear the door open, but I can't withdraw. Not with my face on fire and my fear so fucking apparent. *Focus!* I school my expression into a mask as my fingers finally capture the phone. Slowly, I crawl backward on my hands and knees. "Everything is fine…"

I trail off as my gaze falls on Blake's face. His mouth is open, trapped around a question he hasn't voiced. Heavy-lidded eyes shamelessly rake over my bare legs. My skirt rose up without my realizing it, revealing a glimpse of my lace panties.

To his credit, he recovers first, clearing his throat. A coldness washes over his face, displacing any hint of lust. "Is it done? Where should I send the money?"

"The money…" I avert my gaze and rack my brain for an explanation. There isn't one. "He said it's covered," I lie in the end. "Told me to forget about it."

I can almost hear his eyebrow shoot into his hairline.

"Lyle Harlow told you to 'forget' about money owed to him?" Anger lashes from him, as sharp as a whip. "I thought we were past lying."

"We are," I insist, rising to my feet. "And I wasn't. So don't you lie to me." I size him up, surprised to find that he managed to drive some of the exhaustion from his features. He was always so stubborn, refusing to let anything get in his way. Even me. "Where were you?"

Suddenly, he's eyeing the wall beyond my head rather than meeting my gaze directly. "It's not important—"

"That's not what I asked. You were looking for someone," I say, recalling his phone conversation. *Find her!* "A woman. Masha?"

"There are some things that I can't—" He breaks off and exhales sharply. When I look over, he's watching me, his face carefully blank. "I've spent years being alone," he admits. "Fucking no one. Talking to no one. Being no one. Trusting no one. In one night, I learn that most of that pain was based on a lie. Just…just give me some time, but I promise you…"

He's closer in an instant, guiding my chin into his palm. I shiver at the contact. He's so damn warm. So real. In the rare moments he's like this—open—it steals my breath away. It's unfair; my heart can't guard against him.

"I promise you, I'll try to…be different than before," he says, gazing deep into my eyes. "I'll tell you everything.

Anything. But I'm going to need some time."

"And so do I." I step away from him, making sure that no malice seeps into the action. Maybe just fear. My heart races as I remember his request from last night. Fulfilling it. What did it mean? Apparently nothing. He seems even more standoffish than before, even as he taunts me with… what? Trust? "Maybe we should spend some time apart—"

"No." He grabs my hand, squeezing it tight. "Let me take you to lunch."

"I don't think that's a good idea." I muster up what I hope passes for a playful smile while I gently pull my fingers from his. "What if Hunter shows up this time and blackens your other eye?"

Rather than laugh, he…flinches? Something distorts his blank expression, gone in an instant. Alarm?

I choke out a nervous chuckle. "I mean, it's not like you wanted that to happen or anything…"

My joke shouldn't have made an impact at all. No one would be so cunning—stage a beautiful dinner to give the appearance of a relationship—when his real goal all along was far more sinister.

Draw out Ronan. Cause a scene. Force me to choose between him and my brother.

It's such a sick, twisted thought. And when he stiffens, I know the awful truth.

"You *wanted* it to happen, didn't you?" Disgust makes my voice shake, but he doesn't even blink.

"And if I did?"

"You wouldn't…" Pain claws through my chest and I'm forced to brace one hand against the desk, clutching at the fabric over my heart with the other. The answer is clear in his silence: yes, he would. "So was this all just an act, then?" My throat tightens, choking my voice. "Why?"

"How could I trust you?" He sounds so damn calm. Composed. "You run from me at the gala. You scream at me at the Haven event. You accuse me of abuse. And I'm supposed to believe you'll willingly let me touch you in public? Hold you? Don't be so naïve, Snow. I needed you to trust me again—"

"Naïve?" God, he makes that word sound like some magic spell that excuses his actions. Maybe I am. For one brief second, I actually thought we could…

What? Start over?

Fighting back moisture building behind my eyes, I change tack. "You want me to trust you, but then you lie to me…" Damn it. I'm crying. Tears fall hard, and I taste salt as I attempt to swipe them away.

Warmth grazes my chin. His finger?

"Don't fucking touch me!" I stagger to the opposite end of the room, ensuring that a leather armchair stays between us. "How could you plan something so sick? It's almost like…"

Then a sudden suspicion creeps into my thoughts. No. He wouldn't go that far…would he? As insane as it sounds, I have to voice the accusation out loud. "It's almost like *you* released the recordings."

He's so blank. His mouth doesn't even twitch.

And once again, I've hit on the truth.

"No." I shake my head. "God, tell me you didn't."

His gaze fixates on the wall beyond my head. "What else was I supposed to do, Snow? We weren't exactly on speaking terms. You wouldn't even look at me—"

"Because you disgust me!" I can't catch my breath. Can't breathe. The need for fresh air drives me toward the door, but he steps forward, blocking my path.

"Don't do this," he warns, his tone hardening. "Please. We've made more progress in one damn night than we ever could have if—"

"Progress?" I choke out a laugh, and I don't even recognize the high-pitched trill. "You call lying to me and making my brother look like a fool progress? You can forget about whatever you think you've won. There's no way in hell you could convince me to stay in the same room as you."

Something cold settles in his gaze, turning indigo to ice. "Unfortunately, that's an impossible request. As you yourself suggested, we just put it in writing."

And, now, I know what goal he was after all along: I've fallen into his trap. "You unimaginable bastard."

He has the nerve to frown as if insulted. "I gave you every stipulation you required."

"Damn you! And if I refuse now, what? Will you kick my brothers off the board and steal the rug out from under me all over again?" I don't even need to see his face to know the answer: He would. He will. "Go to hell."

"Snow!"

His hand brushes my forearm, but I shove my way past him, racing for the entrance to the suite. I reach the elevator unmolested and slam the call button for the elevator until the doors finally part. I rush inside, and when I turn, I find him watching me from the mouth of the hall. Shadow encases half of his face, rendering his expression unreadable. Not that I need to see it to decipher him.

"Don't bother wasting your breath on your threats," I spit at him, grasping at the wall for balance as the doors shut. I don't sound confident in the slightest, and I hate that he'll get to relish breaking me for a second time. "Don't remind me of what I promised you. Do to those fucking papers what you did to my house: Burn them!"

Ding!

The elevator descends, and I suspect I have roughly a minute before he'll come after me. Men like Blake Lorenz are wolves; rarely do they let their chosen prey escape. Especially not when the damned soul's already bleeding. Somehow, I manage to make it out of the parking garage on my own, which leaves me on a busy city avenue with no sense of direction.

By fate or by chance, I flag a cab down and have the driver take me straight to the hotel. Curious looks follow me as I race inside and head up to the suite Ronan rented. He must have had the staff looking for me, because he's already in the hall, grabbing me the moment I step off the elevator.

I wait for the insults. The shouting. The lectures. But all he does is take one look at my face and pulls me into his arms, no questions asked. And I can't stop myself from sobbing openly, clinging to his chest with my face buried in the fabric of his shirt. He hasn't changed from the suit he was wearing last night, and going off the dampness on his shirt, he was out all night, hunting for me on foot. Because he loves me.

He may not be perfect, but he'd never manipulate my emotions on a sick whim.

Though he will try to protect me from them.

I draw back from him, raising a hand to shield the worst of my bloodshot eyes from his gaze. "I need to know everything you kept from me," I stammer, knowing that I sound insane. Incoherent. Desperate. "Please." I brace my hand on his jaw when he turns away. "Messages? Letters?"

His jaw clenches in reluctant confirmation.

"Then give them to me. Please. I need to read them. I...I need to burn them."

RONAN LEAVES me alone on the floor of my room with an old shoebox. It must have contained one of his newer purchases for me—piles of which litter my room.

Brushing the emotion churning in my stomach aside, I wrench the lid off.

And my heart is assaulted for a second time.

The damn thing is filled to the brim with envelopes, each one heavy with its own unfathomable burden. Each one from Blake Lorenz—all of them but one. Ronan must have shuffled it into the mix without meaning to, a letter directed to all of us: the Hollingses. It's from the lawyer who managed our trust, and bile seeps up my throat as I wrench it open and flip through the contents.

Dear God. It's a summary of outstanding bills as well as a statement acknowledging the loss of the house and our assets. So, so much gone in just a few days. Because of me and my once-impending marriage to Daniel Ellingston. I let him ruin the Hollings name.

And the worst part?

I'm not even a goddamn Hollings.

My skin chills at the thought. I think it's the first time I ever let myself admit it, even inside my head. I, Snowy Gale, am not a Hollings. After twenty-four years of brainwashing and striving to protect the family name, I've never felt hollower without that heritage than I ever felt in Papa's shadow. Would Daniel have even wanted me if he knew who I really am? A half-Lloyd bastard, my mother's dirty little secret?

Mulling over the answer isn't worth the effort.

But it does give me one slim, pathetic, childish bit of hope at how I can help fix this mess for Ronan and Hunter. Clutching the letter to my chest, I hunt for a leather bag and shove the documents into it. After a moment's hesitation, I stow Blake's letters inside it as well. Then I enter the hallway, knowing I'm in for a fight when Ronan comes to block my path.

"Please," he says, eyeing my bag, his expression strained. "I can't take this."

"I know. I'm sorry—"

"Are you? You want to know all the shit I've kept from you just to keep you from getting worse? The messages that bastard left for you? The police haven't done a goddamn thing, and you just waltz out to dinner with the motherfucker?"

"What are you talking about?"

"Forget it." His expression draws tight, closing against me.

All I can do is shake my head and push past him, knowing he won't touch me. "I'll make this right," I swear as I fumble to get the door open. "I promise. I promise I will."

He lets me go, but I know better than to leave through the main entrance. I slip out through a side door instead and walk the entire way to the James Baylor law offices uptown. Inside the lobby, a receptionist wrinkles her mouth at my outfit. She directs me without comment, and I enter an office at the very back of the building, where James Baylor himself is seated behind a mahogany desk.

"Ms. Hollings." He warily shuffles the documents before him and places them aside. "To what do I owe this visit?"

"How bad is it?"

He wrinkles his nose, jolting the wire-rimmed glasses resting on his nose. "I'm not sure I understand what you mean, Ms. Hollings—"

"Our finances," I clarify, more harshly than I intended. "Please don't lie to me. How bad?"

"Ronan's medical bills are outstanding," the man says with brusque efficiency. "There are the back taxes on the property to contend with, not to mention your family's current expenses."

Like the expensive clothing and hotel suites.

"All of it totals in excess of thousands," Baylor finishes. "Hundreds of thousands."

"B-but what if I can fix it?" My fingers shake as I fish the letter from my bag and place it on the desk. "You can start by telling me that none of this matters. Not if… Not if I'm really not a Hollings."

* * *

AFTER WHAT FEELS LIKE HOURS, James's secretary enters to place a steaming mug of tea before me. Just as quickly, she's gone, and I feel no closer to an ounce of hope.

"So you're saying there's nothing that can be done?"

Mr. Baylor slowly shakes his head. "I'm afraid not."

I pinch my wrist in exasperation—a childish, last-ditch effort to ensure that this all isn't some insane nightmare. But I don't wake up, and there's no reprieve from the dread building in my veins. "Not even if I took a blood test? Had my siblings disown me?"

"I'm afraid there's nothing that can be done about the business," Mr. Baylor admits, his tone grave. "However…" A curious expression flits over his weathered features. Amusement? Shock? He stands and approaches a wooden cabinet on the other end of the room before I can decipher it. "You are your mother's daughter, after all," he murmurs, though I'm not entirely sure if he's speaking to me.

"Sir?"

"You must understand: She instructed me to only reveal this information if you were either married, to have a child, or if you broached the topic yourself. She had it expressed in writing."

"What are you talking about?"

He rummages through a stack of files and emerges with a black folder in hand. Frowning, he hands it to me. "She had me make the arrangements shortly before she died. From Harrison Lloyd—accounts he'd transferred to her long before his conviction."

Numb, I peer at the pages within the file. Stocks. Bank statements. Businesses. All quietly transferred to Elizabeth Hollings throughout nearly fourteen years—right before Harrison Lloyd's downfall.

"It's all yours," Mr. Baylor explains at the exact moment I realize the staggering sum of the combined estate.

"Th-this can't be right?"

"Twelve million dollars. It may seem redundant," Mr. Baylor remarks, "but congratulations, Ms. Hollings. You are a very wealthy woman. Though…there is one catch."

Dazed, I look up and find him shuffling a stack of documents. "What is it?"

"If I were to give you this money now, it could technically be caught up with the rest of your family's estate."

"Oh?" I swallow hard.

"But," he adds, glancing warily at the door. "Far be it from me to suggest anything nefarious, of course. But if you were to find some other way for the money to get into your hands, I could make the arrangements…"

"Like fraud?" I cringe from the thought. Hunter may have been driven to follow Papa's tactics, but I refuse to.

"No," the man says quickly. "Of course not. Think of it as careful accounting."

"And if I were to do that…how would I?"

Mr. Baylor shrugs. "Any way that would see you legitimately receive the funds from another source."

"And then I could use it?" My mind spins with what such a sum could solve. My debt with Harlow. Ronan's hospital bills. Our running tab at the hotel.

"As far as I'm concerned, Ms. Hollings, there would be nothing preventing you from doing so," Mr. Baylor says. "Nothing at all."

Nothing but finding someone willing to give me twelve million dollars under the pretense of free will. Considering my family's reputation and looming scandal…

Well, it sounds easy enough.

NINE

BLAKE

BROKEN GLASS CRUNCHES UNDERFOOT, but I'm already grasping for the next thing to throw. A lamp this time. It strikes the door frame with a violent thud, ripping a chunk of wood from it in the process.

Damn.

Damn.

Damn it!

I'm sorry. How hard would it be to fucking say?

I pretend like I don't know the answer: *impossible.* A romantic sap from a fairytale could declare as much and all would be well. The princess would be his again. Happily fucking after.

But not me. I've been the villain of the story from the start and nothing I do now could erase the past. The things I've done. To her. For her.

If she knew them all she'd do more than run.

She'd fall—like Humpty Dumpty in that fucking story we once made our own—shattered to pieces. Nothing could ever put them together again.

Not all the king's men.

Not all the king's horses.

And as pathetic as it makes me feel, and as much as I swore to never give that woman power over me again…

I'd rather die than watch that happen.

If only death was anything but final when it came to Snowy Hollings. I've been relegated to the shadows once because of her, forced to watch from a distance as she lived on without me. And now?

I'm too fucking close.

Besides, it's not like she has anywhere left to run. I've already covered every base on the gameboard. Checkmate.

I exhale sharply, reminding myself of that point—my ace in the hole. She's as good as a caged bird. It's only a matter of time before she realizes that.

Maybe if I tell myself that lie enough times, I'll finally fucking believe it.

* * *

SNOWY

I WANDER the streets beyond the law offices for what feels like hours before an impulse I can't name drives me into a cab. When the driver asks my destination, I rattle off one address merely out of habit. It's only as the cab finally reaches the crest of a familiar hill on the outskirts of Mayfield that I realize my blunder.

Hollings Manor is a smoldering, decrepit ruin that looks like a stain on the otherwise pristine landscape. As I step from the cab, I can still smell the smoke. Still see the flames licking at the unfeeling sky.

I still feel that pain.

And I hate him for doing this to me. This twisted, broken landscape is the only haven I have left. The overgrown and neglected weeds offer no solace as I wander toward the back of the property, desperate to reconcile my entire upbringing with what I know now.

Did it kill my mother every day, having to look at me and lie?

Or having to see Brandt, a constant reminder of the man whose bed she crawled into every night?

From what I remember, Harrison Lloyd was a cold, unfeeling man, yet he left me, his bastard, more of a legacy than the boy he'd raised as his son for seventeen years. I doubt Brandt had any heartwarming stories of the man to tell. Our dirty little secret was that he spent so much time with me to avoid having to enter his home for as long as he could. If his father wasn't berating him for some stupid slight, then he was hitting him.

Everyone knew of the abuse, but no one said anything. They smiled, and invited the Lloyds over for brunch, and ignored the black eye their son would occasionally sport.

It was the Mayfield way.

But I saw him—so beautiful, so sweet. I saw his desperate struggle to avoid hate. He never wanted to become Harrison. He never wanted to resemble the man he called Father.

And my mother, as charming as she was, must have loved such a disturbed man. After all, she died for him.

I blink, noticing my surroundings for the first time. I'm nearing the lake, stumbling down the beaten path. Tears stream down my cheeks, a hateful reminder of how much like Elizabeth I am. I'm pathetic. Manipulative. Violence and hate must be hereditary aphrodisiacs, because whenever I think of Blake Lorenz, and the awful things he's done to my body...

I don't feel disgust—not like how I should. No matter how badly he treated me, my body sure had no problem orgasming against him. On him. The vulgar memories set my cheeks on fire, and I start to run, aiming for the only refuge in sight.

The boathouse door is locked. I have to force a window open and climb through it. Inside, I find that Blake Lorenz left his exercise equipment behind. Along with something else thrown in the middle of the space as if in afterthought. My heart races as I approach the small object and sink to the floor beside it.

I brush a trembling finger over the cover of a leather-bound book and it doesn't disappear. A heartbeat later, I clutch it to me with everything I have, and the tears fall faster. The worn copy of *Humpty Dumpty* is all I have left, and I imbibe its pages with a million tears and unsuppressed pain. I bleed into the tiny, remaining sliver of Brandt Lloyd, and I know in my soul that I'd eagerly trade away all of Mama's money just to hold on to this moment forever.

Far too soon, the thud of approaching footsteps shatters it. Gasping, I lurch to my feet. Hiding is my first instinct, and I eye one of the old bookshelves in the corner. Then rage sets in, squaring my shoulders and flooding my limbs with reckless energy. Facing the door, I march toward it and throw it open.

"Just stay the hell away from me!"

"I'm so sorry," a woman remarks, her voice a dreamy murmur. "I just… It was such a beautiful house."

Huh? I fixate my gaze on a figure tiptoeing along the edge of the dock, her arms outstretched. Her bare toes stand out in harsh contrast to the gray wood. Around her legs flutters a thin, white nightgown. It and a curtain of wavy, blond curls are her only protection from the biting chill in the air.

Looking up, she notices me, but her eyes are too wide, her pupils unfocused.

"It's you," she says softly, swaying dangerously close to the water. "You're really here. I'm sorry for trespassing, but maybe... You can tell me what it's like."

I blink as recognition conjures a name to my tongue. "Masha?" She seems no less beautiful and young than she did the first night I saw her. But something is wrong. Alarm prickles down my spine and I start toward her, fighting to keep my expression blank. "What are you doing here?" I glance around but don't see Blake—or anyone else for that matter. Did she walk all this way alone? "Are you okay?"

She smiles, but I've never seen a sadder, more forlorn expression. "Is the water too cold?" she asks, turning her gaze toward it. "God, I just hope it isn't cold."

She turns on her heels, as lithe as a dancer, putting her back toward the lake. A sad tilt of her lips is her best attempt at another charming grin. Then she falls.

"No!" Adrenaline surges. Somehow, I fling my heels aside and dive into the water blind. Ignoring the stinging sensation, I open my eyes and strain through the gloomy, dank waters. Sunlight plays over a pale, sinking shape and I swim toward it, grasping, pulling.

I'll never understand how I manage to drag her onshore, gasping and dazed but still breathing. Then I find my cell phone inside my purse, discarded near the dock, and without loosening my grip on Masha's slender body, I call 911.

* * *

MASHA DOESN'T SAY a word during the ten-minute wait for the ambulance. She merely stares up at the sky, her hair a golden tangle beneath her. As the sirens wail in the background, she giggles brokenly. Then tears form in her eyes and roll down her cheeks. By the time the paramedics usher her onto a stretcher, she's sobbing.

While I watch her, my heart breaks. I wish I could pity her. Feel sorry for her.

But all I see in her pathetic, shivering form…is myself.

"Snowy!"

I'm grabbed from behind and whirled around to face a man I almost don't recognize at first. Blake Lorenz looks haggard in a way I've never seen a man look—not even Ronan. My brother always appeared fragile when distraught. Blake radiates fury and pain, seeming ten times larger and more dangerous than any predator.

"What the hell happened?" He's shaking me, I realize as my head is jostled back and forth. He grips my arms so tightly that his knuckles whiten. With his teeth pulled back from his upper lip, he looks crazed, and if I doubted that he had a soul in his twisted, broken being, then I'm proven wrong. It belongs solely to Masha.

"She fell into the lake," I whisper. The moment he stiffens, I suspect that Blake knows damn well Masha didn't simply "fall."

"Mother of God." He releases me so suddenly that I stumble and have to throw my arms out for balance. He races to Masha, who watches him, shivering on a stretcher as paramedics escort her toward the front of the property, where the ambulance must be parked.

He murmurs something to her in what I assume is German. She answers him tiredly, her voice cracking.

"I'm sorry," she says in English. "I'm so, so sorry."

Her words are swallowed by the wind as she's hustled up the path. Blake lunges on the tips of his toes as if intending to follow. At the last minute, he turns to me. One look at my shuddering frame and he strips his suit jacket before draping it around my shoulders.

"You jumped in after her," he croaks, fingering my damp hair. "You saved her—"

"I didn't do it for you." Only God knows where the vitriol comes from.

How is it possible to hate him now, even as he grapples with his sister's distress? Maybe it's loathing directed solely inward, because a part of me wants nothing more than to hold him, and press him for answers, and offer support. I want to know the truth about Masha, which he seems so desperate to hide. I want to know more about him.

But, even now, his expression forms a door, cutting me off from any hint of emotion. "Thank you anyway," he rasps, taking a step back.

And if I were a good woman, I'd let it end here. I'd hold my barbs for another time. I wouldn't want so badly to kick him while he's down, showing him more courtesy than he's ever shown me. But, deep down, I'm just a vengeful sinner.

Like mother, like daughter.

"You can take those documents and you can rip them to shreds," I tell him, hating how breathless I sound.

He's stoic once more, but I'm the one sobbing openly, huddling beneath his warmth even though I want nothing more than to shrug it off. I try, but my fingers won't release the tailored cotton. When gestures fail me, my words are the only weapon I have left.

"I changed my mind. Forget our agreement. It's over."

His jaw clenches, a subtle warning. "I suggest you think carefully—"

"Or what? You'll throw my brothers off the board out of spite? Rescind your offer of assistance?" I don't even need to see the stubborn tilt of his jaw to know the truth. Harrison may not be his biological father, but the man trained him well. He's just as heartless. Just as cold. And I'll treat him the same way my mother did Harrison: like a glorified bank. "Do it. I've decided that I don't need nor do I want your help."

"Oh?" His eyes narrow and I can't ignore how my breath stalls in my chest. "And what the hell do you intend to do?"

I push past him and start toward the path with my head held high, even as my heart turns to stone. "I'll do what I should have done before I ever signed my life away to you."

He inhales sharply, a growl-like sound that stops me dead in my tracks. "You don't mean to…" He sounds doubtful. As if I wouldn't be that stupid. That spiteful.

"Why not?" I can't bring myself to face him. I glare at the trees in front of me instead. So much land tied to a single family's name. Forrest would die to know what's become of his goddamn legacy. If I were to thank Blake for one damn thing, it would be for finally severing any ties I had to it. "Maybe I'll let you have a front-row seat."

The idea forming in my head is too childish to ever enact. So devious. Perhaps only someone as demented as he is would ever propose it. Fittingly, he doesn't even need a further hint to guess my intent.

"No." He advances, and before I can move, my forearm is in his grip. "Hell no. *Fuck* no. I won't let you near it. Do you hear me?"

"Oh yes!" I wrench away from him, but he doesn't relent. Neither do I. I twist and tug until my arm strains in its socket, which draws a cry from my lips.

Finally, he lets me go, and I race up the path. When I'm a safe distance away, I turn for one last quip.

"If you want to play your sick games, I won't be a participant. I'll find another man to make me his toy," I snarl. "Anyone but you."

"Snow…" His eyes practically glow in the faded daylight, more monstrous than human. "Don't. You don't fucking mean it."

I manage to smile, even as tears continue to fall and my legs buckle beneath me. "I do. See you at Bolles. I'd rather auction myself in a room full of strangers than ever trust you again."

Then I turn, leaving him there.

And I run.

TEN

WITH THE HOTEL out of the question and no other refuge in mind, I'm once again forced to rely on pure impulse. Maybe it's the thought of Masha, so pale and innocent, that drives me toward her polar opposite.

"Snowy?" Sloane looks at me like I'm a three-headed demon cursed to darken her ornate doorstep.

I'm standing in the foyer of the Sebastián mansion, clutching a leather handbag to my chest, my clothing drenched and worthless, my eyes bloodshot. Honestly, I don't know what to expect. A warm welcome? A cold shoulder?

Suddenly, the Spanish beauty snaps her fingers to summon a maid. "Hot tea," she demands. "And call my manicurist." She eyes my cracked, worn nails with a frown. Gently, she takes my hand, tugging me inside and toward the winding staircase. "It's about time we had the chance to properly catch up."

Two hours later, I'm bundled in a robe, lounging on a chaise in the upstairs spa of the Sebastián home. Sloane is sprawled on a chair beside me, a mug of tea in her freshly manicured hand. A frown tugs at her mouth, and she lowers her gaze while flicking an imaginary piece of lint from her lap.

"I tried to call, you know? When you didn't return it, I thought… Everything got so insane."

"I know," I say.

Sloane, on a good day, was my friend only in the most superficial of terms. Being seen on my arm got her exposure, and I let her screw my fiancé in secret. Everyone won. Until now. I don't find Daniel lurking in this posh suite, and Sloane seems determined to avoid mentioning him by name—along with any other men rumored to be in my orbit.

"You can bring up the headlines," I blurt. "I won't be upset. It's all lies."

"Really?" Sloane raises an eyebrow, her lips pursed as if to trap a multitude of questions behind them. In the end, she settles on one. "Is he really as bad as they say?"

All I can do is shake my head.

Sloane sighs. "Good. But I'll make sure Daddy doesn't invite him to any future galas—"

"You don't have to do that," I say. "There's nothing between us."

"Like you and Daniel?" Sloane prods.

I glance at her sharply. "What do you mean?"

"You dated him for nearly two years, and in an instant, it's all over." She sounds more wistful than I'd like.

"Well, he did singlehandedly cause my family's ruin," I remind.

"I didn't mean it like that." Sloane bites her lower lip, parting her thick hair with her fingers. "I just mean... He loved you, you know. He really did."

I mull over that statement. Somehow, I don't bring myself to mention the obvious catch to his so-called love—their dalliances behind my back, for instance.

"Just admit it," Sloane adds before I can respond at all. "If you could go back, before everything happened. You would, wouldn't you?"

Would I? I turn away, eyeing the view of the Sebastiáns' estate from a nearby window. It's a far cry from the bustling city landscape glimpsed from Blake's penthouse. Here, the neat gardens and fountains create a carefully crafted fantasy, like the backdrop of a gilded cage.

"I don't know..."

"So that's a yes, then," Sloane counters, her tone cold. "Bad investments aside, at least Daniel never wound up in the tabloids under the guise of assaulting you."

"I don't want to fight," I admit. Instead, I draw my knees to my chest, admiring my neatly trimmed toes with pale-pink nails. "If it makes you feel any better, I need a favor."

"Oh?" She faces me, suddenly animated. "Money? References? A tabloid contact?"

She practically squeals at the possibilities. Apparently, her life has been boring without being caught in the whirlwind that is the Hollings rumor mill.

"No." I draw in a breath and release it with a harsh sigh. "You know men. Like…like the kind who belong to my father's club?"

A perfectly trimmed black eyebrow shoots into a fringe of black hair. "*Que*? Oh, Snowy, you aren't that girl. Those men… It's not like you think."

Her serious tone makes me wonder just what experience she has with Bolles men. But I've tangled with the worst of them all.

"It's not like that. I need you to contact one of them to arrange something."

"Oh?" She leans in, drowning me beneath the sweet scent of her perfume. "Like what?"

"An auction," I blurt, and her eyes widen. "But it's not what you think. And I need your help to ensure that it goes exactly how I need it to."

Riling Blake aside, an auction could have a much more practical purpose. Securing my mother's money, for one.

Mr. Baylor claimed that, as long as a transaction was legitimate, it would be legal. He never mentioned whether said agreement couldn't be scandalous...

"I'm listening," Sloane says, her expression wary. "Okay. Tell me what you need me to do."

Hours later, my plan sounds less insane, at least on paper. In fact, arranging to auction off a woman's body is surprisingly like arranging an engagement party. There are guests to invite and outfits to plan. At least in this case, the venue is already secure. Through Sloane and her wealth of masculine contacts, I have an in at Bolles.

More importantly, I have a date.

Tomorrow night.

* * *

"ARE YOU SURE ABOUT THIS?" Sloane asks from beyond the door of her private en suite bathroom. Her concern seems genuine—the most authentic emotion I've ever witnessed her express. Perhaps she's right to be. I told her only as much as I had to.

One, that I needed to arrange an auction at Bolles on short notice.

Two, that I needed a man to secretly bid on my behalf, with a limit I specified.

"For what it's worth, I'd trust Andrew with my life," Sloane adds. "He's gay. He only joined Bolles because his father is a homophobic *puta* and the membership keeps him off his back."

She's trying to assure me, but I doubt anything can. I'm insane. Any woman would have to be to recklessly throw herself into the fire with only a thin lifeline as protection. Reckless or scorned. Hell hath no fury, after all, and I've been bathed by the flames too many times to fear them now.

"I…I think I'm ready."

Sloane opens the door and gasps at my appearance. Rather than risk crossing my brothers to fetch a gown from home, I was forced to raid Sloane's private collection. Where my wardrobe was designed to sparkle and shine, her gowns were composed with another goal in mind entirely.

"You look like sex," she says, nodding appreciatively.

I agree with her. Wearing a skintight black gown that hugs my nonexistent curves, I look like sex as Blake Lorenz taught me. Dirty, brutal fucking. A screen of lace covers my breasts, and only a strategic placement of the design shields my nipples from view. Two waist-high slits on either side render the skirt little more than an ineffective dangling bit of silk. With my hair wrangled by Sloane's stylist into a tight knot at the nape of my neck, there are no wayward curls to shield my face from view. Or the fierce expression I barely recognize, enhanced by burgundy lipstick and eyes lined in kohl.

Tonight, I intend to take my life back from Blake Lorenz—no matter what it costs me.

"You look…terrifying," Sloane amends, though a bit of sadness seeped into her tone.

I look over and find her frowning. She doesn't recognize this new woman, either. Whether that's a good thing or bad, I've yet to decide.

"I need one last favor," I start after one last glance at myself in the mirror.

"Already ahead of you," she says. "Do you want to take the limo or the Rolls?"

BOLLES WELCOMES me like an old friend. The strained, unhealthy kind with no warmth lost between meetings. How Papa used to taunt me with it, using it like the cruelest punishment, even the night he assaulted me.

Desperate girls spread their legs in Bolles.

Angry, bitter, jaded ones, however? We bare our legs proudly in couture and stroll into the club with our chins jutting into the air. Nothing can reach me through the impenetrable shield hate has formed around my heart. Not the lingering, lustful glances cast my way or the curious, amused ones by the few hostesses already demeaning themselves for the members of this establishment.

Inside, I head directly for the foyer and into the spacious lounge on the bottom level. Chandeliers cast a seductive, soft glow over the inhabitants: men in suits and girls in skimpier attire than mine. They eye me like a new toy placed on the shelf of an exclusive store.

One of them, a smirking blond with his shirt unbuttoned to reveal a muscular chest, approaches me. "I'm Andrew," he says, eyeing me up and down. "Sloane told me all about you."

For a split second, doubt creeps in as his gaze rakes over my breasts. Before I stiffen fully, he winks.

"This way. The arrangements have already been made."

He leads me past the billiard room, into an even wider area. At first appraisal, it resembles a lounge of some kind, with a round platform in the center surrounded by black leather chairs. A silvery spotlight adds a mysterious atmosphere, only enhanced by the dark-blue walls and polished marble floors. Men are already seated, facing what I'm beginning to suspect is a stage. Dressed in expensive suits, they're watching. Waiting.

For the first time, real alarm sinks into my veins, fighting with determination for potency. Do I really intend to demean myself just to make a point? With one glance at the few empty chairs—and the one man missing from this crowd—I have my answer.

Hell fucking yes.

"Don't worry."

I jump as a hand presses against my lower back, but it's only Andrew, gently guiding me forward.

"You're the last…guest of the evening," he assures me. "I'm sure you'll fetch an interesting price."

This must be an event they regularly hold here, I realize. Lingering on the outskirts of the room are other women dressed no less shamelessly. Have all of them been bought and sold already? Disgraced heiresses? Desperate waitresses? Women looking for a thrill, as Sloane admitted to me?

I can't find the pride to pity any of them as I approach the raised platform. There's no announcer there to add pomp and circumstance. No thrilling music to count the seconds down. The moment I brace a heel against the dais, a man calls out, "Five hundred."

"Eight hundred," another says, his casual tone suggesting he just bid on a pair of shoes or piece of jewelry, not a woman.

"A thousand," someone adds to the chorus of bids.

For a painful second, there's no other offer. "Two thousand," someone calls finally— Andrew, perched on a chair in the back. Catching my relieved glance, he nods. "Five thousand," he adds after another man has countered his offer.

Minutes pass, and it almost feels like a strange, thrilling game. One played after too much wine at some rich bastard's soirée. A game of "who can be the biggest show off" by throwing unseemly amounts of money around.

"Six thousand," bids another man, his face obscured by the glow of the spotlight.

There's a moment's pause. Then I hear Andrew wager. "Seven thousand—"

"Ten thousand." A newer voice cuts through the fray and any innocence this event may have held is promptly shattered. The devil enters the room, looking as though he crawled his way from hell. His suit is rumpled, his hair a wild mess. Cold, glaring eyes find me, cutting through every obstacle in his way. "Twenty thousand," he adds before another man can even finish voicing his bid.

A shudder runs through the room. Heads turn, eyeing the newcomer curiously. What was fun and games is now a gladiatorial match, with money as the weapon and my body as the prize.

Andrew, as Sloane insisted, proves to be more reliable than expected. "Thirty," he says, sounding unfazed by this new challenger.

As if shrugging off a fly, Blake flicks a different amount off his tongue. "Fifty."

The confused murmurs grow. Excitement and tension crackle in the air. I'm sweating in my borrowed dress, aware of how my chest heaves with every breath. Sloane warned me to be careful. *"That gown is killer, but one wrong move and your goods will be on full display."*

They must be, because, if anything, the only man standing suddenly looks taller. His voice grates, taking on an increased urgency. "One hundred."

"Two," Andrew says without missing a beat.

"One million."

My jaw drops, along with most of the men's jaws in this room. The wildest amount I ever pictured anyone pledging was maybe a few thousand. And, by anyone, I meant the one bastard who thwarted my original plans for an auction. Never in my most dangerous nightmares did I imagine him putting that much of a price on me. Or a bounty.

"Two million." A slender figure rises from the crowd. Andrew, his face suddenly drawn with concentration. "Four," he adds when Blake unflinchingly counters.

The game ends as other men lose interest. It's a two-man race now, each naming an amount more absurd than the last.

Six.

Seven.

Nine.

Ten...

Oh God no. Terror corrupts my limbs, turning bone and blood to cement. The closer the amount creeps to my limit, the harder I sweat. Quake. Tremble.

He can't. He can't really...

No. He won't.

Teeth bared, he snarls, "Fifteen million." Loudly, as if he wants the entire damn world to hear. To know the price he'd pay for the privilege of owning me. Claiming me.

Dread has me in its grasp even before I force myself to glance at Andrew. His teeth are gritted, but the silence stretches on as he heeds my hard limit.

A second passes.

Another.

Sold.

No one says it. I feel it: possession. Wrapping around my throat, yanking me the few steps it takes to descend the dais. He doesn't beckon me or even call me by name. He doesn't have to. As he glowers like a fucking psychopath, his gaze alone warns any other man from glancing in my direction. It's like I no longer exist, a pawn in his possession, unreachable to any other.

I assume the other women purchased within these walls would approach their buyer with a mixture of curiosity and excitement. They'd submit to this creature who bought them like a commodity.

I run.

Panting, I find that Bolles is a maze of dark, winding hallways and hardwood floors. Floors that echo, taunting me with every footfall that lands in my wake. Slow and steady, but never far behind, he chases me into a foyer. Up a polished set of stairs. Farther. Farther. Farther…

Rounding a corner, I nearly run into a woman leaving a bathroom, her arms laden with cleaning supplies. She gives me an odd look as I lunge past her, closing the door. The damn room is too narrow. There are no hiding spaces—just the sliver of space beside the black marble toilet, its basin blue with cleaning fluid.

He doesn't knock. He doesn't even barge inside. The doorknob turns slowly, as if he's savoring the sound of my racing heartbeat. Relishing in the frantic swell.

I stop breathing as he forces his bulk through the doorway. He seems that damn large—he can't merely step inside. He crams every inch of his body into the narrow space. Slowly, he flicks his gaze over me, molten hot, as he reaches up to tug his tie loose.

"Turn around."

My body obeys, a slave to the ragged tone of voice I've never heard him use before. It's volatile, grinding inside me, irritating raw flesh. A warning of what's to come.

"Bend over."

My hands land on the toilet seat, but I choke down any disgust I may feel. It's primal, this compulsion taking control of my spine. I can't resist. Not even as his fingers graze my throat, practically shaking with possession.

"Open your mouth."

The moment I do, silk is shoved between my lips. His tie. His thumb strokes my jaw until I bite down, muffling any sound I might make.

"You think I'll let them fucking hear you?" he murmurs into my ear. There's a terrifying calmness in his voice, far beyond rage, or anger, or even hate. It's acceptance.

We'll only ever belong together like this. Fit together like this: two halves of the same broken puzzle piece. "Hell no."

Two fingers delve beneath my skirt and find the panel of my thong. "You think I'd let them get a fucking taste of what is *mine*?"

God. My eyelids flutter as he rubs between my folds, easing me open. Warm wetness greets him, and he takes advantage, painting heated flesh with the proof of my arousal.

He growls. I hear his zipper come undone, and a heartbeat later, I'm thrown forward as he plunges inside me. My knees buckle. My arms strain to support my weight as my face is brought ever closer to the water glistening in the toilet.

But he doesn't fuck me.

He breaks me open, grinding every inch of himself he can fit into the cracks. I cry out, muzzled by the makeshift gag. I'm mute to every thrust and groan. No one can hear me whimper. Moan. Scream.

"No fucking way." He never stops speaking to me, listing every transgression committed against him. "I saw them. Looking at you. Fucking you with their eyes. But you're mine—" He bucks his hips, and my arms give out. My chin hits the toilet seat, leaving my ass in the air, my body at his mercy. "Fuck. I should string you up. Never let you out of my fucking sight. Fuck. Fuck!"

He doesn't even give himself the chance to experience his release in full. He pulls out, still impossibly hard. Dazed, I watch him stuff himself into his pants, his face a mask of pure insanity.

"Car," he says simply. "Five minutes."

He strips his coat and tosses it over my heaving frame before storming into the hall.

Five minutes.

ELEVEN

I LEAVE Bolles a captive after entering just a moment earlier with my soul in play. I wagered and badly lost. My tormentor is waiting for me out front, ready and willing to usher me into his dark chariot. Not that he needs it. He'll drag me into Hades with him if he must. By the aid of a vehicle. By my hair.

"In," he grunts, stepping aside to wrench the door to the back seat open.

I move past him, numb. Dazed. As he slams the door behind me, I realize he drove here himself. Radiating tension, he climbs into the driver's seat. A telltale click betrays that the locks engage, trapping me within.

We return to his suite in silence, crowding into the elevator wordlessly. The moment the doors part on the top floor, he commands me forward with a curt nod, his gaze unreadable. With my shoulders squared, I enter the foyer.

Something heavy rams into me from behind, forcing me

against the nearest wall where a framed portrait of a painted landscape hangs. Fabric tears and cold air rushes to assault my suddenly bare torso.

"Turn," he commands, but he does it himself, shoving me back. Darkness taints the blue of his irises as he grabs my panties with both hands. Tears them off. Throws the lace aside. His cock is already captured in his fist, straining to enter me.

Groaning, he lifts my thigh against his hip and shoves the swollen crown inside me.

My cry cuts the air, loud without anything to stifle it. The sound only makes him harder. Madder. He drives into me, grunting, teeth clenched, eyes pressed shut.

"You're so beautiful." Every praise lands like a curse. "So wet for me. God, so wet. Fucking hell…"

He's ruthless, taking me with reckless need. Like he's drowning. Starving. Dying. Only this can keep him afloat, sustain him, keep him alive. Only this gives his life any damn meaning.

He drags me to the floor, rutting me from behind with my face pressed against the marble. Drool coats my cheeks. I can't suck in enough air to gasp. Moan. I claw at the floor, a mass of tense, clenching, churning muscle and nerves, taking as much of him as I can. So deep that it fucking burns. It bleeds.

"That's right," he urges, sounding crazed, as he pulls out only to seek his way into my body through a different route.

A tighter one that clenches against him. He has to dip into my gaping "cunt" to find enough lubrication. "So goddamn wet. Let me in, Snow. Won't hurt… Let me in… Jesus Christ!"

My head rears back as I find the voice to scream. God, it doesn't hurt—it desolates. He claims me in a way only he can, forcing me to accept him. Need him. Crave every fucking burning, painful, stretching inch.

And inch.

"So fucking good," he mutters into the nape of my neck. "So good. Fucking hell. Feel like heaven. Heaven…"

The intimacy of this way of fucking undoes him too quickly. He groans, collapsing against my back. But he doesn't pull out. I doubt he can, gripped so tightly by my body for every spasming, unbidden release.

"Do you know what you do to me?" he demands, grasping strands of my hair. Pulling on them. "Drive…me… goddamn…insane."

I was wrong. Still hard, he flexes his hips, driving into me for another series of punishing thrusts. Too much. Can't take. Blind. Numb. Dumb.

Burning.

My body goes limp before jolting back to life, enslaved to every grinding, harsh, bruising bit of friction.

"You're mine now," he tells me, thrusting even deeper. Faster. Oh God, too fast. "Mine!"

My vision goes white. I'm weightless, robbed of sensation. Just the knowledge of him crushing down on my spine, his presence inescapable as my body rides every dizzying throe. This isn't an orgasm. It's dying, becoming something twisted and new from the ashes.

"You're fucking mine," he promises, his voice hoarse. "From now on, you're fucking mine."

* * *

I COME to on what feels like a bed. How we got here, I have no clue. I smell him sweating and breathless beside me. My inner thighs throb with his release, my body burning in the aftermath of his possession. Somehow, I know without having to look that he's ready to take me again.

It's like we're two cogs of one of those wind-up toys. He's the crank, twisting into me. I'm the part that jumps across the floor at the whim of every motion.

"Touch yourself." He voices the command into my ear, biting the lobe when I don't comply fast enough.

My fingers rise from the bed, trembling and weak. I guide them down my belly until they meet a mass of swollen, slick flesh.

"Holy hell." He inhales, positioning himself to watch every illicit motion. "More," he grates, his eyes glowing in the dark. "Harder. The way I know you've imagined me touching you."

Like a deranged madman, apparently. Rough. Rigidly. Tentatively slipping inside, just to the nail bed before chickening out.

"No." He leans in closer, inhaling the scent on my skin. His hand captures my wrist and the pressure increases.

My fingers have no choice but to enter me. One. Another. "Oh God—"

"Yes." He bites me again, grinding a ridge of flesh on my throat between his teeth. "Fucking yes."

He guides me in and out, but never deep enough. Hard enough. Fast enough. He coaxes me up that dangerously high peak, but never close to the edge.

"The things you make me do," he admits, barely intelligible. "I've fucked my fist for weeks. Come inside my goddamn pants. You make me so fucking… Fuck."

I stiffen as he forces my thumb against the bundle of nerves aching for the most stimulation. One hard flick has me gasping. After another, I'm grinding my hips against my own damn fingers.

"You were made for me," he declares. "For this. To be fucked by me. Fucking me. You're fucking *for* me."

I squeeze my eyes shut against his expression. Too raw. Too dangerous. I focus on the white-hot flames building inside my belly, growing hotter with every twist. Every thrust. Far too soon, he bats my hand aside. Hot air assaults the throbbing flesh. God no. Then I open my eyes and find him hunched on all fours, his head lowering.

He spears me open with his tongue, fucking me with the stiff tip. I lose my voice from screaming. I lose my fucking mind. I only find pieces of it again: on my knees as he takes me from behind, slamming my shoulder against the headboard.

"Fuck," he growls, his face buried against my neck. "I'd give you anything…everything. I'd give you everything. But I can't… I don't. Trust. Can't trust."

He rears back, spilling himself inside me before I can anticipate the searing warmth. For some reason, that last confession resonates more than the others. *I'd give you everything. Anything.*

"Purse," I croak, too exhausted to lift my body from the twisted sheets. "Purse."

Frowning, he rises from the bed and returns a second later, dropping my handbag beside me. Blindly, I reach inside and grab a letter at random. He eyes it blankly as I press it against his palm.

"Read."

I can't find the words to explain his expression. Maybe there aren't any. Just feelings: an aching clench of my heart and a twist of my belly. Things I hate feeling. Things only he can make me feel.

He leaves again, but he doesn't go far. Into a bathroom, maybe? I hear water running. When he pads back to the bed, soothing warm runs between my legs, cleaning me up. He washes me slowly, using the same rag to stroke my backside and down my thighs. Satisfied, he settles beside me, sitting upright. Paper crinkles, manipulated by his large hands. A man like him isn't the type to write letters or read them. They forge contracts and sign lives away with the stroke of a pen.

"Dear Snow…" He sounds worse than I do. Ragged and hoarse. After clearing his throat, he tries again. "Dear Snow. I don't want to hate you. I can't hate you."

My skin heats, and I roll onto my side, hunting his expression. He keeps his face utterly stoic, hiding himself from me, even now.

"And I should. There are moments where I still look at you and I feel it. I despise you so fucking much. Then others… when the light catches your hair, and your eyes seem so goddamn blue, and all I can fucking think about is being inside you. Near you. And that's the worst part," he insists darkly. "You don't want me to crave you the way I should. Need you the way I fucking need you. If anything, you should ignore me. Run away. Because I'll fucking chase you. I'll chase you until you stop running."

He crumples the page in his fist and tosses it aside.

"My first fifteen-million-dollar fuck," he grumbles as he staggers for the door as if drunk. Looking back, he frowns, the expression almost pitying. "I wish I could say it wasn't worth it. I fucking wish I could."

He leaves, letting the door sway in his wake. I'm too tired to track where he goes. Somewhere far from this room, down the stairs, but still in the suite. Like any predator, he won't leave his kill for long.

Groaning with the effort, I feel along the bed for the letter. My heart lurches when I finally find it, clutching it tightly. I roll onto my stomach and unfurl it, straining my eyes to read in the dark.

I seek out every scribbled word in that scrawl I know so well.

Only to find nothing.

Not on this side. Not on the other.

It's blank.

A sickening feeling runs through me like a lance as I drag my bag closer and grab another letter at random. I rip it open, unfurling the pages. There are three of them, each one blank. So is the next. And the next. And the next.

Every single envelope contains a varying number of blank pages.

And suddenly, I know why: He sent me blank, fake letters, knowing that I'd never read one.

I WAKE up sprawled over a strange bed in a strange, darkened room. Gray walls and hardwood floors form a bare, utilitarian prison. At least at first glance—a second appraisal reveals that the door is open, and faint rays of daylight seep through black curtains, revealing a distinctly masculine air. Steel-colored sheets cover the substantial mattress. The frame is dark wood, with simple, sleek furniture rounding out the drab surroundings: a nightstand in the same style as the bed, a leather chaise near one of the massive windows, and a floor lamp placed beside the door to a walk-in closet. From here, I can make out seemingly endless rows of hanging suits.

A terrible realization strikes: This is his room. His bed.

I scramble to my feet, alarmed to find countless balls of crumpled paper mingled in the sheets. Then I take a step and groan as my body throbs in a million different ways. My back aches. My head pounds. A steady burn builds between my legs—in both the front and the back. My cheeks flame as I remember the myriad of ways Blake Lorenz violated my body.

The ways I *let* him violate me.

Fifteen million dollars wasted on one senseless night.

He must be insane.

Dreading what I'll find, I hunt the floor for my dress but find nothing, not even my panties. Facing him naked isn't even a remote option, so I cut my losses and snatch a white shirt from his color-coded closet. On me, it's long enough to reach my knees, providing enough cover to give me the strength to leave the room. Before I do, I notice another alarming detail: My purse is missing, along with the bank documents stowed inside it.

Insane, yes, but even Blake Lorenz wouldn't be so bold as to brazenly search through my belongings. Right? I feed myself that lie, even as the truth becomes clearer with every step I creep from the bedroom on my way to the upstairs hall. I can sense him radiating frustration and rage from the lower level.

He's standing before his desk, facing the doorway. Shadows beneath his eyes reveal he hasn't slept. In days. Unsurprisingly, my bank documents are spread before him. I suspect he's spent hours poring over every one, reconciling the pure folly of my deception.

"Well played," he says coldly. "The pauper's become a princess again." He snatches up one of the pages and throws it so hard that it slides across the desk. "A very wealthy princess. Tell me, did you intend to milk me for so much or did you get caught up in the moment?"

I flinch at the vitriol flung my way. He's furious, but for once, I don't think it's all directed at me. He glares down at his hands, flexing them against the wood. A fifteen-million-dollar fuck, he mused, according to my hazy memories. Last night, he deemed that amount of money well spent.

"You weren't supposed to win me at all," I say, alarmed to find my voice a rasp. My throat feels rubbed raw. No wonder—he bit it. Stroked it. Coaxed a million dollars' worth of screams from it. "I… You weren't supposed to win."

He frowns at the idea, as if I'd suggested he stop breathing on a whim. "You thought I'd sit there and let some other bastard buy you? Own you? Jesus Christ." He throws his head back for a long, disturbing laugh that never goes beyond the surface. When he meets my gaze again, all I find in his eyes is pain, raw and exposed. "There's no fucking amount I wouldn't pay. I'd scrape together every goddamn cent. You remember that the next time you get the urge to play your little game. Though I suggest you consider the welfare of others first."

I suck in a breath at the thinly veiled threat. I've outed Andrew as my accomplice, and the monster before me didn't miss a damn thing. Suddenly, I know his motive for confronting me like this in the first place: to catch me off guard and learn just who nearly outbid him.

His hands curl into fists over the desk's surface. "Who was he?"

"No one," I croak. He must hear the truth in my voice, because his jaw relaxes by a fraction. "I asked him to help me. That's all—"

"You know I had it all fucking planned," he admits, shaking his head. "How I'd make you stay. Make you earn every fucking cent. I'd lock you away. I'd make you crave my cock as badly as I crave you. I'd make…I'd make you need me."

He sounds deranged. No, even worse. He sounds one hundred percent truthful.

"How?" I find myself asking. "By manipulating me again? By lying?"

He shrugs, his eyes narrowing. "By fucking. It's the only goddamn way you seem to hear me. Listen to me. Understand me. When I'm so deep inside you, there's nothing fucking else."

I turn away, my cheeks flaming. The view from the window offers no reprieve. The water looms below, as gray as the storm clouds rolling in over the horizon. It's as if the entire world is trying to warn me in visual clues: *Run. He's dangerous. He's fucking mad, Snow.*

"And, now, I don't need you anymore," I say, voicing what he seems unwilling to.

"You don't," he admits. "You're a free woman. Congratulations—"

"So, now, maybe you'll stop treating me like a goddamn object and listen to *me* for once!" My fingers knot into fists. I could hit him if I were close enough, and it takes everything I have to stay back. "All I wanted—all I asked—was that you talk to me on equal terms. Trust me. Open up to me! All you've done is lie, and cheat, and steal—"

"You want to talk?" He cuts his gaze toward me, his features contorted by shadow. "Fine. Let's talk. But that's the problem, isn't it? I can't say a fucking word to you that doesn't make me want to bash my fucking skull in. None of it means a goddamn thing. But then all of it means *everything*. I can't feel a fucking shred of anything real unless I'm around you."

He's closer, invading my space without care. His fingers capture one of my curls, grinding it into a wild tangle. I stiffen at the deliberate act, but I can't move. My body won't obey any of the frantic commands my brain issues.

"I want to tell you every-fucking-thing. God, I do..." He swallows hard, his expression constricted, as if something is squeezing him from within, causing unimaginable pain. "But at the same time, I'd rather hurt you. Lie to you. Cheat. Steal from you. I'd rather fucking break you than give you an ounce of myself. Because...because if you turn against me again, there won't be anything left. I won't have a damn thing."

Tears spill from my eyes, impossible to stop. It's the first time he's ever directly addressed his past as Brandt. Without mocking. Without taunting. It's the pain I've feared facing for ten damn years, and my heart is no match for it now.

"I'm sorry—"

"I know." His other hand encircles my throat, tightening just enough to render me silent. "And I want to believe that. I do. But, fuck, I *can't*." He moves, using his bulk to steer me back. Back.

It's a shock when my shoulder blades strike cold, unyielding glass. And the look in his eyes makes me suck in a startled breath—a pained stage between determination and recklessness. The same way he was when he set my home on fire from the inside. The same look he was wearing when he bid for me. When he swore while buried inside me that I was his alone.

"There are times when I look at you and all I see is that girl again," he admits, hissing the words into my hair, his breath igniting the sweat gathering along my scalp. "So sweet. So innocent. And all I fucking want to do is…" His fingers form a fist with a chunk of my curls trapped between them. "Crush her."

"Talk to her," I croak, aware of his touch still pressed against my throat. "Just talk to me. Tell me what you feel. Just talk to me, please."

"Feel?" His mouth flattens into a hard line. It's as if he's never heard the word before—or at least not in so long; he's forgotten its meaning. "All I feel is need. I need you in a way I can't fucking stand. Like I've never needed anything. It drives me fucking insane."

"So talk to me," I murmur, though I don't know how I found the sense to speak. I should run. Every instinct in my body is urging me to—but I can't seem to move an inch. "Keep talking to me. Tell me—"

"I need to let the world know you're mine. I had you first. I will always have you first." His eyes glaze over, unfocused.

Suddenly, I'm spun around, forced face-first against the glass. I turn my head, putting one eye to the view while keeping the other trained solely on him.

He looks beautiful like this. A tempest. A raw, violent thunderstorm about to descend. Groaning, he smooths his hands up my bare thighs. A shudder runs through me, an electric current lacing from his fingertips. The higher he goes, the harsher it feels, until my teeth chatter with the force of it.

"I need to hear you," he adds, sounding dazed, even as his fingers find me without hesitation. "How it feels when I'm inside you so fucking deep." He slides a digit inside me and my lips part on cue.

"Hurts," I whisper. "Like…like you're splitting me open. Every time."

He growls, satisfied with the answer. Another finger slides home to join the first, extending the burn. "It should," he agrees. "Because that's what you do to me, every fucking time. You split me open. You make me into a fucking… fuck. Do you know what you taste like?" He laughs, stretching me from the inside out, drawing a moan with every deliberate stroke. "*Snow*. How fucking pathetic is that? Snowy tastes like snow… But you do." He lunges, encasing me from behind. His pelvis presses against my ass, revealing a teasing brush of the erection stiffening against the front of his slacks. "Pure. Clean. Like fucking snow."

He bats a tangle of hair from my neck and lathes the exposed area with his tongue. A groan escapes my clenched teeth, melding with his weary sigh.

"Like this," he rasps as if struggling to remember something, put it into words. "Only like this. Feel…better. Only like this."

There's no explanation. He removes his hands from me to tug at the front of his pants and yank them down. One hand captures my thigh while his hips buck, guiding his cock between my legs. Inside.

"Talk to me," he begs as he builds a slow, torturous rhythm. "Need you. Talk to me."

"You're breaking me," I tell him, my voice cracking into jagged syllables and panting breaths. "Breaking me."

"Yes." He grasps a fistful of my hair, drawing my face toward his. His lips nudge mine and he licks them open, shameless and ruthless. "And look. The whole fucking world can see it. How good it is when I fuck you. Say it."

"So good." Sensations overwhelm me. I squeeze my eyes shut against them, but he growls, nipping my lower lip. Jawline. Any part of me he can reach.

"You watch," he warns. "Watch what you do to me."

I open my eyes to madness. It consumes his entire being, darkening the hue of his gaze, dragging me down with him.

He swivels his hips, deepening his entry. More. More. Too much. "I'm drowning," he croaks. "So wet. Drowning me. Drowning."

The sounds of slapping flesh dominate. He said that this is the only way we can speak: in frantic, driving motions. Whispered curses. Heat. And sin. And skin on skin. All of it swelters, wrapping me in a terrifying, claustrophobic cocoon of fire, and lust, and Blake.

"Shit, I feel you coming," he gasps out.

And I come undone. Literally. I'm a puppet with loosened strings, grasping at the window glass with sweat-slick fingers that don't have a chance in hell of finding traction. He falls with me, to his knees, somehow still inside me. Still moving. Weakly, I fall forward, presenting my ass to him as the world looms below, watching as he claims me. The sky observes unfeelingly as the water churns, laughing at my destruction.

Far too soon, I hear him groan and I'm flooded with fire.

"Like this," he bites out, collapsing against my back. "Only feel like this."

THE INTENSITY of the moment flickers and dies like a candle being blown out. Minutes later, we disentangle our limbs, scrambling to find a safe distance apart. I crawl to the farthest corner of the room while he approaches the desk. Then I notice an incessant buzzing sound: a phone ringing.

"What is it?" he snaps, his back to me. Suddenly, his shoulders slump and he braces his free hand against the desk. "What? She's awake? Keep her in bed until I get there."

A sudden urgency stiffens his spine. He grabs his pants from the floor, wrenching them up. Only one person could spur him into action like this.

"Is she all right?" Without sex or rage to distract, the full depth of my selfishness sinks in. Poor Masha. Her brother should have been by her side last night. Not chasing after me. Though something tells me that the other day's events were not an out-of-the-blue occurrence.

"She's fine." He sounds as though he had to spit out every word, aware of the promise he made. *Talk to me.* After doing up his zipper, he rakes his fingers through his hair and curses. His clothes are crumpled, damp with sweat. Sighing, he peels them off while stumbling for the door.

"I'm coming with you." I don't know where the desire comes from. Maybe it's pathetic self-preservation. I can't face myself alone. I can't face the marks, and the aftermath, without him to consume my attention. Not yet.

He looks back sharply, still tugging his pants off. I picture him heading for the shower. He'll barge into Bolles wearing a day-old suit and a crazed expression, but he can't reveal that part of himself to her. He'll clean and scrape the broken pieces of himself together. He'll put his mask on. Pretend.

In the end, he says nothing, but I sense rather than feel the unspoken command. *Hurry up.*

I lurch to my feet, using the window for balance. Then I follow him up the stairs. He enters the room I woke up in, while I creep into the navy one. I snatch items of clothing at random from the closet and shower, scrubbing at my skin without surveying the damage. Sore. Burning. Bleeding.

I dry quickly and reenter the hall minutes later wearing a black dress and a pair of flats. I find him waiting for me at the base of the steps, his damp hair dripping onto the shoulders of a black suit. Watching me, he adjusts a gray tie, looking no less exhausted than he did before.

"Are you ready?"

I swallow at the grating tone in his voice. "Yes."

Together, we take the elevator down to the lower level. A car is already waiting in the garage, a stern-faced driver at the helm. We have no choice but to share the back seat. Gritting his teeth, Blake holds the door open for me. I swear I hear him inhale as I settle onto the seat. Then he climbs in beside me, slamming the door behind us.

Minutes tick by in silence as the driver maneuvers the car onto the main street. Glaring daylight leaves nothing to hide behind. I still feel him in my skin. Taste him on my lips. Our damp hair drips steadily, creating a pulsing soundtrack. Too loud.

"Masha," I say, breaking the silence. "Is she…all right?" I'm not talking physically.

"I…" He breaks off and swallows. Lightning quick, his hand shoots out, grasping mine.

My eyes widen at the contact. There's no rage in his grip. If anything, his fingers shake, demanding whatever strength I have left to give.

"Her father never saw her for the first five years of her life. Her mother and he divorced. She took Masha away. Kept her isolated. Then she remarried. A monster."

Oh no. A part of me suspects the direction this tale will take. In a sad, ironic way, Masha has the look for it: the tragic princess in a brutal fairytale.

"What happened?" I force myself to ask when he doesn't continue.

I gasp. His grip tightens as he glares out of his window. "The bastard controlled her. Manipulated her. Warped her mind. When she was barely seventeen, he forced her to marry a man just as twisted as he was."

"Oh God." Like a punch to the chest—that's how perspective shifts around me.

Forrest Hollings was no saint, but even he had lines he never crossed. Perhaps he thought he could save me for the highest bidder. Luckily, he died before ever getting the chance.

"Her husband was…cruel," Blake says simply. "It was fucking hell to get her away from him. Her father—*our* father—made me promise to keep her from the motherfucker. And I did. I paid him off. Threatened him. Blackmailed. Nothing ever worked for long. Six months ago, he managed to contact her again, and he hasn't stopped since. I offered him more money. Hired thugs to teach him a lesson. In the end, I brought her here, to the States. A week ago, he found her again."

Raw pain enhances his features, exaggerating the small nuances I missed before. The black stubble growing in along his chin. The overgrown length to his hair. The bruises beneath his eyes, far darker than they first seemed. How long has it been since he's slept?

Maybe not since that night in Hollings Manor.

"She'll be fine in a few days," he adds, though I think he's speaking more to himself than to me. "And if he comes near her again, I'll fucking kill him."

"Have you gone to the police?" I ask, marveling at the fact that he still has my hand. Tension radiates through his skin, as if he's deliberately avoiding squeezing too hard. Crushing me.

"The police don't mean shit to a man with money." He lets me go, and my hand cools without his heat. "If I pay him off, he'll just come back again."

We say nothing else during the rest of the trip to the hospital. Rather than a normal room on a medical floor, Masha has a private suite in a locked unit. A realm I know all too well. Some of the nurses call me by name as we enter, a fact that doesn't go unnoticed.

"How many times?" Blake asks as we cross the quiet unit with its soothing, light-blue walls and gentle atmosphere. His expression is strained as we pass a patient, thin as a rail, trailing an IV pole as she wanders the wing.

How many times have I been in Masha's place? "Too many times," I reply.

His sister is in bed when we finally reach her room. Pale sunlight streams in through a large window, illuminating a vase of yellow roses on her bedside table.

"Son of a bitch." Blake crosses the room and snatches the blossoms from the table, tossing them into the trash. Then he sinks to his knees beside Masha's bed and smooths his hand over her hair, coaxing her awake. A worn smile makes him look like a different man—someone capable of joy.

They converse in German, their voices hushed, and I step into the hall rather than intrude.

Not long after, he returns to my side. "I... She's asking to speak to you."

"Really?" I look over, surprised to find slightly less exhaustion weighing his features down than before.

"If you don't want to, I could—"

"No." I shake my head. "No, I'll see her."

I slip past him and warily enter the hospital room. Masha is upright, propped against a wall of pillows. She looks pale in the faint light drifting in through one of the wide windows, but a fragile smile shapes her mouth.

"Hello," she says, her voice faint and lilting.

I do my best to match her grin, praying that none of my concern shows. She's just a waif beneath white sheets, almost the same color as the linens. Her hair forms a golden halo, which adds some definition to her pale form. Dark circles enhance her hollow gaze, making it seem endless. Penetrating.

"How are you feeling?" I ask, approaching the side of her bed.

She laughs weakly. "You don't have to pretend," she says. "I know that I scared you. I know how I look. At least someone can see the obvious." Her gaze cuts beyond me to the doorway, and a hint of what could be pain distorts the green irises. "I read the papers," she croaks, clutching the blankets draped around her. "He promised me he wouldn't... Be honest with me—"

"They were lies." Driven by an impulse I can't name, I reach for one of her hands and clench it tight. "He never assaulted me."

"But he did hurt you," Masha says firmly. "I know he did."

My lips twitch to form a rebuttal. Maybe not for Blake's sake, but for his sister's peace of mind. As exhausted and frail as she looks, there's a coldness I vaguely recognize in her gaze: resigned fear. She doesn't want to see him as a monster. At the same time, she's not naïve.

"I... He didn't hurt me," I say, but the words fall flat. Hollow.

Masha sighs and stares down at her hands. "You don't have to lie to me." Gingerly, she disentangles her fingers from mine and turns to stare out the nearest window. "Sometimes... I'm so sick of being the victim. The pawn. Even Blake. I love him so much, but he's the same." Her gaze meets mine, burning brightly for the first time during this visit. "Maybe the only way to beat them is at their own game."

I say nothing. Her words resonate deeply enough without requiring agreement out loud. Their game: vicious lies and cruel manipulation. Could I ever be so callous?

"Thank you for coming," Masha says, snapping me from my thoughts.

I awkwardly back away and reenter the hallway, where I find Blake lingering near the doorway, his expression tense.

One glance at me and he grits his teeth, nodding just once. "Let's go."

We return to the car, but I don't recognize the direction the driver heads in.

"Lunch," Blake proposes, sounding hesitant. "Or a walk. Or a fucking drive around the city. Anything to…to just talk."

Hope flares to life in my chest, a painful, pathetic thing. "Okay. A drive."

The driver may be listening, but this moment feels too damn fragile.

"What did Masha say to you?"

I don't miss the careful note in his voice. "Nothing," I say, but the truth is obvious in what I don't voice. She asked me if he was a monster, and I couldn't find the words to deny it. "She looks better, at least," I finish, stumbling over the words. "Healthy—"

"She'll be fine," he says. "I've arranged to have her transferred to a more familiar facility upstate. She'll…she'll be fine."

Again, he alludes to the fact that this isn't her first stint in a hospital. A part of me wants to demand more answers, but I keep seeing her face, that fragile innocence. In the end, all I can do is stare out the window and picture how I must have appeared to my brothers when I was in her place. Maybe I was too selfish to see it before, but now, their concern makes a bit more sense and I hate myself for causing it.

"It feels strange to be back," Blake says, breaking the silence. "I…I thought about you." He takes my hand, this time cradling my fingers against his palm. "Every damn day. God, I thought of you…"

Words fight to squeeze their way past my thickening throat only to fail. I thought of him too. Every moment. Every second. I couldn't not think of him.

"Those days," he adds, his voice deepening, "I play them over and over. They feel like a fucking dream. Sometimes… I wonder if it was even real. If any of it was real."

"It was." It had to be, because those days were all I had left. I still cling to them like an addict to her very last vial of poison.

"I still remember." He laughs, the sound broken, echoing off the close quarters. "Your laugh. Those stories we used to tell."

"Humpty Dumpty," I say, my voice barely a whisper.

"Yes." He nods. His other hand captures my chin, tilting my face toward his. He's closer, his mouth nudging mine, a silent demand to open. He doesn't kiss me when I do. He merely breathes, inhaling every breath I exhale. "I know that things can't ever be like they were. But…I want. I need…"

"I know."

We say nothing else, spending what feels like an eternity trapped in an intimate embrace, sharing the same air. The same space. The same pain.

We can't ever go back. Brandt Lloyd is dead, along with his fiery princess, Snow.

We're the jagged shells of those two innocent souls, left behind, forced to find some semblance of self again.

But maybe we can find a way to meld our broken edges.

Or stab each other with them.

THIRTEEN

BLAKE

SHE ALWAYS WAS the only person in the world who could make the ugliest situations reveal their beauty. Like finding solace in a mental institution or crafting an imaginary world for a boy desperate to escape his own personal hell.

They used to wonder why I spent so much time with her —*them*, the onlookers and gossips and petty, spiteful neighbors. Maybe I was deranged? Or degenerate? Or awkward with people my own age?

But they were wrong.

The silly little girl with stars in her eyes could make an afternoon shut indoors with only books to read compelling. To her, nothing was ordinary. A bad day was the worst one in the universe—for that moment. A good one, the very best, at least until the next.

She always saw magic in every moment.

And she always ignored the darkness in me.

"You're thinking." Her fingers dance a trail up my forearm, luring me back to the present. Halfway up my elbow she pauses, her gaze lowered as if registering the act for the first time. Silently, she pulls away.

But I stop her.

"About us," I say, maneuvering her wrist so that her palm is upright. "You really were a pain in the ass."

She gasps, playfully offended. "I was *your* pain in the ass." Her face falls as the full weight of her words lands between us.

My pain in the ass. Just not anymore.

Something in my expression must change because she sighs and tries pulling her hand away. "I'm sorry—"

"You don't have to walk on eggshells around me." I let her go and turn my attention to the nearest window. The world passes by in a blur, and I indulge the dramatic irony: ten years without her have passed much in the same way.

A blur. Colorless and empty.

"I feel like…" She sighs, fidgeting beside me. Her hands run aimlessly through her hair, twisting the soft curls. "I feel like I've forgotten how to say the right thing. It didn't use to be this hard."

Hard. My jaw clenches at her use of the word and I can't fucking help myself. "Was it easier with him? Daniel Ellingston?"

She inhales sharply. "Please don't do this."

"I don't mean it like that." Fuck, maybe she's right. It's so fucking hard. "I mean in that… He didn't scare you. I do."

She can't deny it. Even now she sits angled toward the door on her end, maintaining a hairsbreadth of distance between us at all times. Her eyes dart warily toward mine and then away again.

"You don't scare me." I have to strain to hear her. "You don't. I scare myself. Because every time you lash out. Every time you flinch when you look at me, I remember…"

She doesn't have to say it.

I remember who you used to be.

A person I can never be again.

"Do you want me to leave?" I keep my tone intentionally soft as my entire body stiffens. I feel like a fucking fool at the gallows, waiting to be hung on her say so.

"No," she says and some of the tension in my body eases. "But… Can I ask you something?"

"Yes." She jumps and as my voice echoes back to me, I realize how goddamn eager I sounded. Feral. "I mean, you can ask me anything."

"Masha's…fine," she says, testing out my term. "But what about you?"

I clench my jaw, steeling myself for what she might say. "What do you mean?"

She swallows hard and then tentatively adds, "Do you still have those nightmares?"

My blood runs cold. Nightmares. That's a delicate word for it—when she really means waking up, shouting like a fucking madman, chasing phantoms in the dark.

"I shouldn't have asked," she says quickly. "It's none of my business—"

"I don't like talking about it," I admit, hating how cold I sound.

She nods, her hands fluttering over her lap. "My brothers had me hospitalized after the gala. Did you know that?"

Her words land like a sucker punch—not that she intends for them to. Redness paints her cheeks. Embarrassment? Before I can be sure, she turns away from me again, eyeing the view passing beyond the windows. "Their one condition was that I see my therapist once a week—and I haven't even called to set up one appointment. Why?" She shakes her head and fingers one of her loose curls. My own hand twitches, aching to tuck the strand behind her ear. Like I used to I realize.

She'd play with her hair whenever that bastard Forrest said something that sent her running to one of her hiding places. I'd chase her down and smooth my fingers through the tangled mess she made. Always.

"Why?" I prod as her silence extends to nearly a minute. "Why not?"

She inhales, her face tilted toward me a fraction of an inch. "Because despite what happened recently… We both know where the true damage is."

An answer springs to my lips. "The past."

She nods. "And I don't think I'm brave enough to go there. Not yet. I can't—"

"I know." I don't smother the impulse to touch her this time. She stiffens when I ease the mangled curl from her grasp. It's still soft, despite the damage done by a forced hair-cut and cheap dye. The damage *I* did.

"Have you gone to therapy?" I can hear the skepticism in her voice.

"No," I admit, frowning. "What could I say?"

That I was convicted of a crime that I didn't commit, accused by the girl I loved. That the man I believed was my father liked screwing the neighbor's wife—when he wasn't smacking me across the face for fucking breathing.

Anger seeps in and for a cruel second, I'm back there. In that place. As *that* kid. I'd take every blow without a word. Or complaint. I never fought back.

Until now, I never understood why.

"Blake?" Snow runs her fingers down the side of my jaw, and I know she's reliving it too. The many times she would trace my bruises while simultaneously pretending they didn't exist. "Are you alright?"

I shrug her off, swallowing hard, squashing those memories. "I'm fine."

But I'm not. My gaze hones in on her fingers, so soft and slim. In them—figuratively—she has a whole wealth of information to use against me, if she wanted to. My past. Her pain. The worst part? I couldn't stop her if she decided to.

If. And if she did, my first instinct is one I never felt when Harrison Lloyd raised his fist. With him, I cowered. But against her?

I *want* to fight. Bite. Snarl.

That bastard could beat the shit out of me, but I never felt wounded. Harrison Lloyd could never truly hurt me.

Snow on the other hand? She could leave me. Turn against me. Hate me...

And there's no need for a goddamn therapist to spell out what would happen next.

Her betrayal cuts deeper than any bruise.

And if I'm at her mercy again...

She'd fucking decimate me.

* * *

SNOWY

WE RETURN TO THE SUITE, retreating to separate rooms as if by an unspoken agreement. The need to lick my wounds drives me into the bathroom and I strip, climbing into the tub and turning the water to the hottest setting. Steaming.

Outstretched beneath the scalding liquid, I feel no closer to sanity than I did the first night I dared to take on Blake Lorenz. God, I was so stupid back then, barely three months ago. I was a fool.

And now?

I'm reckless. My mind goes to Masha and the torment that drove her to the unthinkable. But was I ever any different? I let my emotions shape my weight, knowing what I was doing to everyone around me. I knew the risks.

But when I wanted to fall…I stubbornly fell.

Only one boy was ever there to catch me. To shake his head at my broken pieces and instruct that I put them back together myself. King's men or king's horses couldn't mend me; only I could do that. Only he would force me to.

But, now, that boy's grown up, and the king's lost his softer edge. He'll break me apart sooner than he'll put me back together. It's the only way we know how to coexist.

The sound of a door opening snaps me into awareness. I jump, realizing I never locked the door to the bedroom or the bathroom. Both are easily flung aside, revealing a creature with eyes blazing like hellfire.

"B-Blake?" I scramble to cover myself, not that his eyes ever leave my face. It's as if he fixes his gaze on mine deliberately, honed with rage. "What's wrong?"

"Interesting conversation you and Sloane had," he snarls, throwing something at me.

It lands in the bathwater with a splash and I scramble to catch it before it can sink. The unfortunate object turns out to be a tabloid, its cover soaked through.

"You want me to be honest, but have you been?" he demands while I read the scandalous headline: **ABUSED HEIRESS TELLS ALL.**

My heart sinks as I scan the first few sentences. *With allegations of abuse against Blake Lorenz from heiress Snowy Hollings swirling, a close personal friend of the heiress tells us she regrets her failed engagement to Daniel Ellingston...*

Oh, Sloane. I don't even blame her. Our relationship was always transactional.

"You can't even fucking deny it. I knew it. I fucking knew better than to let down my guard around the *irresistible* Snow." Blake barks out a hollow laugh, shaking his head. There's almost a desperation to the action—relief? "And there it is," he adds nastily, "that goddamn thing only you can make me feel." He forms a fist, bringing it toward his heart as if he means to pummel it from his chest. At the last minute, he storms from the room.

Exhausted, I sink back, tossing the magazine aside. My eyes drift shut, and I focus intently on the warmth seeping into my aching muscles, buying myself more time before I have to face reality beyond these walls. So many false stops and starts. This one feels like yet another vicious yank backward. At the same time, I suspect that the rumor was nothing more than an excuse. The first thing he could latch onto to guard himself again.

Because this scares him.

It's terrifying me.

Eventually the water cools too much. I can't hide here anymore, and I crawl into a towel without bothering to dry myself first. Dripping wet, I enter the hall, wandering with grim determination into that darkened room at the very end.

He's sitting on the bed, his back to me. Faint moonlight sneaking through the curtains gives his hulking shape vague definition, dusting his hair and outlining his shoulders. They're hunched, radiating tension as I cross the threshold.

"Get out."

I don't. Instead, I let my steps carry me carefully over the bare floors, swaying to keep my balance. Both of my hands clutch the towel to my front, and in the end, I let it fall before mounting the mattress. "You don't get to storm away every time something pisses you off," I admonish, my tone deliberately soft. "You promised we could talk. So talk—"

"Stop it." He lurches to his feet and marches toward the windows, stubbornly eyeing the sliver of view visible. "Not now, Snow."

"Come here and *talk* to me." My voice rings out, stronger than it should be considering that I'm breathless, gasping for air.

He growls, almost snarling in frustration. "I said get the fuck out—"

"Then come to bed at least." I flatten my hand against the space beside me, loud enough for him to hear. "Come lay beside me. You look exhausted."

"No." His teeth are bared, visible in his snarling profile. But it's more of a plea than a refusal. Wavering control humanizes him like nothing else. I can see it fighting to combat the hate he seems desperate to cling to.

"Blake," I say, calling him by name. "Come lay beside me."

"I'm not a goddamn child." He turns, his body hunched forward, his eyes narrowed. "And I told you to get the fuck out—"

For the first time, he seems to realize just how I must appear: wet and naked, outstretched on his bed. Submitting. He swallows hard, his expression wavering.

As the cold air assaults my damp skin, I extend my hand. "Come."

A curse escapes through his clenched teeth, but the next second, he advances like a man possessed. The bed lurches beneath his weight as he lies down with his back to me. Carefully, I shift toward him, letting my fingers sink through his hair before he can rake his own through the wild curls. A sigh runs through him, jolting me in the aftermath. He doesn't relax into me. Never lets down his guard.

All he does is close his eyes with a begrudging hiss.

And I give him five minutes of silence. Of peace.

But then I can't resist.

"Do you remember?" I ask in a whisper, still stroking his hair as much as I dare. My fingers twitch sporadically, gliding through the wild strands, but he doesn't call me off. Yet. "You never could sleep when something was on your mind."

He tenses at the mention of the past, his unease acting like a shield, threatening to cut him off already. "I remember a lot of things about the past," he says, his tone laced with warning.

This time, I don't back down from the threat. "So do I."

He sighs but doesn't offer up a cutting retort. Progress? Or maybe an ominous sign.

"I remember that you used to pester me when I couldn't," he admits. "You'd never… You never let anything go."

I nod. "Not until you told me what was wrong."

The answer would always be a multitude of different thoughts or concerns most boys his age wouldn't bother to care about. His future. His family. The perils of the universe.

Something warns me that none of those topics are what's bothering him now. Not even close.

"You always told me in the end," I hear myself say almost wistfully. "Always…"

He doesn't respond this time—but it isn't until I hear the slow cadence of his breathing that I realize why.

He fell asleep.

* * *

I WAKE UP ALONE, unsurprisingly. He had another nightmare last night, shouting at phantoms in the dark. I closed my eyes and pretended to be asleep, though I doubt I fooled him. Despair and dread wafted from his skin like perfume, leaving a trail I can still follow as pale daylight illuminates the otherwise monochrome room.

He's waiting for me in the study, hunched over a breakfast tray piled high with too many foods to name. Bacon. Eggs. Bagels. I can't help imagining a fallen warrior presenting his opponent with a lavish feast as a form of surrender. Or a challenge.

He nods to the chair strategically placed before the spread, and a dare lurks beneath his gaze as he lifts a fork and extends it to me. "Eat."

Smart soldiers choose their battles wisely. With Hunter, I knew his deliveries of meals came only out of love and concern. Blake, however, merely wants to provoke. He needs me to refuse him now; it's the only way he knows how to turn the tables in retaliation for what little vulnerability I coaxed from him last night.

Today, I'm too damn tired to play the game. I sit as commanded and dutifully shovel a spoonful of yogurt into my mouth. He watches, scowling at the subtle defiance. Regardless, with every subsequent bite, his frown lessens. Soon, he's merely resigned as I polish off the serving of eggs.

"Your spoils, princess," he says mockingly while sliding a strip of paper in my direction. A check. One for a disgusting sum. "It's merely for show," he admits. "Our accountants will need to do the necessary paperwork for the transfer."

"I don't want it."

He looks like I've slapped him, and I race to clarify.

"I'd prefer you donated it. To Haven. In honor of women like Masha."

The mention of his sister only earns me a shred of leniency. "So content you are with Harrison Lloyd's money that you can't accept a dime of mine. Is that it, Snow?"

"No!" I push back from the table, gritting my teeth.

Only he can do this to me. Maybe he was right; we can only feel anything when together. Hate. And Lust. And *pain*—all at once. It's an unhealthy mixture, and every time we clash, I feel in danger of overdosing.

"I don't need your money. I don't need anyone's money."

"Don't lie to me," he warns, a cold smile shaping his mouth. "What about Daniel Ellingston's money? When he had some, anyway? You were more than willing to sell yourself to him for it."

It's a low blow, and it takes everything I have in me not to jump at the bait. Something must have happened in between his nightmare and when I woke up. Before that, even. A catalyst for him trying to pick a fight over the tabloid, perhaps. Something has him jumpy, itching for a battle, and my stomach sinks at the thought of what it might be.

"Don't forget that I sold myself to you, too," I say softly.

He frowns and retreats to the windows. The breathtaking view only seems to earn his ire. He scowls at the skyline. "Keep some of the money—"

"Half, then," I concede. "Donate half of it to Haven."

"Fine." He snatches up the check and stows it into his pocket. Then he sighs, and I see a hint of what has him so irritable. Unease. "I...I need..."

"Anything." Damn. I didn't mean to sound so eager. So fucking desperate. But I am. Extortion and blackmail—the only dynamic in which we seem to function. And I'll take it over the fighting or the insults. "I mean… Just tell me what you want me to do."

"Accompany me to a ball. Tomorrow night."

I blink. "A ball?"

"Rumors are rampant, Snow," he says, sounding almost neutral for once. He sinks onto the chair across from me and absently snatches up my hand. His fingers stroke the back of it, grinding warmth into my skin. "They're a bigger threat than expected. They're pressuring me to step down from the board. And I'll admit that I wanted to rip down everything with the Hollings name—but I spent almost half my life being groomed to run that company."

He still wants it. I can see the desire burning in his eyes. The same one that drives Hunter to lie and scheme his way toward the top of the corporate ladder. Power.

"So you need me there."

"No." He hesitates, trying to find the right words. "I *want* you there."

"I pick my dress?"

He shoots me an odd look. "Yes…"

"And no lying. No blackmail. No hidden extortion?" I almost expect him to say yes.

Instead, he shakes his head. "I'm asking you for a favor, Snow," he admits.

One with supposedly no strings attached.

"All right. I'll do it."

"Good." He releases me and rises to his feet. The sudden shift to his expression takes my breath away. It's so easy for him to switch emotion on and off.

A pang runs through my chest, a painful tendril of doubt. "But I want something in return."

"Oh?" He cocks his head. From his posture alone, I can guess what he suspects I'll demand: something humiliating or degrading. Something to shift the scales in my favor.

"I want you…" I inhale raggedly, meeting his gaze, hiding nothing. "I want *you* for a day. You. No lies. No games. No secrets. I want to talk to *you*."

No. I didn't mean to say that. But any excuse I may have dies in the face of his expression. He's guarded again, so damn wary. Like a predator eyeing a trap, he looks me over from head to toe.

"A day?"

"Are you afraid?" I wonder, letting my voice dip to a mocking octave. Perhaps joking can lessen the fear building in my veins, warning that I've gone too far, too fast. "The big, bad Blake Lorenz afraid of one little bargain?"

"A day," he repeats skeptically. "I thought I just paid for the privilege."

I flinch. "Don't mock me."

"I'm not." He runs a hand through his hair, knocking the wildest curls away from his face. "Fine. A day. To do what?"

I stare at my half-eaten plate, suddenly overwhelmed. From the corner of my eye, I notice the bookshelf. It's almost like I knew all along what I'd find there, taken from my purse, shoved to the very end of the selection of books. I stand, aware of him watching, and grab the leather volume before offering it to him.

"I want you to read to me."

"Snow…"

"Please."

He eyes the book like it's something dangerous. A venomous threat waiting to strike. He takes it anyway, crossing over to the threshold of the room, and I follow him without being beckoned, trailing his slow footsteps into the living room, over to the red throne-like chair.

He sits, cocking his head to issue another silent dare. This one I don't shy away from. I sink onto his lap, facing the view. Gradually, my body relaxes into his firmer one. His arms come around my waist as he opens the book. Then, grudgingly, he starts to read.

His voice sinks to a low, grating rasp that transports me to another time. Another place, with another man. But, for the first time, those two halves don't battle for supremacy. They merely coexist: memory and reality.

"And all the king's horses and all the king's men failed to put him back together again."

I shiver as he bats a strip of hair from my neck. And then he reads again.

And again.

And again, retelling the same tale until the daylight fades around us.

FOURTEEN

I STARTLE TO AWARENESS, curled in an awkward position against a firmer surface. Warm fingers part my hair into sections, and a part of me shivers in recognition. I know this feeling. This smell. More and more, my nostalgia acts like poison, and with every breath, I'm overwhelmed by memory.

We used to lie like this sometimes, huddled together like magnets. Though perhaps old Snowy would describe it more poetically: We used to exist together, like two halves of the same broken, abominable creature.

"You're so damn beautiful," he murmurs when I start to stir.

My heart pangs, uneasy. Only God knows how long he let me sleep like this, bundled in his arms. The city glows below us, a hotbed of neon fire and ebony darkness. Damn. I rub my eyes, mourning the loss of time.

"How late is it?" I whisper.

He shrugs, his eyes unreadable in the dim illumination. "Close to midnight."

"But still today." Heart in my throat, I turn, craning my neck so that I can see his face as I reach for the collar of the shirt. "You're still mine. I mean…under our agreement."

His jaw twitches as if to issue a refusal, but in the end, he lets me slowly unhook every button and drag the sleeves down one by one, leaving his chest bare. Why?

Maybe I'm finally letting myself believe what he said: that we can only ever understand each other like this. With physical touch over words. In silence and darkness, and devoid of trust.

His past will always be a barrier to overcome. If he won't tell me in words, then I'll have to feel the damage for myself.

And there's so much of it to discover.

My pulse surges as I stand, circle around to his back, and allow my fingers to knead his shoulders, sensing the tension coiled there. But my finger slips, finding a nasty patch of circular flesh, eerily smooth. "How?" I ask, though I already know the answer.

"Spoiled, rich bastards weren't very popular in prison," he says, his voice rough. "Especially perverted ones."

I swallow hard, tears burning behind my eyes, and withdraw my hands. "I'm sorry—"

"Don't." He grabs my wrist, forcing the contact.

Fighting apprehension back, I spread my fingers out again, flattening my palms along his spine. "C-can you tell me what happened—"

"*No.*" He shakes his head, softening his tone. "I-I mean…I can't go there, Snow. Not like this."

Fair enough. Slowly, I trace a ragged scar, cringing at the images my own imagination conjures: him pinned down, tortured. Because of me.

"How many are there?"

He hesitates. I can feel the vibrations of his lungs as they struggle to trap the answer inside.

"Twenty…thirty," he says finally. "I don't really know."

"Turn around."

He lets me guide him so that he's sitting with his back exposed, still facing the windows. A low sound catches in the air as I sink to my knees. It's like he can sense what I offer without having to see it: submission. I press the silent promise into his skin, brushing my lips along the ridge of his hip. Two scars etched onto him by my foolish mistake.

"Three," I murmur, lathing my tongue over another healed scar. "Four. Five."

He sucks in a breath with every exploration, and I can almost taste the need in his skin, which feeds the ache building inside me. It comes from nowhere, hot like fire— and he stokes it higher with every bit his grip on the edge of the chair tightens, straining the muscles in his back.

He says nothing when I stand and circle to his front. Then I kneel again, meeting his gaze. All I find is…reverence, for once, and it chokes me. Neon colors paint his skin as I shuffle between his legs and work on the front of his pants.

"Goddamn…" He inhales sharply and groans through an exhalation. His large hands cup my scalp, trembling even before I find his cock, which is hardening beneath my touch, and coax him from the cage of fabric. "Jesus, Snow."

I part my lips, and he bucks his hips, gripping my hair tightly in his fist. I'm stuffed to the brim with him. I'm choking on him, and it's a devastating death. I let him use me as he needs to, writhing his way to a slow-building orgasm that catches me off guard. He grunts, flooding my mouth, and instinct nearly overrides the need to please him. My throat contracts, but at the last second, I force myself to swallow.

Every drop.

"Shit!" He shoves me back and I release him with a wet pop, gasping for air. "So good." He smooths his fingers along my face, murmuring praises. "So fucking good."

I rest my cheek against his thigh as his fingers sink through my hair and pet the thick curls. And I don't know how long we remain like that.

I just wish it could fucking last.

FIFTEEN

BLAKE

HOLDING HER IN MY ARMS, I'm at the mercy of the cruelest weapon that Snowy Hollings has in her arsenal.

Peace. Nothing compares to this. Not the money I stand to gain from the destruction of her family's company. Not the years of torment she caused. Not even the true extent of the twisted web I've spun around her.

For a few minutes of golden dawn, she's perfect, her chest rising softly, her hair falling across her face—and the rest of the world fades away. I can pretend like this, for a second, that I've finally won her back.

Screw Lyle Harlow or Daniel Ellingston.

Screw the world waiting beyond these walls. Hearing her breathe, sensing the warmth from her skin, inhaling her scent shouldn't be more than enough to smother the rest.

But it is.

And…for fuck's sake, I want to hate her for it.

My fingers twitch, smoothing the shorn curls from her face. Her delicate bone structure plays with the faint rays of the rising sun, reflecting it off pure white skin. It paints her in a golden hue—a mocking reminder of what she is in the grand scheme.

A trophy I desired to win at all fucking costs.

But she's so much more.

We could have *been* so much more.

Groaning with regret, I stand and carry her in my arms to a leather chaise. She stirs lightly as I set her down on it and back away. Upstairs her scent chases me, even into the shower.

I do my best to scrub her away, pretending that it would be so easy. Snow clings to my skin, but a few lathers of soap can wash her off. It's futile of course—the woman is in my blood.

She's always been there.

Always.

And the moment she sees the monster I really am, she'll run away again.

This time for good.

Across the room, my phone vibrates on a dresser. It's as if the universe itself decided to issue a fucking challenge. *You think you can keep her?*

Think again.

"Blake." I snarl, answering the phone without looking at the ID. For a damn good reason.

No one sane would call this early.

"I warned you, you sick bastard," a man slurs into my ear. "I warned you to stay away from her. Don't hang up," he warns before I even start to lower the phone, intending to do just that. "You listen to me. You think I'll let you hurt her again? Hell no."

"And just how do you plan on doing that?" Somehow my tone comes out level. Some fucking how. Maybe it's instinct, warning me that this time, he isn't bluffing.

"I'll tell you how," he says. "I'll tell her the truth. That's what I'll do. I'll tell her everything. Everything you've done. I'll tell her…that it was you from the start."

* * *

SNOWY

HOT SUNLIGHT WARMS my naked skin. He must have placed me on the chaise in the living room without bothering to cover me.

Because rather than sleep, he spent the night watching over me. Sure enough, I sense his gaze as I draw my legs together and peel my eyes open to a high ceiling.

"Your breakfast is on the table." His voice comes from the upstairs landing, and like any addict, I chase it. He's there at the top of the steps, adjusting a pair of silver cufflinks, dressed to the nines in tailored business attire: a gray suit, a white shirt, and a navy tie. "Eat," he warns when he sees me mount the topmost step. Something unreadable crosses his expression. Uncertainty? Before I can place it for sure, he leans forward, swiping his lips along my forehead, and I'm rendered speechless. "Eat," he insists as I marvel over what's as close to an affectionate gesture as a man like him can give. "I need to go to the office, but I'll return later."

I watch him draw back, a frown tugging at my mouth. How soon the real world chooses to descend. It's as if there's this vicious tug of war between the moments when we come close to a semblance of intimacy and those when he feels farther away than ever before.

Resigned, I grab a robe from my room and find food waiting for me in the study. Blake hasn't left yet, and a thought begins to itch at the back of my skull, impossible to soothe. Ronan and Hunter. Placated or not, they'll happily ambush Blake Lorenz in public if they believe for a second he's hurt me in any way. Sighing, I reach for the office phone and dial the hotel directly, intending to leave a message.

Instead, Ronan answers, his voice gruff. "Who is this?"

"It's me," I stammer.

"Snowy, thank God. Where are you?" He sounds strained, as if it's taking all of his effort to keep from shouting. "I'll come. Just tell me where."

"I'm safe," I say, avoiding the question. "I promise. But…" I glance at the clock. Blake is already late, but Ronan? Never. "Why aren't you at the office?"

"Snowy, what are you talking about?"

"I… Didn't you get a seat on the board?"

He laughs coldly. "You mean that shitty olive branch Lorenz offered? One seat for Hunter and me to fight over between the two of us? I let Hunter take it."

One seat?

The receiver slips from my grip, landing on the desk. I can hear Ronan calling for me, but nothing registers over the rage surging through my veins, deafening me. I'm racing into the foyer before I know it, catching him heading toward the elevator.

"I'll have a car sent around seven to bring you to the…" He stiffens at my expression. When I form a fist and smash it against his chest, he doesn't even flinch.

"One seat?" I shout. "One goddamn seat?"

"It's all I could risk," he says, not even trying to hide it. "With my position already in peril, I would have been laughed out of the building if I'd proposed to restore two

Hollingses now. I made a calculated move by installing Hunter first. I always intended to add Ronan when I could afford to spend the capital."

"A move," I echo. "Perhaps a better word is a *game*. Another way for you to watch my brothers fight over their goddamn birthright."

Danger flashes in his eyes. "And what about my birthright, Snow?"

"I don't know," I admit, stepping back. "I don't even know who you are anymore. You aren't Brandt Lloyd."

Anger. It hardens him like nothing else, twisting his features into a chilling mask. "And who do we have to thank for that?"

I shake my head, blinking rapidly. "I won't let you make me spend the rest of my life apologizing. Not after everything you've done to me!"

"Then don't," he says, his teeth gritted. "And I won't dare expect you to give me anything else. Feel free to leave, Snow."

Exasperation forms a pathetic response. "I don't want to fight. I just… I just want you to stop pushing me away."

He turns, heading for the door. "Stop letting me." Then the elevator doors open and close with him behind them and he's gone.

* * *

I DON'T STORM from the penthouse, crying tears of despair. I pace instead, tearing at my hair as I run over every word. Every phrase. Every kiss and fuck and touch. My parting words ring truer than ever: *Stop pushing me away.*

And his are equally enlightening.

Stop letting me.

God, everything about him feels like a test. A game. How far can he push me before I run? Before I break? How far can Snowy bend before she lets him down again?

A part of me rails at the treatment. How dare he dangle trust like a carrot he'll never let me have? But there's the true heart of the matter: I did have it once. By all intents and purposes, I threw it away.

But that doesn't mean I deserve this. Or do I?

Doubt haunts me every fucking minute I stay within these walls. Rather than leave, I'm driven farther into the maze of rooms, eventually finding my way inside the navy one. Without thinking, I finger an emerald gown and then rip it from the hanger. Another. A whole damn rack of clothing tossed onto the floor. I once thought these pieces of silk and satin made me who I was—Snowy Hollings. But who am I really?

A rumpled pile of couture gowns can't tell me.

Panting, I work my way through the entire closet, grasping, tearing, throwing. Fittingly, the last dress I reach for holds the most significance.

I have no idea how he found it—or if he even looked inside the black garment bag. I hid it at the very back of my old wardrobe, if only to stop myself from trying it on every five damn minutes.

My fingers shake as I undo the zipper now, freeing the dress for the first time in months. As always, an appreciative gasp catches in my throat. This floor-length creation of white silk was my dream wedding dress. Ironically, I chose it without my fiancé in mind. It was the gown of a fairytale princess, with lace sleeves, a sloping neckline, and a body-hugging bodice. In lieu of a veil, I intended to wear flowers in my hair, otherwise adorned only by my wedding ring.

But that was then. Now, it's just another worthless item, but I stop shy of tossing it aside. Instead, I carry it into the bathroom like a spoil of war.

If Blake Lorenz wants to play a game of guilt and blame, then I'll take the next round.

Carefully, I drape my gown over the counter. Then I face my reflection, eyeing the woman staring back. Her eyes are reddened, but she hasn't cried yet. Gritting my teeth, I ensure that she won't.

Then I turn to the shower and run the water as hot as I can stand it.

Hot like hellfire.

SIXTEEN

THE FACT that I find a car waiting for me at seven feels more like an ominous warning than a gesture of good faith. I shiver as the driver ushers me into the back seat, taking care to ensure that my dress doesn't get caught in the door.

A ten-minute drive later, we arrive before an exclusive venue on the outskirts of Mayfield. Blake didn't pick just any event to stage his apparent innocence. He chose the Hollings-sponsored benefit gala—an event that once was the mainstay of our societal events. It blows my mind that I forgot about it in all the chaos.

Despite—or perhaps because of—the rumors swirling around its newest board president, reporters are out in droves tonight, positioned near the entrance of the ballroom behind metal barricades. The moment I step from the car, a frenzy of flashing cameras and shouted questions ensues.

Apparently, my date decided against meeting me at the door tonight. So I enter alone, using one hand to maneuver the skirt of my dress while advancing with my head held high. A pair of ushers dressed in tuxedos allow me inside and I join the fray, a fallen princess among a sea of watchful enemies.

My most daunting opponent doesn't use stealth or violence to unnerve me tonight, however. I find him in the foyer, directing guests, his smile gallant. Until he spots me, that is, and his mouth falls into a hard line that takes my breath away.

His narrowed gaze slices through my delicate ensemble like a razor, ripping down to the bone underneath. I can't stop my fingers from self-consciously covering my breasts, and the motion only makes a muscle in his jaw lurch. Two involuntary steps take him away from the pretty woman in a red cocktail dress he'd been directing, and I can tell he intends to turn back, ignore this slight.

But he can't. Not when I've been this fucking brazen.

"I take it that no other option was suitable?" he murmurs, snatching my wrist the moment he's close enough while positioning his body so that no one else can see the possessive motion.

Up close, I sense just how angry he really is. Fury bellows from his nostrils, mingled with every harsh exhale he takes. His fingers twitch against my skin, reminding me of his earlier confession: *I see that girl and I want to crush her.*

"Tell me I look beautiful," I command him, my voice weak. Beautiful even quaking with rage and pain. Beautiful even in another man's wedding dress.

Something chilling alights his features as his mouth cocks into a cruel excuse for a smile. "You always look beautiful," he declares. "Fucking beautiful."

"Now, kiss me." I can't stop my teeth from skewering my lower lip as his attention turns to it. "Make it good, darling. Good enough to convince everyone here that I don't want to strangle you or that you don't want to…" More-than-strangle me. God, the violence promised in his gaze is too horrifying to give voice to. "Think you can manage that?" I settle on daring.

He scoffs. The next second, I'm in his arms, his palm pressed against my lower back, burning me through satin and lace. His mouth claims mine without warning, his teeth gnashing my tongue when no one can see. I jump at the sharp pinch, but he growls in answer, licking at the claimed flesh. I'm gasping as he pulls away and lowers his mouth to my ear.

"And when do I get to rip this fucking dress from your body and show you just how *beautiful* I think you really are?"

I swallow hard and brace my hand against his chest to find enough leverage to back away a single step. "After you make some speech filled with lies about how much I mean to you. How much you care about me. How much—" I suck in a breath. Damn it. My eyes burn, blinking frantically. I force air into my lungs and soldier on. "How much you love me.

Go on. This is my company too. I don't want to see it ruined. But, after this, I've given you everything."

And he couldn't even give me one promise to cling to.

"Snow—" He grips my arm tighter when I try to pull away. "You wait for me," he demands, his tone rough. "I'll know if you don't and I swear I'll come after you and drag you back. You wait for me."

I pull away, breathing rapidly as I delve deeper into the crowd, imagining him hunting every step I take. But when I finally turn to get my bearings, he's gone. I'm alone in a realm of unfamiliar faces all jostling for a look at the woman with bloodshot eyes in a beautiful dress.

"You certainly know how to make an entrance."

I flinch as someone loops their arm around mine. Sloane. She's cutting a stunning figure in a black gown almost as revealing as the one I wore at the auction.

She tugs me confidently through the center of the room, smirking as we draw attention with every head turned. "I didn't think you'd come."

A hitch snuck into her voice. Perhaps I stole her chance at the spotlight once again? I don't have the energy to decipher her motives. Instead, I let her parade me around like a shiny token, unable to avoid my "date" for the evening.

It's like he positions himself to constantly remain in my line of sight though he never once looks my way. He mingles, and laughs, and talks up a room of people who secretly think him to be a predator. As charming as he can be, however, none of them dare say as much to his face. I now understand why he's maintained his precarious spot at the company for so long when any other man would have been driven out for less scandal.

He's Blake Lorenz and the world has no choice but to acknowledge that fact. He spins lies so emphatically that you start to question the visible truth.

"You're distracted tonight," Sloane teases, her breath tinged with her fourth glass of champagne. "Do tell. Do tell."

"Why?" I disentangle my arm from hers, unconvinced by her playful frown. "So that whatever I say can show up in tomorrow's papers?"

She winces. "I'm sorry. Beautiful Snowy, desired by all. I didn't think you'd mind."

Something in her tone draws my attention. Pain? Whatever it is, she dispels it with a charming grin. "Don't be too upset?"

"Why Daniel?" I find myself asking. "I know you... I know—"

"I was never the one he wanted," she says, her gaze fixed somewhere far beyond this room, I suspect.

"What are you saying?"

She stiffens and shakes her head before plastering a fake smile onto her otherwise blank expression. "Nothing. Oh, he looks dangerous."

I follow the line of her gaze, confused by the statement. Oh God. Marching onto a raised dais serving as a makeshift stage, his eyes aglow, Blake Lorenz looks *more* than dangerous.

He looks insane, hunting for me in the crowd as he takes the microphone.

"I'd like to make an announcement," he declares, and it's as if the whole world stops, turns, and waits.

Dread forms a weight around my heart, growing heavier with every second he holds my gaze. So many unspoken words pass between us in this instant, which terrify me when he finally opens his mouth again.

"Thank you all for coming. Especially given current... rumors swirling around myself."

An audible murmur runs through the crowd. Like any manipulative bastard, he knows the best way to capture every ear here—through intrigue and spectacle.

Satisfied by his captive audience, he continues. "With that in mind, I'd like to start off this night by announcing that not only will I be pledging a generous donation to the Haven Project, but I am officially making Hollings Incorporated a designated benefactor of such an amazing charity."

A part of me bristles at how easily he utilized my donation for his own needs. Does the man have no ounce of shame? Or perhaps he does. There's something in his gaze that sends my heart hammering against my chest. Something raw and real, impossible to ignore: guilt. He doesn't hide it from me for once. He lets me in, allowing me closer than I've ever been to the emotions he guards, even while across a spacious ballroom.

"Haven and the ideas it represents mean more to me than a worthy cause," he continues, his voice thick. "Rape, sexual abuse, and assault are the taboo deeds we usually regulate to tabloids of sordid news stories. But you and I know the dirty, dark secret lurking in most homes, even here in Mayfield. The black eye you use makeup to disguise. The bruises we can't explain away. The illicit touches we excuse because it hurts too much to call it what it is…" He looks at me directly and so many words spill into the air between us.

A million secrets.

A hundred memories.

Perhaps a single, earnest apology.

It feels like an eternity passes this way—but in the end, it must be no longer than a few seconds. Clearing his throat, he turns to the crowd still hung on his every word. "It hurts. So you turn your shame and embarrassment into anger, and you direct it at the people who mean the most to you."

I inhale sharply, steeling myself for what he might confess next. His tormented expression claims it's brutal.

"When I… When I was assaulted," he says hoarsely to audible gasps of shock that erupt throughout the room, "I blamed myself. I blamed the people who I thought were supposed to protect me. And I punished them and myself. But now I realize, even after the physical abuse was over, by continuing to hate, I was only destroying myself and continuing to be a victim instead of a survivor. It's organizations like Haven that offer resources to help young boys and girls who felt as powerless and helpless, as I once did, move on from being victims to survivors... Thank you."

He leaves the stage in a rush as my mind spins, a whirlwind of agony. He meant it, every word. I may not know the man he's become, but I knew Brandt. I knew that tortured look in his gaze, lingering just long enough for him to tell his secrets to me. Only me. I remember the nights his father antagonized him the most. And I remember what snippets of his ordeal in prison Blake Lorenz let slip: *Once, they tried to show him what rape was, Snow.*

"Heavy stuff," Sloane murmurs beside me, snapping me back to the present. She downs her last glass of champagne and grabs my arm. "Come. I want to get fresh air." She's in the process of fishing a cell phone from the cleavage of her dress. It's buzzing, and she frowns at the number before stowing the item back in place. "Come."

"But..." My gaze tears from regal figure to figure, hunting for a familiar face.

There. He's fixated on me, slowly pushing his way through the crowd. They part adoringly. By baring his soul, he's won their fickle hearts over. But mine?

"Just five minutes," Sloane pleads, tugging me forward.

I expect her to head for one of the terraces overlooking a courtyard with a bubbling fountain. Instead, she takes a turn down a winding hallway and shoulders a metal door open.

"Where are we?" My nose wrinkles in the blisteringly cold air. Rather than a beautiful, scenic view of one of the venue's gardens, I make out the shape of a dumpster and a white van parked along a narrow alley. It must be a service entrance of some kind.

Giggling, Sloane tugs me forward, forcing me to heft the skirt of my gown with my free hand.

"Where are we going…" Motion catches the corner of my eye. Then pain. *Wham!*

Stars float across my vision. The world tilts violently sideways, and something firm catches my fall. I throw my arms out, a desperate attempt to get my bearings.

Then blackness.

SEVENTEEN

CONSCIOUSNESS RETURNS IN SLOW, painful drips, and only snippets of sound give me context to my surroundings. I'm lying flat, tasting salt. Night air nips at my skin as the faint roars of traffic allude to the fact that I'm outside. Near the gala?

Scuffling footsteps bolster that suspicion. I recognize the distinct click of high heels, echoed by a heavier, steadier set of footfalls.

"What...what are you doing?" a woman demands, her thickening accent betraying her fear. Sloane?

I try turning in her direction, but my limbs won't obey. My head feels too heavy. Agony shoots through my skull, focused around a single, throbbing point. God...was I struck with something?

"You weren't supposed to hurt her! You were just supposed to—"

A sudden crack echoes and the woman goes silent. Alarm doesn't even have the chance to sink into my limbs before a sound like a car engine revs into gear and the world sways beneath me. Someone has my arm in a vise grip, using it like a leash to shove me against a firm surface. I scramble to regain my bearings, running my fingers over an uneven material in a desperate bid to place it. Soft. Rugged. Carpeting?

"Don't move." An unfamiliar touch shocks my cheek.

That voice…

"Not so fast," I'm warned when I attempt to move. Something chafes against my eyelids when I try to open them, obscuring my vision. "If you can hear me, just nod."

Swallowing hard, I do, once.

"Good."

The pressure withdraws, and my heart races as I try to settle on a possible culprit. Ronan? Hunter? Again, I'm sure I know that voice, but my throbbing head fails to come up with a name. Someone gruff, nervous…well-spoken?

"You'll be safe, as long as you do what I say," my captor warns, furthering the mystery.

Licking my lips, I risk his ire to ask, "Who…who are you?"

There's no reply. Silence mingles with the perpetual sirens that wail throughout the city and my fear only grows. We're moving, I realize. Fast. Away from the venue to somewhere unknown. In a car or a van?

"Where are you taking me?" I croak, trying once again to probe for answers.

For the second time, I receive no response. In its absence, my headache worsens, and pain feeds a million dangerous suspicions.

"Someone offered me more, Little Hollings," Lyle Harlow claimed.

Would the man really be so bold?

Suddenly, the world comes to a stop and I'm jostled onto my side. A door opens and cool air tickles my cheek, alerting me to the fact that we're not outside, but somewhere enclosed. A garage? A hand latches onto my shoulder before I can be sure, and I'm shoved upright onto trembling legs.

"Move," I'm commanded. A warning grip on the back of my throat keeps me from resisting the contact as my captor steers me forward. He's panting.

Straining my ears, I strive to notice any detail I can. Silence, mostly. It encases us in an echo chamber of unsteady footsteps and frantic breaths. There's only two of us, a fact my captor seems desperate to disguise. He's moving unsteadily, creating the illusion of a million pattering footsteps.

"Don't fight," he warns, tightening his grip until I nod frantically in agreement. "Keep moving."

We're in a narrower space now, where the air feels even more enclosed. I jump as a door creaks, opening and closing behind us. We're alone, and the figure I'm with towers above me. Their breath heats my shoulder blades, bearing down on my scalp.

"Stop." He shoves against a firm surface before I can comply on my own. "Sit."

I manage to perch myself on what feels like a metal chair without falling. The skirt of my gown bellows out around me, creating a makeshift barrier between me and the man I sense steadily advancing.

"Put your hands behind your back. Please."

And suddenly, it clicks: I know that gallant tone of voice. Even now, he can't resist the suave air of politeness bred into him—a benefit of ten years of finishing school.

"Daniel." My voice rasps, echoing off our surroundings. "Daniel, is that you—"

"Shut up." He doesn't hit me, but his hand lands over my shoulder, imparting a subtle warning. "Do it," he rasps, damn near begging. "Put your arms behind your back, Snowy."

When I do, he takes them both. Something thin is wound around both of my wrists, tethering them together tightly.

"Now, open your mouth."

Terror threatens to shatter the cohesiveness of my thoughts. *Focus, Snow,* I tell myself. *Don't panic...*

"Now!"

My lips part woodenly, allowing something rough to be shoved between them, which prohibits any attempts to speak. Cloth? Sweat lingers in the fabric, betraying that it's an item of clothing. A glove? Tie?

"I'm going to take the blindfold off," my captor says as his footsteps once again move behind me.

Suddenly, the cloth over my eyes is withdrawn, which allows me to make out a darkened room lit only by a dim floor lamp. Dingy carpet and water-stained walls give no clue of my surroundings—somewhere far beyond the glimmer of downtown Mayfield, I suspect.

Somewhere secluded.

"I'll only tell you this once, Snowy," my captor warns, his tone rough, nearly imploring. "I don't want to hurt you." A shadow flickers over the floor, tall and slender. When he finally comes into my line of sight, I'm grateful for the gag stifling my gasp.

In the harsh, artificial lightning, Daniel Ellingston III looks like a stranger—though I suppose he always has been. A few short months have left his once-coifed blond hair wildly overgrown, with lanky strands falling into his bloodshot eyes. His gray suit is crumpled and unkempt. Faint body odor warns that he hasn't washed in a while, either—him, the man who groomed himself better than I did while we dated.

Alarm spurs my faltering heartbeat, stiffening my posture. At a glance, I can tell he's alone. But for how long?

"Don't look at me like that." Groaning, he runs his fingers through his hair, flicking the worst strands away from his face as his lips contort into a shadow of his infamous grin. "Even now, I can't seem to impress you, can I, Snowy?"

Something warns me not to react. I stare ahead blankly, tracking every unsteady step as he paces in a small circle before me. He's holding an object in his right hand, something he absently taps against his thigh. My brain recognizes the shape, but a part of me refuses to put the proper name to it. The Daniel Ellingston I knew would never carry a gun, especially not one formed of stark black metal. It simply didn't mesh with his image.

What could have transpired in nearly three months since his disgrace to push him to this point?

"I can explain everything." He frowns at the weapon before he tucks it behind his back and out of sight. "You just wouldn't understand," he stammers. "That's why I couldn't tell you before."

Tell me what? I do my best to nonverbally convey the question as calmly as I can. Blank expression. Imploring gaze.

Suddenly, he whirls on his heel. "That smug bastard had it all fucking planned, I bet," he growls, still running his free hand along his scalp. "That motherfucker. He turned you against me. How is that for irony? So much for hating the fucking Hollingses—"

No. The thought feels instinctive, like the little voice most people sense before touching a hot stove or running over pavement visibly slick with ice. *Don't. This might hurt. Tread carefully.*

So much for hating the fucking Hollingses…

"You already know." Daniel pauses his manic march and cocks his head, studying me with a shrewd gaze.

The disguise I fought to uphold fails. I can't stop my eyes from lowering to the gun. He's tapping it again, recklessly against his thigh.

Chuckling, he lifts it, his expression puzzled. "That bastard is more dangerous than he looks. I have to, Snowy," he says in a rush. "I have to carry this damn thing now because of him. And you know it. I can see it on your face."

My face: lips flattened; wide, watering eyes; a throat that won't stop swallowing hard, desperate to fight back the emotion threatening to overwhelm me.

"I thought he'd gotten to you," Daniel says with a hollow laugh that chills me to the core. "But he hasn't, has he? You were always too smart for your own good, Snowy. I should have told you from day fucking one."

Told me what? This time, I don't want to know the answer. It's like I can sense it unfurling anyway, in the shadowy recesses of my mind where only the darkest fears dwell.

"I did what I did," Daniel admits, cutting his gaze beyond my head. "It was wrong. I know that—but I would have never gotten the idea if he hadn't... Fuck!" He slams the butt of the gun into his hip, cursing under his breath. "I should have known the bastard had an ulterior motive. You were never supposed to know. It was never supposed to go public."

A sickening sensation creeps through my stomach, threatening to upend everything balanced precariously inside it.

It congeals into a chilling suspicion that haunts my thoughts before Daniel even parts his lips to utter, "That bastard Blake Lorenz. He set me up, Snowy. That bastard took everything from me. And, now, he's stolen you too."

* * *

"I SHOULD HAVE KNOWN BETTER than to ever trust that son of a bitch," Daniel snarls, though I barely even hear him. His voice takes on a dream-like quality, like something recalled from a nightmare. Distant and formless.

For a moment, this dark, dingy room fades and all I can see is the beautiful backdrop of my dream penthouse and the man who dwells inside it. His blue eyes meet mine unflinchingly, devoid of a single ounce of shame.

"What did you expect?" I imagine him snarling. "After all, you hurt me first. You betrayed me first. You were stupid enough to fall in love with me all over again..."

"Snowy?"

I flinch as warmth brushes my cheek. Daniel. He's frowning down at his fingers, and at a glance, I see why. The tips are glistening red. Dread lances through my chest as my skull throbs in response. How badly am I injured?

"I didn't mean to hurt you," he says, his voice thick. He reaches for me again, but I can't stop myself from cringing. He stiffens and then lowers his hand with a sigh. "I didn't… But I had to get you away from him. You don't understand!"

So tell me. The words wind up garbled by the gag, but he nods in understanding regardless.

"I can't. I…" He stops pacing, balanced on the tips of his toes like a cornered animal ready to bolt. "What the fuck was that?" His head swivels toward the door as his hand shakily raises the gun.

My heart lurches at how his finger twitches over the trigger, and another indiscernible moan breaks from my throat.

"Shhh," he snaps in annoyance, turning to me once more.

He approaches my chair to stroke the side of my face. Clenching my jaw, I do everything possible not to resist the motion. At the same time, I tug my wrists, testing the strength of the binds: alarmingly tight. Inhaling through my nose, I attempt to meet Daniel's gaze, but his emerald irises are unfocused, darting toward the corners of the room.

Where Blake looks perpetually exhausted, Daniel seems like a zombie, reanimated to react on only the basest human responses.

"I know it was wrong, Snowy," he says. "But I thought... We were supposed to be married when it happened. I would have control of the Hollings Estate and you'd never have to know. I'd keep your brothers on, of course. Everything would be as it was..."

He's rambling and my brain struggles to catch up. *Married. Estate. My brothers.*

All of it leads to one chilling conclusion: Daniel wasn't just a greedy fool caught up in an investigation's web. He planned this. He planned to steal my family's company out from under me all along.

And only one man was devious enough to show him how.

"He came to me six months ago," Daniel says hollowly. "Not that I can fucking prove it. He's a clever, clever son of a bitch. He made it seem like an easy way to consolidate my power in the industry. He'd take a small cut and come on as a primary investor—your brothers jealously guarded their board of directors. Damn... You can't blame me for wanting *some* shred of control. They were so fucking arrogant."

And for a good reason. Almost overnight, Daniel managed to betray the sliver of trust placed in him and wreaked havoc on my family from within.

But he couldn't have done half as much damage alone.

"He said that all he wanted was the company," Daniel continues. "Just a few goddamn shares. He wouldn't humiliate your family in any way. All I had to do was allow him to invest and we would… It doesn't fucking matter!" He shakes his head sternly and refocuses his gaze on me. "It all went to shit, Snowy," he croaks. "Suddenly, the fucking Feds were on my doorstep. Everything was in the papers. You hated me. And that sick son of a bitch. He's dangerous, Snowy. He has a bulldog that he keeps on a leash. Some thug named Harley or Larow—"

Harlow. That name echoes off the inside of my skull in a morbid loop. Harlow. Lyle Harlow. Lyle Harlow.

"It's funny… That was the contact who fed me all the information I needed to make the false investments. And he threatened you, Snowy. Threatened to hurt you if I didn't leave the city—"

Another muffled sound escapes me, garbled by the gag. Even I can't decipher the plaintive howl. Perhaps a simplistic word: no. No, no, *no*. I'm shaking my head before I realize it, blinking back burning beads of moisture that escape down my cheeks in searing rivulets.

Daniel bought my contract with Harlow. But that meant another man had introduced him to my father's old lackey. Another man who knew him prior. Had he known the truth all along? Toying with me. Torturing me for days until I finally broke down and revealed the truth.

Was everything that happened since just another lie? Some sick, twisted way for him to save face? I'd thought him the shattered remnant of the boy I loved, but maybe he was more of a monster than a man all along…

"Listen to me, Snowy," Daniel implores, continuing to speak even as my thoughts drift and dissipate.

I'm far beyond this room, reliving every moment and every word. Every fucking touch and caress. Every lie. They're all poison, building in my veins, choking the breath from my lungs.

"Snowy!"

I blink and find Daniel in front of me, his eyes worriedly scanning my face.

"Stay with me—"

"Get the fuck away from her."

That voice. Like a hook, it sinks into my soul and my entire being swivels toward the sound. Rather than a knight in shining armor, I find a shadowed figure dominating the doorway.

He looks like hell, burning and ruthless. Wind has disrupted his curls as if he ran all the way from the ballroom. But he's unarmed, and I suspect he came alone. Honed like a laser, his gaze finds me and narrows, brimming with rage.

"She's bleeding, you fool," Blake says coldly. "What the fuck did you do—"

"Shut up!"

Blake can't see Daniel's face from his position, but I can. Fear sinks into my muscles, and my wrists flex, testing the give of my binds again, ignoring the pain. Dread ramps up, coaxing a terrifying lullaby out of my heartbeat. *Thump. Thumpthumpthump.*

"Just shut the fuck up—"

"Can you hear me, Snow?" Blake eyes me without flinching, even as the barrel of a gun sways in his direction.

In this moment, I could stomach anything—any ounce of disgust or grudging concern. Anything but this: his eyes practically glowing, fixated on my face, begging for a response. *Can you hear me?*

My chin jerks in acknowledgment and he nearly deflates with relief.

"Good. Listen to me, Snow. Everything's going to be all right."

"Don't fucking move!" Daniel has both hands on the gun now, but he can barely steady it enough to point it in Blake's direction. The barrel sways back and forth, dangerously erratic.

"Put the gun down, you fool," Blake snarls. "Before you blow your damn head off—"

"Or yours."

I've never heard Daniel sound so unpolished. So... desperate. He's shaking from head to toe, his skin alarmingly pale—and I realize I was wrong before. He's *terrified.* Riling him up now is the wrong course of action to take—even Blake seems to realize that.

He raises his hands in a gesture of surrender, though his posture doesn't betray anything of the sort. "Put the gun down." As he speaks, he inches forward a careful step.

"I said don't move—"

"Daniel," I rasp, or at least I attempt to around my gag. "Please... Don't do this."

"You believe *him*?" He turns to me, his expression stricken. "Do you?" His hand twitches, and the mouth of the gun yawns before me, endless.

"Stop it, you fool." My blood runs cold at the apparent fear cracking that impervious baritone I know so well. For the first time Blake Lorenz sounds terrified. "Lower the fucking gun," he snarls. "Or point it at me. Focus on *me*—"

"Shut up!" Wide, Daniel's gaze darts from me to Blake. "Now, you pretend like you give a damn about her?" he wonders. "Bullshit! Maybe I should just do it, huh?" The gun centers over me again, but this time his hand holds it steady. "Maybe this is the only way you'll fucking feel a shred of guilt. *You* did this—"

"Daniel, please." My wrists are on fire, but I think I have enough leverage to slide one hand free. Just a little more...

"What the hell was that?" A floorboard creaks, drawing Daniel's attention over his shoulder. Suddenly, his back is to me, his movements erratic. "I said don't fucking move!"

Panic urges my body into motion. I wrench at the binds, my eyes watering as agony crawls up either limb. Skin peels and gives way in searing shreds—until, at last, freedom! The sudden shift in motion throws me forward and off the chair.

"No!" Daniel lunges toward me, his aim unsteady. "Stay there—"

"Get the hell away from her!"

Just like that, chaos descends. A heavy force slams into my body, knocking me to the floor, as a monstrous sound tears through my eardrums. The world explodes into a mixture of clamor and noise. I taste blood. Hear church bells, constantly ringing.

Ringing.

Then…silence.

A coppery scent reaches my nostrils as the weight pinning me to the floor suddenly goes limp, rolling off me. Footsteps tear from the room, leaving me alone with the downed figure.

And all I see is blue.

Glazed.

Empty.

Dying blue.

EIGHTEEN

BRANDT NEVER LET me win our games, not even when I begged to. He always made me fight for a victory, but he never played dirty or used underhanded tricks to ensure one. Blake Lorenz, on the other hand, plays unfairly without even trying. Only a true monster would die now, when I hate him so much. When I'd kill him myself for answers.

He *can't* die now.

The thought hammers against the inside of my skull as I race down the hospital wing on trembling legs.

A doctor dressed in white awaits me at the end of the corridor, his face grim as he surveys some documents attached to a clipboard. "He'll need surgery," he says, his tone stern. "Afterward, we'll have a better idea of where to go from there."

He rushes through a set of double doors before I can question him. Alone, all I can do is sit and wait. It feels like hours pass, though in the end, I'm not sure how long it takes for a nurse to finally emerge from the cordoned off area, her mouth slack with exhaustion.

One look at me and she recoils. When I glance down, I see why: my beautiful, white, ridiculous dress is stained with blood. I'm shaking. Dried tears streak my cheeks, containing smeared remnants of makeup.

"M-Ms. Hollings?" Blinking, the nurse regains her composure. "He's in a room now," she says in a rush. "You can see him…if you want." She utters the last three words hesitantly, her gaze on my face.

I'm too tired to tailor my expression, and I can only guess what she finds in it. Terror?

"O-okay," I stammer, lurching to my feet. My heart pounds as I follow her through a maze of winding hallways, and I can't help the pathetic metaphor that comes to mind: I feel like, with every step, I'm traversing the landscape of my soul —or how I imagine it to be, anyway. Clean and white, save for that one realm only he could dominate. It smells like blood and is stained with shadow and stark reality.

The moment I reach the doorway to his room, I realize that once again Blake Lorenz has already foiled my plans. He's standing, a sight that I have to blink twice just to accept. One of his hands clings to an IV pole for balance while the other holds a cell phone to his ear.

"Find her. Please," he demands, his voice rasping and hoarse. "I need to see her. Just find her—" He breaks off abruptly, spotting me in the doorway. Slowly, he lowers the phone, even as the distorted voice of someone blares from the speaker. "Snow," he says, his eyes widening. "You're here."

"Not for long." I don't intend to sound so cold, but I don't try to soften my tone either. He looks awful. A hastily tied hospital gown leaves his backside exposed, baring his scars to the harsh daylight that enhances every brutal imperfection in the flesh. A bandage clings to his shoulder, already seeping droplets of blood in some places. The doctor claimed the bullet missed an artery by mere millimeters, saving him a lethal or crippling blow.

But it's yet another scar added to the damage he already bears.

"You shouldn't be standing," I hear myself croak.

The next second, he's on the bed, eyeing me from behind a fringe of hair. "What did he tell you?"

He doesn't sound angry for once, or suspicious, or defensive. Just so damn tired. I doubt he slept longer than an hour judging from his bloodshot gaze. He's running on mere fumes now, determined to avoid letting his guard down even for a second. "I know you're angry," he says. "Just let me explain."

"Explain?" I parrot the word in a hollow voice I don't even recognize. "Maybe you can explain how you knew Lyle Harlow before you used him to ruin my family's company."

He winces, gritting his teeth. "I…"

"Were you lying all along?" God, it's unfair how my voice carries more pain than his does. His wound is superficial but mine were always soul-deep, impossible to heal. "Why? Just tell me why? Did you enjoy watching me suffer?"

"No!" He forms a fist and slams it into the bed. When I jump, he clears his throat and forces the fingers apart. "No… I came back, needing money. My father's businesses were under attack in Europe."

I say nothing, remembering what he mentioned about Masha's husband.

"Admittedly, I could have taken any company," he adds. "But real estate is my forte and I needed enough collateral to sever my family from his creditor, once and for all."

"So you took over Hollings enterprises," I deduce.

He nods, his expression weary. "More than that. I wanted all of it—but you have to believe me when I tell you that I had nothing against you or your brothers. Not at first. You were cogs in the machine, insignificant in the grand scheme. But then…" He swallows hard, his gaze darkening. "I reached out to Lyle Harlow for assistance. Your father wasn't the only one who utilized his 'talents'—but the bastard saw right through me, I don't know how. He called me out by name, and he mentioned you. How you jumped at Forrest's beck and call, so eager to do his bidding. I spent years believing the worst Snow, but I never hated you. Not like I did then, hearing him describe it. Then seeing you…"

He blinks as if remembering where he is.

"I lost my fucking mind, seeing you again. Healthy. Happy. I'd always imaged you the same shy, awkward little girl, but you weren't. You were living, when I was just a shell of who I used to be. I can't even think of myself as Brandt anymore."

I remember a chilling snippet from the night he took my virginity. *I'm not him,* he swore. *Not anymore…*

"Still, I planned to avoid you. Leave you to Daniel. But then I saw you." He laughs brokenly, shaking his head. "You weren't just living, but you were *thriving.* Perfect, beautiful Snowy Hollings without a care in the world—"

"You sent the book to my engagement gala," I croak. His slow nod compounds the agony ripping through my chest. Of course he did.

"I wanted to see how you'd react," he admits. "I wondered if you'd even fucking remember."

But I did remember.

I could never forget.

"And then you came to me at the offices," he adds. "And again at my private residence. It's like you were haunting me, I couldn't fucking escape." He sounds crazed, a man possessed. "Seeing you again drove me insane, Snow. I can't explain it, and I know that it doesn't excuse what I did. But I was so convinced you deserved it, every fucking bit. Until the letters. Until I heard you say what Forrest did and I realized…I was no better than that son of a bitch." He looks up, meeting my gaze directly. His eyes are more than bloodshot now—they're blazing, welling with emotion that takes my breath away. Regret? Can I trust it?

God, I don't know.

"I'm not asking for forgiveness," he insists. "Not even reconciliation. I just want…I just want us to start over. Not Snowy. Not Brandt. Just two people who made fucked up mistakes. That's all I want."

I should leave, I know I should. At the same time, a part of me recognizes that this may be my only chance to do something. Say something. Hurt him. Kick him. Scream. Anything.

My lips part, but all I can muster in the end is…

"Lie down before you rip your wound back open."

He does, a reluctant frown tugging at his mouth. "Snow—"

"Stop!" It's not enough to refuse him, I have to throw my hands out in front of me, a physical barrier against more lies. "I need you to listen to me, for once."

Warily, he stays, but one of his hands remains outstretched, reaching for me always.

It takes everything I have in me not to grasp for him in return.

"I love you." The confession spills out unbidden, laced with so much pain. I could choke on it, if my lips didn't keep moving, churning out admission after admission. "God, even after all you've done. Even now… I love you so damn much. I do—"

"And I love you." The ferocity of his statement robs my breath, making me sway on my feet. "God, I love you—"

"But we're not *right* for each other." Tears spring, welling beneath my fluttering eyelids. Blinking doesn't keep them at bay—they drip down, painting my cheeks in spite. "We're not. Not anymore."

Beautiful sweet Brandt and foolish, selfish Snowy.

The people we used to be are dead and gone. In their place?

Strangers. Hell, I barely recognize the caricature I've become.

But I'm growing surer of one thing: she doesn't deserve *this*.

"Just tell me what else you've done," I plead. "Just tell me everything."

Uncertainty makes his eyes so goddamn blue. Like an ocean, swirling with years of agony I could only imagine. Pain I'm partly responsible for—no. *Was.* Shaking my head helps to drive that new perspective in: I refuse to keep wallowing in guilt.

We hurt each other.

"Tell me."

"Riley Haverty," he says thickly. "I sent her. I gave her a donation large enough to convince her to approach you."

A pinch in my chest has me seeking out the wall for balance. I can't lie. This deception stings just as much as the others. "Why?"

He looks away, his jaw tight. "You needed to speak to someone. Anyone."

"Because you care so much about me?"

"No." He laughs, shaking his head. "Because I know what it's like, Snow. You wouldn't talk to me. Maybe Riley could reach you. Get you to show your face again. Believe in something again."

In a way he was right—a sick, twisted, degenerate way.

"And now?" I ask. "What am I supposed to believe in?"

"Us," he says simply. He starts to stand only to clutch his chest and remain seated. "We lost each other once. I can't lose you twice. I can't."

"But..." My tongue flicks over my dry lips, desperate for traction. "You already have."

"Don't say that."

He's so beautiful like this that I could almost forget. The pain. The torment. Almost. But, even now, pleading for forgiveness, he guards his secrets too well. I can't tell if he's even truly sincere or just pretending.

The strangest fact of all? I don't feel a shred of guilt for doubting him this time.

"Please," he says, but there's no real energy in his voice. Just a plea so raw it snaps me back ten years into the past. When I was just a girl and he was *just* a boy, and there was no hostility between us. "Hear me out—and I know that you don't owe me a damn thing. Just listen…"

He waits, and I linger near the door, my heart swelling in my chest. Just a few steps forward would carry me beyond his reach. I *will* myself to move.

But I'm frozen.

"I thought I lost you once," he says and his rasping tone sinks into me like a hook, leaving me flailing for freedom. "At the lake. And even then, when all I wanted was to hate you, I couldn't—even thinking for a second that you were really gone…" His voice trails off, leaving me with only memory to fill in the gaps of what he holds back. Me in his arms. Him begging me to live.

You don't get to leave me. Not until I let you go.

"And, it nearly happened again. I almost lost you, and I know that I don't deserve forgiveness. Not this time. But fuck, Snow." He looks up, capturing me in his endless blue stare. I'm enthralled just as I was all those years ago, forever under his spell. "I would give anything to hate you. I would. Because it would be easier than the need I feel. I need you, even when you're gone, you're the only fucking thing that feels real."

But not real enough to change for.

"I'm sorry." Finally, my body remembers how to move.

And I'm already racing down the hall, leaving him there.

Alone.

NINETEEN

"THIS IS YOUR CHANCE, SNOWY," a soothing voice urges. "Now, once and for all, you can tell the truth you've been holding onto for so long."

My mouth opens, but the words won't come.

Not yet.

Ten years later and the truth shouldn't be so hard to say. Like stone, it sticks in my throat, forming a wall more formidable than the one Humpty Dumpty decided to sit on.

But once upon a time, a beautiful boy convinced me that I was stronger than any fall. No matter what, I could always piece myself together again.

And, in his memory, I refuse to remain shattered.

Licking my lips, I close my eyes and I let the words come slowly. "The past few months have been a whirlwind for me.

My family fell into financial trouble. My fiancé was convicted of a federal crime." Charges that would soon include attempted murder and assault. "And living through it all made me realize one glaring reality: I can't move forward if I don't look back. Starting with the fact that ten years ago, my father, Forrest Hollings. He…" My voice trails off, reverberating throughout the room with the aid of a microphone. Slowly, I open my eyes again, taking in the multiple onlookers giving me their sole attention. Seated across from me is Riley Haverty, her face schooled into the perfect, caring mask of a talented talk show host.

I have to give her credit. She did seem remorseful for her part in Blake's deception. This moment is my payment. My one chance to speak on *my* terms in my own words.

Does it matter that the whole world is watching?

Maybe not. Beyond the stage lights and the rapt crowd are my brothers, lurking in the shadows. Some parts of my story I won't reveal today—I can't. But one day, when it's right, I'll tell them the rest.

As for now?

Breathing deeply, I turn my gaze to the nearest camera and clear my throat, ripping down the wall I've let silence me for so damn long.

"My father, Forrest Hollings, made me lie," I say, my voice growing stronger with each word. "He urged me to commit perjury. And…when I was just a child…he assaulted me."

* * *

HEALING ISN'T ALWAYS CATHARTIC. Not at first—
and especially when your wounds have scabbed over and
healed in hideous, jagged scars like mine.

Purging myself of that pain means ripping myself all over
again and carefully stitching up the torn pieces.

It hurts like hell, but this time I can survive.

I know I can.

Even if I have to face each battle alone.

"Good morning, Ms. Hollings." I look up as I pass the
security booth where a smiling guard greets me with a nod.

Apparently this visit is more welcome than the day I first
attempted to meet Blake Lorenz.

It's funny how time can change your perspective so much.
Back then I was terrified.

And now?

I'm resigned. In my hand is a simple invitation—more like
a summons. Barely a week after my interview went live and
Blake Lorenz chooses now of all times to restate his hold
over my life.

Like hell.

Today, I refuse to cower. Reassessing my feelings, one word
I don't expect lingers on the edges of my mind anyway.

Tentatively, I toy with it, testing it silently over my tongue. *Free.*

Entering an elevator, I find myself swaying on my feet. It's as if a million pounds have been lifted from my shoulders, but as light as I feel, there's an unnerving sense of weightlessness.

One wrong move and I might pitch too far. Trip. Crash.

Or fly.

When I arrive at the top floor, the executive suite is surprisingly empty. The secretary is gone from her usual spot, as is the security guard who usually monitors the property. There are no other employees scurrying about like they did down below.

Save for a lone figure who blocks my path.

His voice reaches me before my eyes finish taking him in. "Snow…"

God, he still looks beautiful. Untouchable, even despite the stiff way he holds his right arm. His hair has grown longer in a few short weeks and his chin is covered in overgrown stubble. As sharp as ever, his eyes fixate on mine, a pulsing, endless blue. "You look…" His lips part before closing again. Then he shakes his head and sighs. "Am I allowed to say that you look beautiful?"

I should refuse him. Run. Leave. My eyes dart to the nearest doorway, a tempting exit.

"Please, Snow." He's closer, advancing a dangerous step. "Please. I just want—"

"What?" I ask, my chin jutting in the air. "To manipulate me again?"

"No…" He frowns and my stomach clenches. "I want to start over."

"So that's why you brought me here?" I keep my chin tilted defiantly, forcing myself to hold his gaze.

"I brought you here?" he says, his brows furrowing. "But *you* invited me here—"

"No. I did."

We turn in unison to find a slender, feminine figure dominating the doorway of the presidential suite. Her blond hair hangs loosely over her shoulders, framing her face and the determined expression on it.

"Masha?" Blake rushes to meet her. "What are you doing here? When did you get back?"

"This morning," she says, enduring his hug. "I wanted to beat the news reports."

"Reports?" Blake turns her to face him. "What reports."

"That we're freed from the debt our father owed," she says softly. "All of it. Forgiven."

"That's impossible." Blake shakes his head. "How?"

"It was simple in the end." Masha looks at me, her eyes blazing. "I played his game. I saw your interview, Snowy," she says, her tone soft. "And to prevent me from giving one of my own, I ensured that we will never have to worry about him again."

"Hanz?" Blake grabs his sister's shoulders, his knuckles white. "You met him? Alone? Are you insane?" His eyes blaze, jaw clenched. But the longer he meets his sister's fearless stare, the more his tense posture deflates.

"We're free," Masha says. Her fingers graze his cheek in a silent caress. "All of us."

She gingerly steps from her brother's embrace, as lithe as a dancer. "I'll meet you at home, Blake. Goodbye, Snowy." With one last nod in my direction, she drifts through the suite, fading into an elevator.

Stunned in her wake, Blake recovers first.

"I swear I didn't lure you here—"

"I guess this means you don't need Hollings Enterprises," I say tightly.

Needling him should be the last thing on my mind. But freedom doesn't shroud me as easily as it does Masha. I still feel the pain underneath it all, biting deeper as he shakes his head, chuckling.

"I guess not," he says, still laughing. "But I still want it—"

"Keep it." Turning on my heel, I start down the hall.

"With *you*." Heavy footsteps advance on my position. Only now do I realize that I've frozen mid-step. Warmth alludes to a body approaching mine, proceeding the fingers that trace my shoulder. "I want to run this company with you, Snow. Together. No games. No tricks."

My breath catches, betraying the weakness I know he can sense. Hope. "How can I trust you?"

There's silence for so long that I assume it's my answer: I can't.

"Wait." His hands encircle my waist before I can even take a step forward. "You won't trust me," he says, his throat rasping. "Not right away. Maybe never, not fully. And I can't lie. A part of me wants to ensure you will, any way I can. Even if I have to lie, or cheat or steal from you to do it. But that's not what I want."

"What do you want?"

"*This.*" His arms tighten around me. "Holding you. Touching you. Knowing that every second of contact is only because you want it to last. I'm on your terms, Snow."

My terms.

"And if I told you to leave me alone from here on out?"

He stiffens. Then gradually his touch withdraws and he paces away. "Then I'll do it. Even if it fucking kills me—but you'd have to say the words."

And he doesn't want me to.

"I don't know if we can ever go back to where we were before," I admit, hating how much that statement stings. "I don't…"

"But we can start over." He's close again. His mouth finds my jawline, his nostrils flaring, taking me deep. "Together. We can start over *together*."

"And how would we cement this deal?" I wonder, tilting my face toward him. "With another contract?"

"We could." His eyes gleam a dangerous hue of blue. "Though I'd prefer something a little more old-fashioned." His gaze fixates on my lips.

"Like what?" I force myself to ask.

He takes his time leaning in, giving me every chance to back out before our mouths connect. Just once. Against my lips, he murmurs, "We can seal it with a kiss."

Mischa grates out something that isn't English, capturing my nipple between his thumb and his forefinger, guiding it to a stiff point. Then even words cease to matter. Our language becomes a series of groans and gasps smothered into silk and skin. His fingers roam without care or reason, fanning over my rib cage, plunging through my hair, and grasping strands so hard that my eyes water.

"Look at me." His teeth find my earlobe, grinding it between them. "Fuck. *Look at me.*"

I do. And the sight of his face, hard with determination, steals my breath away.

He looks too powerful. Too real. Too raw, hungry for me.

He crushes me with his last thrust, refusing to shift his weight even as he empties himself into me. I'm trapped beneath him, forced to bear every lethal pound. It's almost as if he's trying to drive Robert out through his presence alone.

I try to hang on to that familiar monster. I try…

But, with every passing second, his evil is harder to grasp, like smoke chased away by a raging inferno.

And, without his protection, I'm devoured whole.

Read XV now!

"I've given you enough for tonight," he tells me, sliding his fingers free, ripping away my only lifeline to sanity.

My thoughts cloud over. Can't think. I'm forbidden to move—but my hand jumps anyway, the fingers grasping at the air.

"You want more?" His voice… I've never heard it so thick. It's like he's breaking every word off of stone—hammering humanity out of the monster he really is. "Say it, then. You want more." He snaps his fingers, shining, bloody. "Beg."

I don't want more. I shake my head, biting my lower lip.

He steps back, starts to turn.

I whimper. It's the only sound I can make. Not words. I can't say it.

"Do you want it?" He steps forward, bracing one knee on the cushions of the couch beside me. His fingers come to circle my throat, tilting my head back so that I'm forced to stare into those swirling black holes he has for eyes. "How badly do you want to come?" His fingers sweep down, catching a swollen, bitten nipple between them. "Do you need it?"

Fire licks through my veins, but it's nowhere near strong enough. Harsh enough. I *need* more.

"Y-yes."

When he bears down, I can't hide the scream that rips from my throat. It's too soft. Too damn close to a moan.

"Then fucking ask for it—"

"P-please."

His eyes disappear, narrowed into slits. The next second, he's on his knees, his hands on my hips, dragging me forward. His mouth catches me.

And my body does the screaming for me. It explodes. Ignites. Blows up.

Kaboom! It's a scramble to reassemble myself in the chaos. Nothing in the world compares to his tongue. It's soft. Strong. Licking. Sucking. Breaking. Breaking. Breaking.

This time, I don't get just a taste of clarity. I get a full fucking dose. My thoughts go so clear that, for the first time in my life, I don't feel anything. No fear. No pressure. No stress.

Just *nothing*.

Read Submit now!

A WORD FROM THE AUTHOR

Hey there!

Thank you so much for reading! If you enjoyed the story, please leave a review and recommend the book to any friend you think would love this twisted world. You'd have my eternal gratitude. Even a short sentence goes a long way!

Then, come join the rest of us dark romance lovers in my Facebook Group where you can get snippets, sneak peeks of upcoming books and even help vote on aspects of future novels.

Come to the dark side:
https://www.facebook.com/groups/lanasbeautifulmonsters/

WANT MORE STUFF TO READ?
Join my newsletter and get a **free book**! Plus, you get to stay updated with any new releases, random giveaways and exclusive sneak peeks!
https://www.lanaskybooks.com/newsletter

ABOUT THE AUTHOR

Lana Sky is a reclusive writer in the United States who spends most of her time daydreaming about complex male characters and parenting her Cockapoo Joey. She writes dark, twisted romance across several genres. Her titles include everything from mafia romance to vampires.

facebook.com/AuthorLanaSky

twitter.com/lanasky101

amazon.com/author/lanasky

pinterest.com/lanasky101

goodreads.com/lanasky

instagram.com/lanasky101

bookbub.com/authors/lana-sky

For more titles by Lana Sky, please visit:

https://www.lanaskybooks.com